Moment of Truth

His hand on her shoulder spun her round, while the other began to undo the fastenings of her jacket. "Well, I'll be damned!" His exploring hand traveled down from her shoulder and over the small breast. "So you had me fooled after all! Well, well, this is my good day." The grip on her shoulder loosened into a caress, his hand warm through the thin fabric of her threadbare shirt. "If you play at love as well as you do at cards, I'm in luck indeed."

Sonia pulled away with one frantic movement, her hand found the little gun she had pushed into the jacket pocket. "If you come near me, I'll shoot you. . . ."

JANE AIKEN HODGE is the daughter of noted poet and critic Conrad Aiken. Mrs. Hodge's fiction has appeared in the **Ladies' Home Journal**; her first novel, **Maulever Hall**, is a carefully researched spellbinding Gothic romance.

THE
ROYAL GAMBLE

(Original Title: The Adventurers)

Jane Aiken Hodge

 PYRAMID BOOKS • NEW YORK

With the exception of actual historical personages, the characters are entirely the product of the author's imagination and have no relation to any person in real life.

THE ROYAL GAMBLE
(original title: The Adventurers)

A PYRAMID BOOK

Published by arrangement with Doubleday & Co., Inc.
Copyright © 1965 by Jane Aiken Hodge

Pyramid edition published May 1971
Second printing, April 1976

ISBN: 0-515-04052-5

Printed in the United States of America

Pyramid Books are published by Pyramid Communications, Inc. Its trademarks, consisting of the word "Pyramid" and the portrayal of a pyramid, are registered in the United States Patent Office.

PYRAMID COMMUNICATIONS, INC.
919 Third Avenue, New York, N.Y. 10022

Chapter 1

"Sonia! Sonia!" Miss Barrymore's voice came faintly from somewhere inside the castle. Then, nearer, "It's time for your music lesson."

Sonia von Hugel took no notice. She had found where the castle cat had hidden her kittens, and now, sitting on the floor of a turret above the stables, she was stroking one on her lap while the other purred into her ear. She was tired of music lessons, tired of being cooped up indoors. The sun was shining, the first time for weeks, and her father had forbidden her to leave the castle. A battle had been fought, a few days ago, somewhere beyond the mountains, at Leipzig. They had heard the guns for two days and then the rumors had begun to trickle in. At first, Father had been incredulous. That Napoleon might have been beaten at last was surely too good to be true. Father had double cause to hate the French Emperor. The loss of his estates in Hanover had been bad enough, and then, on top of that, had come his son's death. Compelled to join Napoleon's army, Frederic had set off gaily to help him add Russia to his conquests. There had been one letter, from Moscow, then—nothing.

Sonia shivered and then caught the kitten as it fell off her shoulder. That had been almost a year ago now. Poor Frederic—and poor Father. Frederic had been just like him, a sportsman, unromantic, short-tempered, and often impatient with what he called her crotchets. Only he called them *launen* since, like his father, he thought English a ridiculous language. Only Sonia, faithful to her mother's memory, spoke it by preference. "One thinks so much more tidily in English," Miss Barrymore had said once, and she found it true.

"Sonia! Sonia!" Her governess's voice chimed in with her thoughts, and she moved forward to peer down through the turret's narrow windows into the castle courtyard. Barry was standing at the main doorway, autumn sunshine glinting in her red-brown hair. Looking down at her, Sonia experienced a little shock of surprise. Dear old Barry looked actually handsome today, despite that ridiculous coronet of plaits. Old? Well, thirty at least, and to Sonia, at seventeen, anyone over twenty-one was old. And yet, as Barry stood there, her neat figure immaculate as usual in gray alpaca, Sonia felt a sudden qualm of—could it be envy?—and found her hand instinctively smoothing out her own crumpled dress.

"Sonia, where are you?" Miss Barrymore called again, and then, "I can't find her anywhere, Baron." Speaking to Sonia's father, who had just emerged from the saddle room, she dropped naturally into her fluent German.

He shrugged broad, leather-clad shoulders. "Fine-lady airs again. Thinks herself too old for lessons, I suppose, now she's seventeen. But she's not left the castle. I told the gatekeeper to see she didn't. If the French are really in retreat, this is no time for her to be roaming about the countryside."

"You think there is danger?"

"No, no; nonsense. Nothing of the kind. They've never come up this high before. Why should they now?"

"But if the French are in full retreat—and as disorganized as rumors says—may not anything happen? You will think me foolish, but I really believe I should feel happier if you were to post one of the men in the pass to warn us of any danger."

"Afraid, Miss Barrymore?"

"Sometimes, it is sensible to be afraid, Baron."

"For women, perhaps. As for me, I only wish some of the murdering ruffians would come this way. I have a score to settle with them." His hand lingered for a moment on the butt of the gun in his belt.

Her cool gray eyes took him in, from leather jacket to shabby boots. "That is precisely what I am afraid of. There are three men in the castle, and half a dozen women. You have no scouts out, no preparations for defense, and you talk of settling a score with the French." She turned away from him. "But as you say, there is no reason why they should come this way. I just wish I knew where that child was." And raising her voice she called once more, in English. "Sonia, where are you, child? You are making me anxious."

Sonia put down the kitten. Her father could shout and bully forever, but she was too fond of Barry to let her worry. She bent forward to call down from the little window, then hesitated. Its entrance masked by hay in the stable below, this was too good a hiding place to be given away so lightly. She was shaking dust from her skirts before climbing down the tiny, twisting stair when a new noise brought her hurrying back to the window. Something was happening outside the closed main gate of the castle. There were shouts and then, sudden and horrifying in the still autumn air, a shot. She could see nothing, and neither could Miss Barrymore or Father who stood, as if petrified, gazing at each other on the steps below the castle door.

Now there came a loud knocking on the main gate, and shouts from outside, in French and then in halting German: "Open up! Open up in there!"

Father and Miss Barrymore still stood immobile, staring at each other. Then, "Best open to them," said Barry.

"Never!" Father was looking to the priming of his gun.

"Madness!" She saw what he was doing. "Your only chance, now, is to temporize with them."

"I! Temporize! With the French! You do not know what you are saying. My son—" The rest of it was drowned by a fresh outburst of knocking and shouts from outside.

"Open up!" German again. "Or we will break the gate down, and it will be the worse for you. Hurry, there. Your gatekeeper is in need of—attention."

And then a little, horrid pause. "There must be a great many of them," said Miss Barrymore. "For the child's sake, open! Do all they ask; it is the only way."

Father's face was red with rage. "I'd rather die." And then, as she made a sudden dart toward the gate: "No you don't."

Caught in his furious grip, she raised her head and shouted at the top of her voice: "Sonia, if you can hear me. Hide!"

Now there was a new noise from beyond the gate. Confused shouting, some words of command that Sonia did not understand, and then, heavy and unmistakable, the crash of a heavy object against the gate. The huge bolt

7

shuddered in its socket; the hinges creaked, but the gate held firm.

"You see." Father had to shout against the tumult outside. "What did I tell you?"

"You're mad. Think of the child! There's still time—" Once more her words were lost in the clamor from outside.

This time, Sonia could hear a voice counting in French: "One, two, three!" And then a tremendous crash. The huge bolt had held, but the hinges of the gate, rusty with age, had yielded to the pressure from outside, and a group of French soldiers almost fell into the courtyard. Sonia caught her breath at sight of them. She had seen French infantrymen often enough during her country's long vassalage, but never any who looked like this. Their uniforms hung in tatters; some had lost their shakos, others had wounds wrapped in blood-drenched rags, but worst of all were their faces, grimed black with powder, grizzly with unkempt hair and drawn with the fatigue of their long retreat. They seemed, as they stood for a moment, panting, on the fragments of the gate, more like animals than men.

But discipline still prevailed among them. A sergeant pushed forward. The three chevrons on the sleeve of his shabby gray overcoat betokened good conduct. "You're the owner?" Father had never been spoken to in that tone before. "We need food; quickly. All the clothes you have; bandages; wine. Hurry, and we'll forget what's past."

Sonia's hands clenched and unclenched at her sides. She had seen Father in these rages before. Once, he had killed a servant. Now he fired, as she had often seen him practice doing, from his hip. A look of astonishment transformed the sergeant's face. He looked, in his amazement, like the child it was hard to believe he had ever been. Then, almost in slow motion, he bent double and fell to the ground.

Sonia had heard wolves often enough, on winter nights when the snow lay thick around the castle, but the noise the French soldiers made now was, somehow, worse. Their sergeant had led them, bullied them, comforted them since the debacle of Leipzig. He had been their hope, their promise of home. Now he lay still, face down in the mud. They hardly bothered to avoid him as they moved forward, still growling that savage, incomprehensible cry, towards Father and Miss Barrymore. Barry was trying to shout something, but Father was reloading his gun. He shot once more before they overwhelmed him. Sonia buried her face in her hands and sank, shuddering, to the dusty floor of the turret.

There were cries, then screams. Once, Sonia raised her head from her hands and gazed down to where Father and Miss Barrymore lay, very still, on the steps. As she did so, one of the youngest of the kitchenmaids ran screaming out of the main door of the castle. Three Frenchmen were following her. They caught her in the middle of the yard and dragged her into the stable below Sonia's turret. The sounds that followed would echo in her head, she thought, till she died. At last there was quiet. The three soldiers emerged into the yard, straightening their ragged uniforms as they went. And from below, nothing. Not a sob, not a quick-drawn breath. Just silence.

There were no more screams, either, from the castle itself, but a confused moise of shouting and singing suggested that the Frenchmen had found their way to the wine cellar. The sun still shone. It seemed incredible. The cat, one of whose kittens Sonia was convulsively clutching, emerged from the stable entrance and prowled across the courtyard to sniff indifferently at Father's body, and then, more lengthily, at Miss Barrymore's. How long had it been? Sonia had no idea. She was stiff and cold: tears followed each other silently down her cheeks. From time to time she bent, almost automatically, to wipe her face in the kitten's soft and springy fur. She did not seem to be thinking at all.

Then she stiffened, straightened up and gazed towards the castle gate. Surely that was the sound of horses' hooves? Yes, it was louder now, and she heard a strange cry, hoarse like that of ravens: "Hourra! Hourra!"

She had never seen Cossacks before, but she recognized them at once as they crowded into the castle yard over the fragments of the gate. There was no mistaking those wild figures in their loose gray cloaks and fur caps, riding small, active-looking horses and brandishing lances as they crowded round an officer, distinguished only by his small cap and green cloak. Instinctively, Sonia drew a little further back from the slit window. The French were bad

9

enough, but mothers in the village frightened their children with stories of Cossack atrocities. Still, nothing could make any difference now to Father or Miss Barrymore or, judging by the silence, to the other inhabitants of the castle.

The Cossack officer had seen the bodies in the corner of the courtyard and shouted an order to his men, half of whom dismounted, handed their ponies to their comrades and advanced on the castle entrance. At this moment a burst of noise echoed from the main hall. The Frenchmen were singing the "Marseillaise." Another order, and the Cossacks disappeared into the castle. A confused noise of shouting and shots followed; then two of the Frenchmen emerged into the yard, fiercely pursued by a group of Cossacks. Appalled, fascinated, unable to look away, Sonia watched them cut to pieces, there in the castle yard. She half thought that one of them had been among the three who had followed poor Gretchen, the maid, into the stable below her. But it made no difference to Gretchen.

The rest of the dismounted Cossacks emerged from the castle door, wiping their lances on their cloaks. What now? Suppose they searched? Suppose they found her? She clutched the kitten more tightly in her lap, for comfort, and as she did so, saw its mother emerge once more from the small doorway that led to the kitchen, and sniff cautiously at her father's body. The Cossack officer said something to one of his men, then rose in his stirrups and hurled his lance. A horrible howl, a convulsive movement, and the cat was still, pinned against the wooden door. It was the last straw. Sonia bent forward over the kitten, trying to stifle great uncontrollable sobs in its fur.

She was lucky. In the courtyard below, the bustle of imminent departure drowned the noise she made. When she looked up at last, the bloodstained courtyard was silent and empty, save for the bodies that lay so still. Afternoon sunshine, striking across the courtyard now, made them seem if possible more horrible. Slowly, shakily, she got to her feet, tucking the kitten half consciously under her arm. Deliberately, she turned away from the window. She had seen too much already. Hard to believe that this morning she had been a girl, a child, running away from her lessons. What was she now?

And what was she going to do? She moved like a

10

sleepwalker across the little dusty room to the stair and climbed slowly down it. Gretchen's body lay tumbled in the hay at the bottom. She looked away. She had been right. Nothing mattered to Gretchen any more. Avoiding the courtyard, she climbed up to her own room through the tangle of side passages and back stairs down which she had run, in mischief, this morning.

Opening her door, she breathed a sigh of relief. Neither Frenchmen nor Cossacks had got this far in their looting. The cold little room lay bare and tidy as she had left it—a lifetime ago. She moved across to open the heavy wooden wardrobe. Somewhere between here and the stables, almost without knowing it, she had come to a decision. She could not stay here. Her father's sister, Aunt Gertrude, was the only alternative. It meant a long, cold and dangerous ride over the mountains. What else could she do? Ah, there they were. She reached to the back of the wardrobe and pulled out the suit of her brother's clothes that she had rescued from her father's furious holocaust after his death.

Fortunate that Frederic had preferred the modern, loose-fitting trousers to old-fashioned, form-clinging net inexpressibles. She pulled them on, tightening them at the waist—Frederic had been a robust young man—then added his enormous sheepskin jacket and turned to the looking glass. How furious Father had been when she carried it off from Mother's room. This was no time to be thinking of Father. The reflection in the glass was reassuring. Except for her hair. The long golden braids Father had insisted on would have to go. She fetched scissors from her workbasket. One, two! That was better. Now the tanned little face could easily have been a boy's. Wide-set brown eyes looked back at her from the glass, remembering horror. No time for that. She found an old fur cap of Frederic's, tucked the ragged ends of hair into it and prised up the loose board under which she kept her treasures. Not very much money, but it would have to do. She would not think about the Frenchman she had seen pull the purse from Father's belt. Her mother's pearls would be her independence from Aunt Gertrude. And beside them, dusty under the floorboards, lay the little gun with which Frederic had taught her to shoot before he left, laughing, for the wars. She picked it up, made sure that it was loaded and in working order, and slipped it into the big pocket of the jacket. There. A few immediate necessities in a small bag that would hang behind her saddle, and she was ready. And high time too. The light outside had changed again. It would be evening soon, and she had far enough to go. Suppose the Cossacks had found her pony, out to graze in the field behind the castle. Cross that bridge when you come to it. Worse and more immediate was the fact that now she had to cross the castle courtyard and go out the main gate. Thinking about it would only make it harder. She looked around the room. Would she ever come back? Frederic's gauntlet gloves hid cold hands too small for the figure she intended to present. It was time to go.

The main stairs this time, and old Agnes, the housekeeper, lying in a curiously small black heap, clutching the newel post, very still. Then the main hall, a shambles, where Cossacks had cut down Frenchmen as they drank and looted. Everything topsy-turvy and everywhere blood. A sigh of relief at the open door, turning to a little gasp at the remembered state of the courtyard. Don't look at Father and Miss Barrymore. Someone has moved her body a little. Don't look: you have enough to remember. The French sergeant's body lies right across the main gate. Step over it, and wonder what would have happened if Father had kept his temper. What's the use of wondering?

Outside, Hans, the gatekeeper, lay where he had fallen. And that was all. Otherwise, everything was, incredibly, as usual. The dark woods around the castle, the rising ranges of mountains beyond, should they not have changed to match the change in her? Absurd! She turned and hurried down the path that led to the plateau behind the castle. No sign of horses' hooves here on the muddy path. It looked as if the Cossacks had ridden off the way they had come, down the valley. Doubly lucky if they had done so for it would mean that they had missed not only her pony but the village higher up the valley.

Marmion was grazing peacefully on the banks of the stream and Frederic's old saddle was still hidden under the straw at the back of the shed. She shrugged away an uncomfortable memory. If Father had not been so bad-tempered, it would not have been necessary to deceive him. But then, if he had not been so bad-tempered, he might still be alive. Poor Father, poor Miss Barrymore . . . It was still no time to be thinking of them. She picked up the saddle and went out into evening sunshine to call Marmion.

"Ridiculous English name," Father had shouted, and, "But I am English," she had answered, courting the inevitable explosion of his rage.

Saddling Marmion, she felt the memories jostle through her brain. Was this how it felt to drown? Had she died a little, with the others, today? And yet it was good to be alive, riding up the valley, feeling the cool wind in her face, watching cloud shadows on the mountains. Shameful to feel this; and suddenly, with shame, came a memory she had so far contrived to suppress, the memory of Gretchen's face as she ran from her pursuers, and the sounds she had made, in the stable below, when they caught her. Sonia gritted her teeth. Death had been too good for those Frenchmen.

The village lay quiet as usual in late sunshine. She had been right. Neither Frenchmen nor Cossacks had found their way here. The familiar village noises, of dogs, and hens, and clamorous children seemed to call to her from a remote past. She had ridden here yesterday, with her father; that was in a different life. She jumped quickly down from her pony, defying memory, and rapped loudly on the door of the cottage—it was little more than a hovel—where lived the head man of the village and his wife, who had been her foster mother.

Greeted with rapturous astonishment, she told her story in the fewest possible words and realized, as she did so, that she sounded almost callous. Well, better that than tears, uncontrollable tears, as they would be if she let them flow. "You must go up there," she said, "at once, and do—what has to be done." She bit off the words. What need, after all, for speed?

"But you will come in, and rest yourself, and eat?" Old Urse sounded doubtful as she spoke. Dearly though she loved her, she thought her cottage no place for the young lady from the castle.

"No." Sonia was surprised at the clear decision of her own voice. "I must ride over the mountains, at once, to my aunt."

13

"Of course: the gracious lady your aunt." The old woman sounded at once relieved and surprised that Sonia had come to so proper a decision. "But it is not safe for you to be riding about the mountains alone."

"Who could go with me?" The question was unanswerable. Long years of war had taken their toll and there was not a young man nor a horse in the village. "I shall travel faster alone."

It was obvious truth. The old woman made her eat some coarse brown bread and drink a mug of milk, all she had in the house, then bade her a reluctant—or was it a relieved—farewell? All the time, easy tears had been pouring down her brown old face, and at last, helping Sonia to mount, she looked up at her. "You do not cry?"

"There is no time for tears." Sonia looked down at her from a stretched face, white-gray under the tan. "Good-bye, Urse. Make your husband go up—quickly."

"Never fear, Baroness, I will go and find him at once." And the old woman turned, once again with the smallest suggestion of relief, and ran off down the village street.

Baroness! Sonia turned the unexpected title over in her mind as she rode up the mountain track. Of course, old Urse, ignorant as she was, would assume that with Father's death the castle must be hers. She shivered, remembering how Father's mourning for Frederic had been embittered by thoughts of Cousin Franz who must now succeed to title and estate alike. He had been—yes, he had actually been angry with Frederic for dying, and had taken pleasure in taunting his daughter with her lack of expectations. "A pauper, that's what you'll be when I die. Best make up to your Aunt Gertrude while there's time. Miser that she is, she'll be your only hope. No use expecting anything from those English relatives you set such store by. Never did anything for your mother: why should they for you?"

The thought of Aunt Gertrude, unpleasant enough in itself, was, for once, almost a welcome distraction from darker memory. A harsh, black widow, she lived a life of near-Trappist solitude, her Calvinism so fierce that anything she found herself enjoying was, automatically, bad. Father had always maintained that her threadbare black gowns were the miser's badge and that death would reveal her as a rich woman, but Sonia did her the justice of thinking her stringent life the result of a charity as genuine as it was unlovely. The idea of sharing, indefinitely, in this silent, angular woman's life of prayer and thin broth was not a happy one. But why should she expect happiness? After today, she thought she would never hope for anything again.

It was getting colder. Surely she had been riding for a long time along the twisting little path up the valley? She had never come this way alone before, having visited Aunt Gertrude only reluctantly, when her father made her accompany him. But the ride from the village had never taken more than an hour or so. Could she have taken a wrong turning? The path had only forked once, that she remembered, and that had been very soon after leaving the village. At the time, deep in thought, she had taken the right-hand branch, almost without thinking. Now, remembering, she realized that it had been the better marked of the two. Could she have been wrong in choosing it? The path to Aunt Gertrude's isolated house led nowhere else; the other led up the next valley and over a spur of the hills to a village she had seldom visited. She paused and looked about her. Nothing but thick pinewoods and, somewhere below, the sound of the invisible stream. It might be either valley, but if it was Aunt Gertrude's she should reach the little plateau on which the house stood any minute now. Instead, as she rode on, the path began to climb steeply. She stopped again. Fool that she was, she had indeed taken the wrong turning. And it would soon be dark. No time to rage at herself for her mistake, nor yet for the excuses that rushed into her mind. Rage and excuses were equally useless. She must decide what to do. Apparently, she had already decided, for Marmion moved forward again. If she turned back, it would be black dark before she reached Aunt Gertrude's house. A wolf, howling somewhere behind her in the forest, settled the question for her. Another twenty minutes or so, surely, should bring her to the village, where, as she remembered, there was a little inn. Most important of all, she had now put two ranges of hills between herself and the line of the French retreat. The chances of encountering more fugitives—or more Cossacks—were infinitely less if she went on than if she went back. So debating, she had been riding steadily onward all the time, and sighed with relief when at last the path turned downwards and grew wider. Now, too, she began to hear village noises; a cow lowed, a dog barked at her approach and its voice roused others, further away. No screams, no glow of fire. The French had not been here, nor the Cossacks. She reined in Marmion for a moment while she settled the fur cap over her ragged hair. She knew no one in this village, since all her family's dealings had been in the other direction, where the main road lay. It had been bad enough telling her story to old Urse; to strangers, she would not. For tonight, she would be the boy she seemed. Safer so, and fewer questions to answer. She thought rapidly, concocting a story that would account for her belated arrival. For it was almost dark now. She was glad to ride in among the first cottages and see the flicker of firelight and the glow of smoke rising from rudimentary chimneys. The inn, which stood at the crossroads in the center of the village, was merely a cottage a little larger than the rest. A rough shed to one side served as stables and Sonia, taking Marmion there, was disconcerted to see a handsome black horse already installed. She had hoped to find the inn empty, but even in the half-light she could see that this was no peasant's mount. Well, at least she was prepared. She settled Marmion as best she could and crossed to the inn door, which opened directly into one fairly large room serving as kitchen, taproom, everything. To her relief, there was no one there but the landlady, busy over black pots on her primitive cooking-stove.

She looked up as Sonia entered, revealing a kindly, anxious, weather-beaten face. "Another one!" She came forward, wiping her hands on the ragged cloth that served as an apron, then exclaimed again as she got a clearer view of Sonia by the dim illumination of a tallow dip. "All alone?"

"Yes." Sonia had been afraid that she did not look very old, and plunged straight into the story she had invented of being separated from her father as they rode home from visiting a sick relative. It did not sound very convincing, even to her, but the woman had other things on her mind. "Madness to be out today at all," she said. "I have been hearing such tales. Did you not meet them? The French, or worse still, those murdering Cossacks? But come in, you must be perished with cold." She did not wait for an answer to her question. "Sit down by the stove. Yes, there's a room you can have, though it's not much of a one, our best one being already taken by a gentleman who rode in half an hour ago. My husband's out scouring the village for something for his supper. You look as if you could do with a bit of something yourself. Here, let me take your bag; I'll put it in your room for you; it's just through there." She dropped Sonia's little bag through a door in the corner of the room. "There, I must get back to my cooking; the other gentleman's starving, he says. He's been riding all about keeping out of the way of those ———— French." She used an adjective Sonia had never heard before. "I was afraid, when he first came in, that he was one of them. Speaks funny, he does, not a bit like you and me. Comes from the north somewhere, he explained. Well, it takes all kinds to make a world, they say, but why the good God thought fit to create French-men and Cossacks is more than I can understand." And she retired, muttering, to her stove, from which an admirable smell of soup was beginning to spread through the room. It was odd to be hungry. Sonia sat drooped forward, her head in her hands, gazing into the fire and trying not to think.

The landlady's voice roused her. "There you are, sir! Come and warm yourself." And then, with a respect she had not shown Sonia, "You will not mind sharing the fire with this young gentleman?"

As she spoke, the stranger had advanced into the room. "Of course not." His figure, in the dim light, was unmis-takably a gentleman's, and so was his voice. He sounded young, too, about the age Frederic had been when he rode away to the wars. Sonia breathed a little sigh of relief. Nothing very formidable here.

Or—was there? He was surveying her with very clear, very steady gray eyes that looked older than the thin brown face. He was slight, almost willowy—Frederic would have made two of him—but just the same she felt, as they exchanged silent, inquiring glances in the half-light, something of strength, of steel about him. Now, he seemed to come to a decision. "My name is Vincent, Charles Vincent, at your service." It was a relief when he looked away from her to pull a stool towards the stove, dust it with a very white handkerchief and settle astride it.

"You are English, then?" His name had confirmed something his accent had already suggested to Sonia, and she spoke, without thinking, in English.

"My father was." He answered in the same language, but with, surely, the hint, now, of a French accent. "And you?"

"My mother." She should follow his lead and introduce herself but had not thought, when concocting her story, to provide herself with a name.

He seemed not to notice the omission. "A remarkable meeting," he said, still in English. "I am glad to find a compatriot, or half of one"—did his tone mock her, or himself?—'with whom I can practice my phrases. I am grown, I fear, lamentably rusty. But you—you speak like a native."

"My mother spoke nothing else."

"Spoke?" He was quick, this stranger, uncomfortably quick. "I am sorry."

"It is a long time ago." Aware of his sharp eyes on her face, she was glad that, despite the fierce consoling heat of the stove, she had not removed her huge, all enveloping sheepskin jacket.

"I am still sorry." He sounded it. "But, surely, you must have some family. What are they thinking of to let you— excuse me—young as you are, be wandering about the countryside at this, of all times?"

"It happened by accident." Once again she plunged into her story which sounded even thinner, now, than it had the first time. It was almost a relief to be interrupted by a loud knocking on the door. The landlord, who had returned some time before, hurried to open it and admit two Austrian officers, who swaggered to the fire, demanding food, wine and beds for the night in tones that admitted of no denial. The elder, and spokesman of the two, interrupted the landlord's obsequious promise of the best his house could offer, by turning sharply on Vincent. "And who are you? You've got a damnéd Frenchified look to me!"

"No wonder for that." Vincent's voice was calm. "I had a French mother—an émigré," he added, as the man's hand went to his sword. "You would like, perhaps, to see

18

my papers?" He reached into an inside pocket and produced them.

The man looked them over rapidly. "Hmm." Suspiciously. "Worked for the King of Saxony, did you? And what does that make you but an enemy? A spy perhaps?"

"Look a little further." Vincent was cool as ever. "And you will see that I have a *laissez-passer* from Schwartzenberg himself. You will hardly wish better authority than his?"

"Schwartzenberg, eh?" The man's tone changed. "Charles Vincent," he pronounced the name abominably, ". . . interpreter . . . pass freely to Allied Headquarters . . . Speak a lot of languages, do you? Jabber, jabber, parlez-vous . . . Russki and all. Well, I suppose the old man knows what he's about. But what are you doing here, hey?"

"Looking for Allied Headquarters. Perhaps you can tell me where they are to be established?"

"If you will tell me when the French will stop running. Not this side of the Rhine, if you ask me. Never hoped to see them panic so. Ruled the world for twenty years, and now, look at 'em. Running like hares. You should have seen them at Leipzig when the bridge blew up. Drowned themselves in their terror; thousands of them."

"I know. I was there. I'd never have believed Napoleon could make so obvious a mistake as to chance all on one bridge. It must be true, what they say, that he's not the man he was, since the retreat from Moscow."

"Moscow? Were you there?" Sonia, watching and listening, noted the new respect in his tone. This Charles Vincent might be young, but he was evidently a man to be reckoned with.

"Yes," he answered casually. "Conscripted, like so many others, into the French army. I never want to see service like that again."

"Took French leave, did you? Plenty did."

"No; invalided out; frostbite."

"Oh. So now you're an interpreter—and the boy?" His tone sharpened.

"Lives in these parts. Lost his way in the mountains, dodging the French. He was just telling me about it." It was a much better story than Sonia's and she breathed a sigh of silent gratitude. "No papers, of course."

19

"I suppose not. Speak German, do you?" His tone, as he turned to Sonia was not unfriendly.

"Of course I do."

"And you live—" He interrupted his own question: "Ah, at last," as the landlord appeared with a great flagon of the local wine and four heavy mugs. "That's better! And how about food?"

"Presently, presently, your excellency."

"And beds?"

"Well, there lies a difficulty, your honor." Nervously. "These two gentlemen had already bespoken our only two rooms."

"No difficulty about that. They'll have to share. No objections, I suppose?" He spoke impartially to them both.

"Not the least in the world," said Charles Vincent. And "No," said Sonia. What else could she say?

Chapter 2

Sonia watched in silent, stoic despair as the landlord moved the little cloakbag into Charles Vincent's room and dumped a straw mattress in the corner for her, but the two Austrians, on being shown her room, were loud in their complaints and argued that Vincent should change with them.

He refused with unruffled cheerfulness: "First come, first served is the rule of the road, as you well know. Be grateful to me, gentlemen, that I consent, for your sakes, to accommodate this boy, who doubtless snores like one of those new steam engines." He had been superintending the landlord's operations in his room as he spoke and now returned to the fire, a pack of cards in his hand. "And now, what say you to a game of whist while we wait for this meal, which should be delicious, judging by the time the good woman is taking to prepare it."

"Cards? Why not?" said the older of the two Austrians. "But unless the boy plays, we shall lack a fourth."

"How about it, urchin? Will you join us?" Vincent

returned from the corner of the room with a small bench to be used as a card table and put it down close to the stove. "What's the matter?" he added, "have you caught cold?"

Sonia was still sitting huddled up in her heavy jacket. "A little, I think." And then—anything to distract attention from her appearance—"Yes, I can play whist."

"Excellent. Cut for partners, gentlemen?"

To Sonia's relief, she found herself partnering Vincent against the two Austrians. To his, he found her an admirable partner. Whist had been her father's only indoor relaxation. One of her earliest memories was of him playing three-handed with her mother and Miss Barrymore and losing his temper because his wife could never keep track of the cards. When her mother had died, Sonia had, inevitably, taken her place at the card table, since Frederic was too like his father to be bullied into submission. Sonia, on the other hand, realized, even as a child, that if Father was playing whist with her and Miss Barrymore in the little parlor Barry had made so snug, he was not downstairs, drinking himself black-tempered in the dining hall. Besides, she had a natural aptitude for figures. It was no trouble to her to keep count of the cards in her head and Father was soon hailing her as an infant prodigy.

It was soothing to concentrate on the cards that were played, and the deductions to be made from them. The Austrians, clearly, had not played together before, and as the older was an extremely rash, and the younger an absurdly cautious player, they were at odds in no time. Vincent, on the other hand, played very well indeed and was soon paying her the compliment of assuming that she too knew what she was doing. After the second game, gathering up the cards and shuffling them with careless expertise, he looked across at the older Austrian. "It passes the time," he said, "but would be more amusing if we played for a small stake. A dollar a hundred, perhaps? Picayune, I grant you, but you will forgive me if I suggest no more, since I shall doubtless have to pay the boy's losses as well as my own."

Losses? Sonia gave him a sharp little look. Judging by the experience of the first two games, they were more likely to win handsomely. This did not, however, seem to occur to the Austrians, who had been drinking steadily and who were not anyway equipped to draw the swift deductions she and Vincent had from those first two hands. They agreed, carelessly enough, and the game continued.

When the landlady finally announced dinner, there was a pleasant little pile of winnings by Sonia's place and the Austrians were grumblingly surprised, exclaiming at what they called their opponents' run of luck.

Vincent agreed with them blandly as they drew up their stools to the table. "You shall have your revenge after dinner, gentlemen. The luck must change presently."

Once again, spooning up thick soup, Sonia gave him a sharp glance. He must know as well as she did that the two of them had held only reasonably good hands. Skill, not luck, had won for them. He met her glance with cool gray eyes. "Shall we take them on again, urchin, or will it be too long past your bedtime?"

"Of course not." She was, in fact, drooping with fatigue, but not too tired to calculate. Vincent was drinking a great deal less than the Austrians, but enough so that they would not notice this. Surely if they played for another hour or so, he must fall asleep at once when he finally went to bed, which would much simplify the looming problem of sharing his room. Besides—she felt the surprising weight of her purse—it would be pleasant to arrive at Aunt Gertrude's with a little money for immediate expenses, and she had no doubt that they would continue to win after dinner, as they had done before. It would take a most unusual run of luck to make up for the Austrians' bad play.

The soup was followed by a dish of sauerkraut and the old fowl that the landlady had been systematically boiling towards tenderness. Vincent and the older Austrian were discussing the chances of a rapid Allied advance against the French and Sonia was interested to see the deference with which the Austrian listened to Vincent's view that all would be lost in talk. "They discuss: Napoleon acts." He was carving the bird with thin, skillful brown hands ... hands ... For a little while, she had forgotten. Now, with a rush it all came back: the soldiers swaggering out of the stable below her, coarse hands busy about their clothes. Vincent had served her now, but the food was dust and

22

ashes. She jumped up, headed blindly for the door and got outside just in time to be horribly sick in a corner of the yard.

Returning, pale and chilled, to huddle again by the stove, she was teased, inevitably, by the Austrians. "Drop too much, eh?" For once it was the younger one who spoke. He swayed towards her, tankard in hand. "A drop more will put all to rights. Come on, drink up!"

"No, thank you." She leaned away from him, but he pushed the tankard toward her. "Drink up, I say, boy!"

"No!" She pushed the mug away so violently that some of the wine it held spilled down his jacket.

He swore, and reached for his sword, but, somehow Vincent was between them. "Leave the boy alone. He's had a hard day—as have we all. Besides," he added lightly, "if you kill him, which I am sure you would find easy enough, who will make our fourth at cards? You are to have your revenge, remember?"

"Revenge," he muttered, stupid with the wine he had drunk. And then, his anger forgotten as quickly as it had come, "And I am to sit next the stove this time. The luck will change, so; I am sure of it." He picked up his stool and moved it to the position Vincent had occupied earlier in the evening. The other Austrian crossed the room to join them, belching contentedly. If he had noticed the little scene by the stove, he gave no sign of it. "Back to work, gentlemen," he picked up the cards and shuffled them clumsily, with great butcher's hands.

"You are well enough to play?" Vincent was still standing between Sonia and the others. His face and voice alike suggested that she had better be.

"Of course." Nothing for it but to take the hint, though she longed, almost unbearably, for quiet, the dark, the forgetfulness of sleep.

"Good. Well, gentlemen, what's it to be? Another round with the same partners or shall we cut again? It's all one to me, though it looks as if the urchin here may be a dead loss as a partner. Shall we cut again?"

"No, no," growled the older Austrian. "We were to have our revenge, remember. If the boy's taken too much, that's your worry."

"Oh, very well." Vincent shrugged, having achieved, Sonia was sure, exactly what he intended. Settling herself

opposite him, she watched the brown hands deal as expertly as they had carved. They were good hands, long,
graceful, bearing out her first impression that whatever
else he might be, he was a gentleman. He was watching
her. Slowly, reluctantly, her eyes rose to meet his cool
gray ones. Cool? Now they were smiling at her out of a
totally serious face, telling her—what? They were giving
her courage, that was it. Don't despair, they were saying.
Well—she gathered up her cards for the first game of the
new session—at least she would concentrate. The Austrians, clumsily arranging their cards, were still talking about
the luck changing. They had no idea . . .

How odd it all was. She had hardly met any men of her
own class save Father and Frederic. When Miss Barrymore
had suggested that it was time to be considering marriages
for her, time for her to see something of the world, and
be seen by it, Father had merely growled that peace
would be time enough for that. "If it ever comes." She
knew nothing about men, had always expected to be
helpless with shyness when she was first plunged into
society . . . Well, of course, this was not exactly society . . .

"Clubs are trumps, partner." Vincent's voice warned her
that the game was about to begin. She shook herself out
of her abstraction and concentrated her attention on the
game. Vincent obviously wanted to win, and she owed it
to him to do her best. Leading a significant singleton
knave of diamonds, she looked at him thoughtfully across
the table. Handsome enough, in a brown, burned-down,
high-polished sort of way, and with the manner and
charm of a complete gentleman, he was, she began to
suspect, most likely one of the class of professional gam-
blers of whom Frederic had spoken so furiously. But then,
Frederic had lost a year's rents at hazard and had always
maintained that the dice had been loaded. He might well
have been right, but—here she trumped her partner's
diamond lead—Vincent did not need to cheat.

Curiously enough, it was just at this point in her
thoughts that the older Austrian brought his hand down
with a crash on the table and said, "The devil's own luck!
I never saw anything like it." And then, after a little
pause, "I have a pack of cards somewhere. I suggest we
finish the evening with them."

24

Nothing seemed to shake Vincent's calm. "By all means, if you would prefer it. They could hardly be greasier than mine." He had no intention, it seemed, of taking offense, and conversed casually about indifferent subjects while the Austrian fetched and shuffled the cards, then slammed them down on the table and cut the pack to Vincent, whose deal it was.

"Let's see how you prosper with those," he said.

"You think the luck will change with the cards?" Vincent's voice was cool. "Well, I have seen stranger things."

"I dare swear you have," growled the Austrian, picking up his cards. "Well; we shall see."

Sonia sorted hers with a hand that trembled a little. If she had wanted to win before, she was desperate to do so now. The only way to prove the Austrian's insinuations false was for her and Vincent to continue their winning streak with the cards he had produced. And this time her hand was a wretched one, with nothing higher than a knave. Sorting it, she met Vincent's eyes with her own anxious ones. He smiled at her reassuringly, and cut for trumps. They were spades, her longest suit: things might not be so bad after all.

They won that game by a narrow margin, thanks mainly to the younger Austrian's failure to return his partner's lead, and the next two easily, since they held better cards, and were now playing together as if they had done so all their lives. This ended their second rubber and once again the little pile of coins by Sonia's place grew higher.

Having paid up, the older Austrian rose abruptly to his feet. "It's growing late," he said, "and we have far to go in the morning."

Vincent gathered up the cards and handed them to him. "They did not change your luck," he said quietly.

The Austrian gave him look for look, then, suddenly, he laughed. "Very well," he said, "I admit it. You outplayed us. But you had the devil's own luck too, admit! I've never seen so many lucky leads. If I didn't know you'd met for the first time tonight—well, I might be wondering."

Vincent laughed lightly. "Don't wonder," he said. "We did meet for the first time tonight, and we were lucky, weren't we, urchin?" He pocketed his winnings. "And," he added significantly, "we all have more important things to

25

do than quarrel over a game of cards." He yawned. "You're right. Time for bed, urchin, and if you snore, I'll strangle you."

The moment of tension had passed. They said good night as amicably as if the hint of cheating had not hovered over the card table. Shutting and bolting the rough but heavy door of their room behind them, Vincent laughed and stretched largely as he moved over to his bed. "A good day for me, urchin, when I chose to back you up in that tale of a cock and a bull you told. I don't know when I've won so much so fast. But now, what am I to do with you? Running away from home, I suppose? Brutal parents? All that? Join the army and see the world? I don't recommend it, and I should know; I tried it. Look where it got me: Moscow and frostbite." He had thrown off his jacket and now sat down on his bed and began to pull off his boots. "Give me a hand, will you?"

Reluctantly, Sonia crossed the room and knelt down beside him. This friendly inquisition was worse than anything she had imagined. She could feel the clear eyes considering her, as she knelt, awkwardly, by the bed. Absurd to imagine they could see right through her disguise. It was just—she did not want to be so near to this slight, steel-keen stranger. Something in her vibrated as she reached out, reluctantly, for the first boot. But she had done this for Father often enough. For all she was worth, she pretended she was doing so now. As for her hope that, by bedtime, Vincent would be, if not actually drunk, at least too fuddled to do anything but fall asleep, she might as well give it up at once. He was leaning forward now, alarmingly close, to give her a searching look as she knelt with the second boot in her arms.

"You smell very good, for a country boy. Eau de cologne, I'd say. There's more to this than a boy's truancy, or my name's not Charles Vincent. Let's think: Saxony, Württemberg? Or one of the minor families, maybe? Runaway princes are two a penny these days, but there might be something in it, still. Come on, boy, I'm your friend, I promise. I owe you something for the way you returned my leads tonight. Tell me who you are, and I'll see you safe to your friends. And no need to look so scared either. I told you, I'm on your side."

Sonia had dropped the boot and backed away towards

26

her pallet in the corner to which the dim candlelight hardly reached. She managed a convincing yawn. "I'm too tired to talk now." In her turn, she sat down on the straw mattress and began to wriggle her feet out of Frederic's boots. "In the morning—"

"Afraid I'll recognize you, eh?" To her horror he crossed the room, soft-footed, knelt on the floor beside her and began to help her with the right boot. "One good turn deserves another, and besides—should I have been serving you kneeling, all this time? Maybe you should have the good boot? How about it? Saxony? Württemberg? The Bavarians are on our side now, so not one of them. Or—French, perhaps? One of the marshals' sons? That would explain it." He laughed. "And spent the evening, cool as a cucumber, drubbing a couple of Austrian officers at cards! By God, I hope it's that. And no need to fear me, either. I had a French mother, remember. I'm on no one's side but my own—and now, yours."

Worse and worse. She racked her brain. Had the King of Saxony sons? The fat old King of Württemberg certainly had, but were they not too old? As for the French marshals, she knew too little about them to pretend to be one of their sons.

He had taken off her second boot now, and was still kneeling on the floor, looking up at her. His face was in the shadow but she was uncomfortably aware of those clear, considering gray eyes. "Thinking up a new story? Wasting your time. I haven't played cards with you all evening for nothing. You're no fool; but nor am I. The truth or nothing, see. But the morning will be time enough. Only don't think you can get away before I wake; I'm the lightest sleeper I know."

She had been thinking that very thing. It seemed that he was right: he could indeed read her mind. He rose and stood over her, speaking more gently now. "You're exhausted," he said. "It's late for urchins, even royal ones. To bed with you. We'll talk in the morning." And then, as she still sat there, looking up at him: "Bed, child." He reached down to help her out of the heavy jacket she had kept on all evening.

"No. I—I want to say my prayers. Do you go to bed; I'll blow out the candle when I've done."

"And then steal away, I'll wager, while I'm snoring. I'm

27

too old a bird to be caught with that kind of chaff." And
with the words, one iron hand on her shoulder spun her
round, while the other began to undo the fastenings of her
jacket. "Well, I'll be damned!" His exploring hand traveled
down from her shoulder and over the small breast. "Not
an urchin, but a baggage. So you had me fooled after all!
A prince indeed—how you must have laughed. A camp
follower, more like; and French, no doubt, as I suggested.
Well, well, this is my good day." The grip on her shoulder
loosened into a caress, his hand warm through the thin
fabric of Frederic's threadbare shirt. "If you play at love
as well as you do at cards, I'm in luck indeed."

His hand on her breast sent a strange tremor through
her and at the same time, she remembered Gretchen's
face, and those of the soldiers who had killed her. Her
hand found the little gun she had pushed into the jacket
pocket; she pulled away with one frantic movement, and
faced him. "If you come near me, I'll shoot you."

"Dear me." His voice was as calm as when he
confronted the angry Austrian. "How very melodramatic.
Do, my dear baggage, put that gun away; I'm sure you're
a lamentable shot, and besides, think of the excitement in
the house. Surely not what you want at all? As for coming
near you, heaven forbid, if you feel so strongly about it.
There've been enough women in my life, and will be
again, I hope. I don't need to trouble myself with a
half-grown spitfire. What's the matter, though? Following
a lover in the army? I must say your spirit does you
credit. I don't suppose he's worth it for a minute." And
then, impatiently, "Oh, do please put that gun away. Tuck
it under your pillow if you like, and shoot me if I come
near you in the night, which, I promise you, I won't. If
I've got to have my face scratched, I'd rather a cat than a
kitten any day. You're safe enough with me, infant."
Ignoring the gun, which she still held in a trembling hand,
he moved across the room to pick up his jacket from the
big bed. "I had a feeling the pallet would be my lot, and I
was right. Shall I turn my back while your ladyship gets
herself to bed? Don't shoot me in the back, mind, with
that deadly weapon of yours, which, by the way, you have
forgotten to cock."

"Oh!" She looked down at the useless gun, then dropped
it from a limp and shaking hand.

28

"That's better. Now, you see, I am very busy trying to make this pallet endurable. Into bed with you, baggage. We will talk more in the morning."

With his unexpected kindness, reaction had set in violently. Tears followed each other silently down her cheeks as she got herself into the big cold bed, and once there, she buried her face convulsively in the pillow to smother the sobs that began to rack their way up through her.

"Well," came the cool voice from the other side of the room. "Are you safe, Rapunzel? Can I turn round?" And then, with a little laugh: "I thought there was something odd about that hair. You must let me recut it for you in the morning."

A sound, half hiccup, half sob, was the only answer. He had moved across the room to where the candle stood on a rough chest, but now paused. "What's the matter, Rapunzel?"

"N . . . nothing," she managed. "Leave me alone."

"Or you'll shoot me? We've been through all that before. Come, Rapunzel, you'll feel better if you tell me, and, who knows, I might be able to help you. Not a camp follower, are you? You had me fooled with that little self-possessed air of yours—and besides, what an angel with the cards! But—a child, in a world too big for it. Best tell your Uncle Charles all about it. No need to beat about the bush. You've seen me for what I am; I saw those bright eyes of yours summing me up tonight. I make money by my skill at cards—but I don't cheat, mind you. I've got to live, haven't I? Have you ever tried to live on an interpreter's pay? Foolish question, but what I'm trying to tell you is, I may be an adventurer, but I'm a gentleman, just the same, and word of honor, I'll help you any way I can."

As he intended, the long speech had given her time to master her sobs. And—she believed him. She could hear him moving a little nearer and, instinctively, buried herself more deeply in the bedclothes. "Reaching for your gun?" asked the amused voice. "Don't bother. It's all right. I don't eat babies. Only, I thought, if I sat down here"—she felt his weight, solid, at the foot of the bed—"you might find it easier to tell me about it. Had a bad day, haven't you? Very bad, I'm beginning to think. French stragglers, or Cossacks?"

"Both," she managed.

"Good God. No wonder you didn't want me to touch you."

"No, no." She raised her head from the pillow to answer more clearly. "Not me, but . . . Gretchen . . ." And so, bit by bit, among sobs, she got the whole story out. At last, dry-eyed, she looked at him through the shadows. "I won't ever forget it," she said. "I'm different, now. I used to want—oh, all kinds of things. Girls do, I suppose. I don't want them any more. If that's what men are like—" She broke off, then started again. "I meant it, when I said I'd shoot you if you touched me."

"I know you did. But—you will forget, you know. Gretchen and the others, they're dead; they don't care any more. They wouldn't want you to remember. Tomorrow, the sun will rise; it will be a new day, a new life. I had a friend, a good friend; the only one, in fact. My mother didn't like me much; I never knew my father. Well, this friend of mine and I, we joined the army together. He was always singing, always joking, always laughing. Me, I'm a gloomy sort of man, underneath; and plenty to be gloomy about. But Mark laughed, he sang; if there was anything to enjoy, he enjoyed it. And—I shot him, with this hand." He held it out, steady in the candlelight.

"What?"

"Retreating from Moscow. He was wounded, crossing the Beresina, and dying by inches. I carried him as far as I could; we had no horses, no wagons, nothing. At last he said, 'Put me down, Charles.' I put him down, in the snow, and he looked up at me for a moment. We both knew what I had to do. We had seen what the Russians did to stragglers. Well, you've seen the Cossacks. You know. But, do you know, I was crying. He looked at me, then he smiled: 'Charles,' he said, 'remember something, for my sake. Remember that it's never as bad as you think it is.' And then, 'Quickly, Charles.' So I shot him through the heart. And since then, when I begin to feel gloomy, I think of Mark. 'It's never as bad as you think it is.' And now, go to sleep, Rapunzel and think that tomorrow must be better than today. Besides, you've got a friend now: Charles Vincent who shot his last one. We're birds of a feather, you and I: no ties, no affections, not

30

much to be sentimental about. You hate men, you say: well, I don't very much care for women. If you'd met my mother, you'd know why. But I've got more sense than you, Rapunzel. I'm going to marry, one of these days— I'm going to marry a great great great deal of money. I don't care who brings it; she can be humpbacked, or harelipped, so long as she's rich enough."

"Where will you find her?" For the first time since morning, Sonia had forgotten her own troubles.

"You're no fool, Rapunzel, are you? That's exactly the question. Money looks to money. If I'm to get my heiress, I'll have to put a better show before the world than I can at present. For the moment, you see me—or you would if the light was better—with all my worldly possessions about me. Well, not counting my horse, out in the stable. But, thanks to you, I'm richer tonight than I was this morning. Suppose we kept it up; I'd be richer tomorrow than I am today. And, Rapunzel, so would you. Money's a powerful consoler, you know."

"What do you mean?"

"I'm not sure that I know myself. But if we played as well as that together, tonight, meeting for the first time . . . Suppose we practiced. We'd be unbeatable, Rapunzel. I'm on my way to Allied Headquarters, looking for work as an interpreter. There should be plenty of it, God knows. And—there'll be rich men there, and long, anxious evenings with death, perhaps, in the morning. Play will be high; the players' minds not always on their cards. Well, nothing wrong with that." He sounded as if he was arguing with himself. "They can afford to lose it; I should be glad to win it; all perfectly honest and aboveboard, you understand, Rapunzel. I may be an adventurer, but I'm no cheat."

"Of course not."

He laughed. "Those Austrians weren't so sure. 'Devil's own luck,' indeed. You play like an angel, Rapunzel. How about it? Forget Aunt Gertrude. Join forces with me; we'll make a fortune, I promise you. Enough of one, at any rate, to set up house handsomely, wherever the fortunes of war take us. And then, for me, my heiress, and why not a brilliant match for you? I've always noticed that it's the girls who don't care who get the men. Of course," he added thoughtfully, "I don't really know what

31

you look like—as a girl—but you're quite a presentable boy. And you've got spirit—that's the thing. With money behind you, and no clutter of feelings to hold you back— think of the advantage of it. A marshal of France, perhaps? An English duke? Why not?"

"You're mad."

"I don't believe so."

"But how?"

"I've been thinking about that. You'll be my sister. Nobody knows anything about me; still less do they care. My mother was married to my father; I have her marriage lines. But that's all I know, except that he was English. They met in Brussels in '92; she had fled there with her family when things got too hot for them in Paris; he was a young Englishman, making his tour. I suppose he must have been of reasonable family or he wouldn't have been doing so. Anyway, it was *coup de foudre* on both sides; they were married within a fortnight of meeting. Then, the French revolutionaries defeated Austria at Jemappes and took Brussels. My mother never told me exactly what happened; all I know is that my father went back to England while she and her family escaped just in time, first to Liége and finally to Coblentz. I was born there. We never heard from my father again. So"—he shrugged—"you can see that there is no one to be surprised if I suddenly turn up with a sister."

"Your mother's family?"

"All dead, I think. They were greedy. When the émigrés were told to return to France or lose their estates, they went back, all but my mother, and paid the price of their greed on the scaffold. It made my mother the bitter old woman I remember. That and being abandoned by my father. And the émigré life, of course. Pride and penury; makeshifts and make-believe; all the gossip and backbiting of a court, without any of its advantages. I tell you, I was glad to find myself in Napoleon's army. There, real things were real. Even frostbite ... But of course, my mother's friends washed their hands of me—she was dead by then; there's no one to care, or remember, whether I had a sister. And as for you, it's simpler still. Who's to know you were not killed up there at the castle today? You're dead, Rapunzel. Forget Aunt Gertrude and her daily prayers; be born again as my sister; we'll make our fortunes, I promise you. I have—I am paying you the compliment of talking frankly—I have a certain gift for dealing with people." He laughed. "You should have seen old Schwartzenberg. He meant to have me locked up, and ended by giving me letters of recommendation."

"So now you are dealing with me."

"Exactly! I told you our minds worked well together. You see through me; I understand you. Together, we'd be unbeatable. Come, Rapunzel, say yes. You don't want to molder your life away on a mountain peak when the world's in the melting pot. I tell you, anything may happen in the next few weeks. If the Allies beat Napoleon, I've my letters of recommendation from Schwartzenberg. If, on the other hand, he proves too many for them after all—and it wouldn't surprise me; he's a miracle that man— but if he does, here I am; fought at Moscow; French . . . We can't lose, Rapunzel. Come on, the world's our oyster."

"Which we with sword will open? Well—why not? It couldn't be worse than living with Aunt Gertrude; that's one thing certain.'"

He laughed and rose from her bed. "You flatter me unspeakably, Rapunzel. Now—sweet dreams, sister dear. We'll make our plans in the morning."

Chapter 3

"And what, may I ask, are you doing here?" She looked at him coldly across the castle courtyard, a tall woman in a severe black dress that threw up red lights in her dark hair, where it showed under the bandage. If she was alarmed at his sudden appearance, she was very far from showing it.

Charles Vincent had been looking about him. Yes, this was the place: the broken gate, sawdust on the castle courtyard, and silence, where there should have been all the noises of life going on, all these spoke of yesterday's disaster. "You must be Miss Barrymore. Rapunzel thought you were dead." He had taken off his hat and now moved towards her.

"The question is not who am I, but who are you?" She must be in her thirties, with that air of composure and command, that highly formed face. "And who is Rapunzel?"

"Do you know, she never told me her name. But—your pupil, undoubtedly, and safe."

"Thank God for that. I have been frantic with worry."

"You do not sound it." They had exchanged, by now, a long, considering glance, gray eyes locking with deep blue ones.

"What's the use?" She liked what she saw: the brown face, the slim figure in the plain coat, and above all the gray eyes that met hers so squarely. Her voice became more friendly. "You think I should be in strong hysterics? There's been too much to do. We had—I expect Sonia told you—some trouble here yesterday."

"Sonia," he said. "A pretty name. And the other one?"

"Does it matter?" Impatiently. And then, "Well, Von Hugel, if you are interested."

"I am." And then, as if it explained something, "She thought you dead."

"Only stunned. But—where is she? And how much did she see?" Odd to be taking it so entirely for granted that he was Sonia's friend, and hers.

"Everything, I am afraid. You will find her—changed, I think. I am glad you are alive."

She looked at him quizzically. "Thank you. So am I. But, where is she? Why are we standing talking here? And who are you?"

"Charles Vincent." He answered the last question first. "An adventurer: we met last night at a village inn. She was still in bed when I left this morning." And then, at her quick movement: "No need to be anxious. She's all right. I told the landlady to have an eye to her. She won't run away again. I am come for her clothes."

"Oh?"

"She ran away in some of her brother's. Very sensibly. She was going to an old dragon called Aunt Gertrude, but lost her way. I think I have persuaded her to forget about Aunt Gertrude and come with me.

"With you? In what capacity, may I ask?"

He looked at her admiringly. "You're a cool one. Not as a mistress, if that is what you want to know." He laughed. "She pulled a gun on me."

"Good." She had stood, all this time, dominating him from the top of the castle steps; now she turned. "We might as well talk inside," she said. "And by the way, I can defend myself quite as capably as Sonia."

"I am sure you can." He followed her into the castle hall. Here, too, there were signs of yesterday's struggle: broken chairs, the big table still lying where it had been overturned; and everywhere the signs of swift, aimless looting.

"Not a pretty sight." She had been following his eyes. "Which of these bands of brigands do you adhere to, Mr. Vincent?"

"Why, none of them, ma'am. I told you, I am an adventurer. Charles Vincent is my interest, he and no other."

"Very creditable, I'm sure." Dryly. "And where, pray, does Sonia come in?"

"Why, she's an angel with a pack of cards. We are going to make a fortune together, she and I. We won a little one from a couple of Austrian officers last night. And we had never played together before. A bit of practice, and the sky's the limit."

"And you expect me to countenance this project?"

He looked at her thoughtfully. "That is exactly what I have been wondering. But tell me, ma'am, what else have you to suggest for her? I don't know whether there is some hearty young squire in the district who's dangling after her, but I can tell you, it's no use. She won't be touched; not after what she saw yesterday. And I shouldn't think there was one anyway; she's a child, still. Just as well, if you ask me. Of course, I've only seen her in boy's clothes, and her hair cropped; not at her best, I grant you, but no beauty, surely. Not yet, anyway. And no portion, from what she tells me. Well, there you are. Marriage is out. What's left? Aunt Gertrude and the cousin who inherits. Charity either way. You know more about them than I do, but it doesn't sound much of a future to me for a spirited girl like Rapunzel."

"Rapunzel?"

"Because of the hair. Had to call her something, you understand. You wait till you see her."

"I can tell she is not at her best. Well, what are we waiting for?"

"You mean, you'll come?"

"Of course I'll come. She's in my charge, after all. I'm all she's got, poor lamb."

"Not quite all, ma'am. She's got me too, now."

"An adventurer?"

He looked about him at the hall, with its bloodstains. "An adventurer, yes, ma'am, but not a murderer." Was it the deep voice that gave him his charm? He certainly had a way with him. "Well, what about it?" More pressing now. "Do we pack her things? She's been a long time alone."

"I—" For the first time she hesitated. "I suppose so. You don't know the cousin; I do. And you haven't seen Sonia as I have. And you say she won't be touched. She'd not be safe from him; not here; not at her Aunt Gertrude's. You may be an adventurer, but you strike me as a gentleman."

"Thank you," with an ironical bow. "She is to be my sister, ma'am. You had best be our aunt."

"Another Aunt Gertrude? You are too kind. And—you are going a little too fast for me. I did not mean to imply that I would lend any countenance to this lunatic scheme of yours. Your sister indeed! I never heard such nonsense! And a fortune to be won at cards: I've heard of them lost that way often enough, but that is something quite other."

"Well, is it? After all, what's lost must be won. And I tell you, Rapunzel and I play together like . . . like . . ."

"Like angels. You said that before, and I am prepared to take your word for it. You seem to forget, or, very likely, you do not know, that Sonia comes of two ancient and aristocratic families. What would either the Von Hugels or the Delvertons in England think of me if I were to allow her to become a card sharper?"

She had spoken with the easy confidence of her ten years' seniority, but now, gray eyes flashing, he was formidable. "Who said anything about card sharping, ma'am? And as for family; it's true I know nothing of my father, but my mother was a duke's daughter. And much good it did her. When you've seen duchesses mending lace for a

36

living—as I have—you come to set less store by ancient lineage. Pride makes no porridge, ma'am. Will these Von Hugels and Delvertons of yours provide an income for your Sonia? A dowry when she marries? She did not seem to think so."

"I'm afraid she may have been right. At least so far as the Von Hugels are concerned. As for the Delvertons, I know little about them, except that Sonia's grandfather cut off her mother for marrying her father."

"Not exactly encouraging."

"No, but I still think it my duty to take her back to England. Indeed, what else can I do? Sonia does not know it, but her Aunt Gertrude has never approved of me. She was very angry when the baron engaged me, years ago, and is not a woman to forget or forgive. She would never consent to my going there with Sonia—and still less would I consider abandoning Sonia to her Calvinist mercies. So, sir, if you are really on your way to Allied Headquarters, and will give us your escort so far, I shall be deeply grateful to you."

"And what then?"

"Why, surely I shall be able to make some arrangements to get us to England."

"I admire your optimism, ma'am. Are you aware that to get to England at present it is necessary to sail from Prussia to Sweden, and so across the North Sea? A difficult and expensive journey at the best of times. Impossible, I should have thought, for two unaccompanied ladies in the depth of winter. Now, think a little, again, of my plan. You come with me to Allied Headquarters and we set up house together. As brother and sister, or as cousins, if you prefer it: I can see that it would save her the trouble of changing her name. With you for chaperone, we shall be the pink of respectability. I believe I have omitted to explain to you that I have letters from Schwartzenberg strongly recommending me as an interpreter—I was able to be of some small service to him at Leipzig. Well then, we have our reason ready for following the Allied advance, and if Rapunzel and I contrive to make ourselves a little money on the way, what's wrong with that?"

"And then what? Do you expect Sonia and me to play the part of camp followers for the rest of our lives?"

"Nothing of the kind. For one thing, I expect to be rich

in a few months. For another—I do not think you quite understand the significance of the battle that has just been fought. Barring a miracle, Napoleon is beat, ma'am. And—I think he has had his share of miracles. I was with him at Moscow—and after; and I can tell you, he's not the man he was. He makes mistakes, now, and he can't afford to. And worse still, they know it in France. I'm half French, and I have my sources of information. If he retreats to the Rhine—and I don't see what else he can do—he is likely to find revolution waiting for him at home. No, I've no doubt about it, his days are numbered. I see no reason why the Allies should not be in Paris by Christmas, if they can only unite their counsels instead of fighting each other as hard as they do the enemy. And from there, think how much easier it will be for you to return to England."

"I see," she said thoughtfully. And then, with a little laugh that made her look, suddenly, much younger, "You are a very persuasive man, Mr. Vincent."

"You mean, you agree?"

"Well," she temporized. "At least to this point. I will pack up Sonia's things and my own and come with you to this inn—she has been too long alone already. It will be time enough to think again when we are safely at Allied Headquarters."

"I agree with you entirely. But—I beg you will pack as little as possible, and—how about a horse for you?"

"Good gracious!" Once again she was the wise elder. "Do you really expect me to come gallivanting about the country with you on horseback? The family carriage is quite unharmed in the stables, and I have already persuaded the coachman that it is our duty to go looking for Sonia. I had meant of course to go to her aunt's, but he has had such a fright, poor man, that I don't think he will care where she goes, so long as it's away. Besides, he does not like Sonia's cousin overmuch."

"I suppose the carriage actually belongs to the heir?"

"I expect it does, and the horses too."

He laughed. "I can see we will deal admirably together. I am very far from being the only adventurer."

The night's bad dreams had prolonged themselves into a daytime nightmare of memory, and Sonia was sitting huddled wretchedly over the inn stove when she heard a carriage draw up outside. She jumped up at once, to hide in her room—"You'll never get away with it in the daytime, and at close quarters," Vincent had warned her before he left. Then, her hand on the door, she paused, peering out through the leaded window. Surely, she knew that carriage? Vincent jumped out and turned to hand someone down. Then she was running, disguise, everything forgotten: "Barry! Barry!" She threw herself into her governess's arms. "You're not dead!" Tears, easy, relieving tears ran freely down her cheeks.

"Not in the least." Miss Barrymore returned her embrace heartily, then held her at arm's length to look at her. "Though I might well die of shock, here and now, at the spectacle you present. Back indoors with you, child, and let's see if we can make a lady of you."

Charles Vincent, his arms full of boxes, shook his head gravely: "It will surprise me if you can," he said. "And—sadden me too. I shall miss my courageous urchin. But—before you effect your transformation, our Austrian friends are gone, I trust, Rapunzel?"

"Yes, hours ago. A dispatch rider came for them. I hope it was right: I listened at the door. They have orders to report at once to Allied Headquarters at Weimar."

"Admirable urchin. You see"—to Miss Barrymore—"my first prophecy has proved correct. The Allies are advancing already."

"And so you expect us to throw our bonnet over the windmill and follow you to Weimar?"

"Well, what else can you do? You surely do not propose to wander about the countryside unescorted?"

Sonia was looking at Miss Barrymore with huge bright eyes. "You mean you are not going to make me go to Aunt Gertrude?"

"Do you want to?"

"I'd as soon be buried alive. But I was afraid you would think it the proper thing for me to do."

"Perhaps it is, but, do you know, I cannot bring myself to like your aunt any better than you do. No, my idea, if you agree, is that we should make every effort to get to England."

"To England!" Sonia's eyes were larger than ever. "But

39

Grandfather Delverton has never had anything to do with us."

"I know. It's a chance to take, but I do not see how he can disown you entirely, circumstanced as you are. And— if he does, at least I shall be on my home ground. If your family fail us, I suppose we shall have to have recourse to mine."

"Have you family? You have never spoken of them."

"And you thought me sprung, fully armed, from the head of Jove? Yes, I have family from whom, it is true, I parted in anger, but that was many years ago. Who knows, they might be quite glad to see me back? And if not, we shall just have to find ourselves some genteel occupation or other."

"Nonsense." Charles Vincent had just returned from depositing the second load of boxes in the bedroom. "I am a true prophet, and I tell you that by the time you reach England, you will be rich enough to snap your fingers at both your families."

Sonia gave a sudden little crow of pleasure. "You mean our plan still holds? We are to be brother and sister and make our fortune at cards? You do not object, Barry?"

"I am entirely composed of objections, and you are most certainly not going to be brother and sister; I never heard of such a crackbrained scheme."

"No, no, we settled all that," said Vincent pacifically. "We are to be cousins, but we shall make our fortune just the same. I, Charles Vincent, have spoken. And by the way, I have been thinking about you, Miss Barrymore. Would you very much mind if we invented a husband for you?"

"A husband?"

"Yes. The more I see of you, the less convincing you strike me as likely to be in the character of a chaperoning spinster aunt. And—respectability is to be our watchword, you know. Would you very much object to passing as Mrs. Barrymore—a widow, I suppose."

"Taking brevet rank, like a housekeeper?" She shrugged. "I don't care ... if you think it advisable ... it is all madness together."

"I think it essential."

"Very well, then. You, with your fertile imagination,

will doubtless be able to invent a convincing end for my late husband."

"No trouble at all. Gloriously killed, poor Mr. Barrymore—I imagine you would rather not change your name—? Let's see; you've been with Sonia several years, have you not? You must have married very young: a runaway match, perhaps, from the schoolroom. What's the matter?"

She had gone very white. "Nothing. Nothing at all. And then, I take it, he left me, rejoined his regiment and was killed?"

"Exactly. Most gallantly, of course—you insist on the army? I had thought of Trafalgar."

She shrugged. "Oh, very well. I really think we have all run raving mad. Come along, Sonia, I can't bear to see you looking like that for another moment. And as for your hair!"

"Skirts again!" Sonia sighed. "I enjoyed being a boy." Over her head, Miss Barrymore's eyes met Vincent's in a look of shared satisfaction. Convalescence had set in.

But the journey on which they started, next morning, was enough to shake even Elizabeth Barrymore's strong nerves. Inevitably, in their search for Allied Headquarters, they were following the line of the French retreat. It was nearly a week since the battle of Leipzig, but it would be years before this once fertile countryside recovered from its scars. Whole villages had been burned to the ground and every bridge destroyed so that they had to make several long detours to find bridges or boats. The sites where the demoralized French troops had bivouacked were marked by every possible kind of horror, and the two women soon learned to respect Charles Vincent's orders when he rode back to the carriage and told them not to look out of the windows. They had grown almost used to the sight of dead men and dead horses lying by the roadside, but there were other, worse, horrors from which it was best to turn away.

The journey seemed to go on forever. There was, of course, no hope of obtaining post horses, so their own must be favored as much as the appalling condition of the roads would allow. They met no one except a few Cossacks and other troops marching to join the Allied army, and an occasional group of French deserters or, perhaps, stragglers. In the whole countryside, life seemed to stand still, and it was with great difficulty, each night, that they contrived to persuade peasants who still had houses to allow them the use of a room. Again and again, Elizabeth Barrymore had cause to appreciate Charles Vincent's foresight. When she had been packing up her and Sonia's things, back at the castle, he had insisted that she devote a large portion of the available space in the carriage to supplies for the journey. Thanks to him, they could pay for a night's shelter with what was infinitely more precious than money—food. For the looters at the castle had missed one storeroom full of half-cured hams and smoked cheeses.

"I don't care if I never see another bit of ham as long as I live," said Sonia petulantly as they left the half-destroyed cottage where they had spent the second night of their journey. "And as for the smell of camphor!" She gave an angry shake to the handkerchief she carried.

"There are worse smells." Charles Vincent was holding the carriage door for them, but looked over her head as he spoke and away down the burned and blackened village street to a corner where, arriving the night before, they had seen a pile of bodies, those of horses and those of men, all mixed huggermugger.

"How can you!" Sonia shuddered angrily and jumped into the coach. Elizabeth followed with a reproachful backward glance at Vincent. And yet, in a way, she had to confess herself relieved at the almost hostile relationship that seemed to have developed between her pupil and their protector. Well, a quick glance took in Sonia as she drooped listlessly in her corner of the carriage, it was not surprising. Their first meeting had been so romantic, melodramatically so; further association was almost bound to bring disillusionment. Sonia in her brother's clothes might have had a certain glamor. In her own utilitarian stuff gown, with short hair straggling around her pale little face, she looked at the moment, merely pitiful. No wonder if Vincent treated her with an older brother's casualness.

She seemed to lose no opportunity of grumbling at him. He bore it admirably, as he did all the miseries of that grim journey, and Elizabeth, searching her heart as to her wisdom in so rashly throwing in their lot with his, had to admit to herself that everything he had done so far justified her decision. His *laissez-passer* from Schwartzenberg saw them safely through any encounters with Allied troops; his presence, riding beside the coach, seemed enough to scare away the demoralized groups of French stragglers they encountered. These poor creatures, without discipline, food or money were reduced to trying to sell their golden earrings for food—but mostly the peasants refused the bargain. The French army had lived off its conquests too long. The days were gone when they were hailed as liberators; now the country people's hatred for them was such that they even risked disease by refusing to bury their dead.

Watching one of Vincent's encounters with a wretched little group of wounded Frenchmen, Elizabeth thought she saw money change hands. She could hardly blame Vincent for his sympathy for these rags of men, whose countryman, on the mother's side at least, he was, but she could not help feeling a little anxious. They had pooled their slender resources before starting out on what seemed, more and more, their desperate venture and the total result had been very far from cheering. After a slight battle with herself, she raised the subject when they stopped an hour or so later to eat cold ham and rest the horses.

"How much did you give those Frenchmen?" There seemed no way of wrapping up the question.

"Only a couple of dollars." He grinned at her ruefully, and she found herself liking him better than ever for taking the inquisition so well. "I know I had no right to, without consulting you, but—I served with one of them on the retreat from Moscow. I could not let them go with nothing."

"Of course not—" But Sonia interrupted her.

"You mean to tell us you gave our money to some of those murderers? What right had you!"

"The right of humanity, urchin." His voice was gentle. Like Elizabeth, he must be remembering what she had gone through.

"Humanity! What humanity do they show? I tell you, when I see them dying by the roadside, I'm glad. 'There's one less of you at least,' I tell myself."

"I think you must be forgetting, Miss von Hugel, that I am French myself."

43

The formal address, which he so seldom used, pulled her up short. "I—I'm sorry. I forgot. Anyway, you don't act like a Frenchman."

He smiled wryly. "I suppose I am to take that as a compliment." And then, to Elizabeth: "Just the same, you have every right to be angry with me. It was unpardonable to make so free with our common resources. Here"— he pulled out his purse and handed it to her—"take this and look after it for me, in case I am tempted again. And now, it is high time we were on our way. The sooner we get to Weimar and you and I start earning our keep, urchin, the better for all of us."

"But—" Elizabeth checked herself. It would be time enough, when they got to Allied Headquarters, to raise her doubts about Vincent's plans. She had gone along with them so far because it seemed the only thing to do, but surely, at Headquarters, some other solution of the problem would present itself. If they could sell the carriage, for instance, might it not provide funds for the journey back to England?

That night the rain that had fallen steadily since they started turned to snow and the air became bitterly cold. Vincent, riding on ahead to a half-destroyed village, had found them one room in a cottage where, they learned, Napoleon had lodged only the week before. They slept, all three of them, fully clothed on the carriage rugs around the stove, and Sonia, waking with chattering teeth at first light, summed up the feelings of all three. "We can't get to Weimar too soon for me," she said.

"We'll be there tonight." As usual, Vincent was already up and now left them alone to make what toilet they could.

"Lord, I look a fright." Sonia was coming her hair with the help of her pocket looking glass. "How do you stay so tidy, Barry?"

"Long hair's a great advantage." Elizabeth was rebraiding her plaits, preparatory to winding them round her head in her neat coronet. "Never mind, darling, perhaps there will even be a hairdresser in Weimar."

"And we will rest and rest and rest, and you shall go and call on that Goethe you talk so much about, while I pay my respects to the Grand Duke. Perhaps he will ask us to dinner. After all, Father ..." She stopped and bit back tears. "How could I forget? Poor Father ..."

"Never mind, my lamb." Elizabeth crossed the room to put her arms around her. "I am glad you can forget, sometimes. And I think it is an excellent notion that you should pay your respects to the Grand Duke, even if you are in mourning. So long as you feel up to telling him about your father."

"Oh. Yes; I suppose I must." And then, "Oh, Barry, I do hope we don't meet Cousin Franz in Weimar."

"So do I." Inevitably, Elizabeth remembered the carriage and Vincent's remarks about adventurers.

But when they reached Weimar that evening, the empty silence of its narrow winding streets told them they were too late. Vincent, who had gone to make inquiries at the main inn, came back with a rueful face to confirm this impression. "Headquarters moved on yesterday," he said. "To Gotha, it seems. The only good thing about it is that there is plenty of room in the inn."

"And no one to play cards with." You could trust Sonia in her present state to look on the dark side of things

"You could hardly expect to do so anyway, in the public rooms of an inn." Once again Elizabeth felt it best to postpone the inevitable argument about Vincent's plans.

"What! You mean that I am to be cooped up in a private room!"

"Of course you are, my dear child. Nor, I am sure, would Mr. Vincent suggest anything else."

"I wish you would call me Charles." He had been following the exchange with close attention. "Of course you are quite right, Miss Barrymore, as always. And no need to make such faces at me, either, Rapunzel. When we establish ourselves, reputation will be our strongest card. No one must be ashamed to be seen at our house. You will have to be above gossip, my poor Rapunzel, like Caesar's wife."

"We are to have a house?" Sonia asked.

"We shall have to. And give delicious little dinners to which the card table will be a logical conclusion. I promise you, they will pay for themselves soon enough."

"That is all very well." Elizabeth interposed what she thought an insuperable objection. "But what is to pay for the house?"

45

He laughed. "How I wish I knew! But don't look so gloomy, Rapunzel. Who knows what successes I may not have while you two ladies are cooped respectably up in your private room."

"It's not fair," Sonia began, but he had already turned away to make their arrangements with the landlord of the inn and she had to vent her irritation on Elizabeth, who bore it as patiently as she had done all her charge's explosions of nerves on this trying journey. It would be a long time, she thought, before Sonia recovered her normally equable temper. And no wonder.

Now, suddenly, Sonia burst into tears. "Why am I so horrible, Barry? I hate myself—I hate everything!"

"Never mind, my lamb. It will pass. Everything does, sooner or later. Oh!"

"What is it, Barry?"

"Keep your head down. I'm very much afraid it is your cousin Franz on the other side of the street."

"He's bound to recognize the carriage. Oh what *shall* we do? I wish Charles were here."

"So do I. Oh dear, he's seen it; he's coming this way. Do you think there is the slightest chance that he will conduct himself like a gentleman for once, and let us keep the carriage?"

"I shouldn't think so. But perhaps he won't have heard of Father's death. Do we have to tell him?"

"Shh—" And then, in well-simulated surprise and her best German: "Why, it's the Herr von Hugel. How do you do, sir?"

"The *Baron* von Hugel," he corrected her, leaning his broad red face in at the carriage window. "Cousin Sonia!" His surprise seemed as false as they knew their own to be. "What can you be doing here in Weimar? And—surely—in my carriage?" And then, as the merest of afterthoughts: "Allow me to present my condolences on your father's unlucky death—and my congratulations on your own"—a significant pause—"equally lucky escape."

"You have heard, then?"

"Of course. Did you hope I might not have, little cousin? What an innocent you are, to be sure. Did you really not know that I had a faithful friend in your household? Lucky for me, was it not, that he contrived to escape the massacre brought on, I understand, by my

46

uncle's folly. Oh yes, I have heard all about your disaster and am even now on my way, hotfoot, to your side. I suppose you were looking for me, little cousin, and no wonder! Nor was your confidence misplaced. No need to look so anxious; I will marry you at once. It is my duty as head of the family. I never thought I might come to think of it as such." And then, as if really seeing her for the first time, "Good God! Did they cut your hair too?"

She stared at him with wide, uncomprehending eyes. "I do not know what you are talking about, Cousin Franz."

He laughed. "Bravely spoken! So that's to be your line is it? Well, I must say I admire you for it and promise I will never cast it up against you when we are married. Though I confess it will be a relief to me if your first child is not born for—well, shall we say a year or so at least."

Now at last she understood him and turned first white, then scarlet with what Elizabeth was glad to recognize as more rage than confusion. "Your spies misinformed you, sir. And even if what you think were true, I would rather die than marry you."

"Strong words, cousin. And what, pray, do you intend to do instead? Your father left you penniless, you know. I would not like to see you reduced to begging—or worse."

"I am going to England—to my mother's family. Miss Barrymore goes too."

"Splendid!" His sarcasm was heavily obvious. "Your mother's family having shown such tender concern for her welfare—and yours. But of course you must know your own business best, cousin—and with the estimable Miss Barrymore for companion, what harm can come to you? Though I confess it strikes me as a somewhat rash journey for two ladies to undertake unescorted—even if one of them is somewhat advanced in years." And then, condescending at last to return her greeting: "How do you do, Miss Barrymore. I am delighted to see that you are not dead, as I had been led to believe."

"Your source of information does seem to have been a trifle unreliable, does he not?" She had been thinking rapidly. "And—Miss von Hugel and I do not travel unaccompanied. Mr. Vincent has kindly undertaken to escort us."

"Vincent? And who, pray, is he? Some friend of yours?" His tone suggested the worst. "As head of the family, I must object to my cousin's undertaking such a journey in such fly-by-night company."

"Make your objections, then, to me." Charles Vincent had come up behind him during this speech. "Charles Vincent, at your service."

A measuring glance passed between them. On the face of it, they were unequally matched enough, for Von Hugel loomed nearly a head taller than Vincent and broad to match. But his eyes fell first and there was more bluster than confidence in his voice when he spoke. "As head of her family, sir, I ask by what right you have undertaken the charge of this young lady."

"These young ladies, sir; a very different matter. Why— by the right of friendship, if I may claim it—and as a fellow Englishman."

"English, are you? I might have known it, though there's something damned Frenchified about your speech."

"There is. Do you want to make anything of it?"

"Oh, no . . . not the least in the world." Now the bluster failed completely and he turned to Sonia. "I am glad to see you have so swaggering a defender, cousin. I shall await news of your—adventures with interest. But before we part, since that seems to be your desire, there is a little matter of my carriage to be discussed. Go to England, on your fool's errand, if you insist. I have done my duty in offering to marry you; do not expect me to break my heart over your refusal. Tarnished goods, cousin, tarnished goods—" And then, quickly, aware of Vincent's involuntary movement towards him, "But pay me, first, for my carriage with which you have made so free, and be grateful my strong family feeling prevents me from having you taken up for its theft as I should."

"Name your price." Charles Vincent's voice crackled.

"Well, let us consider: I would not wish to be hard on you, cousin." Once more he spoke to Sonia. "And indeed it goes hardly with me to let you go like this. Think again, my dear: my offer is still open. Think before you refuse me. To be Baroness von Hugel, after all—and, I promise you, I do not intend to rot in the country as your father did. Trust me to make my mark in the world, and whatever height I rise to, you shall be at my side. Today's events—and what led up to them—shall be forgotten; as my wife you will command respect. Which is more, I can tell you, than you can hope for if you choose to throw in your lot with Miss Barrymore and her"—he paused—"friend."

"My friend, too," said Sonia, and, simultaneously, "That is enough," in tones of ice from Vincent; and, from Elizabeth Barrymore, who had quietly been counting the contents of her purse, "Take that—and go."

"Thank you." He began, elaborately, to count the money in his turn, but was interrupted by Charles Vincent. "If I were you"—his voice was more dangerous than ever—"I should not linger here any longer. I have spared you, so far, as Miss von Hugel's cousin, and, as you have pointed out, the head of her family. If you stay much longer, I may find it impossible to restrain myself. And—one thing more—you have made enough slanderous speeches, today, to merit death ten times over. If I ever hear of your doing so again, I will find you out, wherever you are, and make you sorry you were born."

"A very gallant defender." Von Hugel crammed the money into his pocket. "I congratulate you, ladies." But his voice shook on the would-be mocking words, and his back, as he turned, without so much as a bow, and left them, was that of a beaten man.

"Well, he's gone," said Elizabeth.

"And our nest egg with him. Have we enough left for beds for the night, or must I turn highwayman?" Vincent's voice was incorrigibly cheerful.

"Oh, we can manage, I think, for a couple of days." Elizabeth kept her voice light to match his.

"A couple of days!" Sonia's voice shook. "And what then?"

Vincent handed her out of the carriage. "Why, by then your Uncle Charles will have turned up something—or other. Don't look so down in the mouth, Rapunzel. Rome wasn't built in a day."

"No, but it was destroyed in one. You must wish you had never saddled yourself with us. Alone, you'd be at Frankfurt by now."

"Yes, and talking to myself from very boredom. At least with you, Rapunzel, and Miss Barrymore for company I shall never be dull."

"You amuse yourself, I take it, with my tantrums! You

49

heard what my cousin said. I've no reputation, no fortune, nothing. Why do you trouble yourself with me?"

"Because you're an angel with the cards, remember? Don't frown and fret so, Rapunzel. Think what a setdown you gave that miserable cousin of yours. And think, too, how furious he will be when he realizes he made us pay merely its market value for the carriage. With things as they are, the horses alone are worth three times what we paid him."

"Really?" she brightened up at once. And then, "But we can't afford to sell them."

"Quite true. And that is why I must leave you two ladies to your own devices this evening. Make the most of the private room I hired for you before this little contretemps, and I will see what gold mine I can find in the streets of Weimar. And don't fret, Rapunzel; your turn will come."

It was a long, gloomy evening. Elizabeth could not help feeling that this reverse was largely her fault, since it had been her idea to take the carriage. The fact that Charles Vincent had not even hinted at reproach made this somehow even harder to bear. But there was worse. The money she had been compelled to give for it had been mostly his. So much for her idea of selling it to pay for their journey to England. Reluctantly, hesitantly, she had to admit to herself that there was nothing for it now but to subscribe to his plan for them. She did not like it, but she liked the alternative still less. And at least, Vincent's care for them on the journey had confirmed her first impression of him. He might call himself an adventurer, but he was a gentleman just the same, and could be trusted. Anyway—rather him than Cousin Franz.

Anxiety kept her long awake. She lay ramrod still so as not to disturb Sonia, a quotation, familiar as despair, echoing in her mind: "I have offended reputation." But what else could she do? How protect Sonia? After today's meeting, it was doubly necessary to get her safe to England, away from the scandal Franz would almost certainly spread. Very well then, face it, Vincent's plan was their only hope.

She slept at last, but restlessly, and woke early. Sonia was still asleep, looking a peaceful child again with her hair curling wildly on the pillow. Elizabeth dressed quickly: let her have her moments of peace. Downstairs, in the main room of the inn, Charles Vincent was drinking coffee. Watching him for a moment unobserved, she thought he must have made a long night of it. There were dark circles under his eyes, and his face was drawn under the tan. And, disconcertingly, something tense about the way he sat, hunched over his cup, brought home to her how young he was. All last night's qualms came back with a rush. Most of the time, he seemed so completely the man of the world that one tended to forget that in happier times he would hardly have completed his education. Had she been mad to throw in their lot with his—to burden him with their problems as well as his own?

He looked up and saw her. "Good morning." Now his face and voice were as usual. "And good news."

"Really?"

"The best. We are solvent again—affluent, you could almost call it. Here, treasurer, take this. I have saved out enough for the hotel expenses. These are our savings."

"Good God." She was amazed at the weight of the purse he handed her. "You cannot, surely, have won all this at cards!"

"No." Again a fleeting shadow crossed his face. "I met a friend—a cousin, to be precise. He is in the entourage of M. de Saint Aignan."

"The French Minister to Weimar?"

"Yes. They too are on their way to Frankfurt."

"Then perhaps we shall have the pleasure of meeting this generous cousin of yours."

"I doubt it." There was certainly something odd about him this morning.

Chapter 4

In England, early that November, Lady Elinor Burnleigh faced her brother across the elaborate equipage of a country house breakfast. "In that case, I will come too." A formidable woman, handsome as a thoroughbred, she

51

had only recently abandoned the last pretense of youth. Her tone was that of one who is used to being obeyed.

And yet, "Impossible." The Earl of Denbigh had never used either the word or the tone to his elder sister before. Now, seeing how she arched aristocratic eyebrows at him, he qualified the bleak rebuttal. "You know as well as I do, Elinor, what things are like in Europe. It is no place for a lady."

"Lady Burgersh is there."

"Yes, and remember what you said when you heard she was to accompany her husband. 'Unsuitable' . . . 'unladylike' . . . those were the mildest of the words you chose to describe her conduct. Surely you cannot wish, now, to imitate her?"

Thus convicted out of her own mouth, Lady Elinor changed her ground. "Naturally I do not *want* to go." She used the tolerant tone of seven years' seniority. "But if you insist on accepting the mission Lord Castlereagh thrusts upon you, I feel it my duty to accompany you. My father charged me, on his deathbed, to look after you. I do not consider it as consistent with my duty to him—or to you—to let you go jauntering off to Europe by yourself. Heaven knows what absurdities you would commit, without me beside you. The very least of it will be one of your giddy fits. You know you have never been perfectly strong since your accident. I often think it has only been my constant care that has kept you alive."

"Do you, Elinor?" An odd note in his voice. "Now, it's a strange thing, but I have recently begun to wonder whether it was not your perpetual cosseting that has kept me ailing. Does it occur to you that I have never had one of what you call my giddy fits when I was away from home?"

"You've never admitted to one, but that's another story. But it's all of a piece with the rest of your ingratiude to me. And as for the idea of your setting up as a diplomat— I confess I find it vastly entertaining. Does Castlereagh really think you a match for those wily Europeans? You know perfectly well that you always believe the best of everyone till I undeceive you. Without me, you will be their dupe, very likely their laughingstock. Think how easily you are led! You have come near enough, once, to disgracing the name of Burnleigh. I cannot risk having it happen again."

"That is enough, Elinor." He put down his cup and saucer with a little definite click of porcelain on mahogany and rose to his feet to stand over her. Tall, lean, fair and elegant, he yet contrived to give an over-all impression of grayness as if there had been too little sunshine in his life. While she looked up at him, bridling astonishment, he went on in the same tone of calm finality. "It is my fault, I know. I have run in leading strings so long, I suppose you thought it would go on forever. I should have said this years ago, when Father died, but—I suppose I was sorry for you. I played you a cruel trick, did I not, in being born, so tardily, when you had been bred to the idea of being heir to Burnleigh? A peeress in your own right— hereditary bearer of—what is it?—the clove orange at coronations? It was hard to lose all that. I have always known how you felt—and Father too. If I could have waived my claim in your favor, I would have done so. You know that I did my best."

"A boy's best!" Her voice was full of an old scorn.

"No!" Blue eyes she had always thought gentle blazed in his face. "A man's. You and Father tricked me out of the best thing I ever tried to do. And destroyed my chance of happiness. If you had only let us get away to America, you would be Countess of Denbigh now—in fact, if not in name—and I—"

"President of the United States, no doubt!" Mockingly, "With that scheming hussy at your side, who knows what you might not have become."

"I said, that is enough, Elinor." Dangerously quiet now: "What you and my father have done to me is done. We will not discuss it further—nor will I allow you to speak ill of the dead."

"The—" she paused. "Of course. I am sorry, Giles. Forgive me. It is my anxiety for you that makes me speak. I cannot bear to think of you going so far away, all by yourself."

"But I shall not be going alone. Philip accompanies me."

"Philip! Now I know that you have taken leave of your senses. What earthly use can that scatterbrained ward of yours be to you? Except to get you into more scrapes than you might have managed for yourself."

"On the contrary. I expect Philip to make himself extremely useful as my secretary. Lack of occupation has been his trouble as much as anything. That, and too much money. I wish I could have persuaded his mother to let him go to the Peninsula as he wished, but even she admits that to accompany me to Allied Headquarters in Germany must steady him a little."

"And he agrees to leave his London"—she paused—"pursuits, to rough it with you on the Continent?"

"You never liked Philip, did you? I have often wondered whether it was not, in part at least, knowledge of your disapproval that drove him to some of his wilder exploits."

"I might have known you would prove it all my fault, as usual. Well, don't come crying to me when he disgraces you, as I have no doubt he will."

Surprisingly, he laughed. "Elinor, what must I do to persuade you that I am no longer the boy you used to bully—oh, for my own good, of course. Perhaps, when I return from Germany, you will contrive to bear in mind that I was thirty last birthday—old enough, one would think, to make my own mistakes. As for Philip, he is in debt again, of course, and—"

"Involved with a woman as usual. You do not need to mince words with me, Giles. Her demands must be serious indeed if he is prepared to flee her so far. Poor Philip, he always liked his comforts. How wretched he will be as a camp follower."

His laugh, this time, was an angry one. "Not perhaps the happiest phrase for a diplomatic mission. And I think you do less than justice to Philip's affection for me. It has not, I can see, occurred to you that Philip's motives for wishing to go with me may be very much like your own. It would amuse you, I am sure, to think that he too wants to look after me, and bores me dreadfully with talk of warm clothes and the medicines we must take with us. Really, I think it quite heroic of me to let him come."

"Lunatic would be a better word. Oh—"

The door of the breakfast room had burst open to reveal Philip Haverton himself. Young, slight and dark, he was dressed in the height of London fashion, his striped

54

waistcoat, high cravat and profusion of jewelry presenting a marked contrast to his cousin's country blue coat and buckskins. He stopped and flushed at sight of Lady Elinor, disapproving, teacup in hand. "I—I beg your pardon Lady Elinor. I did not know you were down yet." And then, eagerly, to Denbigh. "News at last. There is an urgent messenger this instant arrived from London." He handed him a letter. "Do you think it is our marching orders? Will there be time for me to order another half-dozen cravats before we leave? I knew I should have gone to town last week. My man tells me I have only four dozen shirts to my name, and as for cravats—he is quite in despair. Tell me quick, Giles, what's the news?"

"I shall know when you give me a chance to read this." Denbigh moved away to read the letter by the window.

" 'News at last?' " Even at thirty-seven, Lady Elinor would have been a handsome woman if it had not been for her trick of either frowning or raising her eyebrows, as she did now. "You mean this project has been on the tapis for some time?"

"Did you not know? Castlereagh has been urging Giles to go ever since hostilities recommenced this summer. There is the devil to pay among the Allies, you know—oh, I am sure I beg your pardon, Lady Elinor." It was significant that though he called her brother Giles, he always gave Lady Elinor her title. "They need someone like Giles to hold them together. He'll do it, if it's possible. How about it, Giles? When do we leave?"

"At once. We have won a great victory, at Leipzig. Lord Castlereagh writes that the way is open to France—if only the Allies will take it. My instructions await me in town. A frigate is standing by to land us at Cuxhaven. Lord knows where Allied Headquarters will be by then: the French are in full retreat. Come, Philip, there are a thousand things to be seen to, if we are to reach London today. You will excuse us, Elinor?"

She inclined her head in stately acquiescence, but, inevitably, had the last word: "Believe me, no good will come of it."

News of Leipzig reached another English breakfast table that morning. In his luxurious little house behind Park Lane, the richest man in London sat alone, as usual, over his tea and mutton chop. As usual, too, Henry Fessingham, M.P., was reading—this time the latest government report on the condition of the agricultural laborer in the southern countries. Drinking lukewarm tea, he grunted irritably, ran his fingers through shaggy gray hair and folded down the corner of the page that had annoyed him. "Starvation wages!" For lack of any other audience, he had been talking to himself for years. "And what will happen when peace comes—if it comes—" He paused, impressively, as if addressing the crowded House of Commons, drank more cool tea and turned over the page. "Rack and ruin," he went on. "Enclosure; selfishness; going to the dogs. Can't say I didn't warn 'em. Not known as Cassandra in the House for nothing. But what's the use?" He pushed back his chair and walked across to the window. Outside, late autumn sunshine brought out the colors of the last roses in the town garden that stood, said London gossip, in the place of wife and child to him. It was a long time, now, since the last exasperated mamma had given up hope of snaring this elusive prey for her daughter. Twenty years ago, he had been London's most eligible untitled bachelor, highly susceptible, and present at all the *ton* parties. Then, suddenly, he had given it all up, abandoning Almack's and applying himself instead to Parliament and finance. It was too provoking, said London's mammas, to see so much money put to so little use. They saw his plain coats and knew nothing of the schools he financed—nor would they have approved if they had. As for his garden, the privileged few who had managed to see it raised affronted hands: all that money to contrive a country garden in the heart of town! And not one glasshouse, either. Sent away with posies of seasonable flowers, violets or roses or even the stylish new chrysanthemums, they shook their heads and told each other that poor Fessingham got odder every day.

This morning, he looked out at his garden gloomily enough. "The roses need pruning," he told himself. "But what's the use? 'Weary, stale, flat and unprofitable—' " He threw open the window for a closer look at the roses, and then stopped, arrested by the sound of bells. One after another, London's churches took up the melodious tale, which was punctuated, presently, by the heavy note of gunfire. Henry Fessingham stepped out on to the terrace and selected a last perfect rosebud for his buttonhole: "A victory at last," he told himself, "let us devoutly hope it is against France, and not those unlucky Americans. Yes— definitely they need pruning." He returned to his breakfast parlor and was about to ring the bell when a footman bounced unceremoniously into the room, then recollected himself and snapped to attention: "News, sir, splendid news. Boney's beat—soundly beat at last. In Europe somewhere; I forget the name of the place."

"Excellent." Coolly as ever. "In that case, James, I believe I will celebrate with some hot tea and a fresh roll. One of the ones you have in the servants' hall, perhaps . . . oh, and James . . ."

"Yes, sir?"

"What is that you are holding?"

"I quite forgot. An urgent message from Whitehall, sir."

"Then you have best give it to me." He took the letter and read its brief contents. "My carriage at once. For Whitehall. Give the orders, will you, and forget about the roll and tea."

Giving the necessary orders, James let it be known that the master got queerer every day. He tapped his forehead significantly: "Money and gardens, and politics," he said. "And not a chick nor child to bless himself with. Queer as Dick's hatband, if you ask me."

"Nobody did," said the butler repressively. "And Lord Liverpool don't seem to share your views. The carriage at once, didn't you say? For Whitehall? I know what that means, even if you don't."

It was late when Fessingham returned home, and the huge flares were already burning in their sockets on either side of his front door. The butler himself was hovering anxiously in the front hall. "The Earl of Denbigh is here, sir." He came forward to help his master out of his heavy greatcoat. "And Mr. Haverton."

"Good." Fessingham dropped York tan gloves on a mahogany chest. "They stay to dinner, of course. You have given the orders?"

"Yes." The butler's tone was reproving. "You will find them in the blue drawing room, sir."

"Thank you." He picked up the dispatch box he had

brought home with him, crossed the hall and opened the door of the blue drawing room. "You have lost no time, gentlemen."

"I thought there was none to lose." Denbigh and Fessingham greeted each other with the casualness of old friends, while Philip Haverton stood a little to one side, concealing unwonted shyness by sucking the gold head of his cane. "You have our instructions?" Denbigh asked, before turning to present "My ward Mr. Haverton."

"Yes. I am delighted to make your acquaintance, Mr. Haverton. You accompany your cousin on this mission?"

"If there is no objection." Haverton sounded like a schoolboy, at once bashful and excited.

"Not the least in the world. I am glad my friend Denbigh will have company on what I am afraid must prove an arduous journey. The frigate *Careless* awaits you at Harwich; your instructions are here." He put the dispatch box down on a side table. "We will discuss them when we have dined, and then—my carriage is at your disposal, gentlemen."

"You mean we leave at once?" Philip Haverton's tone betrayed that he had had very different ideas of how he would spend the night.

"If it will not inconvenience you." This to Denbigh: "The wind is fair. Who knows how long it will continue so? I am sorry to put you to such fatigue." He was still speaking rather to Denbigh than to his companion. "There will be time, I hope, for sleep when once you are on board."

"But not for the farewells Haverton intended saying. Can it be done briefly, Philip? In two hours, say, while I confer with Mr. Fessingham? But no sitting down to a hand of cards, mind. I'll not wait for you so much as five minutes."

"Oh, thank you, sir." Philip's worldly air was constantly being marred by his blush. "I promise you, I won't so much as look in at Boodle's—but there is someone—I ought to say gooddbye."

"Should you? Well—don't let her make you a Cheltenham tragedy of it. And no promises, mind: I never made a woman a promise but I lived to regret it. Right—two hours, then."

"Two hours!" He consulted the jeweled watch that hung

with a number of seals from his fob. "Then if you'll excuse me, sir?"

Fessingham saw him out, then returned to his friend. "He will be useful to you?"

"I hope so. On my public business, that is. As to the other—of course he will know nothing about it."

"Quite so." Fessingham put his dispatch box on a table by the fire and drew up two chairs close to it. "You'll take a glass of madeira?"

"Thank you. And then, I hope, you will tell me what purpose I can serve in Europe when we are almost too nobly represented there already."

Fessingham laughed. "Trust you to put your finger on the point. That is exactly it. We are too well represented. There is Sir Charles Stewart at the court of Prussia, Cathcart with the Russians and your friend Aberdeen with the Austrians. It was all very well when our various ministers were at the courts to which they were accredited. But now that all the monarchs have insisted—most foolishly, if you ask me—on following their armies, they—and the ministers—are thrown far too much together for comfort. It's the deuce of a situation, you know."

"That I can well imagine."

"Yes. The Grand Alliance against Napoleon has been an uneasy one at the best of times. Well—I don't need to remind you that all our present allies have been on his side at one time or another. The Emperor of Austria gave him his daughter—Prussia was his humble servant for years—and even the Czar would have continued his friend if he'd let him. Attacking Russia was Napoleon's fatal mistake, I think. The Czar's a strange man—but a leader of men. He—and English gold, of course—are what keeps the Alliance going."

"And I'm to represent the English gold?"

"Precisely. And not only to see that the attack is pressed with all possible vigor, but to make sure of a just and reasonable peace when the end comes—as I am sure it must."

"And your just peace?"

Fessingham laughed. "I was afraid you would ask that. There of course, is exactly the difficulty—and, by the way, one of the points on which I particularly rely on you to keep me informed. There are as many views as to what should happen to France as there are Allies. More, I expect: the question is which one is right."

"Is it true that the Czar wants to put Bernadotte on the throne of France?"

"So I have heard, and it may not be as fantastic a notion as it sounds."

"It seems crazy enough to me. One of Napoleon's own marshals who turned against him? I'd as soon expect a Bourbon restoration."

"And you may be nearer the mark than you know. My informants report that there's an increasingly powerful secret society both in and out of France working for the restoration of Louis or even of his brother the Comte d'Artois. You'll want to watch out for them. And that brings me to the other side of your commission. You are going, you know, as my representative as well as Castlereagh's. You do not mind?"

"If you do not, I hardly see why I should. I only hope I have enough"—he paused—"discretion."

"I am sure of it. That is why we have chosen you. And—you have other advantages. You are comparatively unknown—and unmarried." A sharp glance from under bushy eyebrows. "Lady Elinor did not object to staying behind?"

"She objected, of course."

"But she stays?"

"Yes."

"Good. And young Haverton?"

"Will act as my secretary—in the rest of my business."

"Yes. I wish we could have found someone trustworthy to send with you, but it is not easy. At all costs, we must keep your real errand secret. And now, since we have reached the subject, let us have another glass of madeira and discuss codes and ciphers like a couple of master spies."

Chapter 5

"Lord, look at the crowds." Sonia turned from the high gabled window. "You'd think the whole world had come to Frankfurt."

"And you'd be about right." Elizabeth shook out the fine cambric frill she was sewing. "Charles says it was little short of a miracle he found us these apartments."

"With his usual modesty." Her tone was sardonic. "And I have no doubt he has agreed to pay far more for them than we can afford."

"Well," said Elizabeth reasonably. "We can hardly grumble at that, since he has been franking us ever since he met that providential cousin of his."

"Yes—his mysterious cousin. Shall we never meet him? Is Charles ashamed of him, d'you think? Maybe all his fine talk about being a duke's grandson was nothing but moonshine and he doesn't want us to meet his fat burgher kinsman." She turned once more to look out the window. "Look at them! Grumble, grumble, grumble all the time about their sufferings under Napoleon—iniquitous taxes, forced levies ... and all of them as fat as butter, looking as if they'd never suffered in their lives."

"And making a pretty penny out of the Allies too, by all reports. I can see why they're in no hurry to have Headquarters move on again. Another month or so of this and they'll have gone far to recoup their losses under the French."

"A month? Do you really think it will be so long?"

"Impossible to tell. I was asking Charles only this morning." And then, as he entered the room, "Ah, Charles, the very person. Now you can tell Sonia yourself what you think the chances are of Headquarters' moving on."

"Poor." He dropped his heavy greatcoat on a chair and moved over to the big stove in the center of the room. "At least for the time being. They sent a peace offer to Napoleon, you know, by M. de Saint Aignan and intend to await his answer here. After all, it makes a change after the discomforts of the campaign."

"Yes," said Elizabeth, "they seem to be entertaining themselves pretty well, what with parades and dinners and the opera. It must, as you say, make a pleasant change. Think of the road here."

Sonia shivered. "Don't talk about it. But tell me, Charles, isn't M. de Saint Aignan the man that mysterious cousin of yours works for?"

"Yes. My cousin has returned to France with him—and why you call him mysterious beats me."

"Why, because you never brought him to call on us."

"And why should I, pray? Has it not occurred to your scatterbrain that a cousin of mine might be a trifle surprised at finding me equipped with a couple of relatives he had never heard of."

"Oh." Sonia took it in. "And now he's gone back to France, without a penny of his money. He must be very devoted to you, Charles."

Vincent laughed. "He means, I think, to have a friend at court in case the Allies contrive to pull themselves together, stop dining and wining each other, and march on Paris."

"Oh, God, if they only would." Sonia picked a rose out of a vase on the table beside her and began systematically shredding it to pieces. "I'm so tired of Frankfurt I could scream."

"Well don't," said Charles Vincent. "The landlady would undoubtedly complain. As for Frankfurt, you were glad enough to get there, so far as I can recall."

"Of course I was! After that grisly journey: I shall never forget it."

"Nor will Elizabeth, I imagine." And then, as she snatched another rose out of the vase, "Blücher sent those roses: I expect him again tonight. He may be surprised to find them so diminished."

"He sent them to me, did he not?"

"To you and Elizabeth. His gracious hostesses, if I remember the phrase aright. He would hardly call you gracious if he could see you now."

"No? Well, let me show you just how gracious I can be." She swept across the room to the chimney piece where the landlady had arranged a prized collection of china figures, snatched up a Dresden shepherdess and threw it at him with all the force she could muster.

"Tut, Rapunzel." He caught it neatly as she turned and ran sobbing from the room. And then, to Elizabeth, "My fault, I suppose."

"Not really. Poor child; I wish I could convey to you how unlike she is to her usual self."

He smiled his wry, delightful smile. "I'll take your word for it. Poor child indeed. That was a bad day she went through."

"A terrible one. I cannot help feeling guilty for having been safely unconscious through it all."

"You should be grateful you were. I do not imagine you could have helped trying to intervene. Your unconsciousness most certainly saved your life."

"I suppose so. It's a sobering thought. But—seriously, now we are alone, do you think we really have a chance of making enough money to get ourselves to England?" How strange to find herself asking this, committed to this fantastic line of conduct. But for the thousandth time she asked herself, What else could I have done?

"I'm sure we can." His confident tone was reassuring. "We've done pretty well this last week, you know. Well—everything is on our side. It is not merely that there are no ladies in Frankfurt: there are no homes. The men dine each other, day after day, with the same food sent in from the same inn, the same company, the same speeches. No wonder if we have been mobbed since we started keeping open house. I think our problem will continue to be rather to limit the number of our guests than to find them." And then, on a different note: "And no need to look so grave, either. I know you don't much like it—nor, I suspect, now it's real to her, does Sonia, but they can well afford to lose what we so badly need to win. We give them a pleasant evening and win from them money they'd lose elsewhere, if they did not here. Well, then?"

"I know. But it's true: I don't like it. And—you're acute: I think it has been a new shock to Sonia—poor child, as if she had not had enough already. It seemed, I am sure, a good deal more romantic in the idea than it does in the execution."

He laughed. "Like so many other things. Well—'poor Sonia' if you like, but if you ask me, part of her trouble is

63

that our guests are such singularly unromantic figures. I am sure she had visions of gallant young cavalry officers and elegant aides-de-camp—and then to find herself playing with old Blücher with his red nose and stink of garlic. Well, to be fair, it is hard on the child."

"Of course it is. She has had so little pleasure in her life. Indeed, I have been wondering: Could not you be a little sweeter to her, Charles. A few compliments? A little praise would do wonders with her, I am sure."

"No." There was something rigid about the monosyllable. And then, on a lighter note: "Never mind; I am bringing a guest tonight who should please her—a young man straight from England, and such a popinjay as you never saw, brimful of the latest airs and graces. I am sure you can rely on him to cram-feed Sonia with compliments. And in the meantime, had you not better go and see that she is fit to be seen when they arrive? And, which is more important, prepared to make herself pleasant."

She paused at the doorway. "Do you think I should play instead of her?"

"No." He could be very firm. "Everything depends on the correctness of the appearance we present. You must be the chaperone, Elizabeth, at your work in the corner—though I confess it seems a great waste of you."

"Why, thank you." She swept him a curtsy, half stately, half mocking. "If you would only make a few pretty speeches like that to Sonia. Poor child, she's starved for compliments. Her father and brother never did more than admire her sauerkraut or her soup. You would be amazed how she would react to a little judicious praise! But you take her almost as much for granted as her brother did."

"Well." He was standing with his back to the window so she could not see his face. "Are you not grateful for that?"

She laughed a little. "You're no fool, are you, Charles? And—I'm not sure you're not right."

She found Sonia in wonderfully restored spirits. The new dresses she had ordered when they arrived at Frankfurt had just come home and she was trying on a ravishingly becoming creation of lavender-colored gauze over satin. "Now, at least, Charles cannot say I do not *look* like a lady." She turned from her glass to greet Elizabeth.

"If you would only try to behave like one."

"Charles lectures me so I cannot help but tease him. Don't do this, don't do that, don't walk in the streets alone, nor yet ride Marmion—and you know he's always too busy to accompany me, and you, poor darling, have no horse. I sometimes think I shall go mad cooped up here. And no colors either—" She returned to the subject of one of her fiercer arguments with Charles. "Poor Father—you know I'm not heartless, Elizabeth, but it was all his *fault*. After what I've seen, mourning just seems silly."

"Charles is right, just the same. You should be grateful he did not insist on solid black: I quite thought he would."

"Running a gaming hell in black! Really, that is too rich. How completely I was deceived in Charles! To set out on an adventure and find oneself saddled with a Methodistical preaching parsonical bore is really the outside of enough, and so I shall tell him if I have to sit through many more of his sermons."

"I wish you will not."

"I'm sure you do, darling Elizabeth." She was trying on her new bonnet and flashed Elizabeth an entrancing smile in the glass. "You wait and see: I will be the very pink of propriety tonight and old Blücher will send me twice as many roses tomorrow. *He* says my hair will start a new rage, 'damme if it won't.' "

"I think it very becoming too." One of Elizabeth's first actions on reaching Frankfurt had been to get the town's foremost hairdresser to restyle Sonia's ravaged locks, and her pointed little face was now surrounded by a halo of soft golden curls which were indeed extraordinarily becoming, giving width to the narrow, striking little face. But Charles, appealed to by an exuberant Sonia to say if she didn't look all the crack, had infuriated her by merely asking how much Herr Schumacher had charged.

Now, Elizabeth changed the subject. "You are dressed already: I must make haste or our first guests will be arriving."

"Guests!" Sonia made a face. "Fat old men, stinking of schnapps and garlic—it's all right for you, sitting at your work, but if you but knew how tired I am of whist. Why can we not play something exciting like hazard or loo?"

"You know perfectly well that Charles is right about that: you could not be sure of winning."

"We don't always anyway."

"Of course not. And a good thing too. Come, Sonia, quit your grumbling, there's a good child. I know this is not an ideal life, but we might just as well make the most of it. Oh—and Charles promises a new guest tonight, a young man this instant arrived from England. He should be able to tell us what chance we have of getting there."

"Why did you not tell me? Quick, Elizabeth, come and let me help dress you. I do wish"—they were in Elizabeth's room now—"I do wish you had bought yourself some new clothes. You could look so striking, you know, if you would only make the effort. A dark green gown to bring out the red in your hair and there would be no knowing you. Your shoulders are much better than mine—you know they are—and look at you, buttoned to the neck like a dowager of forty. Oh, Barry, do buy some clothes!"

"I do not need them." Elizabeth took a demure, high-necked gray gown from her closet and hung it over a chair. "I am the chaperone—you, my love, are the great attraction and you know it. It would hardly do for you to be wearing your brown stuff schoolroom gowns."

"Poor Father." Sonia's face clouded. "But he was not really kind to me, was he, Barry? I'm not a brute, am I?"

"Of course you're not. Come, we ought to be downstairs setting out the refreshments."

Sonia laughed. "How surprised our guests would be if they knew that the man who opens the door is our only indoor servant. I nearly went into stitches the other night when Sir Robert Wilson sent his compliments to the cook. I wish he had left a tip!"

"Yes, it's a pity the custom of vails does not seem to obtain in Frankfurt. We should add quite a tidy sum to our takings that way." And then, seeing another April cloud blow across Sonia's face, "Never mind, love: it is a strange life, but it will be over soon, and all forgotten."

It was hard to believe, half an hour later, that Sonia had needed such encouragement. The long narrow drawing room was crowded now, and she was the center of an animated group of officers, all begging her to be their partner when they sat down to cards. If she thought them middle-aged and portly, she concealed it very well as she smiled up at Sir Robert Wilson and shook reproving curls at old Blücher who loved a pretty girl almost as well as a game at cards. "So many roses," she said, "and at this time of year. You really should not, General."

"My dear," he said, "what else is there to spend money on? You are our only pleasure: you must let us render you our homage, and our thanks."

"You are too kind." As she swept him her graceful curtsy Elizabeth found it hard to believe in the termagant who had, earlier, been shredding red roses one by one. She was glad to see that Charles, approaching across the room, had been a witness to the whole scene. He must admit that Sonia could behave when she wanted to.

He was followed by a dark young man, conspicuous in this group of uniforms and epaulettes by his civilian dress. And what dress! It was a long time since Elizabeth had met a London dandy, but she found it in a way reassuring to see how little the breed had changed. This young man looked as if he must have eased into his dove-gray coat with a shoehorn, while this, with his brilliant striped waistcoat and skin-tight trousers, made him stand out among the shabby uniforms like a dove among crows. She would have felt sorry for him if he had not been so evidently contented with himself.

His sweeping bow, as Charles presented him, almost caricatured itself. He was Philip Haverton, and enchanted to make their acquaintance. While he divided his speech courteously between them, his eyes were for Sonia only, and Elizabeth was able to watch from a little behind as he began to pay his court to her. In answer to the questions she put him, he was very ready to describe what he called his intolerable journey: six dreadful days on a stinking tub of a boat, beating this way and that between Harwich and Cuxhaven—nothing to eat but salt biscuit and pease broth and nowhere, positively nowhere in the wretched cabin to hang up one's clothes—he had really feared his man would shoot himself. Indeed he had been in the gravest doubt whether he would be fit to be seen today—here he flicked an imaginary speck of dust from his immaculate lapel—his man had been up all night. And how glad, now, he was that he had insisted. A speaking glance gave point to the compliment. He would not have missed this meeting for the world. "You are English, too, Mr. Vincent tells me."

"Yes, but I've never been there. I cannot tell you how I

long to go. Do you think we could make the journey, Mrs. Barrymore and I?"

"Impossible! The roads between here and Cuxhaven—I could not begin to describe them to an elegant young female. And then, you must remember, Hamburg is still in French hands. Though it's true my cousin says leaving his garrisons behind is one of Napoleon's mistakes ... No, no, Miss von Hugel, your best plan is to follow the victorious Allied advance and go home in comfort from Paris."

"So long as it is victorious! They seem to be mighty slow in starting."

"That's what my cousin says, but I hope now he's here he will knock their heads together for them. Oh—I should not have said that. Do me the favor of forgetting it, Miss von Hugel: I am but a novice diplomat yet and I am afraid such delightful company has made me forget discretion."

"Never mind," said Sonia kindly. "Nobody heard. But who is this remarkable cousin of yours? I do not recollect to have heard of him."

"Well of course not. As I was telling you, we only arrived yesterday. Even Giles Burnleigh takes longer than twenty-four hours to make his mark. Or the Earl of Denbigh, to give him his full title, about which, to do him justice, he's not the least in the world a stickler. There's nothing high and mighty about Giles: you should have seen him on the boat, drinking rum with our ruffian of a captain as if it was the most natural thing in the world. I sometimes wish I could persuade him to live a little more up to his dignity—would you believe it, Miss von Hugel, he did not order so much as an extra cravat for this mission! I only hope he will meet with the respect he should ... He is busy today, presenting his credentials, calling on this prince and that bigwig—no need of me, I'm glad to say. Though I did not look to have such luck as this. But tell me about yourself, Miss von Hugel. How do you contrive to speak English so beautifully, and have never been there?"

"Barry taught me—Mrs. Barrymore, I should say." She turned to bring Elizabeth into the conversation. "Good God, Elizabeth, what is the matter?"

"Nothing." But Elizabeth was very white. "A spasm; it

68

will pass. Look, Sonia, they are bringing out the card tables."

It created the diversion she had hoped for. Young Haverton forgot his solicitude for her in trying to secure Sonia for his partner, and she was able to subside into the chair by the lamp where, night after night, she acted the chaperone over her embroidery. Tonight, she hardly paid attention to the arrangement of partners, nor the chances of the game, and yet it seemed only a moment before Charles was breaking up the party. Sonia rose from her place near the stove and crossed the room to her: "Are you better, Barry? I never knew you to be ill before."

"Nor am I." Elizabeth had herself well in hand now and was able to condole with young Haverton on his losses. Not that they seemed to weigh heavily on him. "To tell truth"—here a languishing glance for Sonia—"I was not paying proper attention to my cards. I am only grateful that you avoided the misfortune of being my partner, Miss von Hugel. But, tell me, do you attend the ball the Czar gives tomorrow for his sisters the Grand Duchesses? I had been wondering whether to go, since aside from the two royal ladies, and Lady Burgersh, who, you know, is never out of her husband's pocket, there would be no partners but the fat Frankfurt fräuleins. But now—Miss von Hugel, put me out of my misery: tell me you will be there."

"I believe so. You'll be well enough, won't you, Barry?"

"My love, I should be desolated to disappoint you, but—"

"You *can't*," wailed Sonia, "my very first dance." And, almost at the same time from Haverton: "Oh, pray, Mrs. Barrymore, think again. My cousin does not go: he is not so strong as one could wish—the result of an accident many years ago: he *says* he'll be too fagged for it. It's all very well for him"—a querulous note in his voice now— "he's met all the bigwigs. Of course I saw them at the review this morning—and a damned disappointing lot they are, too—excuse me, Miss von Hugel. The Czar's well enough, if it were not for that stoop of his, and the King of Württemberg keeps some kind of state, but the King of Prussia merely looks cross, and the Emperor of Austria stupid—and even the Czar—do you know, I saw him this afternoon, walking round town with Nesselrode in a round

69

hat and a green coat my man would have been ashamed to wear. It's very disappointing. But he must make some kind of appearance at the ball, since he gives it for his sisters—Say you'll be there, Miss von Hugel."

"Of course we go." Charles Vincent had joined them. "Our guests are leaving, cousins."

He returned to the subject of the ball later when the last guest had gone. "What possessed you to say you might not go, Elizabeth? You must know how important it is to us?"

"Important?" She was tidying the room. "I hardly see why. We have too many guests already. Was it a good evening, Charles?"

He and Sonia had been counting their winnings. "Good enough so that we can afford to indulge ourselves tomorrow. Besides—our position is not so secure that we can afford not to be seen on such an occasion. I had trouble enough getting the invitation from Pozzo di Borgo."

"Divine Pozzo." Sonia burst into her melodious laugh. "Have you seen that Kalmuck of his? I saw him in the street this morning, dressed in a tapestry depicting Leda and the Swan—upside down. I thought I'd die laughing."

"I hope he didn't see you?"

"Who? Pozzo? Does it matter?"

"Of course it matters. The Czar, his master, is likely to be the arbiter of the world's destinies. I have hopes of being presented to him tomorrow."

"Have you, Charles?" Elizabeth finished stacking glasses on a tray. "Is that why it is so important we go?"

"In a way. He fascinates me, that man. Imagine the contradiction in terms: a liberal-minded monarch, an autocrat talking constitutions ... Call it a whim if you like, but I long to meet him."

"A whim? Yes, I can understand that. Like the one that brought Sonia and me to Frankfurt. But when you begin to talk about liberal principles and constitutions— Charles, you make me wonder about your motives."

He gave her a quick look. "Is it so strange to wish to go to a ball where half the sovereigns of Europe will be assembled? What is the matter with you tonight, Elizabeth? Has something happened to disturb you?"

"She's not well, poor Barry," Sonia intervened. "But

you'll be better tomorrow, won't you? Think of my dress! Even Charles will think me a little beautiful in it."

"Shall I?" His voice was teasing. "I do find it so difficult not to think of you in that filthy leather jacket and your brother's breeches. No, no"—he threw up a hand in self-defense—"don't throw it. Our landlady values those figures highly: she told me so only this morning."

"I cannot imagine why." But she replaced the china horseman on its stand. "Anyway, I can see there is no need to save any dances for you. Which is just as well, as I have nothing left but the waltzes, and I am sure you do not waltz."

"No more are you going to."

"Not waltz! But it is all the rage. Elizabeth, tell him—"

"It may be the fashionable thing here, but you will not find young ladies doing it in England. Ask your friend Lady Burgersh if she means to—and she is a married woman."

"I wish I was too, and free of your intolerable bullying. I suppose you mean me to confine myself entirely to those dreary polonaises the Czar has introduced—just walking about the room in time to the music and saying 'yes,' and 'no' and 'quite so' and 'precisely' to your partner."

"No, no, my English friends tell me that country dances and quadrilles are quite unexceptitonable, but the fact remains that English young ladies do not waltz, and you, my dear, are to be an English young lady."

"Your dear, indeed! Your dupe! I wish I had gone to Aunt Gertrude!" And with this Parthian shot she turned and flounced out of the room.

"You are very patient with her." Elizabeth had known that this question of waltzing must arise, and was relieved that Vincent had taken so definite a stand.

"I wish I could shake some sense into her, but it would not do; would it?"

"Absolutely not. She has had enough of violence, poor child."

"Just the same, I hope she does not disgrace herself at this ball. I am afraid you have a good deal to endure from her tantrums."

"Nothing of the kind. I love Sonia." She spoke more sharply than she meant to.

"Something *has* happened to disturb you. I wish you would tell me what it is."

"Nothing—everything. Sometimes I think I was mad to embark on this adventure."

"You are tired, that's all. Things will look better in the morning."

"They could not look worse." And then, seeing his surprise: "Forgive me. You are right, of course. I am tired. Don't look so anxious, Charles. If we must go to the Czar's ball I'll do my best to act my part."

"I knew I could count on you. And Sonia . . . you don't think she'll fly out into one of her wild starts?"

"I hope not. But do remember, Charles, she's only a child, hardly out of the nursery. And then, that shocking experience . . ."

"That's all very well." He locked the night's takings safely away. "But even shocking experiences pass . . . even children must grow up in the end. You've had your troubles too, Elizabeth, and I don't notice you having tantrums all the time."

"Give me time." There was something odd in her voice tonight. "I may come to it yet. Charles—"

"Yes?"

"Was I mad?"

"What do you mean?"

"To throw in our lot with you. I've often wondered whether you don't regret it."

"I? Never. And you? I know it cannot suit you to play the merry widow night after night, but"—reasonably—"what else could you have done?"

"You're right of course." Her voice was dull. "Good night, Charles. I won't fail you at the ball tomorrow." Only, later, alone in her room, she gazed long and tearlessly at the reflection in her glass, remembering the young girl who had laughed there once. At last, savagely pulling down her long hair, "A merry widow," she told herself, "I wish I was dead."

And yet, next day, she found herself not quite immune to the thrill of preparing for the ball. It was more years than she cared to remember since she had worn her midnight-blue ball gown, but it still fitted her perfectly

72

and did wonders for her clear complexion and heavy auburn hair.

Sonia had never seen her in it. "Good God! Barry! You look"—she paused—"different."

"Well, I should hope so. And you look like someone who is not going to be ready in time. Do you want to miss your first two dances with Mr. Haverton?"

"It's the buttons. Did you ever see so many buttons?"

"They make for an admirable fit." Elizabeth began dexterously to fasten tiny buttons up her pupil's back. "There." She stood back to admire the finished effect. "I told you this silver gray would suit you. You look like an angel."

"An angel in mourning?" Sonia had wanted silver tissue, and had bowed most unwillingly to councils of propriety. "Still." A smile for her reflection in the glass. "I suppose it could be worse. Shall I wear my pearls?"

"Of course. There is nothing like a string of pearls to convey a suggestion of respectability."

" 'Assume a virtue if you have it not?' "

"Precisely. I am happy to find that our hours of Shakespeare have not been entirely wasted. And that reminds me—Charles is right, you know, about the waltzing. I am afraid we *are* very much in the position of Caesar's wife. Suspicion must not touch us. You really like this life, do you not, of balls and cards, parades and morning calls?"

"Of course I do."

"Very well, then. Don't hazard it. If any one starts asking questions about us, we are finished. And reputation once lost—well . . ." An expressive shrug finished the sentence.

"Oh, my poor Barry, do you wish you had never met me?"

"I wish we were safe in England, and all well."

"Dismal creature." Sonia made a face at her. "But never worry yourself about me. I shall amaze you tonight. While the others are waltzing, I shall imitate Aunt Gertrude in a corner." She made a face so like her aunt's that Elizabeth could not help laughing.

They were in high spirits and the greatest charity with each other when they joined Charles Vincent, and his gift of two charmingly arranged bouquets of hothouse flowers added the finishing touch at least to Sonia's pleasure.

He was quick to recognize the hint of doubt in Elizabeth's voice as she thanked him. "Don't worry; this is not next week's rent; I made a little killing this morning. Haverton and I took on a couple of fat Prussians whose brains, I think, must have been in their stomachs. You will find Haverton is my dearest friend. Just as well, I think. From all I hear, that guardian of his is a perfect dragon. I do not want to fall foul of him if I can help it."

"Denbigh?" Quick anxiety in Elizabeth's voice. "Is he better? Does he attend the ball?"

"No. I am not quite sure, from what Haverton said, whether his indisposition is genuine or diplomatic, but it is certain that he stays home tonight. He is not, his cousin says, a great attender of balls. In England, he lives entirely in the country with a starched puritanical tyrant of an older sister. It's as good as a play Haverton says, to see how he is enjoying his liberty on this mission. Well, are we ready?"

"You've forgotten something." Sonia had been prowling restlessly about the room.

"Oh?"

"To tell us how well we look."

"I beg your pardon." A caricature of a deep bow for each of them. "Ladies . . . words fail me—"

"They don't usually." Tart disappointment in Sonia's voice.

"Never mind, Rapunzel. Just wait till young Haverton sees you; he'll supply the compliments in which I am so woefully deficient. Remember, I'm a mere cousin— When did your brother notice your clothes?"

"Never. But you're not my brother—not even my cousin, thank God."

"How deeply I agree with you. But come, Cinderella, the carriage is waiting." And then, as Sonia flounced out of the room first, to Elizabeth: "May I congratulate you on the effect you have achieved—both the effects?"

"Thank you. But why not gratify the poor child?"

"She'll have gratification enough, before the evening is over."

He was right. The Russians had cast their net wide in sending out their invitations and the Assembly Rooms were full of plump merchants' daughters, so bejeweled and beribboned that Vincent whispered to Elizabeth it was hard to believe the tales they had heard about Germany's impoverishment at Napoleon's hands. Some of these girls were handsome enough, in a bold and buxom way, but there was no one, as Haverton lost no time in telling her, to hold a candle to Sonia. "Or to Mrs. Barrymore, if it comes to that. How glad I am that I took the precaution of securing dances with both of you in advance: You are going to find yourselves the belles of the ball."

It was true, and inevitable. The two Grand Duchesses, though both charming girls, were beings set apart; Lady Burgersh had eyes only for her husband; Sonia and Elizabeth found themselves the most eligible unmarried ladies in the room. Or rather, Elizabeth reminded herself ruefully, in the world's eyes, Sonia was the only unmarried lady. She, like the Duchess of Oldenbourg, was a widow. She must not forget. Vincent helped to remind her as they moved through the march-like polonaise together. "You will waltz with me? It will seem odd, I think, if you do not."

At all costs they must avoid seeming odd; it was what she herself had told Sonia earlier that evening. "You think so?"

"I'm sure of it. And I'm equally sure you waltz to perfection."

"It seems hard on Sonia."

"No need to worry about her. She sits it out with Haverton, having already given him his share of dances."

"Oh?" Her voice was doubtful.

"You may well say, 'Oh.' Do you think there is anything in it?"

"I devoutly hope not."

"I too. She would drive him distracted in six months. She needs a man to manage her, not a pretty boy like that. Look at her now."

She was dancing and flirting outrageously with old Blücher. "It was bound to go to her head." Elizabeth's voice was pleading.

Vincent was watching Haverton who was making his purposeful way towards them through the crowd. "Of course," he said almost absent-mindedly. "Within reason. There is something going on. Have you noticed?"

"Noticed what?"

75

"The Czar has disappeared—and so has Schwartzenberg, and Lord Aberdeen."

"Are you sure? There's such a crowd of different uniforms, I don't see how you can tell. The Czar was here a few minutes ago; I saw him dancing with Lady Burgersh."

"He's gone now. Ah—Haverton, how are you?"

"All the better for the news." He made his bow to Elizabeth. "Have you heard?"

"No—what?" Vincent had left Elizabeth to ask the inevitable question and was making an elaborate pantomime of indifference. Turned half away to pick a sprig from one of the orange trees with which the rooms were decorated, he was, she knew, listening with all his attention.

"The very best. The long delay is over. The armies are to march at last."

"I find it hard to believe." Vincent tucked the twig carefully into a buttonhole. "You will tell me next that they have decided which way to go."

"Well, that does seem to be the difficulty. It is an open secret that the Austrians want to cut across Swizerland—but the Czar won't hear of it. He's full of scruples, you know, about neutrality and so forth."

"It does him credit," said Elizabeth warmly.

"I suppose so, in a way, but those Swiss—they think they can go on forever running with the hare and hunting with the hounds."

"All they want is peace and a quiet life."

He laughed. "Don't we all. But they are striking up for the country dances. You have not forgot your promise, ma'am."

"Indeed, no. I only hope I have not forgotten the figures."

"You will remember soon enough. Do you dance, Vincent?"

"Alas, I cannot. I was just making my apologies to Mrs. Barrymore. I have to leave town on urgent business—my cousin, you know"—this for Elizabeth. "You are arrived most timely, Haverton, since I was going to seek you out and ask if you would be so good as to see my cousins safely home when the ball is over."

"Of course I will," Haverton colored with pleasure and took Elizabeth's hand to lead her out to the dance.

She paused for a moment to give Vincent one wry, expressive glance. "You forgot to tell me when we might expect you back. It is *The Magic Flute* the day after tomorrow. Sonia has her heart set on going."

"I will do my best to be back." His warm, approving smile conveyed his gratitude for the way she had picked up her cue. "But I am sure Haverton will escort you if I find myself unable to get here in time."

"I shall be only too happy. And now, Mrs. Barrymore, let me remind you. It is the simplest thing in the world: a whole figure at the top, hay on your side, set and half right and left, chase round one couple, swing corners and a half poussette."

"And you call that the simplest thing in the world!" But they were facing each other now, ready to begin the dance, and she must forget her puzzlement over Vincent's sudden departure and concentrate on following Haverton's energetic lead. Dutifully turning away from him for the hay, she thought that it was impossible to help liking him. But Vincent was right, he was hardly the man to keep her irrepressible Sonia in order. She met her now, coming up the dance flushed and entrancing. Sonia held her hand for an extra moment as they turned each other: "Where's Charles?"

"Gone. I don't know where. Haverton takes us home."

"Oh, fiddle!" One of her all too expressive grimaces, and she was gone, with a little skip to regain her place. Elizabeth moved on in her own direction, smiling to herself. That had hardly been the reaction of a girl in love. But—where *had* Charles gone?

It was a question that she and Sonia were to ask each other many times in the next few days. She had half expected to find a note from him when they got home, explaining his sudden decision, but there had been no word. The servant reported that he had come home, changed into riding dress, hung a tiny cloak bag behind his saddle and ridden away into the night.

"I hope he left us some money." Sonia returned to the question over a late breakfast next morning.

"Not a great deal—but enough for a few days. He said he might be back tomorrow."

"And you believed him? Had you thought he might not come back at all? And a pretty pickle we'd be in then.

And—besides; what if Headquarters move before he returns. All the talk, last night, was of an advance at last. We are going to invade by way of Switzerland, Philip says."

"Philip?"

"Mr. Haverton, if you prefer. Poor thing—how I torment him! He is dying to present me to that guardian of his he's so much in awe of. I can't think why—a worn-out hypochondriac. I wonder what Government were thinking of to send him. Though I'm glad they did, of course, since he brought Philip—Mr. Haverton, I mean."

"I wish I knew what you did mean, Sonia."

"Why, to enjoy myself, of course. Don't pull your long face at me, Barry. Come, admit, I deserve a little pleasure in my life. As for Phil—Mr. Haverton, he can take care of himself, I am sure. And admit, it's useful to have him at our beck and call now Vincent has left us in the lurch. What would we have done last night, else?"

"I am sure Charles would not have left us if he had not been sure we would be well taken care of."

"I wish I had your confidence. You'll change your tune if you find he's left us here, high and dry. After all, what do we know about him?"

"Very little; it's quite true."

"Too little by half. Have you noticed how different he has been since he met that cousin of his in Weimar? Odd starts, and disappearing for hours at a time, and—I don't know—just different, somehow."

"Yes, I have wondered whether perhaps he had something on his mind. His debt to his cousin, perhaps. You must admit that meeting was very timely for us all."

"Too timely. I tell you, Barry, I'm beginning to wonder if there isn't something very havey-cavey about Charles Vincent—and whatever he's doing, remember, we're involved in it. We're his cover, you know, and a very useful one too . . . Have you noticed how often, when the talk turns to politics, he lets us do the talking—and how closely he listens. If he's not a secret agent, I'll eat my new bonnet."

"You'd better not. If you are right in your suspicions, it may be the last you have for a while. After all, Sonia, say what you will about Charles, he's been supporting us for over a month now."

"Yes—and very pretty that is going to look when we get back to England and it comes out that we are no more his cousins than the man in the moon's. Have you thought of that, oh wise and considerate Barry?"

Elizabeth sighed. "Have I not! But Sonia, what else could we have done?"

Sonia crossed the room to give her a quick hug. "Don't look so grave, Barry; I only meant to tease you. I'm sure we were right to do what we did, and, after all, if the worst comes to worst, I can always marry Philip."

"On the strength of two days' acquaintance?"

"Why not, if they've done his business? Why else do you think he wants me to meet his fierce old cousin? So take that anxious look off your face, Barry dear, they'll look after us if Charles does not return."

"I hope to God he does," said Elizabeth with so much emphasis that Sonia gave her a quick, anxious glance.

"What's the matter, Barry? Are you still not feeling well? It's not like you to take things so hard."

"I'm blue-deviled, that's all." She managed a lightness she was very far from feeling. Please God she would never have to explain . . .

Chapter 6

"May I come in, sir? Or are you busy?" Philip Haverton pushed open the door of Denbigh's study, stamping snow off his boots as he came. "I wish you could come out," he went on. "The sun's out at last and you should just see it glitter on the snow. Besides, Cousin Elinor said I must see you got plenty of fresh air and exercise, and you know you have done nothing but write, write, write ever since we got here. But do I interrupt you?"

"You seem to have done so." Denbigh put down his pen and leaned back to look quizzically up at his young companion. "What's the news in town?"

"The very best. Everyone says the armies are to march at last."

"You said that the other night when you came back from the Czar's ball."

"I know, but this time it's true. Something has convinced the Czar that the Swiss must be made to let the Allies pass through their country."

"Has it indeed? Now I wonder what?" He sanded and sealed the letter he had been writing and rose from his desk to tower half a head above his slender cousin. "He seemed set against it, last time I saw him. But it's certainly good news if it is true."

"I am sure it is. I have it from a most reliable source."

"Oh? And who might that be?"

"My friend Charles Vincent. You know—I told you of him the other day. He is but yesterday returned from Basel and says the negotiations have begun already."

"Does he so? And what kind of a man is he, pray?"

"Oh, complete to a degree. It's surprising, too, because he's nothing much to look at. Wears his hair any old how—plain coats—almost shabby, you could say, and yet, no getting away from it, there's something about him. He's only my age, if that—never been to a university—no tour—nothing. And yet, somehow, people listen to him. I wish I knew how he does it."

"By having something to say, perhaps?"

"Well, that, of course. He's the best-informed man in town, Stewart says. Half English, half French; speaks I don't know how many languages; a most remarkable man. I heard a rumor, this morning, that the Czar is interesting himself in him."

Denbigh laughed. "You're a wonder for rumors, Philip. But I had heard one too. That your Vincent has a very pretty cousin." His glance sharpened as Philip colored up to the eyes. "Oh, Philip, not again . . ."

"You just wait till you see her, Giles. She's . . . she's . . . this is quite different from anything else. I wish you would let me make you known to them."

"All in good time. But don't, I beg, let yourself get in too deep before we know more about the girl. I tremble to think what your mother will say when she learns I have let you involve yourself with a young woman who is wandering about Germany, in these times, with no better chaperon than a male cousin of mixed birth and dubious antecedents."

"But that is not the case at all. Surely I have told you that she has her other cousin with her, too. A widowed lady of the most unimpeachable respectability, a Mrs. Barrymore." And then, alarmed: "What is it, Giles? Not one of your attacks?"

"No, no, nothing to signify." He was very white under the tan he had acquired on their journey. "Mrs. Barrymore, you say? I knew a family of that name, many years ago, when I was at Cambridge. No connection, of course. As for her 'unimpeachable respectability,' I'll believe that when I see it."

"Then you will let me introduce you to them?"

"I suppose I must. I confess I should like to know precisely what your Mr. Vincent was doing in Switzerland. You spend a good deal of time with him, do you not?"

"Theirs is the pleasantest house in Frankfurt. I wish you would let me take you to visit them."

"I am beginning to think I should. The play there is very high, they tell me. Stewart was grumbling the other day about the sums he had lost there."

"Charles Stewart is a fool."

"I did not say he was a wise man. I said he had lost considerable sums at cards, at the house of these friends of yours."

"I hope he did not suggest there was anything out of the line about their play."

"Gently, Philip, gently. No, I have heard no hint that the play there is not everything that it should be—only, it seems, they are very skilled players. 'The devil's own luck,' Charles Stewart calls it. 'And a face like an angel.' Rather a public sort of an angel, surely, Philip?"

"Sir, she is the only woman I shall ever love."

"You have loved at least half a dozen since you left the university, to my certain knowledge. Are they so soon forgotten?"

"You won't understand! This is different; entirely different. I want to marry Miss von Hugel; to care for her, protect her."

"You think her, then, in need of protection?"

"No, no! Why will you keep twisting my words? If you had only ever been in love, you would understand."

"You are so sure that I have not?"

81

"How could you have? Your sister is the only woman in your life; always has been; always will be. No wonder if you do not understand what I feel, what I suffer ... Only, come and see her. Then, perhaps ..."

"Perhaps I shall understand what it is to love? Very well, when shall we go? They keep open house, do they not, these friends of yours?"

"And why not? You yourself have often said how tedious this masculine society is, with its dinners, its overeating and hard drinking. You will find nothing of that at Charles Vincent's. It is a most genteel establishment; nothing that even Elinor could fault."

"Those are strong words, Philip."

"I intend them to be. But—when shall we go?"

"Tonight, if you like. But I do not promise to play cards with these paragons of yours. For there are two of them, are there not? Did you not say—a Mrs. Barrymore?"

"Yes, Sonia's cousin and chaperone. A most delightful person; you cannot help but like her."

"A widow, you said?"

"Yes, a tragic case. Married practically out of the nursery—and widowed at Trafalgar. She's been with Miss von Hugel ever since. Can't be a day over thirty—less, very likely. Sorrow's aging, of course. Twenty-eight, maybe. Striking-looking woman. I rather hope her sorrows are over: Charles Vincent's very much attached, or I miss my guess. Stands to reason. Why else would he submit to petticoat government as he does? I mean, if they were his sisters it would be different, but cousins ..."

"Well, I shall look forward to meeting them. In the meantime, I have work to do."

"And I must have a word with that man of mine. Do you know, he had the effrontery to suggest, this morning, that I spoil too many cravats? Something about a shortage of starch—I am seriously considering getting rid of him."

Denbigh laughed. "War's terrible, isn't it, Philip?"

It was unlucky that Charles Vincent chose that evening to bring in a very lively group of young Russian officers on leave whom he had encountered over dinner at Frankfurt's best inn. Elizabeth had been far from pleased at their merry arrival, and indeed her first instinct had been

to retreat upstairs with Sonia and leave Charles to entertain them. But it was hard to resist their delight in encountering two "real ladies," as one of them put it with
the formidable frankness of the drunk. And they had so
obviously made an effort to pull themselves back into
sobriety when they saw what kind of a house they had
come to . . . She ordered coffee and hoped for the best.

They soon settled down to two tables of whist, and
Elizabeth, at her embroidery, congratulated herself on the
sobering effect of concentration on the cards. She returned, however, from a brief absence, to find that
Charles Vincent had sent for wine and was pressing his
guests to abandon their coffee cups and let him fill their
glasses instead. This made her angry on many counts. She
had no doubt these handsome, well-cared-for boys could
afford to lose their money, and, indeed, were much safer
here than if Vincent had left them on the town. But—she
never liked to see it happen. Nor did she like the part
Sonia played. Worst of all, she had noticed Vincent's habit
of working casual allusions to the progress of the Allied
armies into the conversation on such occasions. Busy with
their cards, muddled with what they had drunk, his guests
were all too likely to give a careless answer to what
seemed a careless question. Where were these answers
reported? She did not know, and blamed herself both for
wondering and for not trying to find out.

Today, she had had enough. She put down her embroidery and moved over to Sonia's table. A hand had just
finished; the moment was opportune. Sonia and her partner were being congratulated by their opponents on their
run of luck.

"Luck, nothing," said the fair young man who had
partnered Sonia. "Where did you learn to play,
sweetheart? You're a m . . . m . . . miracle." He pronounced the word with drunken dignity, though in the
fluent French they all talked.

"I've played all my life." Sonia was carelessly collecting
the cards for a new deal when Elizabeth intervened.

"It is getting late," she said, "and you know we promised ourselves an early night. I am sure these gentlemen
will excuse us, my love."

A babble of protests countered this suggestion. "What,
stop before the luck turns?" "You cannot be so cruel!"

Worst of all, Sonia's partner, elated with wins and success, put out a long arm to pull Elizabeth towards him: "The first ladies we've seen since home"—he was maudlin now—"and they want to run away and leave us."

"Sir!" But he was beyond caring for her anger, and the next appeal followed close on the first: "Charles!"

This was the moment when their servant flung open the door and announced, "Lord Denbigh, Mr. Haverton."

It could hardly have been worse. The scene that met Denbigh's eyes might have come from some Hogarthian "Card Sharper's Progress." Close to the door, Elizabeth had her back to it, but there was no mistaking her angry attempts to free herself. While Haverton looked on, appalled, and Vincent hurried across the room, Denbigh acted. His iron hand fell on the young Russian's shoulder. Gasping in subdued pain, he released Elizabeth who turned to face her rescuer.

"Lord Denbigh!" Her face was white as the cards on the table.

He too was suddenly white. "Miss Barrymore!" And then, on a note of extraordinary bitterness: "I beg your pardon. I believe I should say, 'Mrs. Barrymore.'"

"Oh, God, Giles!" There was a note in her voice that Sonia had never heard before. She would have said more, but now the whole room was in confusion. Everyone talked at once. Vincent and the oldest Russian had converged upon her tormentor and were demanding that he apologize; someone knocked over a chair; someone else dropped a glass; Philip Haverton seized the opportunity to take Sonia's hand.

"Gentlemen." It was Denbigh's voice, not Vincent's, that suddenly commanded silence. "You will apologize to these ladies, and leave, at once."

Contrite silence. Then the Russian who had knocked over the chair picked it up again; the one who had broken the glass began a long apology to Sonia, while Elizabeth's molester broke, in his shame, into rapid unintelligible Russian.

"That will do." Once again Denbigh's voice dominated the room, and the Russians filed sheepishly out, escorted by Vincent, who spared only one look, eloquent of apology, for Elizabeth. "And now," Denbigh spoke impartially

84

to Philip and Sonia, "I should like a word with Mrs. Barrymore—alone."

"But—" Elizabeth's protest was swept aside.

"There is a piano, I see, in the next room. I am sure you perform delightfully, Miss von Hugel. And Haverton, here, would like nothing better than to turn the pages for you. Shut the door behind you, Philip." And then, as they retreated: "A little late in the day, surely, to be coming the heavy chaperone?"

She had sunk into a chair, but threw back her head to give him look for look. "And a little late in the day, too for you to come back into my life."

"I was told you were dead."

"By your father, I suppose. Or that sister who loved me so dearly. And you believed them, of course, implicitly."

"Why not? I was ill, you know, for a long time after my father found us that day. When I recovered, my first thought was to write to you. My letters were returned, unopened."

"Who franked them for you, I wonder? Did you really think they would reach me? But I was just as foolish. I went on expecting to hear from you . . ."

"You consoled yourself soon enough."

"Consoled?"

"By marrying your cousin. Did I ever have the pleasure of meeting him? My condolences, by the way, on your bereavement."

"My—" She paused. "Oh, thank you."

"And I"—he was still standing over her, his hand taut on the back of her chair—"I have allowed myself the luxury of faithfuless all these years. Faithfulness to a memory as false as"—he broke off and took a rapid turn up and down the room. "I have no right to say it. Forgive me. It is all a very long time ago. What I cannot understand is the situation in which I now find you. You—proud Miss Barrymore (I beg your pardon: Mrs. Barrymore)—to find you running a gambling den—perhaps worse. Tell me, what are your plans, yours and your friend Vincent's?" No mistaking his accent on the word "friend." "Did you really think there was the slightest chance I would let my cousin marry that pretty little piece in there? Or do you intend blackmail? I take it money must be an object with you. I cannot believe that you—the

Elizabeth I remember—you cannot like this kind of life. Why did you not apply to me for help, if it is merely a question of money?"

"Apply to you?" While he was talking, her anger had had time to cool and crystallize; now she spoke with a deceptive calm. "To you, who let your father take you away, that day, without a murmur, without an attempt at resistance? To you—who never, so far as I knew, made an attempt to see me again? Do you remember what your last words were, before you collapsed: 'When I am twenty-one, I will come back.' It was not a long time, you know. I waited—but, as you say, that is ancient history, why talk of it now? When we were young, and romantic, and a little wild, perhaps, we thought we would find a new world, and happiness together. It was a dream, no more. Look at you now: Lord Denbigh, the courtier, the diplomat, the successful man. And you might have thrown it all away, for me, who am—what you see. I hope you are duly grateful to your father and sister for saving you. Indeed I can see that you are, since your first instinct is to do the same for Philip Haverton. But I think you can spare your pains in that regard. I doubt if Miss von Hugel would have him, even if he had twice your fortune. He may be your cousin, Lord Denbigh; he is still a very silly, vain young man. Sonia's worth two of him, and, I hope, knows it. Leave him alone; he'll get over it. And now, I do not think that we have anything else to say to each other. Allow me to wish you a very good evening." She rose with a rustle of satin and held out her hand. "I hope we shall not meet again."

"Elizabeth!"

"Mrs. Barrymore, you mean, who consoled herself so easily. I wonder if you ever thought what it was like, for me. Of course—you were ill, unconscious. I did not have that comfort. Would you like, just for a moment, to think of my journey home, across England, alone, unprotected?"

"Unprotected? But my father said—"

"And naturally you believed him. As you did when he told you I was dead. Are you still so credulous? Is it safe for you to be engaged on a diplomatic mission?"

He gave an angry half laugh. "You'll be amused, ma'am, to learn that is precisely what my sister said."

"Your loving sister? Does she still run your life for you? What a fool I was—what a childish fool to think I could detach you from so powerful an influence. Oh, I hoped, I suppose, for a while, or pretended to myself that I hoped. But all the time, in my heart of hearts, I knew—you did not really want to break away, to give it all up. If you had—you'd have come back to me. I've thought of it so often, when I read of your career, your first appearance in the Lords, even your twenty-first birthday celebrations. Did you think of me at all, that day? Did you think, 'I promised I would go to her today?' Or did you think, 'What a lucky escape?' It was my fault, I expect. I was so sure of myself, wasn't I? I was going to save you from your sister's dominance—and dominate you myself. Was that what you thought—if you thought of me at all?"

"I tell you: I thought you dead."

"Of course. 'When lovely woman stoops to folly, And finds too late that men betray—' Only I didn't even have the common decency to die. I believe I owe you an apology for being alive."

"And a widow. I never married."

"Of course not. Your sister would not let you." And then, impulsively: "Oh, forgive me. I should not say these things."

"Why not? If you think them. I am only sorry to find you have thought so ill of me, all these years. I wish you had written—"

"Again? After having my first letter returned? Allow me to have some pride. It's all I have had—" She stopped for a moment. "It's all ancient history now—forgotten, unimportant, is it not? Forgive me if I have said anything to offend you. After all, we were—friends, once." And then, on a note of relief: "Ah, Charles, there you are. Did you get rid of the poor young things without bloodshed?"

Charles Vincent closed the door behind him. "Oh yes, we are the best of friends again. They send you so many apologies that I have quite lost count: their first leave since the campaign began; the excitement of ladies' company at last—and such charming ladies ... I am afraid they will call on you in the morning, to apologize again, in person. I am only sorry, sir, that you have had such an unlucky introduction to our house."

"Lord Denbigh is just leaving." Elizabeth did not give

him a chance to speak. "Perhaps you would summon Mr. Haverton who will doubtless wish to accompany him."

"Of course. Sonia's making a terrible hash of *'O Giove omnipotente'* anyway. I don't know how Mr. Haverton can bear it."

"I expect love is deaf as well as blind." Her eyes challenged Denbigh. "I have been telling Lord Denbigh that he need have no fears for his ward in our house. I don't promise he won't lose a little money, but he will not run into debt, as he might elsewhere. Nor into any other trouble, if I can help it."

"If you mean Sonia, I don't think she cares a snap of the fingers for him." He opened the door of the music room. "Sonia! That is enough. One more of your high notes and I shall start catewauling too. Lord Denbigh is just leaving. Come and make your curtsy."

"You speak as if I was a child." She came pouting into the room, her looks a brilliant mirror of Haverton's admiration. "Elizabeth, tell him I'm not a baby any more."

"I can tell you that," said Denbigh. "You are far too beautiful. And I thought you sang divinely. Come, Philip, we must be going."

Chapter 7

Sonia's curiosity was as inevitable as it was hard to bear. "Fancy you knowing Lord Denbigh!" She was sitting on Elizabeth's bed, much later that night. "And you never said a word about it, you strange creature. He's not half so high in the instep as I had heard; a little fierce when he arrived, of course, but that was to be expected. Lord, what a scene that was!" She had obviously enjoyed it. "I've never been so surprised in my life as when he sent us off to the music room like that. Philip went meek as a lamb, did you notice? But what on earth could he have wanted to say to you, Elizabeth, and behind closed doors, too? Come, tell; I'm dying of curiosity. If you tell me, I promise I won't breathe a word to a soul. If you don't, I shall do my best to find out. Do you know what they call him—Denbigh, I mean? Philip told me: 'The Unattainable.' All the girls in London are after him, Philip says, have been for years, and not so much as a nibble. I couldn't understand it when Philip talked about him. I mean: I ask you, past thirty and subject to dizzy attacks. It hardly sounds the most romantic thing in the world, does it? But now I've met him, I can understand it all. Don't you think there's something very attractive about an older man? So masterful, so completely the gentleman. He made Charles and Philip look like a couple of boys on their promotion."

"Sonia, you must not speak of them by their Christian names. How many times am I to tell you?"

If she had hoped to deflect Sonia, she was disappointed. "Oh, very well, Miss Prudence." And then, with a wicked laugh: "But you're a fine one to be preaching at me. All alone for a half-an-hour tête-à-tête with a gentleman—and The Unattainable, at that! Be grateful the three of us are so discreet or you'd not have a shred of reputation left."

"I haven't. I never have had. I can see I shall have to tell you, Sonia—and trust you."

"You can."

"I think so. Well, then, you are wrong about your Unattainable. I was engaged to him once. Worse than that: I ran away with him."

"You! Miss Prudence! I don't believe it!"

"I learned my prudence the hard way, Sonia. I hope you may never have such a lesson. Did you never wonder why I came so far from home to look after you?"

"Often. So attractive as you were—are, I should say."

"It makes no odds. Has not, for years. I ruined myself when I was your age—just eighteen."

"I can't believe it. You and Lord Denbigh. It's not true!"

"It is, though. He was at Cambridge, enjoying his first freedom from a tyrannical father and the older sister you speak of as a dragon. My father's parish was not far out of the town. Giles Burnleigh—as he then was—came to him for coaching. Oh, he was young then, and full of ideals. He did not wish to take advantage of his rank and secure a degree he had not earned. Father thought him

89

brilliant. He was too busy—poor father—with his reading and his parish work to see that I thought so too. And I was right, I am sure of it. Giles had the seeds of greatness in him, Sonia; I felt it. And yet—he had no chance."

"Why not? What do you mean?"

"I mean his father and his sister. His father was a Tory of the old school; rich as you please; master of I don't know how many rotten boroughs; Government's most faithful supporter. Giles's career was planned out for him when he was in short coats. As for his sister, she looked forward to the day when she would act as hostess for the First Minister. And Giles wanted to come out as a Whig. More than that—oh, he had wild ideas then. He was all for the reform of Parliament. No more rotten boroughs; representation for the new towns—sometimes he even talked of 'one man, one vote.' "

"Good gracious! What did his father say?"

"There was a terrible scene. Giles came straight to me afterwards. We had never talked of love, you understand, but I think we had both known ... At least he came straight to me. His father had told him to change his views, and make a public retraction—he had made a wild speech in the Union. Otherwise, he said, he could not prevent him taking the title, when he died, but he should not have a penny to go with it. Everything would go to Elinor."

"Did he mind?"

"Not in the least. I think, really, he was relieved. He felt freed, you see, from a great burden. Those were the days of uneasy peace with France; he thought it shameful. Freed of the burden of his estates, he felt there was nothing to prevent him from doing what he had always wished: emigrating to America."

"To America!"

"Yes. He said that was the land of liberty—of opportunity. He had no doubt of making his way there, and I am sure he was right. I thought it the very thing for him. And then—he asked me to go too."

"And you agreed?"

"Yes. I loved him. We were both under age, of course. There was possibility of marrying before we left, but when we got there we were sure we would be able. We traveled as brother and sister, and, believe me, Sonia, behaved as if we were. I remember sometimes almost wishing he was not such a complete gentleman. Anyway, we got safely to Liverpool and there our luck changed. We had been to the docks, inquiring for a ship and had found one that was sailing the next day. We were walking back down one of the narrow streets near the harbor when we heard screams, the sound of hooves. It was a runaway carriage, heading straight for us. And Giles—he stopped those horses in their tracks, Sonia, but received a blow on the head in doing so. He said it was nothing and we went back to our hotel. Then, later that night, he swooned dead away. I could not rouse him. I'll never forget that night. The landlord of the inn sent for a doctor—a good enough sort of man, but he gave me little comfort. Rest was the only thing, he said—as for taking him on board ship next day, it would be to sign his death warrant."

"So what did you do?"

"Nursed him as best I might. He had regained consciousness, but was still subject to dizzy spells, when the inevitable happened—his father arrived. The delay had been fatal."

"What happened?"

"He blamed it all on me, of course. Giles was easily led, he said. I had influenced him, dominated him . . ." She colored. "Well, in a way, it was true. And he called me—" She paused. "He was old, and angry, he probably did not mean it. But Giles flew at him and I had to separate them. It was dreadful, Sonia. And all my fault: I felt it then, I feel it still. And—Giles collapsed; he was not strong enough for such a scene; it brought on one of his fainting fits. His father turned to me: 'You see what you've done. I hope you're satisfied.' That was the last thing he said. His carriage was outside. He had Giles carried down to it. They were gone in half an hour."

"He left you there?"

"Indeed he did. Luckily, I had enough money to get home, but it took time. When I got there, my reputation was"—she paused for the word—"blasted. I waited for Giles to write, or come to me. He never did. Presently, I read in the papers that he had gone abroad—for his health. Don't look so angry, Sonia. He told me tonight that he had written; his letters were returned. He made

91

inquiries, and was told I was dead. I told you—his father was a very powerful man."

"Surely you wrote to him?"

"Once. It was returned; unopened. Father was very good to me, in his absent-minded way. The rest of the family would have nothing to do with me. But—he heard about your mother; how lonely she was in Germany; how badly she needed a companion who would also help to look after her child. I was tired of being pitied. There were rumors in the newspapers that Giles was about to engage himself to a young lady he had met in Rome."

"They weren't true, apparently."

"No, but I didn't know that. And I've never regretted coming to you."

Sonia reached out to hug her. "It was the best day of my life. Lord, though, no wonder you looked so queer the other day when you heard he was here. Elizabeth?"

"Yes?"

"He'll ask you again of course?"

"Good God, no. It's all over, years ago. Besides—he thinks I forgot him—married again."

"Of course! I never thought of that. No wonder he looked so angry. But—you'll tell him?"

"I'd rather die. Sonia, let me say this, once and for all, and then, please, we won't talk about it again. I broke my heart for Lord Denbigh years ago, no use pretending I didn't. But—it was years ago. My heart will never break again: I'll see to that. It's too painful. I hated him for a long time, but now, I don't even hate him. Why should I? It was not, after all, so much his fault as I had thought. But—I have my pride, Sonia. Indeed, it's about all I have. It made him angry to think I'd forgotten him and married—well, that's all the revenge I'll ever have."

"Revenge? You don't sound like yourself, Barry."

"No? I seem so cool and composed to you, so complete-ly the governess? Well, so I am—now; that's what he did to me. And nothing—nothing in the whole world, Sonia, would make me turn back and be that desperate girl again. There are advantages, you see, about getting old: things don't hurt so much."

"Old? You, Barry? Nonsense."

"I feel old, and that's what counts. As for Lord Den-bigh, I confess I dreaded the meeting, but it's over now, and no reason why we should not behave like the formal acquaintances we are. And, now, please, Sonia, the subject is closed."

"Of course, if you say so." And then, incorrigibly, "He's wonderfully attractive, though, your Giles. And such manners! Did you hear him say I sang divinely? I do hope Charles was listening. He liked me a little, don't you think?" She leaned on Elizabeth's shoulder to study her own reflection in the glass. "I don't see how you could forget him."

"It's all over, I tell you, years ago. And now—it's very late, and I'm tired."

"And sad, poor Barry. Was he very unpleasant?"

"Sonia, I don't want to talk about it. Not now—not ever. I've told you what I have so that you'll spare me—please."

"Poor darling, I'm sorry. I'm not even to tell Charles?"

"No one. And now, good night."

"Let me help you undress first; you look so tired, darling Barry."

"No." It was almost a cry. And then, "Thank you, but, no, and—good night."

"Sweet dreams, Barry." She dropped a light kiss on Elizabeth's cheek and turned away.

Sweet dreams? Dreams of what? Elizabeth stood, dead still, ice quiet as the door closed behind Sonia. Now, at last, she was alone, free—to do what? "I won't cry." Was she talking to herself? An angry swoop took her across to her glass, to make herself reassemble the white face into its habitual mask of calm. "I won't think either." Shaking hands pulled the pins from her heavy hair. "Above all, I'll not remember." Now, tearing the comb through the still entangled braids, she felt excused for the prickling of tears behind her eyes. The pain was salutary . . . reviving. At last, she was able to meet her own eyes in the glass, darker than usual with unshed tears: "Sweet dreams, Mrs. Barrymore."

Philip Haverton was quite as full of curiosity as Sonia, but very much less hopeful of having it satisfied. One look at his guardian's face, over breakfast next morning, taught him to abandon even such hope as he had allowed himself. Under his tan, Denbigh was gray with fatigue, his face drawn with midnight thought. This was no day for even the most casual breakfast table conversation. Philip applied himself strenuously to rolls and coffee and pretended not to notice that his companion was eating nothing.

At last Denbigh pushed back his chair and stood up. "I am not going to forbid you going to that house, Philip, but I do beg you will have a care what you do—and what you say."

"What I say?"

"Yes. I have been interested in Charles Vincent for some time, and what I saw last night confirms everything I have heard. How much, do you imagine, had those young Russians babbled, in their cups, about Allied troop movements?"

"You mean—"

"He is certainly a—well, call it a collector of information. The question I have not yet been able to answer to my own satisfaction is for whom he collects it. It was he, you know, who produced the secret correspondence on the basis of which the Czar has agreed to march through Switzerland. Well, so much the better, of course. But— why did he do it? Be very careful, Philip. Lose your money in his house, and even your heart, a little, if you must, but mind you don't lose reputation too."

"But you can't think Miss von Hugel—or Mrs. Barrymore, for the matter of that—would let herself be involved in anything underhand."

"Knowingly? Probably not. But think what an admirable cover that gaming house of theirs makes for him."

"Not a gaming house, cousin—a few friends for cards—"

"A few drunken young men, without enough sense of the proprieties, or respect for their hostess, to prevent them behaving as they did last night? Come, Philip, you're no fool; use the sense you have; see things as they are. I do not want to have to send you home."

"You couldn't!"

"If you speak like that, I shall wonder whether I should not. But don't look so downcast; I don't want to if I can help it. Just—be careful, Philip. Now we are to be on the march at last it is more important than ever that there should be no discord between the Allies."

"We really are to march, then?"

"The Austrians are gone already; the Russians and Prussians are to follow them at once. I'll never understand how Napoleon came to leave the bridge at Basel intact. Now that the Swiss have let us through—for a consideration—the way to France is open."

It was true. Napoleon was back in Paris trying to galvanize the Chamber of Deputies into action and setting about assembling a new army. The Allied armies poured unopposed across the Rhine and were amazed to find themselves absolutely welcomed by the French peasantry.

"It means nothing," Charles Vincent said. "They're tired out, that's all. And so used to seeing soldiers march past that they greet them automatically."

"You get more French every day," said Sonia accusingly.

"And why not? I see nothing to be ashamed of in being French. We've held the world at bay for twenty years, which is more than you Germans can boast of."

"I'm not German! I'm English, and so are you. I wish you'd never met that French cousin of yours: you've been different since. What's the matter with you? What's on your mind, Charles?"

He laughed. "What do you think? My responsibility for two elegant young females, of course."

Elizabeth looked up quickly, ready for a storm at his teasing tone. But Sonia surprised her. "Charles, don't—" Her voice was pleading. "Be serious, just for once. What have you got yourself into? Who are these friends of yours you never let us meet?"

He put down the paper he had been reading and looked at her thoughtfully. "Who are they, kitten? Why—people I don't want you to meet."

Now she was angry. "Don't call me kitten! I'm not a baby, nor yet the fool you think me, Charles Vincent!"

"No?" His voice was still indulgent. "And I've been neglecting you, Rapunzel? But don't be anxious. I'll make your fortune yet, you see if I don't. And there's always Philip Haverton, if all else fails."

"Oh, you're intolerable." The door slammed behind her.

Elizabeth looked up from her sewing. "I do hope you don't wish you had never met us."

95

"Of course not. I might well ask you the same thing. Sonia's right enough on one point. I have neglected you shamefully since we came to Basel. And—I hope you will forgive me—I would very much rather not explain what I have been doing. Will you bear with me?"

She bit off her thread. "I imagine we shall have to. I only hope you know, yourself, what you are doing."

"Nothing I shall ever regret, I promise you."

She gave him level look for look. "I do hope you are right. But tell me one thing; the landlady was asking me only this morning how long we intended to stay here."

"Oh—yes." Thoughtfully. "Not long, I think. There is talk of a Peace Congress to be held at Châtillon. I propose we move on there so soon as the roads are safe."

She shivered. "Yes. Have you heard that it is the French now who pray, *'Domine de Cossaquibus liberate nos?'* "

"Lord, deliver us from the Cossacks. Yes, I know. Now they know they're on enemy territory, there's no stopping their pillage—and worse. It's uniting the French as Napoleon's tyranny never could."

"Sonia's right: you do sound more French every day, Charles. But—not for Napoleon?"

"The two things do not necessarily go together."

Chapter 8

"What do you think, sir!" Philip Haverton burst into the study of the house Lord Denbigh had taken in Châtillon. "Guess who I just saw in the street."

"Napoleon?" Denbigh put down his pen and looked at him quizzically.

"Good God, no! By all reports he's busy beating us somewhere between here and Paris. No—much better than that: Charles Vincent. He and the young ladies reached town only this morning. Oh, I'm sorry, sir." He had seen the change in Denbigh's face. "Are you not pleased?"

"Why should I be? Or displeased, for the matter of that. It is no concern of mine—so long as you conduct yourself with discretion, Philip. What did Charles Vincent have to say for himself?"

"That's what I wanted to tell you. He says there are white cockades hidden in every attic in France. He is sure that if the war goes on much longer, Napoleon will be forced to abdicate and the Bourbons will be back on the crest of the wave."

"The Bourbons? After all this time? Does he so? I must tell Castlereagh that when he gets back from Troyes. He tells me there is a good deal of pro-Bourbon talk in England these days—and still more against negotiating with Bonaparte."

"You mean, the conference here is a complete waste of time?"

"Worse, if you ask me. We should not be seen to negotiate with Napoleon. For one thing, he only gave his minister, Caulaincourt, a free hand so long as things were going against him. Now that he's taken the field again, and scored some victories, he'll never come to terms. I was never more glad of anything than when Castlereagh arrived to relieve me of my duties at the conference."

"You still seem busy enough. I only wish you would let me do more of your writing for you."

"I wish I could." And then, aware of how much Philip minded being excluded from his councils, "So Charles Vincent thinks the Bourbons have a chance, does he?"

"Yes—I have never heard him so positive. He says the Comte d'Artois is in Switzerland already."

"So I have heard. But it's his older brother, you know, who would succeed as Louis XVIII if there should really be a Bourbon restoration."

"Yes, of course. But Vincent says Artois would be king in fact, if not in name."

"He thinks that, does he? Well—I wonder. You will be calling on him and his cousins, I collect?"

"If you do not object?"

"And if I do?"

"I do hope you will not." And then, with an effort: "Would you not care to come too? After all—if you and Mrs. Barrymore are old friends—" It was the first time he had managed to raise the subject since that unlucky night at Frankfurt.

"Old friends! Hardly the phrase I would have chosen. No, I'll not accompany you, Philip, but say everything that is polite from me to both of them. And if Charles Vincent chooses to talk politics, listen, Philip; listen, and don't talk."

"You want me to spy on them!"

"Oh, my dear Philip, must you behave like a public school boy on his first point of honor? We are all spies here, one way and another. Of course, if your feelings are too nice for the business, you are welcome to go home. But consider a little: it is the peace of the world that is at stake. I suppose you hardly remember what peace is like, and even I, since I was grown up, have only enjoyed that brief breathing space after the Peace of Amiens. And that was more like a pause between rounds than real peace. Surely the sight of the misery here in France means something to you? The beggars in the streets, the starvation, the penury? Have you noticed that you hardly ever see babies or little children? There are no young men, no fathers—"

"But this is France, sir. They're the enemy."

"Philip, will you never grow up? Do you really think that the Frenchwomen who crowd around the carriages, begging for a sou, a crumb of bread—can you look on them as your enemies? They have suffered from this twenty years' war far more than we have at home. What English town has suffered as Troyes has? It is for their sake, quite as much as for our own, that we must work for a lasting peace. If I had to spy on my own mother to ensure that, I would do so."

"But your mother is dead, sir."

Denbigh burst into a roar of delighted laughter. "Philip, you will be the death of me yet. Don't worry; I'll never send you home; you provide me with far too much entertainment. And now, run along and pay your courtesy call. And if you find they have got several Bourbon princes concealed in their attic, mum's the word; at all costs we must not spy on our friends."

"I believe I shall like it here," said Sonia. She and Elizabeth were busy arranging their few possessions in the salon of the house they had taken in Châtillon while Charles Vincent turned quickly through the pages of the *Moniteur*.

"Even though you are among the dreadful French?"

"They seem so friendly. You can't think of Marthe as an enemy, somehow. She adores you, Charles. I can't think why."

"Because I praise her cooking, of course."

She made a face at him. "It's more than you ever did for mine. What I want to know is, can we afford her?"

"We can't have the house without her, so the question is academic. Besides, the town's as full of diplomats as it can hold—"

"So we are going to make that El Dorado fortune at last?"

"I don't see why not. If you keep your mind on your cards. Oh—I met a friend of yours this morning, Philip Haverton; I doubt if he will wait till tonight to call on you."

"Oh, good! He's just what I need after a course of your crabbing, Charles. And his handsome guardian—does Lord Denbigh intend to call on us too?"

"That I cannot tell you. He is very much occupied, Haverton tells me, with the business of the conference, since Castlereagh has been at Troyes."

"Will he come, Liz, do you think?" And then, "You're very quiet, love, do you not feel well?"

"I'm trying to check the inventory of the house, that's all. Yes, Marthe?"

"There's a gentleman below, a M. Haverton."

"Show him up," said Elizabeth, and "No Denbigh then," said Sonia. But she greeted Haverton like an old friend, let him hold her hand for an extra minute and accepted his carefully selected compliments as her natural due. "And now"—she was arranging the flowers he had brought her in a vase—"tell me all about Châtillon. Shall we like it here, do you think? And more important still, how long must we stay here? When does the march on Paris begin? Surely that formidable guardian of yours must know. Does he intend to visit us, by the way?"

Haverton colored. "He sent his compliments, of course, to you both." A glance for Elizabeth, but she was still very much occupied at the other end of the room. "As to the march on Paris: I wish I could tell you, but you know I am the merest of hangers-on, my cousin tells me nothing. Mr. Vincent, I am sure, knows infinitely more than I do of what goes on in the world."

"You think so?" Vincent put down the *Moniteur*. "Well, it says here that now Napoleon's in the field he'll have the Allies back on the Rhine in no time."

"But should we believe that?" asked Sonia. "I thought you said even the French now prefer to get their news from England."

Vincent laughed. "Setting up for a politician, Sonia? It's true that one must take the *Moniteur* with a grain of salt, but they would not claim victories at Montmirail and Montereau without some grounds. What does your cousin think, Haverton?"

"He thinks the Allies should have marched on Paris long ago."

"He's right, of course. It was madness to give Napoleon time to assemble a new army. But even so I'm sure it's only a matter of time."

Sonia sighed impatiently. "Time ... time. I begin to wonder if we shall ever get to Paris, and as for England ... I hardly believe in it any more."

"England," said Vincent thoughtfully. "Yes, it seems very far away."

"Not to me," said Haverton. "Not now that we can send couriers by way of Paris. It only takes eight days to get an answer. Why, I can even tell you who is playing at Drury Lane."

"Just the same," said Sonia, "I don't believe in it."

"What else can you tell us about England?" asked Vincent. "Are they still united against Napoleon?"

"Oh yes, my cousin says there's a strong party against even negotiating with him. There's actually talk of a Bourbon restoration." And then, coloring to the eyes, "Oh, I believe I should not have said that. I beg you will forget it." And he took a somewhat shamefaced leave, promising however to return in the evening.

"He's a very silly young man," said Elizabeth dispassionately.

"Is he not?" Sonia laughed and moved Haverton's flowers into a corner. "Do you know what I think? I believe Lord Denbigh has warned him against us. What do you say, Elizabeth? Oh, she's gone. Do you know, Charles, I'm worried about her."

"Worried? But why?"

"Charles, you're impossible. Can you think of nothing but your 'affairs of state'? Here you are, living in the same house as Elizabeth and you have never even noticed that she hardly eats a thing—I suspect she doesn't sleep either —and you wonder why I'm worried."

"Leave her alone, Sonia. She'll come about—I have a great respect for Elizabeth—too great a one to harass her with my concern."

"Oh! So I'm in the wrong as usual. I might have known it. I can only say, if that's your idea of respect, heaven preserve me from your affection!"

He merely picked up the *Moniteur.* "Do you want to know what Marie Louise wore to the opera the other night?"

"No, I do not. Do you imagine, because I am a woman, I think of nothing but dress?"

"What has become of young Haverton?" asked Vincent some ten days later. "It seems to me I have not seen him ogling you for a week or more, Sonia. Has your magic ceased to work on him, do you think?"

"What a brute you are, Charles." Sonia said it amicably enough. "It's quite true, Philip hasn't been near me for all of a week. I expect that fierce cousin of his has forbidden him our house. What do you think, Elizabeth?"

"I think you talk a great deal of nonsense. And it is time I went to see Marthe." She was rising to leave the room when Vincent stopped her. "One moment; there was something I wanted to ask you. Would you have any objection to our having a small party tonight?"

"A party? But do we not every night?"

"Are you so weary of it? I'm sorry ... But tonight I thought of something rather different. Could we not invite our guests for a change?"

"Instead of just letting them happen," said Sonia. "Why not? And who are you going to ask, Charles?"

"Philip Haverton among others. Will you have any objection to that?"

"Not the least in the world, so long as he comes."

"Oh, he'll come all right; I'm sure of that. It must be merely some point of punctilio that keeps him away."

"And you mind it for my sake? How good you are to me, Charles." She dropped him a mocking curtsy.

Under Vincent's direction, the wine flowed fast and freely that night. He had brought home a curiously miscellaneous collection of guests, among them, to Elizabeth's irritated surprise, the young Russians who had behaved so badly at Frankfurt. "They have come to ask your forgiveness," he explained in an audible aside that made it impossible for her to welcome them anything but kindly. She was surprised, too, that he delayed settling the party down to the card tables that always stood ready at the far end of the room. Or—was she surprised?

He had led the conversation, now, to the subject of Bernadotte, whose Army of the North was making so unaccountably snail-like an approach on Paris. "But I must not criticize him to you"—this to the youngest of the Russians. "I believe your Emperor has a great opinion of him."

"The Czar—God bless him? Yes—back in Freiburg a friend of mine heard him tell the King of Prussia he would not rest till he had marched on Paris and made Bernadotte Emperor of France."

"Nonsense!" This was an Austrian officer. "Can you imagine Unser Franz letting his daughter be turned adrift to make way for Mme. Bernadotte? Not to mention his grandson. A regency's what the French need."

"Or the Bourbons?" This was Vincent, casually.

"Louis the Undesirable?" asked the young Russian. "You might as well try to make me King of France. The Czar's just as likely to allow it. The Bourbons had their day twenty years ago."

Sonia was distracted from this conversation by Haverton's voice. "Miss von Hugel, may I have a word with you?"

"Why not?" She let him lead her away from the arguing group to the other end of the room. "I did not see you arrive. Indeed, I quite thought you had given us up."

"To tell truth, I meant to. But—I cannot. I'm ashamed to admit it, but it's too strong for me. I have tried to keep away—but Vincent's invitation, today, was too much for my resolution."

"Oh? You make it sound as if we had the typhus here, Mr. Haverton. Is this household really so dangerous?"

"I believe so, and, what is more important, so does my cousin."

"Your handsome cousin? So that's why he has never visited us. Is he so afraid of losing his money?"

"You know it's not that. Miss von Hugel, let me warn you as a friend: you are moving in deep waters. Listen!" His uplifted hand silenced her and they listened, for a moment, to the babble of voices at the far end of the room. The argument was going fast and furiously now, the Russians insisting that they had not endured the disgrace of Moscow to see a Bourbon restoration, the Austrians upholding the claim of their Archduchess to hold the throne of France for her son, and a lone Prussian maintaining, *sotto voce,* that only the destruction of Paris could make amends for what had happened to Berlin. "You notice," went on Haverton after a moment, "that Vincent says nothing. He merely listens."

"Well," Sonia flared up. "It wouldn't be much good saying anything when they are all shouting so."

"It's like you to defend him, but, cousin or no cousin, you must face the facts. My cousin says—"

"I knew it." She interrupted him. "I told Elizabeth, last time you came, that Lord Denbigh had warned you against us. You had best listen to his warnings, had you not, and stay away?"

"Miss von Hugel—Sonia—how can you be so cruel? You must know that I love you more than life, more than honor itself—"

"That is evident enough," she said dryly, "since you betray your cousin's confidence to me. I think you had best leave, Mr. Haverton, before you say anything else you will regret."

"Not till I have finished." Now his perseverance had a touch of dignity about it and she listened despite herself. "I have told you I love you, Miss von Hugel. You must realize that I want to marry you, to take you away from this den of conspirators. Only say yes, and you shall be in England within the week, this sordid interlude forgotten as if it had never been."

She swept him a fierce curtsy. "You are too good, Mr. Haverton, but let me remind you that these conspirators, as you choose to call them, are my dear friends. I do not intend to forget them."

"And is that your only answer?" Lamentably crestfallen now.

"What more do you want? Should I thank you for the generosity of your offer?" And then, more gently: "I suppose I should. Then, 'Thank you, Mr. Haverton.' And you will thank me, one of these days, for letting you off so."

"Never!" But she had moved away from him, towards the group at the other end of the room. The tone of the conversation had changed while she had been occupied with Haverton. Now they were discussing the feeling of the town. "I don't like it," said an Austrian. "When we first arrived, they greeted us almost like liberators, but since these late successes of Napoleon's things are very different."

"It's true." Sonia was glad of the chance to join in. "It's been quite different, the last few days. When we first came, we were pestered by crowds of women, begging. They called down blessings on our heads if we gave them a sou or a few kitchen scraps. Now they crowd around us in a sullen silence that is as bad as threats. One spat on the hem of my gown yesterday."

"Nonsense," said Charles Vincent. "You are imagining things, Sonia."

"As usual, I suppose you would say?"

"Well"—his tone of avuncular tolerance maddened her —"you said it, Sonia, not I." And then, "Now, gentlemen, what do you say to a hand of cards?"

Sonia surprised everyone by revoking that night, and was irritated to have Vincent make her excuses. "Miss von Hugel is tired, we had best call it a day."

"That suits me," said the youngest of the Russians. "We are making an early start in the morning."

"Forward, I hope," said Vincent.

The Russian colored angrily. "What do you think? We are going to make Napoleon sorry he was born. Montmirail and Montereau will be remembered for all time as his last victories. Any day now, Blücher's army will join ours, and then"—he clapped his hands together— "finish."

"Do you go to bed, Liz," said Sonia when they were all

gone. "You have looked exhausted all evening. Charles and I will tidy things here." And then, when they were alone, "I have just been warned against you, Charles."

"Against me? By whom?"

"Philip Haverton, of course. That cousin he talks of so much has his eye on you—or so he says."

"He's welcome." Vincent went on expertly packing wineglasses on a tray. "He does not seem to have stopped young Haverton coming here."

"It's not for lack of trying."

"Oh? The attraction was too strong, was it?"

She had not meant to tell him, but his teasing tone was too much for her resolution. "If you really want to know, Philip asked me to marry him tonight."

"Did he so? I told you I'd make your fortune, Rapunzel."

"Charles!" She whirled to face him. "You cannot, for a moment, imagine that I accepted him!"

"No? But why not? He's an admirable *parti*. Yours to command. Young, rich, handsome, as silly as he can hold together and with no particular vices, except a tendency to play high, of which I am sure you could cure him."

"Thank you! You flatter me beyond measure. It had not, I take it, crossed your mind that I might not want a husband who was mine to command. Good God, how can you be so stupid! Marry Philip Haverton? Why, I would as soon marry you!"

He laughed and picked up a couple of empty wine bottles. "But I haven't asked you, Rapunzel."

"Oh, you're intolerable. I should have known it would be a waste of time to speak to you. But I thought you should be warned."

"What? That you are contemplating matrimony?"

"No, stupid. That Lord Denbigh has his eye on you. I'm not a fool, Charles, though you choose to treat me as one. I have known—and so has Elizabeth—this long time past that we are not living on our winnings. Or—not solely. The fairy gold goes on coming in, does it not, from that generous cousin of yours? I think it is time you told us what you do in exchange—or for whom you do it. Like it or not, we are involved, Elizabeth and I. Should we not know just what we are involved in?"

"Nothing you will ever regret, I promise you."

"I think we are the best judges of that."

"Do you? That's unfortunate."

"You mean, you do not propose to tell me."

"Frankly, no. The best way of keeping a secret is—not to know it. Specially for a woman."

"A woman! I might have known we could come down to that."

He laughed. "Well, you're not a boy any longer, Rapunzel." And then, checking her angry retort, "More's the pity, perhaps. And—thank you for your warning, but believe me, all will be well in the end."

"You think so?" she smiled up at him mischievously. "What end, I do wonder?"

"Time will show. And now, it's long past your bedtime, Rapunzel, and I have letters to write."

"To that cousin of yours, no doubt. Telling him everything our guests said tonight. Sometimes, Charles, you make me sick. To hear you pumping those simple young Russians—I tell you, I was hard put to it not to intervene."

"I am glad you contrived to restrain yourself. Do I have to tell you, Rapunzel, that war is not a pretty business? Think of the sights you and I have seen together and tell me I should not do everything in my power to make an end of it—if you can."

She shivered. "Must you remind me? I try so hard to forget."

He gave her a strange look. "There are some things, Sonia, that one ought not to forget."

"You want me to think about it? About Father! And Gretchen! I never told you about Gretchen, did I, Charles? Shall I? Shall I tell you?" Her voice rose almost to a scream.

"Careful. You'll break something." He took a tray of glasses from her shaking hands. "I'm sorry, Sonia, I should not have said that. But—you must try to understand. Come the peace, I'll be as punctilious as you please; till then—"

"Come the peace," she interrupted him, "I hope what you do, or do not do, will be no affair of mine."

He opened the door for her with elaborate courtesy. "I am sure your wish will be granted, Rapunzel, and so, good night."

Sonia and Elizabeth both slept late the next morning and came downstairs to learn from the maid, Marthe, that Vincent had already gone out. "He had a visitor, very early," Marthe explained, "and went out without so much as a cup of coffee."

"Oh? Anyone we know?" Sonia was pouring her own coffee as she spoke.

"No. I never saw him before in my life. He'd come from far, if you ask me, and—fast." She looked as if she would have been glad to say more, but Elizabeth changed the subject.

"And the news in the town?" she asked.

"There's talk of a new attack." Marthe shrugged. "Of course you can't believe all you hear. Only—madame"— to Elizabeth—"would you let me do the marketing today? It might be—safer."

"You think we should not go out?"

"I would feel happier if you did not. Well—you know how it is, madame. We've had it bad enough, we French, for years past—there's not a family in town that doesn't mourn a husband—a brother."

"But you can't blame us for that," said Sonia. "This war is none of our seeking, Marthe."

"Could you convince Mme. Béguèt of that, who lost her husband at Moscow? Or Mlle. Moisson who lost two brothers at Trafalgar? And besides, there are the Cossacks ... They have done things in the countryside that I could not tell you of, mademoiselle."

Sonia was very white. "And I have seen the French do things—oh, forgive me, Marthe. It's no use, is it?"

"No use at all. Only, I wish you will stay at home until things are quieter. So long as Napoleon is on the offensive —I'd feel safer. But here comes monsieur. Ask him what he thinks."

Charles Vincent pooh-poohed the idea. "It's nothing but a flash in the pan on Napoleon's part," he said. "Stay indoors today, if you like, and go out tomorrow to hear the news of victory. I am only sorry that I shall not be here to enjoy it with you."

"Not here?" Sonia's voice rose. "What do you mean?"

"I have to leave town for a few days."

"Leave town now? Leave us alone here? You can't, Charles. Elizabeth, tell him he can't."

"I must." He turned to Elizabeth. "I received an urgent message this morning. It leaves me no alternative but to go."

"Oh, absolutely." Sonia dropped her sewing and jumped up to face him, eyes flashing. "Duty calls, does it, Charles? Of course, we should know by now that when that happens you cannot be expected to spare a thought for us. If the French should be so inconsiderate as to retake the town while you are gone—well, it will just be our bad luck, will it not?"

"Don't be absurd, Sonia. Napoleon's miles away, involved with Blücher. And—even if by some fantastic chance the Allies should be forced to retreat, the members of the conference here have diplomatic immunity."

"Yes, dear Charles, but we are not attached to the Congress."

"That is precisely why I saw young Haverton this morning and asked him to have an eye to you while I am away. And his cousin too, of course."

"Haverton!" said Sonia.

"And Denbigh?" said Elizabeth.

"He would be a powerful friend, if need were. But of course it will not come to that. You are starting at shadows, ladies."

"I do so hope you are right," said Elizabeth.

"Right?" said Sonia. "Charles is always right, aren't you, Charles?"

Chapter 9

Charles Vincent rode away that night, promising to return as soon as he could, though Elizabeth privately suspected that his "few days" might be very much more like a week. She did not at all like to see him go, and was angry at her own dependence on him, angrier still at the idea of being thrust upon Denbigh's protection. How could Charles! But of course he knew nothing about that old affair. It was her own fault for refusing to let Sonia tell him. And yet—she could not really regret this. Sonia's conscious looks when the days passed and Denbigh never came near them had been hard enough to bear. Absurd, of course, to have minded. She let her work fall in her lap and considered it for a moment. Yes—that was it. As she had said to Sonia, there was no reason in the world why she and Denbigh should not meet, now, as mere acquaintances. Indeed, she had had her words of casual greeting all rehearsed and ready. But—to be treated as a leper, to be given no chance to show how completely she had forgotten the past. It was only reasonable to have felt this acutely.

She jumped to her feet. Now, he might at last feel compelled to call and promise his protection. Well, if he came tonight, he would not be admitted. She rang the bell and told Marthe that since M. Vincent was away, they would be at home to no one. "We'll make an early night of it," she concluded.

"And a good thing too." Marthe already assumed all the familiarity of an old family retainer. "You don't look well at all, madame, and so I was telling mamselle only the other day."

"Nonsense! Too many late nights is all my trouble. We'll all be the better for a quiet evening."

Even Sonia admitted herself glad of it. "No cards tonight, thank God." She had wandered into Elizabeth's room in her negligée, brushing her hair as she came. Now she moved over to the window and drew aside the heavy curtains to look out into the darkness. "It's snowing again. Lord, what a brute of a winter. Charles will be perished with cold—and serve him right. What's behind this new start of his do you think, Elizabeth?"

"I've no idea." Elizabeth had her own doubts about Charles but did not mean to discuss them, even with Sonia. "Shall I give your hair a brush for you?"

"Do." Sonia sighed luxuriously. "Who cares about Charles anyway? We two can manage excellently on our own account, can we not?"

"Of course we can." Elizabeth wished she were sure of it.

"I just hope he gets pneumonia for his pains—or frostbite," Sonia went on. "And without us there to nurse him either. That would teach him we're not the useless creatures he seems to think. Oh, there's someone at the door."

"Never mind. We're not at home, remember."

"I should think not indeed. Imagine Philip Haverton's face if I received him like this!" A glance in the glass showed she was well aware of how she looked with her golden curls loose about her face. "I imagine it *is* Philip."

"I expect so."

"I wonder if Lord Denbigh has come too. He should, you know, after being left in charge of us like this. I wonder what he thinks of that."

"I would much prefer not to know."

"Oh, I don't believe he will mind it so much. After all, his affair with you is an old old story. You said yourself it was over and done with. He might be glad of a chance to show he had forgiven and forgotten."

"Forgiven?" Elizabeth bit the word off angrily. "As to forgetting, it's clear he's done that right enough."

"Yes, he really should have called, just once, should he not? Having warned Philip against me, though, he could hardly come calling on you, could he?"

"Warned Haverton? What do you mean?"

"Did I not tell you? Oh, no, of course—it was Charles ... and it's been such a day. Poor Philip, he made me a proposal in form last night. I'd be more flattered if I didn't think it was mainly because Denbigh had told him not to. We're a very suspicious set of characters, I'll have you know. Lord"—she broke off to laugh—"how angry that poor Denbigh must be at being saddled with looking after us." And then, casually: "I refused Philip, of course, and he concealed his relief gallantly. Poor thing, suppose I'd accepted him! I'd have loved to see Lord Denbigh forbidding the banns."

Elizabeth's hands clenched in her lap. Quiet, she told herself, quiet: the child does not mean to be cruel. "You're talking nonsense, my love, and you know it." With an effort she recaptured the old, governess's tone. "Off to bed with you, child. I meant it when I said I wanted an early night."

"Of course. Poor darling, you *do* look tired." Her expressive glance rested on their reflections side by side in the glass. "Sleep well, darling Liz, and be better in the morning."

"Don't call me Liz!"

"I beg your pardon." A laughing curtsy. "Dear Mrs. Barrymore, forgive me. How cross Lord Denbigh sounded when he called you that at Frankfurt, remember? I collect he thought you should have been wearing the willow for him all this time. Will you never explain?"

"No!" Explosively. "Sonia, I asked you not to talk about it."

"You're angry with me!" A child's surprise in her voice. "I'm sorry, darling Barry. I'll never do it again—word of a von Hugel." She moved to the window. "Look at the snow! How cold Charles will be. And serve him right. When will he come back, do you think?"

"When it suits him. Good night, Sonia."

Elizabeth woke next morning with a curious sense of something wrong. She lay for a few moments, eyes still closed, trying to work out what it was. Well, plenty was wrong, of course. Sonia had been tiresome last night; she winced a little at the memory and wondered if Sonia would ever quite get over the shock she had had. And then there was Charles—but that was not it. And her own private misery, but that would be with her, she thought, always. She sat up in bed. Of course. She had not heard the Allied sentries going their rounds through the streets. Usually, their exchange of command and challenge was the first thing she heard in the morning. She jumped out of bed, threw her negligée around her and hurried over to the window.

The first sight that met her eyes was a group of French dragoons, lounging nonchalantly on the street corner, surrounded by an eager little crowd of black-gowned women. As she watched, the crowd grew; a courier in the uniform of the National Guard galloped down the street. It was impossible to believe—and yet, appallingly, true: the town must have fallen to the French in the night. She huddled her clothes on and ran next door to Sonia's room. The curtains here were still drawn and Sonia peacefully asleep. "Quick"—she shook her—"wake up. The French are in the town."

"What?" It was usually a long business waking Sonia, but not today. "It's not true?"

"I'm afraid it is." Now, remembering Sonia's previous experience, she wished she had not waked her so suddenly. But Sonia, though white, was admirably calm. "What do we do, Barry?"

"Hope for the best—and keep ourselves as quiet as possible. I wonder ... !" She had been so occupied with what was going on in the street that she only now noticed an unnatural quiet in the house.

"Marthe?" Sonia had noticed, too.

"Yes, I suspect she has taken French leave." She peered, cautiously this time, from behind Sonia's curtains. "Yes, there she is—look."

Sonia joined her, buttoning her bodice as she came. "Talking to those dragoons! I'd never have thought it of her." Her face, white before, was chalky now. "If she tells them of us—"

"Wait here; watch. I must make sure that the door is bolted. Thank God there's only one." It had been, before, a source of irritation that their little house, squeezed between two shops, had no back entrance. Now, running downstairs on silent, stockinged feet, Elizabeth felt it a crowning mercy. And the front windows, downstairs, were securely shuttered as they always were at night. She drove the great bolt of the heavy front door into its socket and stood for a minute leaning against the door, breathing fast and wondering how long its hinges would hold. Like Sonia, she could not help remembering the scene at the castle; the gate slowly yielding ... But this was a town ... the French were, basically, a civilized people ... that other time, after all, it had been largely the fault of Sonia's father. Arguing so, she was trying in vain to convince herself, before trying to convince Sonia, when she was roused by an agitated whisper from the head of the stairs. "She's coming back—Marthe—alone. What do we do?"

The latch of the big door rose and fell, unavailingly, since it was held by the heavy bolt. A whisper—from outside this time—Marthe's voice, her quick dialect French: "Madame! Let me in, madame, quickly, before they see."

"Don't!" Sonia's voice, almost simultaneously from above.

But already, Elizabeth was pushing the big bolt back. She had come alone, Sonia said. They could not afford to lose a friend. A blast of cold air, and Marthe almost fell

112

into the hall. "Shut it! Shut it, quick!" And then, as Elizabeth did so, "You know, then?"

"The French are in the town?"

"Yes. Since early this morning. The Allies are in full retreat. Troyes has fallen too. I have a friend"—she colored—"a dragoon; I saw him in the street. He says the Little Corporal has them on the run at last. Won't stop this side of the Rhine, he says. Oh, don't look so scared, mademoiselle, you'll be all right, you and madame. We're not brutes, we French; we know our friends. Still"—she started a little, as a noise of shouting swept down the street outside—"you'd best stay quiet. I wish M. Vincent was here."

"Trust him not to be, when he's needed." Sonia turned from Elizabeth to Marthe. "You didn't tell them about us."

"Of course not. What do you take me for? You have been good to me, you and madame. I tell you, we are not barbarians, we French. But—I wish you were part of the Congress."

"So do I." Elizabeth was disconcerted at finding Marthe thus aware of their precarious status in Châtillon. "We shall need all our friends."

"That's what I thought." Marthe was more a fellow conspirator now than a servant. "That's why I thought I'd best find out what I could from Jacques—my friend." She explained. "He says they have the strictest orders that none of the delegates to the conference is to be molested in any way. He has a list. The mayor gave it to him."

"That's a pity. We won't be on it."

"Precisely, madame. But—it could be worse. The main army is not coming here to Châtillon at all; only the National Guard and a few dragoons to keep order. It's but to stay quiet, madame, and all should be well. Only— if you could get some kind of document—just in case anyone comes to the house. Do you think M. the Duke of Vicenza?"

"Caulaincourt? Of course." Elizabeth had been thinking along the same lines. "I will write him a note at once."

"And I will take it for you, and wait for his answer. Only—admit no one when I am gone, madame. We may not be barbarians, we French, but we're not angels either. Jacques has some stories to tell about what's happened in

113

our villages ... Don't open the door, madame. And—are you armed?"

"Armed? Mr. Vincent must have taken his pistols, but—Sonia—your little gun?"

"Of course." She ran upstairs to get it. "Not much use against a crowd." It looked very tiny in her hand.

"As a weapon—none. But as an arguing point." She held out her hand. "Is it loaded?"

"Of course. Here you are."

"Thank you." It fitted neatly into the capacious, unfashionable pocket of her dress. "And now to write M. Caulaincourt."

Ten minutes later, she shot the bolt behind Marthe and turned to face Sonia. "And now—breakfast."

"Food? I couldn't touch a thing."

"You'd better, Sonia. It may be a long wait—goodness knows where Marthe may have to go to find Caulaincourt. And one's much braver on a full stomach."

"Suppose she does not come back?"

"Marthe? Why should she not?"

"Why should she? Or—bringing Jacques and his friends. And you talk of eating!"

"I don't just talk of it." She had already crossed the hall to the big flagged kitchen. Marthe had made up the stove before she went out, and the room was pleasantly warm after the early morning chill of the rest of the house. "I'm going to do something about it. Coffee, I think, today, and—yes, there are some rolls. Marthe won't betray us; she wouldn't look after us so well if she didn't like us a little."

"I'm glad you're so sure." But when they were ready, Sonia did, in fact, drink a little hot coffee and nibble at a roll, and Elizabeth, forcing herself to eat and talk as if nothing was the matter, saw with relief that her color was beginning to come creeping back.

"Just the same." Sonia had been holding the heavy coffee cup in both hands to warm them. Now she put it down on the kitchen table. "Where *is* Marthe?"

"Following Caulaincourt all over town, I expect. As Napoleon's representative at the Congress he's bound to be busy seeing that none of the foreign ministers is molested: that would be the last thing Napoleon would wish." Elizabeth wished she felt as calm as she contrived to sound.

"I just hope Marthe really is looking for him, not just sitting in a café, drinking with that Jacques of hers. Odd, don't you think, that we never so much as heard of him before today?" And then, "What's that?" The kitchen was at the back of the house and yet they could hear the confused noise of shouting from the street at the front. Without a word, they rose and ran up the narrow stair to Elizabeth's bedroom. Looking out cautiously from behind the curtains, they saw that the street was now crowded with people. It seemed a good-humored enough crowd, and the sound that had alerted them was the cry, now repeated, of *"Vive la France, vive l'Empereur!"* The cause of it was a detachment of the old Guard, now disappearing into the main square of the town. The crowd closed in across the road behind them. All the civilian population of Châtillon must be there, Elizabeth thought, and all in holiday mood. She saw Mme. Béguèt, who ran the grocery where Marthe shopped, talking with unwonted gaiety to Mlle. Moisson of the butcher's shop. And there, too, was Marthe's friend, Geneviève, who worked a few doors down the street . . . Surely there was no danger in these people who had been their friends. Mlle. Moisson always let Marthe know when her father was slaughtering . . . Geneviève had drunk many a glass of sirup "to the ladies' good health." Absurd to be afraid of them. Or—was it?

Since the Guards had disappeared, the crowd had stopped shouting and had made, instead, a great murmuration, like a swarm of giant, contented bees. Now, further down the street, the note changed, rose to an angry whine, then clarified itself into words: *"Les Anglais! A bas les Anglais!"* And then, a phrase Elizabeth had read about but never thought to hear: *"A la lanterne!"*

Sonia's cold hand caught hers. "What is it?"

"Someone's coming." It was possible, now, to see a kind of ripple in the crowd where a passage was being forced through it.

"English?"

"I'm afraid so. Madness."

"Gallant madness."

115

"Very dangerous gallantry." Elizabeth was straining her eyes, trying to see who was coming. "I hope it's not—"

"Haverton, of course. Coming here."

"And Denbigh with him. I thought he had more sense."

"Or less courage? See, the crowd falls back before them."

"It's lunacy, I tell you. What can have possessed Giles Burnleigh?"

"I expect Philip made him come."

"You mean he would not let him risk his life alone. Oh, my God!" For now, when the two men were well in sight, forcing their way nearer and nearer through the crowd, its mood began to change. So far, the French had been content to shout insults—and stand back. After all, Denbigh and Haverton were both armed, and showed every sign of meaning business, and the crowd was largely composed of women. But Elizabeth had seen Marthe's friend, Geneviève, bend to pick something up from the snowy street. Now she had a cobblestone in her hand. Mlle. Moisson was saying something to her: encouragement: dissuasion? She raised her arm and threw. The stone missed Haverton, at whom it was apparently aimed, but, fatally, it hit a young woman standing behind him in the crowd. She screamed, put her hand to her head and brought it away covered with blood. In an instant, the temper of the crowd had hardened. Every hand now held a weapon; sticks, stones and, here and there, a dagger glinting in chill February sunlight. Elizabeth saw Denbigh say something to Haverton; they increased their pace, and—she realized what he must have said. He had decided that they must on no account draw the crowd towards their house; at whatever risk to themselves, they would continue on their way down the street, running the gauntlet to draw the crowd away. And now stones and sticks were beginning to fly. Sonia gasped as a jagged cobble caught Haverton on the cheek, but Elizabeth had already left her and was running downstairs.

For a moment, the bolt stuck, then she had it back, flung the door open and stood on the doorstep, a little above the street. Luck was on her side; the two men, advancing steadily, were now almost level with the door; Denbigh had his arm round Haverton, whose wound was bleeding freely. The crowd had hesitated, satisfied, for an instant, with what it had achieved. Best of all, a little hush had fallen. Women were nudging their neighbors, whispering together ... Somewhere further down the street a man raised the cry again of "Death to the English," but, for a moment, it was not taken up. Elizabeth seized her chance: "Is this how you treat your friends? We are not Cossacks!" Her clear voice sent the fluent French ringing down the street. "We are here to bring peace, not the sword." And then, as the crowd still hesitated, muttering, uncertain: "Mme. Béguèt, you know us for your friends. Speak for us."

"It's true." Mme. Béguèt interposed her enormous bulk between Elizabeth and a virago with a spit. "They've never kept me waiting for my money. Not like some I could name." The remark obviously had point, for the crowd shook with a little ripple of laughter.

It gave Elizabeth the time she needed. "Come." Denbigh had managed to force his way towards her, half carrying Haverton, who drooped against him, blood pouring down his face. Now she met them, got her arm under Haverton's other one, and helped Denbigh lift him up the steps to their front door. Sonia was waiting there, and as Haverton collapsed on a bench in the hall, she shot the bolt behind them.

"Thank you—that was—timely." An angry roar from outside gave point to Denbigh's words. "I hope your door is strong. And—I apologize, for both of us, for bringing this trouble upon you. Listen to that." A hail of missiles was rattling against the shuttered windows. "Have you shutters upstairs too?"

"No."

"A pity. We must console ourselves with the thought that they are most of them women. Their aim will be poor. And—it should not be for long. I sent a messenger to Caulaincourt, the moment I heard the news, reminding him of your predicament. He is sure to arrange for your protection."

"I sent to him too." Elizabeth bent over Haverton, who was sitting groaning, his handkerchief to his face. "How are you, Mr. Haverton?"

"Blood!" He took away the soaked handkerchief, looked at it and turned, if possible, paler than ever. "A doctor! I

117

must have a doctor; I shall bleed to death. I shall be marked for life. Look at it come!"

"Nonsense," said Denbigh. "It's only a scratch. Put back the handkerchief, if you don't like the sight of blood. You wouldn't want to soil your waistcoat, would you?"

Sonia darted a look of bitter reproach at him and bent tenderly over Haverton. "Lean on me, Mr. Haverton. It is the shock, merely; you will be better soon."

"Here." Elizabeth returned from the kitchen with a handful of Marthe's clean polishing rags. "Use these to stanch it."

"Dirty kitchen cloths!" He waved them away impatiently. "Infected with who knows what vile French disease?"

"On the contrary." Elizabeth's voice was sharper now. "Marthe is very particular about her kitchen cloths. Come, Mr. Haverton, it was very gallant to come to our rescue. You do not, surely, wish to spoil the effect by bleeding all over our furniture. Here, Sonia"—she handed her a threadbare tablecloth—"spread this over the sofa in the salon, and let Mr. Haverton rest there a little. He will be more comfortable so." She moved towards the stairs. "It's time we found out what's happening outside." Inevitably, instinctively, she spoke to Denbigh.

"Yes." He joined her at the stair foot. "I don't like this silence. May I come too?"

"Of course." No time to think of the strangeness of this meeting. And yet, as she led him upstairs, she could not help being acutely aware of the feel of him behind her, the familiar firm tread ... Don't think about it ... In her room, the disordered bed, her negligée tossed across a chair still spoke of her hasty rising. She hardly spared them a thought, leading the way to the window. "Carefully ... You think they may be planning something?"

"I'm afraid so." Like her, he was looking out cautiously from behind the curtains. "They're in a strange state. You were mad to take the risk you did. They might have torn you to pieces."

"I had to do something."

"Lucky for us you did. But then—you were always one for doing." And then, more dryly, as if disconcerted by the note of familiarity. "I can only apologize for involving you in this danger. But I am sure you will believe me when I tell you it was no idea of mine."

"I thought not."

"No." Oddly, he seemed almost apologizing. "I thought it best simply to send to Caulaincourt on your behalf."

"You were always practical."

"You think that?" He checked himself. "Look! We were right to be anxious. I'm afraid they mean to burn your door down. Is there a back way out?"

"No."

"Windows?"

"Too small to escape by."

"The roof?"

"There's no way up to it."

He shrugged. "Then we shall just have to stay where we are. What a fortunate thing it's been such a cold winter; it should take them some time to get together enough wood for a good blaze. The snow will slow them up, too. But—how much water have you in the house?"

"Not much. Marthe fetches it each morning. I sent her to Caulaincourt. I wish she'd come back."

"Best not count on it. We'll use what you have to soak the inside of the door. It's a pity there's no window above it."

"Yes." The shouting had started again outside. Elizabeth could not help a little shiver of fear.

"Where's the water?" His voice was bracing and she realized, with an angry pang, that he knew exactly what she was feeling. Intolerable that this stranger—for that was all he was—should be able to read her thoughts.

Did he feel her hostility? Notice how carefully she avoided touching him as they passed each other in the hall? "Be grateful for the shouting," he said. "It may well bring us help. Caulaincourt doesn't want violence. He and the mayor have made a special appeal on our behalf. They'll be furious when they hear of this."

"I shall find that a very poor consolation." But she had got her second wind now, and they worked quietly, side by side, drenching the front door with every available drop of water, even what Marthe had ready on the stove for cooking lunch. By tacit agreement, they had left Sonia to minister to Haverton behind the closed door of the salon.

"That's all the water. Now what?" As she spoke, she was angry with herself for turning to him so naturally for orders.

119

"Damp rags, if you've got any. Five minutes—ten—may make all the difference. But first, let's see how they are getting on." This time he led the way upstairs.

It seemed to Elizabeth, looking cautiously out, that the crowd had thinned a little. She said so and Denbigh agreed with her. "A bad sign, I'm afraid. The good citizens have gone home to cook their lunch. Those that remain—" He did not finish the sentence.

"But fewer of them to fight."

"You were always a fighter, weren't you?" Must he keep reminding her? "Yes, I think it's time we counted our weapons. Here, if I mistake not, comes the torch."

A man was running down the street from the direction of the baker's shop, carrying a flaming brand from the fire. "Your gun's loaded?" Denbigh went on. "Mine; Haverton's—we'd best see how he is. Can Miss von Hugel shoot?"

"Better than I do."

"Then fetch them, would you? Here, at the top of the stairs, is the best point for defense."

Haverton was looking much better—and considerably ashamed of himself. Sonia had wound a competent-looking bandage round his head and, Elizabeth suspected, given him a bracing lecture while she was doing so.

His first words were an apology. He was ashamed—had always been made ill by the sight of blood—deplorable behavior, just the same . . .

"Never mind that now." Elizabeth cut him short. "The mob are trying to burn down the front door. Lord Denbigh says we must defend ourselves at the top of the stairs."

"Good God." Could he have forgotten about the mob? His glance now took in the drenched front of her dress. "And I've been malingering here."

It was too true to be answerable. She turned and led the way upstairs to find that Denbigh had been busy in her absence building a barricade of furniture from which they could command the front door.

"Good." He too made short work of Haverton's attempt at an apology. "You and I to fire, Philip, from here and here. Miss von Hugel, if you will, to load for us. Mrs. Barrymore to keep watch—carefully—from the window and let us know what to expect." As he spoke, he was

120

helping the two girls through the gap he had left in his barricade. His hand was ice-cold on Elizabeth's and, glancing at him quickly, she noticed for the first time how pale he was. Well, she told herself, no wonder . . .

While she was downstairs, a flight of stones had broken her bedroom windows. Splinters of glass lay everywhere on the floor; the curtains billowed in the cold wind; the shouting from the street sounded as if it was in the room. She approached the window, carefully, as Denbigh had told her to, her feet crunching on broken glass. Looking out from among the billowing curtains, she saw that the crowd below were too much occupied to notice her. Smoke, the smell of burning and the crackle of flames told her that the fire outside their front door must be burning merrily. All eyes were fixed upon it, except at the far side of the street, where a sort of whirlpool in the crowd seemed to indicate that an argument was in progress. Yes, now she saw Marthe, who had jumped on to the steps of a house on the other side of the street and was shouting to the people nearest her. Impossible to hear what she was saying, but impossible, equally, not to hope. Holding her drenched skirts clear of the glass she ran back across the hall to report. "I'm sure she's on our side," she concluded.

"Let us by all means hope you are right," said Denbigh. "For that door is not going to last much longer. What's that?"

Once again, Elizabeth ran back to look, spurred on, this time, by the sound of horses' hooves. Shouts and then screams from the square beyond; the crowd eddied, broke and began to scatter as a detachment of the National Guard rode into the street.

Reporting this to the others, "I never thought I'd be so glad to see French soldiers," she said.

"How do you know they are on our side?" asked Sonia.

"Of course they are." But Denbigh was suddenly whiter than ever; he swayed where he stood. "How tedious," he said, "my apologies—" and fainted.

"Good God!" Elizabeth was by his side in an instant, anxiously feeling his flickering pulse. "What can be the matter? Was he hurt too, do you think?"

"He said nothing." Haverton too had bent over Denbigh, as he lay half supported by the barricade.

121

"How white he is!" Sonia had fetched sal volatile from her bedroom. "D'you think he's dying, Elizabeth?"

"Of course not. But I wish his pulse was stronger. We must get a doctor—" She stopped, remembering, and at that moment the front door, downstairs, toppled backwards, into the house in a cloud of smoke and steam. "No." Her hand closed over Haverton's as he picked up his gun. "They're friends—look!"

The smoke was clearing now, and they could see a group of soldiers, occupied in clearing away the fire that had been built against the door. Now one of them advanced into the hall, looked up and saw them. "Don't fire." He spoke in French. "M. the Mayor and M. the Duke of Vicenza are here. We are your friends." It sounded oddly, from him.

"Good." Elizabeth did not give Haverton time to speak. "Then be so good as to fetch a doctor, at once."

"A doctor? Yes, madame, at once—but here is the mayor."

The mayor was complete with sky-blue swallow-tailed coat and tricolored scarf. Beside him, Caulaincourt or, to give him Napoleon's title, the Duke of Vicenza, looked almost dead with fatigue. It was the mayor who spoke, bursting into an eloquent flood of apology. He was appalled ... horrified ... he had come as quickly as he could ... the damage should be made good. He struck an attitude: "We French do not make war on ladies."

Elizabeth interrupted him. "Has anyone gone for the doctor?"

So far, they had noticed Haverton's bandage, but not Denbigh's motionless body, which had slipped still further down behind the barricade. Now Caulaincourt gave a quick series of orders. One man hurried off to fetch a doctor, two more came up to help carry Denbigh into Vincent's room, others began the task of setting things to rights. Elizabeth, directing the men who carried Denbigh, listened with half an ear as the mayor's stream of apologies continued. Denbigh stirred a little as he was laid down. His eyelids flickered open, then closed again. She was able, at last, to give her attention to Caulaincourt, thank him, as prettily as she could, for his timely intervention, and beg that the ringleaders of the crowd should not be pursued and punished. "I'd much rather not know who it was, monsieur," she said, "and besides—we have to go on living here, at least for a while."

"Quite so." He was no fool. "You will be glad, though, to know that it was your servant who came to us."

"I thought so." She looked around to see how Sonia had received this heartening news. But where was Sonia? And Haverton . . .

Once again, Caulaincourt showed his quick wit. "I believe M. Haverton's bandage has slipped," he said. "Mlle. von Hugel is fixing it for him—in there." The upper hall was clear now, and the dragoons were downstairs trying to replace the charred front door. Caulaincourt's gesture took Elizabeth across the hall to Sonia's bedroom, where she found her impatiently adjusting a new bandage round Haverton's head. "And don't touch it this time. Elizabeth! How's Lord Denbigh?"

"He stirred a little. I wish the doctor would come." And then, hearing a familiar voice, she hurried out into the hall. "Marthe." She went to her, hands outstretched. "How glad I am to see you safe."

Marthe cut short her thanks. "I hear milord is injured. Where is he? I'm not too bad a nurse, though I do say so."

"In here. Will you watch over him till the doctor comes?" Elizabeth breathed a sigh of relief as she saw Marthe settle herself by the bed, and then turned to Caulaincourt, who was taking his leave. There was something she must ask. "What is the news, monsieur?"

She had always liked Caulaincourt and he did not fall short of her respect. Meeting her eyes squarely, "Better for you, I think, madame, than for us," he said. "It's only a matter of days—a flash in the pan, no more." He shrugged. "I wish it were otherwise, but the facts must be faced. A week, or less, short of a miracle, and you will be masters again. In the meantime, I will leave a guard on the house. May I ask, as a favor to me, that you keep Lord Denbigh and M. Haverton here? It will be safer for you all."

"Of course."

"Ah, here's the doctor." And he took his leave as the little bustling medical man hurried into the hall, with his black bag in one hand and his tricorn hat in the other. Elizabeth made short work of his exclamations of sympathy, hurrying him to Denbigh's bedside. He lay exactly as she had left him, very white, very still ... Marthe had applied a cold compress but confirmed that he had not moved. "There's death in his face, if ever I saw it."

Elizabeth clutched the back of a chair as the doctor bent to examine his patient. "Well, no wonder." He pushed aside the thick fair hair. "You would hardly expect him to be dancing the schottische after a blow like that. Look!"

"Good God." Elizabeth bent forward to look at the bruised swelling. "Will he—"

"He was lucky," the doctor interrupted her. "A little further forward—here"—gentle fingers touched Denbigh's temple—"Anything might have happened . . . death . . . madness . . . loss of memory. With injuries to the head . . . there is no knowing . . ."

"He had a similar one, many years ago," she said. "And has, I believe, suffered from giddy spells ever since. Might there be a connection?"

"There might indeed. Who knows? The new blow may have affected scar tissue left from the old one. Well"—he shrugged and picked up his bag—"it is in the hands of God."

"You mean there is nothing you can do?"

"Nothing that you could not do better. Prayer—and cold compresses. Marthe knows . . . absolute quiet . . . rest . . . I'll come again tomorrow. There may have been a change by then. Frankly, there may never be one."

"You mean—he might remain like this?"

"It's possible. I've known cases . . ." He saw her expression. "But just as likely that he'll be shouting for his breakfast tomorrow morning. But if there is damage to the brain—Well, let me know if there is any change. Don't leave him alone, of course. Not for a moment. Anything might happen." And on this gloomy note, he left.

"Will he die?" Sonia was standing at the foot of the stairs.

"Not if I can help it. Best let the doctor look at Mr. Haverton's wound while he is here." And she returned to sit by Denbigh's bed, almost as immobile as he. Twelve years ago, she had sat there, but then there had been hope as well as fear. Now—

"Don't look like that." Marthe returned from taking the doctor downstairs. "He always expects the worst, that one. I promise you, madame, we'll have milord right as rain in a day or so. Look, his color's coming back already."

"Oh, Marthe, do you really think so?"

"That's right, madame, let the tears come, you'll feel better so. I'll watch milord. And as for praying, like the doctor said, I'd rather make him a good dish of broth any day. And you can tell him I said so."

Amazingly, Elizabeth found her tears giving way to laughter. "What should we do without you, Marthe?"

Chapter 10

"There!" Angrily, Sonia adjusted the knot of Philip Haverton's bandage. "If it slips again, you can just fix it for yourself. Anyone would think you were a baby, the fuss you make." She had been busy mopping up water in the drenched front hall, and now flounced back to her task, angry with herself for being so angry.

"I'm sorry. I'm so ashamed of myself—"

If the abject apology was intended to disarm criticism, it failed. "And so you should be." It was, somehow, a relief to take out the bad temper that haunted her these days on this easy victim. "I'm ashamed of you, I can tell you. You might as well admit that it was all your fault in the first place. I'm sure Lord Denbigh would have had more sense than to risk stirring up trouble by coming to visit us."

"Visit you! We were coming to protect you. But it's true; it was my idea." He still sounded as if he hoped to be congratulated on it.

"That's just what Elizabeth said. The whole business is your fault. It's no thanks to you we weren't killed."

"I meant it for the best." Flushed and wretched, he looked the boy he was. "I had no idea . . ."

"No, of course not. And then, when Lord Denbigh meant to go on by, and draw the crowd away from us, you have to go and get gravely wounded"—her tone mocked him—"and faint, and have to be brought in, and cosseted and bandaged ... and all the time Lord Denbigh was really hurt."

"I know. I told you I'm ashamed of myself. What more can I say?"

She pushed the heavy household mop she had been using into his hands. "Stop saying and try doing, for a change. Marthe and Elizabeth are busy with Lord Denbigh; it's the least we can do to begin clearing up this mess. Or are you still too weak?"

"Of course not." He took the mop and began awkwardly dragging it across the soaking flagstones of the hallway.

"Not that way!" She snatched it back from him. "Like this! Have you never used a mop before?"

"Why, no. Have you?"

"Of course I have. I wasn't brought up in luxury, with an adoring mother who spared me the sight of blood. What happened when you were a boy, and grazed your knee?"

"She bandaged it up for me." He had got the knack of the mopping now and was moving down the hall away from her. Now he spoke over his shoulder. "I love my mother, Miss von Hugel. You may say what you like of me—I deserve it all but—not my mother."

"I'm sorry!" Suddenly, she was in tears. "Why am I so horrible? I can't help it. I don't mean to be. Sometimes I hate myself!"

"Miss von Hugel—Sonia—don't say that. It's my fault; all of it. I deserve everything you said to me. You were right to be angry; absolutely right. You're so brave, so wonderful, after all you've been through—it's no wonder if you can't bear to see me such a craven. I can't bear myself; I'm not worth your tears." He had dropped the mop now, and moved back down the hall towards her.

She stamped her foot. "I'm not crying for you; I'm crying for me, don't you understand! No, don't touch me, I can't bear it."

He withdrew the arm he had wanted to put round her. "Then let me fetch Mrs. Barrymore to you."

"How can you be so stupid! Elizabeth is busy; we should be helping her, not quarreling like children."

"I'm not quarreling with you, Sonia. I'd rather die; don't you know—"

126

"That's just it." She cut short the declaration. "I'm quarreling with you! Oh, God, I wish I was dead!"

"You mustn't say that; it's wicked." He sounded genuinely shocked.

"Wicked." Once again her voice mocked him. "We mustn't be wicked, must we? Not in this best of all possible worlds! I do believe you're going to start preaching to me. The Reverend Mr. Haverton will deliver his well-known sermon on the goodness of God. Oh, God, that's funny!" But her laughter was hysterical.

"Don't say such things." He looked wildly round the hall, as if for inspiration. "I wish Mr. Vincent was here."

"Charles?" She stopped laughing as suddenly as she had started. "Why Charles? What's he got to say to anything?"

"Well, after all, your cousin . . ." More and more, he felt himself out of his depth with her.

"My cousin! Of course: invaluable Cousin Charles. Who rides off when the enemy attack and leaves us"—she paused—"to your protection."

"That's not fair."

"Who said anything about fairness? Do you really think this is a fair world, Mr. Preacher Haverton? What a deal you have to learn, haven't you, besides how to bear the sight of blood."

Now, at last, he was angry. "That's enough. You'll make me ashamed soon of being ashamed." And then, with obvious relief, "Ah, Mrs. Barrymore, how is he?"

"Marthe says he's better. I think it's true. His color's coming back; he's breathing more easily; I would almost say he was just asleep."

"Thank God for that. The doctor seemed to think—"

"Hush," said Sonia. "No need to frighten Elizabeth with what he said."

"Was it so bad?" Elizabeth asked. And then, "Don't tell me—Marthe says he's always gloomy: it's his policy. What did he think about your wound, Mr. Haverton?"

"I may be marked for life." Dramatically.

"You'll have to pretend it was in a duel." Sonia's voice was unsympathetic. "You'd hardly want to plead guilty to a cobblestone flung by an old woman."

"Sonia!" Reprovingly. "But how do you feel, Mr. Haverton?"

"There's nothing wrong with me." His glance challenged

Sonia. "Except guilt. Mrs. Barrymore, I don't know how to apologize—"

"Please don't try. Things happen . . . it's no use—" She broke off as she got her first full view of Sonia's face. "Sonia, darling, what's the matter?"

"Nothing." Sonia was crying again. "Everything!" She ran past Elizabeth and upstairs to her room.

Elizabeth turned back to Haverton. "Oh dear, I'd meant to ask her to sit with Lord Denbigh while Marthe makes lunch. We must eat, after all."

"Let me!" His voice was eager. "He's used to me."

"Yes, that will be best, I think. And Mr. Haverton, did you hear Caulaincourt ask that you stay here?"

"Yes—I am so sorry. There seems to be no end to the trouble I am causing you."

She laughed and shrugged. "Never mind that. Besides—I propose to make you useful, and to begin with, if you would sit with Lord Denbigh, Marthe and I can look out some bedding for you. I'm afraid it will have to be a pallet in his room. What happens if Charles comes back, I can't think, but we'll cross that bridge when we come to it."

"Has he gone far?" And then, coloring, "Forgive me, I have no right to question you, but it seems strange . . ."

"That he should leave us now? He was misled, like the rest of us, by the talk of a new Allied advance. Goodness knows where he is by now, or how he will get back. We are much indebted to you, Mr. Haverton, for your presence and protection."

"After what I have brought upon you—you are too good, Mrs. Barrymore. Do you not realize—Miss von Hugel certainly does—that it has all been my fault? If we had stayed at home, as Denbigh wished, none of this would have happened. And then, to crown it all, I have to faint, like a baby, at the sight of a little blood. I don't know how I can bear myself—or you me."

She laughed, and handed him a great pile of fusty blankets which she had been pulling out of a deep chest. "I shall see to it that it is you who do the bearing. And as for today's events, how do you know that it's all your fault? The crowd was in a dangerous mood; anything might have directed them against our house—suppose we had had no one to protect us." And then, as he obediently

128

carried the blankets upstairs: "You mustn't too much mind what Sonia says, you know ... She has her own troubles. Well, don't we all—"

He stood aside to let her pass ahead of him into Denbigh's room. "I can't imagine you with troubles, Mrs. Barrymore. You seem—I don't know—above them, somehow."

She had moved over to the bed. "No change?" To Marthe: "Mr. Haverton will sit with him a while, so that you and I can put our heads together. Have I thanked you properly, Marthe?"

"I don't want to be thanked." She rose from her stool by the bed. "I want to know what in the world we are going to eat today—not to mention tomorrow, and the next day. And milord here should have nourishing broth when he wakes—how, I ask you, am I to make a nourishing broth with nothing in the house but lentils and black bread?"

Elizabeth smiled her relief. Marthe grumbling was Marthe back to normal. "M. Caulaincourt left a couple of dragoons on guard at the front, Marthe. I rather think that one of them—well, he looks remarkably like your Jacques. Do you think if we gave him a little money he would find us something to eat. For do you know, I find myself ferociously hungry."

"Jacques, is it?" Marthe's eyes sparkled, but she did not change her grumbling tone. "I've got a word or two to say to Jacques about the time they took to get here. Here, let me." She snatched away the blanket Elizabeth had been laying over the pallet in the corner of the room, and then, beginning to make up the bed with deft, vehement movements, "But it's true, Jacques could find food in the Sahara. Leave it to me, madame. And you, monsieur"—she gestured to her stool—"sit here, do, and damp milord's brow, like this, when he stirs. He'll sleep a day, two days, perhaps, and wake good as new. And why you have to send for that jackanapes of a doctor to frighten you when you have me, Marthe, in the house is more than I can imagine. Jacques shall fetch the herbs for a tisane he shall have when he wakes—he'll be showing the doctor the door himself. But, madame"—her tone had changed again—"do you know that mademoiselle is crying her heart out in her room? Listen! Her head's under the pillow, but you can hear it just the same. No, no, not you, m'sieur," for Haverton had started to his feet, "but should you not go to her, madame? Leave all to me." She pocketed the money Elizabeth had handed her. "If we don't have *coq-au-vin* for dinner, I'll never speak to Jacques again."

Elizabeth looked quickly round the room. Haverton had settled once more by the bed, with his sponge and aromatic spirits. Marthe, while she talked, had finished making up the pallet in the corner. The room was reasonably warm, since it was over the kitchen and, mercifully, its windows had not been broken as it was at the back of the house. Now, in the silence, she could indeed hear the sound of muffled sobbing from Sonia's room. "Let me know if there is any change." She turned towards the door.

"Of course. You will go to her?" Haverton was returning to normal. She noticed him anxiously rolling up his frilled shirt cuffs.

"Immediately. No need to look so troubled. She'll get over it. It's been a hard morning."

For the first time, the understatement made him smile. Impulsively, he reached out, caught her hand, and kissed it. "You're a wonder, Mrs. Barrymore, an absolute wonder."

She smiled down at him. "Rather a disheveled one, at the moment. Sonia and I will both feel better when we have tidied ourselves up a little. It's wonderful what appearance does for a female."

His hand had gone up to the bandage round his face. "Mrs. Barrymore, before you go—do you—does she—do you think me a complete poltroon?"

"Of course not, Mr. Haverton. You had no time to be a hero, that was all. Don't be too angry with yourself; it's a terrible waste." And she was gone.

Sonia's sobs were rather more habitual, by now, than passionate. She was prone on her bed, face in the pillow, arms hanging down beside her, presenting, Elizabeth could not help thinking, a well-composed picture of despair. "Well"—she closed the door behind her, and managed her briskest tone—"crying won't clean the hall."

Sonia turned over and sat bolt upright, revealing a face streaked with tears. "I'm hopeless," she said. "I can't bear myself. What's the matter with me, Elizabeth? First I hide

130

while Father's killed, and then, when I get another chance really to *be* something—I spend my time looking after a greater coward than myself. And then—" Elizabeth had begun to speak but her words came pouring on: "As if that wasn't bad enough, I take it out on poor wretched Philip, who behaved no worse than I did. After all, he was hurt."

"Not very badly," said Elizabeth fair-mindedly. "Remarkable, isn't it, to have grown to his age and still faint at the sight of blood. I suppose we should be grateful that Lord Denbigh's wound didn't bleed too or we should doubtless have had Haverton collapsing on our hands all over again. As it is, he is sitting with his guardian in as complete a state of guilty conscience as anyone could wish to see. What on earth did you do to him, Sonia?"

"Told him all the things I should have said to myself. I told you—oh, I wish I was dead."

"You'd make a very unattractive corpse. Come and have a look at yourself. And I must say, I'm not much better—and stop talking nonsense, do. Have you really been feeling guilty all this time because you stayed hidden that day at the castle? What good, pray, could you have done by getting yourself killed—or worse?"

"Like poor Gretchen." Sonia shivered uncontrollably. "I know; I keep telling myself that; but it still doesn't make sense somehow. And leaving you like that. How can you expect me to forgive myself that?"

"Well, you thought me dead, didn't you? There's not much you can do for the dead."

"But you weren't." It was so obviously a relief to Sonia to pour it all out that Elizabeth let her go on, although her mind, all the time, kept racing off after immediate problems. Was Marthe really right about Denbigh? Was Philip Haverton fit to be looking after him? With an effort, she pulled herself back to what Sonia was saying.

"You sent me help, didn't you? What more could you have done? And marvelously surprised your foster father was when one of his corpses turned over and groaned. And then, be fair to yourself: you found us Charles Vincent. Where would we be now, I wonder, if it were not for him?"

"Charles Vincent!" Sonia seized a comb and began to tear it angrily through her tangled hair. "How can you

131

speak of him! It's all his fault—all of this: he should never have left us alone. Much he cares what happens to us."

"I didn't say he cared, I said he had been very useful to us, and so he has."

"So long as we were useful to him. But you know as well as I do, Elizabeth, that he's not really trying to make money at cards any more. Those young Russians the other night—he didn't bring them to play, he brought them to find out what they knew of the Czar's plans. And when he'd learned of the new advance, he started off at once, without the slightest thought for us—to tell—who?"

"I wish I knew." Elizabeth did not try to deny the truth of what Sonia said. "But, to be fair, he did think that the Allies were advancing, and we would be perfectly safe here."

"I don't suppose he thought about us at all. And what makes you think he will ever come back to us? Unless, of course, he thinks we may still be useful to him. He makes it pretty obvious that he doesn't trust us, after all, by telling us nothing about what he is doing."

Elizabeth took the comb from Sonia and went to work in good earnest on her hair. "Now I look on that as a prime instance of his consideration for us. If he really is a spy—and I must confess I find it hard to imagine any other explanation for his actions—do you really want to know about it, and be, therefore, implicated? I must say, even as things are, I feel guilty enough about letting Denbigh and Haverton stay here—suppose they find themselves involved in whatever Charles is doing . . ."

"What!" Sonia interrupted her. "They are to stay?"

"I thought you knew. Denbigh can't be moved—and besides, Caulaincourt particularly asked me, and I must say from every other point of view I am delighted to have them."

"As a protection?" Sonia's voice dripped irony. "An unconscious man and a swooning boy! Oh, my God, it needed only this . . ." She showed every sign of collapsing into fresh despair on her bed, but Elizabeth dropped the comb, took her by the shoulders and shook her.

"That's enough, Sonia. We haven't time for hysterics." And then, more gently, "Dry your eyes, child, and help me tidy the broken glass. We shall all feel better when the house is shipshape again."

"How practical you are." It was almost an accusation, but Elizabeth ignored it. She kept Sonia busy for the rest of the day getting the house back into some sort of order. There was no news. Caulaincourt had promised to keep them informed, and did indeed send a messenger to let them know that a glazier would come, next morning, to repair their windows. Eagerly questioned, the messenger, who seemed friendly enough, only shook his head: "We are waiting for news too, madame. We have heard nothing since the news came of the Allied retreat. Anything may have happened."

"And the conference?"

He laughed. "Goes on as if nothing had happened—and gets nothing done as usual; it is not from those messieurs that peace will come." He left, once more urging Caulaincourt's request that none of them leave the house. "Where you are, and so guarded, you are safe; the town is in a strange state; best take no chances."

The glazier actually came next morning; the house was tidy again; Jacques had made his peace with Marthe by producing a huge basket of provisions and she was contentedly busy cooking on her charcoal stove. Upstairs, Denbigh still slept, but even the doctor, paying his morning visit, admitted that it was more lightly: "It is only a matter of time now. Nothing to worry yourself about, madame. Today, tomorrow, he will wake, as good as new . . . Keep him quiet then for a few days . . ."

"We could hardly do anything else," said Sonia. "Is there any news, Doctor?"

"From the army? None yet." He shut his bag with a snap. "This silence is a bad sign—for us. I do not think you ladies need disquiet yourselves. Patience for a few days, and your friends will be masters here again."

"You think so?" asked Haverton eagerly.

"I am afraid I am sure of it. If this advance had been anything but a flash in the pan, more would have come of it by now. And besides, there are rumors today, from the south. Lord Wellington is on the move again: Soult will never hold him: the Emperor has been whittling away his forces while they've been in winter quarters. It is cavalry from Spain that made our late victories possible. We shall pay for it now the weather's improving and Wellington's on the move. So you see, ladies, if Schwartzenberg or

133

Blücher don't come to your rescue here, your own army may."

"Wellington!" There was awe in Sonia's voice. "Oh, if only it were possible."

"I think it more than probable. You'll stand my friend, ladies, if the redcoats come this way?"

"Of course." When she returned from seeing him out, Elizabeth found Sonia and Haverton in eager conversation.

Sonia turned to her eagerly. "Philip knows Lord Wellington! Just think if he gets here first. Our troubles will be over. What is he like, Philip? Is he as proud as they say?"

"Not proud, exactly, but he stands no nonsense. I don't know him well, you know; he's my cousin's friend, not mine."

"But you do know him?" Elizabeth was glad to see that Sonia appeared to be friends with Haverton again.

"Oh yes, he'd recognize me, I suppose, if we met in the street."

"Oh, how I hope you do! Just think, Elizabeth, the English at last! What a joke it would be if we were safe away before Charles so much as returned." The excitement dwindled from her voice. "In England. Suppose my grandfather will have nothing to do with me."

Elizabeth laughed. "Let's wait to cross that bridge when we've crossed the channel. So far as we know, Lord Wellington is still south of Bayonne. He'll have to be a miracle worker indeed to get here before Charles returns."

"But a miracle worker is just what he is," said Haverton.
. And, "How do we know when Charles will get back?" said Sonia.

"Just as well if he doesn't for a few days"—Elizabeth was determinedly practical—"since we've no bed for him."

Next morning, Philip Haverton woke on his pallet to see Denbigh sitting up in bed and staring at him. "Thank God, you're better." He jumped up and hurried across the room to him.

"Better? Oh, yes, I remember. The French—but what happened, Philip; where are we?"

"At Charles Vincent's house. Caulaincourt asked that

134

we stay here. I'm sorry: I was afraid you would not be best pleased. But what else could I do?"

"Nothing, I suppose. Though you're right: I'd rather be anywhere than here. But what's happened?"

"Nothing—that we know of. The French are still masters of the town: the Congress is still sitting: Aberdeen sends every day to ask after you: so, to do him justice, does Caulaincourt. Neither of them has any news of the armies. It seems fantastic—but there is one thing: a strong rumor going round the town that Wellington is on the move in the south."

"Wellington?" Denbigh swung his legs out of bed. "Then it's time to be up and doing. Is Charles Vincent back, by the way?"

"No, not yet. Should you get up?"

"Well, that's something to be thankful for. Of course I should. I've lain here long enough—too long."

When he got downstairs half an hour or so later, Denbigh found Elizabeth busy polishing the furniture of the hall. "I am so glad to see you better." She gave a final rub to the oak chest she was working on. "I am afraid the results of our flood the other day are going to last a while. We never had a chance to thank you properly, Lord Denbigh. I suspect you saved our lives."

"And you ours. If it comes to thanks, I do not know where I should begin."

"Shall we call it quits, then?" She crossed the hall and opened the dining room door: "Marthe has coffee and rolls ready for you. She thinks you mad, I warn you, to get up so soon, and will undoubtedly tell you so. Sit down, and I'll tell her you are ready."

"Let me do so myself. There is no reason why you should wait on me."

"Why not? You are our guest, after all—and our patient. Ah, Sonia, tell Marthe Lord Denbigh is ready for his breakfast, will you?"

Sonia paused for a moment in the doorway. In contrast to Elizabeth, who was swathed in a voluminous apron, she was ravishing in a morning dress of soft pink that set off the gold of her hair. "Are you really better, Lord Denbigh? I am so glad to see you up, but—should you be? The doctor said that was a terrible blow you received. You should have heard him expecting the worst. We were quite

135

in despair, were we not, Elizabeth?" And then, when Elizabeth did not answer: "But are you really none the worse?"

"Not the least in the world, thank you. In fact, aside from a little weakness and a ravenous appetite, I feel better than I have since I can remember."

"Really? The doctor was full of gloomy prognostications about shifted scar tissue from an old wound. Perhaps, after all, it has done you good."

"I really believe it may have. But I am afraid I have been a monstrous trouble to you ladies—"

"Nothing of the kind," Elizabeth interrupted him briskly. "Sonia, Lord Denbigh is waiting for his breakfast." And then, as Sonia vanished in the direction of the kitchen, "The latest *Moniteur* is on the dining table, my lord; I am sure you will want to see what they are saying in Paris."

"Thank you." He picked up the paper. "But I wish—" He stopped. Elizabeth had left the room while his back was turned. He sighed, shrugged and looked at the paper. He was still studying its description of the Allies' total rout when Sonia returned with a tray. "Marthe's out shopping," she said. "She's the only member of the household who's allowed out, you know. I can't begin to tell you how bored I am. And poor Mr. Haverton's nearly distracted for lack of shirts."

He had jumped up at sight of her, and now took the tray. "You should not have troubled, Miss von Hugel. I am quite able to wait on myself."

"If you're anything like your cousin, you're not. Philip can no more—" And then, coloring, "Must we be so formal? Am I really to call you Lord Denbigh, and my lord? After all, we may be housemates for goodness knows how long."

"I hope not." And then, laughing, "I beg your pardon, Miss von Hugel; how dreadful that sounded. But I am sure you understand what I mean. This *must* be only a temporary reverse."

"That's what Marthe says." She was pouring his coffee as she spoke. "She's got a friend, you know, a French dragoon. He says the French army's at the end of its tether; it's only Napoleon who can hold them together.

Lord, what a man he must be. I wish I could see him, just once."

"I most sincerely hope you never do—unless as a captive. But will you not join me in some coffee? I feel ashamed to be sitting eating and drinking here alone. I have been a terrible trouble, I fear, to you and to Mrs. Barrymore."

"Not at all. Nothing ever troubles Elizabeth, and as for me, I enjoy it." She poured herself a cup of coffee and settled across the table from him. "I never thought to find myself breakfasting with a genuine English lord. Tell me all about England. Will I like it, do you think? And will they like me?"

"I do not see how they can help it."

"Oh, not compliments, please! I have all I can stand of those from Philip. But, seriously, my English—will it pass, do you think? I have tried so hard, but it never seems quite right. Oh, I can manage the words, I think, but the accent"—she made a face—"I should hate to sound, in English, the way Philip does in German. I do so want my grandfather to like me. Do you know him at all? If only he would turn out to be rich, and kind, and make me his heiress so that Elizabeth and I could live happy ever after. We are quite paupers, you know; it is the most dispiriting thing."

"But surely, Mrs. Barrymore—her widow's jointure—"

She made another face. "Law terms; I don't pretend to understand them. All I know is, that if it were not for Cousin Charles—" She stopped and colored becomingly.

"Ah yes, Mr. Vincent," he spoke at random, to cover her embarrassment, "when do you expect him back?"

"Goodness knows. We don't even know where he's gone, you know. He's the most complete mystery, is Cousin Charles."

"Sonia!" Elizabeth spoke from the doorway. "I am sure Lord Denbigh would rather read his *Moniteur* in peace. And besides, your room needs tidying."

"Bother my room!" But she jumped to her feet, with a soft swish of muslin. "I have been seeing to it that our invalid ate a proper breakfast, and see, he has, every bit of it, and looks much better as a result. It's not just calomel pills and jalap, you know, that go to a cure: one must keep the patient cheerful."

"And very delightfully you do it." Denbigh had also risen to his feet. "But talking of nursing, I must thank your Marthe for all her care of me. And for the trouble she has taken over my clothes, too. I am sure I had Philip's blood all down the front of this shirt."

"And so you did," said Sonia cheerfully. "But don't, I beg, thank Marthe for that, or she'll give notice on the spot. She's no laundress, she told us so the day we engaged her, and we've never dared ask her to wash out so much as a handkerchief for us."

"Good heavens!" He looked appalled. "Do you mean that I am indebted to you!"

"To me!" She interrupted him with a peal of laughter. "I hate to think what would happen to that elegant shirt of yours if I so much as laid hand to it. No, no, Elizabeth's the miracle worker here. It's she who cured you, I'm sure. She sat up all night with you the first night."

"Elizabeth!"

"Mrs. Barrymore," she corrected him. "Of course I nursed you, my lord. What else could I do? But Marthe's the one you should really thank. She's a born nurse whereas I'm afraid I am but a reluctant one." And on this chastening note she picked up the breakfast tray and got herself fairly out of the room.

Chapter 11

That seemed an endless day to Elizabeth. And yet it went quietly enough, with Denbigh busy writing in his room, and Sonia and Haverton playing cards in the salon. As for her, she kept out of the way until they all met, perforce, over dinner which she had set late on purpose. Then she found herself equally grateful to Denbigh for his easy flow of talk and to Haverton for his bland unawareness of anything awkward in their situation. Following Denbigh's lead, she roused Sonia to an animated discussion of the novels of Horace Walpole and Mrs. Radcliffe, for which she had a passion, and found herself disconcertingly in agreement with him in preferring a book called *Sense and Sensibility* by a Miss Austen.

Sonia too had enjoyed this book when they read it aloud together, and her eyes lit up when Denbigh told her Miss Austen had published two more novels: "I must try to get them for you."

"I can't think why," put in Haverton. "The most tedious stuff—all about a set of country nobodies. I tried to read one of them—*Pride and*—something-or-other—and never got beyond the first chapter. Oh, Mrs. Barrymore, you can't be leaving us so soon."

But Elizabeth was firm in making their apologies. It had been a long day, they would make an early night of it.

Following her reluctantly upstairs, Sonia flared into mutiny. "How could you, Liz? I was just beginning to enjoy myself!"

"I'm sorry, my love, but you must see how strangely we are placed."

"Well, it's no fault of ours. I don't see why we shouldn't enjoy it. After all, we've lived hobnob with Charles for long enough, why should we draw the line at Denbigh and poor Philip. What an entertaining talker Denbigh is—I could have listened to him forever." She laughed contentedly to herself. "Charles will find his nose quite out of joint when he returns. And such manners—he makes one feel like a queen, somehow. As if one were the only person who mattered in the whole world. Only"—once again the little laugh—"then I see him doing just the same thing to you."

"Yes." Elizabeth could not quite keep bitterness out of her voice. "Don't be taken in by those English good manners of his, Sonia. It's pride that makes him polite; nothing in his heart. It's for himself that he's courteous, not for you, don't you understand?"

"Is that why you are so rude to him?"

"I? Rude? What do you mean?"

"Dear Liz, don't fly out at me, but you know as well as I do that he keeps trying to thank you for your nursing and you never let him."

"Poor man." Her tone belied the spurious sympathy. "It's torture for him to be obliged to me."

"How do you know?"

"Because of the way I feel myself." Fiercely. "Sonia,

139

that's enough. It's bad enough to have him in the house; please don't talk about it any more."

"Liz—I believe you do hate him!"

"Would that be so surprising?" And then, on a note of suppressed violence, "Good night, Sonia."

"So early? But it's true, you look worn out. As for me, I shall finish making over my pink muslin. Do you think Lord Denbigh will remember to get me Miss Austen's new books?"

"I expect so." She closed the door of her room and sat down with a little sigh of exhaustion at her dressing table. Useless to go to bed. Thoughts she had kept down all day by constant activity swarmed out now to torment her. She sat, biting her knuckles, staring at nothing, angry with herself for being so unhappy. She heard Sonia moving about in her room, singing a little song to herself. Then Denbigh and Haverton came upstairs, talking quietly, and closed their door behind them. Was that Denbigh, laughing *sotto voce* at something Haverton had said? She bit so hard on her knuckles that tears started to her eyes. The house was quiet now, settling to sleep. A timber creaked on the stairs, mice scuttled in the garret above her, the old clock ticked on the landing below. Useless to go to bed; absurd to sit here, hands clenched, exploring misery.

Do something then, but what? If she could only go down, go out, walk through the snow until exhaustion made her sleep. Impossible, of course. If only I were a man ... She remembered thinking this before, long ago, in England. It's all over, she had told Sonia. True? False? Is anything, ever, really finished? If she could only stop *thinking!* She was on her feet suddenly, movement as necessary as breathing, when a sound outside hurried her to the window. Shouts some way off, running footsteps, a couple of shots. The street below was dark and quiet, but further off, where it opened into the square, she could see lights, moving figures. Whatever the excitement was, it seemed to have passed them by, and she let the curtain fall and moved over to the closet to get out her nightgown. She would not sleep, but must rest. "I can't be ill." This habit of talking to herself seemed to be growing on her. "Sonia needs me."

Suddenly she dropped the nightgown on her bed and stood, head up, listening. The night was clear and cold;

140

that noise at the window could hardly be hail. It came again; now unmistakably a pattering of small stones. She blew out the candle, felt her way to the window, opened it a crack and leaned out. "Who's there?" she whispered.

"It's I, Vincent. Open the door, quickly."

"Coming." She hurried downstairs and unbolted the big door. Charles Vincent slid through the crack as she opened it, and turned, all in one movement, to close it behind him. "Hush." He bent towards her and blew out her candle. "They're coming back."

It was true. She could hear a confused noise of foot-steps and voices approaching from the square. By the sound of it, the French were knocking and making inquiries at any house that showed a light.

"The kitchen?" she breathed.

"Yes—safe enough there, with a candle." The footsteps had passed their door now. "Lucky they didn't get a good look at me." He paused, as she closed the kitchen door behind them and relighted the candle. "Though they may be back for all that, when they draw a blank. They know I must be somewhere in the street. Play for time, if they come. Tell them you'll only open if the mayor comes in person, to guarantee you. It's not unreasonable; three women alone. Why, what's the matter?"

She had laughed, suddenly. "You're behind the times. We've Denbigh and Haverton here. And as for the door, it's been broken down once already. Never fear, they'll not even expect us to open to them. I expect that's why they went by. Of course they're bound to return, present-ly, and very likely with the mayor. But—why?"

"Later." Impatiently. "Plan first, explain afterwards. Where can I hide?"

"In my bed." Both of them started and turned at the new voice. Marthe was standing in the doorway of her room, which opened off the kitchen. "If you can convince me I should hide you, which, for the ladies' sake, I'm inclined to do. We've had enough trouble here. But—why are they after you? You're French, after all, or so you always said."

"Yes, so I am. How old are you, Marthe?"

"Forty." The question did not seem to surprise her so much as it did Elizabeth.

141

"Then you can remember what it was like, before ..."

She nodded. "I thought it was that. Yes, I can remember, m'sieur. I can remember faces too. I only hope, for your sake, and the ladies', others' memories are less good. That last visitor of yours came in the daytime: madness. But never mind that. For what it's worth, I'm on your side. I don't remember much good of the Bourbons, but I don't remember much harm either. If they'll bring us back peace, I'm for them. Better than another Terror, anyway."

"The Bourbons?" Elizabeth gasped.

"Of course. I've been working for them since I met my cousin at Weimar. Oh, for the money, at first, but now—I've just been to see the Comte d'Artois: he's a man: he'll save us."

"Hush." Odd how Marthe had taken command. Footsteps in the street and a low, impatient knocking on the front door. "Into my bed with you. They may believe me; they may not. And you, madame, you came down for a hot drink for Milord Denbigh who is a little worse tonight, and should not be disturbed." As she spoke, she had been pushing the big kettle to the center of the stove. Now she raised her voice. "All right, I'm coming; no need to wake the whole house." And then, in the front hall, "Who is it, at this ungodly hour of the night?"

Elizabeth looked quickly round the kitchen: no sign of Vincent's arrival here. She followed him into Marthe's tiny bedroom, and saw at once what she had meant. The bed was too low for him to hide underneath, but it had a deep hollow in the middle where Marthe's solid form had lain. He lay down, flat, and she covered him with bedclothes and finally the plump duvet. "You can breathe?"

"Just." His voice was muffled.

"Good. Don't move till I tell you." Back in the kitchen, she could hear Marthe still haranguing their visitors. The cold draft through the house showed that she had opened the front door to them, but had not yet, apparently, let them in. Now she heard her say:

"Wait there, while I call madame." And then, loudly, as she approached across the hall, "Mme. Barrymore?"

"Yes." Elizabeth met her at the kitchen door, talking, like her, loudly and in French. "What is it?"

142

"It's that Jacques and his friends. They want to know if we've let anyone in tonight."

"Let anyone in? Us?" Elizabeth was pleased at the surprise she managed. "After what happened before? What do they take us for?"

"You see." Marthe had turned back to the open door. "We're making a tisane for Milord Denbigh, who's worse tonight, thanks to you and your friends. Come in and search, if you must, but don't blame me if you make him ill again and find yourselves in trouble tomorrow. The Duke of Vicenza's not a man I'd like to have for an enemy. But, come"—she opened the door wider—"I don't expect you to believe me; I'm only Marthe who you've known—how long? Naturally I'd make a practice of harboring traitors."

"Traitors? But what is all this?" Easy enough for Elizabeth to sound puzzled.

"A likely story of a cock and a bull. Some information of a royalist rendezvous, of all things, over the other side of town. And when they got there, stamping their great boots, no doubt, and talking in their great voices—why, the birds were flown, if there ever were any birds, which I personally doubt."

"But I tell you, Marthe." Jacques the trooper's voice from outside. "We saw him; he jumped out of a window and ran away."

She laughed her great hearty laugh. "I wager he did. And whose window was it, pray?—that of the mistress of the house? And her husband out with you, I expect. You'll look a pretty fool in the morning, Jacques, but come on in, go the whole hog while you're at it. Perhaps he's in *my* bed now, your fugitive: you'd best make sure, hadn't you?" And then, as the men outside hesitated and shuffled their feet: "Well, hurry up; make up your minds and don't keep me standing here freezing the house. We've got a sick man upstairs, remember."

Jacques stepped into the hallway and made an awkward bow to Elizabeth. "We don't want to incommode you, madame, not after what happened before. It's true, is it, what Marthe says?"

"Of course it's true." Elizabeth's conscience pricked her as she told the lie, but it had to be done. "Come and see for yourself, if you must, but quietly, I beg."

143

He had been looking quickly round the hall as she spoke and now passed her, with an apology, to glance into the kitchen. As he did so, a voice from the top of the stairs made them all look up. Denbigh was standing there in his dressing gown. His face was pale in the lamplight, his hair tousled, and he seemed to be supporting himself with difficulty on the newel post of the bannisters. "What is all this, Marthe? Am I to wait all night for my tisane? And why on earth is the front door open freezing the house? And what in the world are you doing here?" He seemed to see Jacques for the first time as he emerged from the kitchen. "Haven't we suffered enough at your hands? I'll have something to say to the mayor in the morning."

"A thousand apologies, milord." Jacques retired hastily across the hall. "Marthe, make my apologies, explain . . ."

"I'll explain, all right." She banged the big door behind him. And then: "Hush; wait till they've gone."

She and Elizabeth stood, suspended, listening as the scuffling of footsteps died away down the street. Denbigh straightened up, tightened the cord of his dressing gown, smoothed his hair with an automatic gesture and came slowly down the stairs. "Now," he said quietly, "I would be glad if someone *would* explain."

"How much did you hear?" Marthe had retired to the kitchen, leaving Elizabeth to face him as he descended the stairs.

"You want me to apologize for eavesdropping?"

"No, no; your intervention was most timely; I must thank you." Impossible, somehow, to strike the right note when talking to him. "But—I wonder if you would not, perhaps, prefer not to know the rest of it."

"Oh? A conspiracy of silence—entirely for my own good, of course? I think not; thank you just the same. Give me credit for knowing you well enough to be able to tell when you are lying. You did not at all like telling that soldier there was no one in the house. I suppose it is Vincent."

"Yes." Useless to deny it. "He was just going to explain—"

"Well, then, by all means let us adjourn to the kitchen, where, I assume, you had him hidden, and let him do so.

Since I am already involved in this lunacy, I think I must be allowed to know what it is all about." He held the kitchen door courteously open for her.

Vincent had just emerged from Marthe's bedroom, looking more exhausted and disheveled than ever. "Phew!" He smiled his engaging smile at Denbigh. "I hope I never go through so hot a five minutes again. Thank you, Elizabeth—and you, sir. Marthe tells me you supported her story in the most timely way."

"I hope I shall not live to regret it."

Vincent laughed. "So do I. Ah, thank you, Marthe." She had been bustling about between larder and stove, and now brought him a great bowl of steaming soup. "I need this. I had my last real meal in Nancy."

"Nancy?" Denbigh pushed up a chair for Elizabeth and settled himself across the table from Vincent. "I think I am beginning to understand."

"Not so bad as you feared, eh? Yes, Marthe; why don't you go to bed. I'll thank you properly in the morning." And then, as she closed the door behind her: "What did you think I was?"

"An adventurer."

"Well, so I am. Or—so I have been. I was explaining to Elizabeth when we were interrupted that I first began to serve the Bourbon cause simply for the money. We had a little difficulty, in Weimar; I happened to meet a cousin of mine; he paid me well to act as his informer at Allied Headquarters and, mind you, I earned my money. But it's all different now."

"Oh?"

"Yes. I've been to Nancy, as you guessed, to meet Monsieur—the Comte d'Artois. He's—I hadn't expected him to be so ... If only he could be king, our troubles would be over."

"His brother would hardly approve of that." Denbigh's voice was dry.

"No, of course not. I know it's impossible; though from what I hear of Louis le Désiré, he won't stand the pace for long, and then, Long Live Charles X."

"Your enthusiasm does you credit." Dryer than ever. "But aren't you getting a little ahead of your game? What makes you think the Bourbons have the slightest chance of returning to the throne? It's twenty years: they're forgotten; strangers, and, what is worse, tarred with the brush of the emigration."

"Marthe remembers—enough to hide me, which is enough for me. And—you don't know—how could you what is going on in Paris. I had a messenger from there—that's what sent me to Nancy. He says Napoleon's days are numbered. If you hadn't made the mistake of negotiating with him here at Châtillon there might be revolution already. As it is, the Bourbon party are bound to think the Allies are committed to Napoleon's cause—or at least to that of a regency for his son. But—break off negotiations, march direct on Paris, and you will be amazed what you will find."

"As easy as that? I wish I could believe you. But who are these silent Bourbonists? We've heard nothing of them."

"Of course not. Fouché's secret police are everywhere. So long as Napoleon is in power, they dare not make a move. Look what happened to me tonight. I've had an exciting journey of it, I can tell you, to Nancy and back. Everyone's our enemy: French, Allies ... to be stopped by anyone is to be finished. But—just wait till Napoleon falls; it will be a different story then. Our friends are everywhere; I'm ready to bet there's a white cockade hidden, ready, in half the houses here in Châtillon, and as for Paris ..."

"Yes," Denbigh said again. "But who?"

"I can trust you?"

"I think you must. If there is really anything in it, and you have proof, I will take you to Headquarters to tell your story to Castlereagh. He is impatient, I know, already, at the way the negotiations are dragging on, and I have heard talk of pro-Bourbon feeling in England. There is certainly a large and vociferous party there against any negotiations with Napoleon. But—we must have names, and proof."

"As to names, what do you say to Dalberg, Jaucourt, Vitrolles, and—if the Bourbons are succeeding—Talleyrand."

"Talleyrand! Now you're talking. But—your proviso ..."

"I know. But Talleyrand's never backed a doubtful horse yet; you can't expect him to start now. But I have it

146

on no less authority than Dalberg's that he is ready to come out strongly for the Bourbons—"

"When they are already winning."

"Yes."

"And your proof of all this?"

"None, so far. But I understand that Vitrolles is to get out of Paris as soon as he can safely do so and make the conspirators' proposals to Monsieur. If he could be persuaded to come here—with proof?"

"Then we would go, at once, to Castlereagh and the Allied Ministers. In the meantime, what are we to do with you? You endanger the ladies by staying here, endanger yourself, if you leave. And—I need you, alive, to make contact with Vitrolles. Elizabeth, what do you think?"

"Of course he must stay here." How strange, how sweet and painful to have him use her first name. But—it means nothing, she told herself; it's the old habit, no more.

"I think so. But how?"

"In my room. I can share with Sonia. If the house is searched, we'll just have to improvise."

"Talking of improvisation," said Vincent, "you seem to have some explaining to do too, Elizabeth. Am I to understand that Lord Denbigh is at present occupying my room, and as an invalid?"

"Good gracious," said Elizabeth. "Of course, you don't know anything about it. You're not the only one who's been having adventures, Charles."

Sonia was fast asleep when Elizabeth crept into bed beside her some time later, but woke her early next morning. "What on earth are you doing here?" And then, on a note of sudden excitement, "Charles?"

"Yes, he came back late last night."

Sonia jumped out of bed. "With a fine upstanding story of why he abandoned us so cavalierly, I have no doubt. I look forward to his excuses."

Elizabeth laughed. "His main excuse was a detachment of the National Guard at his heels."

"The French? After Charles? But why?" And then, on quite a different note, "Elizabeth! He's not hurt?"

"Of course not. Charles has as many lives as a cat. But he'll have to hide for a while."

147

"To hide? Oh, poor Charles, he'll hate that. But what on earth has he been doing?"

"Espousing the Bourbon cause, and with a good deal of effect, too, by the sound of it. You and I owe him an apology, I think, Sonia."

"You mean, he's not a spy, after all?"

"You were so sure he was? Well, so was I. And, of course, so he is. It's odd, isn't it, what a difference it makes who you are spying for. Anyway, he's in my room, and we'll have to keep him hidden so long as the French hold the town."

Sonia turned to make a face at herself in the glass. "And that won't be child's play either. I don't see Charles staying cooped up for long with the peace of the world at stake—as he would say. And you can't bully Charles, either, not as you can Philip." She gazed thoughtfully at the flushed cheeks and sparkling eyes of her reflection. "Heigh-ho, what a household! As if it wasn't bad enough having Philip on our hands, now we have to hide Charles. Let us pray, devoutly, for an Allied success. I can't tell you how sick I am of being cooped up in the house like this. I'm sure it's unnecessary, too."

"You wouldn't think so if you'd been awake last night, when Charles arrived."

But over breakfast, Denbigh took very much the same line as Sonia. "We go home today," he announced. "We are more than grateful to you for all your hospitality"— the speech seemed to be directed somewhere between Sonia and Elizabeth—"but we must not be trespassing upon it further. You cannot help but be glad to see the last of us."

Elizabeth was busy setting a tray for Vincent, who must remain abovestairs. "You think yourself well enough for the move?" Her voice was casual.

"Entirely—thanks to your nursing. I have to thank you, also, for—"

"Oh, fiddle!" She had spilt the hot milk. "Fetch a cloth, Sonia, would you? And ask Marthe to take up Charles's tray." To Denbigh: "You will see him before you go?"

"Yes, of course." He had risen to close the door behind Sonia. "No, don't go," as Elizabeth made to follow her. "You must let me thank you for all you have done."

"And if I do not wish to be thanked?"

"You will have to indulge me." He moved forward to face her across the breakfast table. "Elizabeth—I have thought of you constantly since that day at Frankfurt.

"Oh?"

"I was shocked—disturbed—surprised. I am afraid I said more than I intended or like to remember."

"You were never anything but courteous, Lord Denbigh."

"Elizabeth! Don't keep me at arms' length like this. Don't you understand—I want to help you."

She raised her eyes to look him full in the face. "You are too good, my lord, but the time for that is past. My life is—what it is. There is no room in it for help from you."

"But I owe it to you—"

"Then you will just have to bear the burden of the debt, my lord."

"Oh—" He bit off the words. "Forgive me, Elizabeth, I am a bad hand at an apology. Don't you understand, I'm appealing to you, by the past, by our old affection, to let me help you now. This is no life for you—involved in God knows what—so situated that I have not felt able even to visit you—with no one but that scatterbrain cousin of yours to protect you. Who knows what lunacy he may involve you in next? Only say the word, and I'll have you in England within a week—and that engaging child too. Once there, my sister—"

"Oh, no, not that." Her laugh was dangerously near hysteria. "Not Lady Elinor!" She stood very straight, facing him, her hands clenched on the back of a chair. "Lord Denbigh, let me tell you, once and for all, that I would not accept your help if you were the last man on earth." And then, on an entirely different note: "Ah, Marthe, there you are. Take this up to M. Vincent, would you? I am sure he must be ravenous this morning. And remind him to keep away from the windows." She had moved towards the door as she spoke, and now whisked herself out of it before Denbigh could say another word.

"She's had no breakfast." Sonia had returned and was busy mopping up the spilt milk. "And no more have you," she added as Denbigh rose to follow Elizabeth. "Is everyone gone mad this morning? No use going after her, if that's what you had in mind. You can see she's in no

149

mood to be thanked. Thank me instead or, better still, tell me you think there's no reason why we should go on being cooped up in the house. If you can go out, why can't we?"

"I would not advise it. As Mrs. Barrymore said, you should have seen the National Guard last night."

"They were really after Charles?"

"They were indeed. I don't like to think what would have happened if they had caught him. It was lucky for him that Mrs. Barrymore was still awake."

"And of course I had to sleep through it all. Sometimes I just can't bear myself."

"You? Absurd child. Only consider what pleasure you give to others."

"Me? Do you really mean it?" And then, pouting, "But I wish you would not call me 'child.' I am eighteen, you know."

"A very grave and serious age. I wish you were safe home in England, Miss von Hugel."

"So do not I. Besides, I have no home."

"How can you be so sure? Have you written to your grandfather?"

"No, why should I? He never wrote my mother; Elizabeth and Charles are all the friends I have."

"And very good ones too, but it is different for them. This is not at all the kind of life you ought to be leading."

"I don't see why it's different for Elizabeth. Charles, of course, is a man, and they are always to have everything their own way, but aside from being a little older, and having so much more sense, how is Elizabeth any different from me?"

"Why, in having been married, of course. You must see that it makes all the difference. I do wish, Miss von Hugel, if you will not do it yourself, that you will let me write to your grandfather on your behalf. I could send it in the diplomatic bag. There is no reason why you should not have an answer in a week or two. Only give me his direction, Miss von Hugel. I tell you, I should not like to see a daughter of mine in your situation."

"But I am not your daughter. And as for Elizabeth— oh, good morning, Mr. Haverton, have you roused yourself at last? Shall I give you some coffee, though it's more than you deserve, coming down so late."

"I could not bring myself to face the fact that it was to be my last meal in this happy house." He took the full cup from her. "Do we really leave today?"

"Yes." Denbigh had risen from the table and spoke from the doorway. "As soon as you are ready, Philip."

"What's the matter with him?" Philip asked as the door closed behind Denbigh. "Blue-deviled, like me, at the thought of leaving?"

Sonia laughed. "I doubt it. Counting the moments till he's safe away, I should think. Though—I don't know. He's very kind, isn't he? Not a bit frightening when you get to know him. He wants to write to my grandfather on my account."

"And have you sent back to England? You won't let him?"

"Of course not. I'm very happy where I am. Besides, I couldn't think of leaving Elizabeth."

Elizabeth appeared at the very last moment when Denbigh and Haverton were standing ready in the hall. "I am so sorry." Her hands were covered with flour. "I have been helping Marthe with her baking and quite forgot how late it was. Are the streets quiet?"

"Yes, absolutely." Sonia came running downstairs. "I've just had a look out of my bedroom window. You'd hardly think it had all happened, would you?"

"No," said Denbigh. "But it did. We are enormously indebted to you, Mrs. Barrymore."

"Nothing of the kind," said Elizabeth almost tartly.

And, "Nobody thanks *me*," said Sonia.

Denbigh took her hand. "I wish you will think about what I said to you. Let me write to your grandfather on your behalf. I am sure Mrs. Barrymore will agree that it is much the best thing for you."

"Of course—if she wishes it."

"Which I do not."

"Very well. But if you should change your mind ... And now, we must not keep you longer from your baking. My thanks again." A deep formal bow for Elizabeth. "And to you too, Miss von Hugel. Come, Philip."

Haverton turned from an anxious consultation of the glass. "Am I fit to be seen with this bandage?"

"I hope so," said Sonia. "Since I put it on ..."

The big door closed behind them. "Well," said Sonia, "so much for that. And now, I am going to see Charles."

"In his bedroom?"

"I don't remember that that prevented you from visiting Lord Denbigh, my love."

"He was ill." Elizabeth's color was higher than ever. "You know perfectly well that that was quite another matter."

"Oh, I do, do I? And so, I suppose, was your running away when he tried to thank you. You are to be free to behave as madly as you please, while I'm to be all prunes and prisms. You should have heard Lord Denbigh on the undesirability of my position here. If I were his daughter, he would not like to see me so situated. It's all very well for a widow, like you," and then, horror-stricken at the change in Elizabeth's expression, "Oh, Liz, I did not mean it. Why don't you explain to him?"

"Why should I? It's no affair of his."

"You really don't care any more?"

"Of course I don't." Angrily. "I wish you'd stop chattering, Sonia, and turn your hand to something useful."

"I will. I'll fetch down Charles's tray. You know how much Marthe's got to do." And before Elizabeth could protest further, she had crossed the hall to tap on Charles's door. "Charles! It's I, Sonia. May I venture into your den and fetch your tray?" And then, as he opened the door for her, "So you decided to come back to us at last! And with the National Guard at your heels, too, adventurous Charles. How I wish I'd been awake to see it!"

"Sonia! I owe you an apology." He spoke as if the words had been fretting his mind for a long time. "You were right and I was wrong. I should not have left you. If anything had happened, I'd never have forgiven myself."

"That would have been a great comfort to us, I'm sure. No—don't shut the door, Charles. Elizabeth's shocked to the marrow already, poor darling. Did we ever decide, by the way, just what kind of cousins we are? Not very close, I imagine, judging by the way you abandon us. No thanks to you we weren't murdered in our beds—or worse."

"Don't! Sonia, you can't possibly say anything that will make me feel worse than I do already."

"Then I'm wasting my time, am I not?" She picked

up his tray. "No need to look so conscience-stricken, Charles. We've had a splendid adventure—and been splendidly protected. Well—of course Haverton was very much what you'd expect. Do you know, he actually swoons at the sight of blood. But you should have seen Lord Denbigh. He was superb. Now there's my ideal of a really gallant gentleman; I believe there must be something in what they say about English breeding after all. Such manners, such an air—and then, his courage . . . but of course Elizabeth will have told you all about it, I won't bore you any more with the story of our adventures; you must tell me, instead, about yours. I wonder, though; Lord Denbigh is so wonderfully kind, perhaps I should let him write to Grandfather on my behalf."

"What do you mean?" Elizabeth, hovering in the hallway, was surprised at the vehemence of Charles's question.

"Why, Lord Denbigh thinks it most compromising for me to be gallivanting about Europe with only a couple of giddy cousins for protectors. He wants to write to Grandfather by the diplomatic bag—did you know it goes by way of Paris and Calais, by courtesy of Napoleon? He says he could get an answer in a week or so, and then, if it was favorable—which, with such a sponsor, you would think it must be—who knows? He might even escort me home. Think, what pleasure—and what comfort, to travel, as it were, in the diplomatic bag. And how could Grandfather reject me, so protected?"

"You cannot be serious! And leave Elizabeth here alone? After all she's done for you?"

She snatched up his tray. "You need to take some lessons in manners from Lord Denbigh. Try it the other way, Charles: 'Oh, Sonia, don't leave us. How could we manage without you?' I cannot imagine how you expect to succeed in diplomacy—if that is really what you are playing at these days—I can only say I pity those poor Bourbons."

Chapter 12

Sonia yawned enormously. "This is the outside of enough! Two whole days and neither Haverton nor Denbigh has thought fit to call and thank us for our hospitality!"

"But Lord Denbigh wrote." As usual, Elizabeth was busy sewing.

"Yes, a diplomat's letter, full of polite nothings. Do you think he's forbidden Philip to call? Does he really think our reputations so tarnished?" She looked, as if for reassurance, into the big glass over the hearth. "Perhaps I should have paid more attention to that terrible lecture he read me. Shall I write him, Liz, and ask him to write Grandfather on my behalf?"

"Why not do it yourself?"

"Write Grandfather? I'd never dare. Besides, I don't mean to leave you, Liz; not till the adventure is over. I mean to be there when the Allies march into Paris, if it's the last thing I do. No, no, Grandfather can wait. But Denbigh's another matter—and Philip! Think of his staying away two whole days." Once more she consulted her reflection almost anxiously.

"Perhaps you have teased him once too often."

"Much more likely he's waiting for a new waistcoat to be sent home. Or maybe his scar's not healed to his satisfaction. Yes, of course, that will be it. And as for Lord Denbigh, I'm sure it's all your fault, Liz. He must have been affronted by the curt way you said good-bye. Baking indeed! I ask you!"

"I think it much more likely that he was grateful." Elizabeth could not quite keep the bitterness out of her voice.

"Liz, what's the matter?"

"Nothing." She might as well have said, "Everything." Deep in a private misery, she had not even the spirit to try and dissuade Sonia from her lighthearted new habit of calling her Liz. But what had happened to the old respectful relationship of pupil and governess? Would she be able, now, to influence Sonia in any new crisis?

"Well, at least—" Sonia had wandered away to the window. "It's thawing at last. Listen to the rain! Philip will never come today; he might get his ruffles wet. But I can't imagine Lord Denbigh being sopped by a little thing like the weather, can you? Charles is raging, by the way. He says if he can't get out soon, he'll go mad. So shall I, for the matter of that, and I'm not confined to one room as he is. Don't you think we could venture today, Liz, just to find out what the news is?"

"Caulaincourt particularly asked that we do not."

"Oh, fiddle!" And then, on a new note: "Look! Here comes Philip." She was back like a flash to the glass to pat her curls into place. "I shall give him a tremendous scold, I promise you." And then, as Marthe showed him in: "Well, there you are at last. Better late than never, I suppose."

"And full of apologies." He was his immaculate self once more, a neat court-plaster patch over his scar. "But I have news that will make you forgive me. The Allies are on the advance again. Unless Napoleon achieves one of his miracles, my cousin thinks Châtillon will be in our hands again tomorrow. And I suspect the time for his miracles is past. My cousin sent me to tell you."

"That was kind of him," said Elizabeth. And, "You would not, of course, have come on your own account," said Sonia.

"How can you be so cruel? Mrs. Barrymore, intercede for me. I have positively not been fit to be seen these last two days. Why—what's the matter?"

Sonia had gone off into a peal of laughter. "Just what I said! Forgive me, Philip, I must be grateful to you for proving me right. But where is your cousin? What is *his* reason for not visiting us?"

"Oh—I clean forgot. He sent his respects, and thanks for your hospitality. He was summoned urgently to Chaumont yesterday. Something's going on there. Lord knows what. He never tells me anything."

"I don't wonder," said Sonia. "Charles! Is this wise?"

"Why not?" Vincent strolled across to the window. "The French are beating the retreat. The episode is over. Oh, good morning, Haverton. What now, do you think?"

"My cousin says—" He colored and stopped. "My cousin has gone to Chaumont. He left a message for you."

"Oh?"

"Yes. If you have news for him, he says, will you go to Chaumont."

"Thank you." Vincent's eyes were very bright. "I'll remember that."

In London, the air smelled deliciously of spring. There, too, it had been the hardest winter in living memory, and with the first hint of milder air there had been a hurried, overnight dismantling of the booths that had driven a thriving trade on the frozen Thames since Christmas. Now, Henry Fessingham returned from his morning walk in his garden with a snowdrop in his buttonhole.

A footman met him at the garden door. "A messenger, sir, from Whitehall."

"Good." He took the little packet of letters into the study, shuffled quickly through them and opened the one in Denbigh's handwriting first. It had come fast, he saw with satisfaction. The courier service through Paris was working well. "But a mistake, nonetheless," he murmured, as he spread out the letter on his desk and prepared to decode it. "Much better to accept no favors from Bonaparte. Mistakes all round ..." He frowned as he began to read the brief letter. Denbigh always wrote shortly, and to the point. He wanted an investigation made into the background of one Charles Vincent: "Half French, half English; I know little more about him, except that he is the cousin of an old acquaintance of mine, a Mrs. Barrymore, and also of a young lady called Sonia von Hugel, whose grandfather is English. His name is Delverton and he's a parson, somewhere, I think, in the home counties. As for Mrs. Barrymore, her father (also called Barrymore—she married a cousin) used to be vicar of Trumpington. My sister may, perhaps, know something of him." Fessingham would never know what it had cost Denbigh to write those words. He concluded, briefly: "Vincent has approached me as a Bourbon agent, and might be a valuable asset—if I can trust him." He ended with a reiterated emphasis on the urgency of the business. "He promises to come to me, shortly, bringing an accredited representative from the royalists in Paris. It is urgent

156

that I should know to what extent he is to be relied upon."

Fessingham looked quickly through the other letters. Nothing urgent there. He rang the bell: "My carriage, at once, and while it is preparing, send me Mr. Jones."

Mr. Jones, his secretary, took his orders with his usual competent calm: two vicars, both elderly, one called Delverton, the other Barrymore and perhaps still resident at Trumpington. "Yes, indeed, I'll have the details for you when you return."

"Thank you." Fessingham pulled on his gloves and went out to the carriage which was already at the door. It was his coachman's pride that it could be ready, day or night, in five minutes.

Lady Elinor Burnleigh had opened up her brother's house in St. James's Square. It was too agitating, she told her friends, to be cut off in the country at a time like this. "After all, anything might be happening to poor Giles."

She was sitting in her morning room when Mr. Fessingham was announced. "Henry Fessingham! Not bad news, I hope. Show him in at once." And then, to her companion, "No, no, my dear, don't go. I may need your support."

Shown into the room a moment later, Henry Fessingham found them both apparently busy with their netting. Lady Elinor dropped hers at once and rose to hurry towards him. "Mr. Fessingham! My brother! I have been so anxious—"

"No need to be." He took her hand reassuringly. "He writes that he is in the best of health."

"Thank God for that. Oh—in my anxiety, I clean forgot. Allow me to present Miss Cerne, who is helping me to bear the suspense of my brother's absence."

"Enchanted." He took the soft little hand in his and gave her one of his quick, comprehensive glances. A pretty child, just out of the schoolroom, huge dark eyes almost hidden by the tangle of black curls; a general effect of some wild creature of the woods, half tame, half timid. "You are staying with Lady Elinor?" However urgent his business, he knew he must play out the social game if he wanted his hostess's help.

"Yes." The voice was almost inaudible. "Since I left

157

school. Lady Elinor is so good ..." She stammered to a blushing halt.

"The daughter of my oldest friend," put in Lady Elinor briskly. "I mean to take her to Paris with me."

"To Paris?"

"Surely it won't be long now?"

"I hope not. But—surely you will not wish to visit a defeated, an enemy city?"

"Why not? It's still Paris. And—Giles will be there, will he not?"

"I expect so." He suddenly felt sorry for Giles Burnleigh. "And that brings me to the purpose of my visit. I had a letter from your brother, only this morning."

"And none for me!"

"He wrote in great haste, and on official business."

"Which must always come first. Did he condescend to send me any message?"

"His fondest love," Fessingham improvised, and then, more happily: "He shows his confidence in you by urging me to consult you on a point of some importance."

"Oh?" The frown vanished as she raised her eyebrows.

"Yes. He wishes me to trace a Mr. Barrymore, who used to live at Trumpington. He thought it possible that you might have some idea of his whereabouts."

"What!" She half rose, then seated herself again with her back to the window, but Fessingham could see that she had gone very pale, leaving two telltale patches of rouge on her cheekbones. "Mr. Barrymore?" She managed a lighter tone now. "Well, that is ancient history! My dear"—to Miss Cerne—"I had no idea that Mr. Fessingham's visit was a business one. Perhaps, after all ..."

"Of course, Aunt Elinor." The girl jumped to her feet, dropping her netting, which Fessingham retrieved for her.

"A charming child." He closed the door behind her. It would be kinder to give Lady Elinor a moment to recover from the unaccountable confusion into which Mr. Barrymore's name had thrown her.

"Is she not? Her mother died when she was a baby; her father married again almost at once. It's the old story of the neglectful stepmother, so I have made myself responsible for her education. She does me credit, does she not? A little town polish before the season—that's why I thought Paris would be just the thing. And Giles will be there to

158

take us about. He will be surprised, I think, at the change in her."

Oh ho, thought Fessingham, so that's it, is it? You've been bringing up a wife for your brother, have you? I wonder ... The glimpse he had had of Miss Cerne had not suggested any formidable intellectual equipment. She had doubtless, at her school, been taught to sing, and play; to embroider and gossip. She might even have been made, reluctantly, to read a few bound volumes of *The Spectator*—

"I am educating her in politics." Lady Elinor might have read his thoughts. "She is quite a child, of course, but such an eager child to learn; I cannot tell you what a pleasure it is to me. But you were asking about a Mr. Barrymore, a clergyman?"

"Yes. Or rather about a cousin of his daughter's. A Charles Vincent."

"Vincent? I cannot say I ever heard of him. But then, my acquaintance with the Barrymores was of the very slightest. I cannot think what possessed my brother to suggest me as a source of information."

"I suspect that he was reaching for straws."

"But why? What earthly interest could he have, after all these years, in the merest of boyhood acquaintances? He went to Mr. Barrymore, you know, for coaching, when he was a student at Cambridge. I am almost sure that the old man has died since—he was old then. I remember thinking it an absurdity altogether. As for the daughter—goodness knows what became of her—what does become of clergymen's daughters?"

"This one married a cousin, a Mr. Barrymore, and has crossed your brother's path in France, with this other cousin, Mr. Vincent, about whom he is inquiring."

"Oh," she pounced on it eagerly, "married, is she? I'm surprised at that."

But delighted, thought Fessingham. I wonder ... Best pursue it a little further: "Not only married, but widowed—" He let it hang, watching her reaction.

"Hmm—" This pleased her less. "Widowed? Or—a grass widow? And wandering around occupied Europe with a cousin I've never heard of. It sounds all of a piece to me ..."

"All of a piece with what? I must beg you, Lady Elinor,

if, as I begin to suspect, you know something—anything about Mrs. Barrymore, that you will tell me. It may be of the utmost importance."

"In that case—" She had recovered her composure by now, though it had taken her, he thought, a considerable effort. "It is all such ancient history, I would rather have spared her—and my brother, but if you think it really important—my duty?"

"Absolutely." He could see that she was longing to tell him; the minimum of encouragement would do it.

"Very well, then. It's not a particularly edifying story, I'm afraid, but you know my brother well enough to make allowances."

"Of course."

"He was very young, you know, when he went up to Cambridge, and very earnest. He insisted on going to Mr. Barrymore for coaching—said his college tutors were fit only for drinking with. My father adored him; let him have his way in everything. Folly. I told him so, but he never listened to me. So there was Giles, young, impressionable, and going, daily, to the Barrymores' house. Mrs. Barrymore was dead; the daughter kept house for her father; she was older than Giles—she saw her chance—and took it."

"You mean?"

"They eloped. I would never have believed it of Giles—but he was hopelessly under her spell. She must have held out for marriage. They were going to America, of all things. I'm sure Giles's heart wasn't in it; he made such a point of paying his debts and saying his farewells that, inevitably, I found out what was in the wind. My father caught them in Liverpool; it was a lucky thing for Giles that he did. I don't like to think what would have become of him."

"What did happen?"

"Giles collapsed. There'd been an accident. I never did hear the rights of it. Her fault, I have no doubt. Father brought him home and I nursed him back to strength. It took a long time; then we sent him abroad; it was all over . . ."

She's not telling it all, Fessingham thought. No use asking more questions; she's told all she's going to. "A sad story," he said. "I'm glad to think Miss Barrymore recovered sufficiently to marry her cousin."

"Don't waste your sympathy on her. A scheming hussy; you can see that the experience soured poor Giles about women. Well, can you wonder? Is he seeing much of Mrs. Barrymore?"

Fessingham repressed a smile at the giveaway question. "I don't know. A good deal, I imagine: it must be a very small society. But you can tell me nothing more about Mrs. Barrymore's family?"

"Nothing whatever. It was a painful episode; best forgotten."

"Quite so." He found himself more and more wondering about that elopement. What had really happened? What was Lady Elinor concealing? "You would not expect your brother to be on particularly friendly terms with Mrs. Barrymore now?"

"I should have thought it most unlikely." She colored disastrously, the natural red showing up her rouge almost as brutally as pallor had done. "But—she involved him once; anything is possible. I am sure of one thing, she should not be trusted, not for a moment. Of course, I have no idea why you have thought it necessary to make these inquiries, but my advice to you is, do everything in your power to protect Giles."

"Yes. Quite so. Well, for the moment there is not much to be done, but if the Allies do take Paris, I think I shall treat myself to a quick visit there."

"Admirable, Mr. Fessingham. Precisely what I had hoped you would say. I know what a good friend you are to Giles. And if you have no objection, Juliet and I will accompany you. You will understand now what I have in mind for her. Poor Giles trusts no one—can you wonder? First Elizabeth Barrymore, then all those matchmaking mammas in full cry after him. But Julie is something quite else again. He thinks of her—I have seen to it—as a younger sister."

"And what of her?"

"Oh, she adores him, of course. It was inevitable."

"Poor child." Fessingham rose to take his leave.

"Nothing of the kind! Lucky child, you would say, if you knew the home I took her from. I've made that girl, Mr. Fessingham, and—for a purpose. I do not expect to be disappointed." She rang the bell at her elbow. "You must see a little more of her before you go. She's no empty-headed schoolgirl, you'll find." When Juliet joined them, she proceeded to prove her point by a series of leading questions to which the girl responded with the eager docility of an examination candidate. Yes, she had seen Mr. Kean and thought him the greatest actor since Garrick; she was passionately devoted to the music of Beethoven; she had read Miss Edgeworth's new volume of *Tales of Fashionable Life* and quite doted on *The Absentee;* and then, coloring more than ever as Fessingham interposed a question: Oh no, Lady Elinor did not allow her to read Lord Byron's poems.

Fessingham sighed inwardly for the poor child and rose to take his leave. Lady Elinor took his hand warmly: "Dear Mr. Fessingham, so good of you to visit a lonely spinster. And so kind to undertake to squire Juliet and me to Paris. Only think, Juliet my love, Mr. Fessingham has undertaken that we shall be the first Englishwomen to enter the town."

Fessingham, who had undertaken nothing of the kind, had to admit himself outgeneraled. Still, all in all, he thought the advantages of taking Lady Elinor and her protégée with him might well outweigh the drawbacks, many and obvious though those were. There was no blinking the disconcerting nature of what he had learned. More disconcerting still was the fact that Denbigh had not thought fit to tell him of his early involvement with Mrs. Barrymore. Well, there could be all kinds of reasons for that. But—he would be glad to get to Paris and not altogether sorry to have the formidable Lady Elinor, and her charming, silly Juliet, as reserve cards.

At home, he found Mr. Jones already returned. Mr. Barrymore was indeed dead; Mr. Delverton was very much alive, a hunting parson in the Cotswolds. "Admirable, Jones. I shall drive down there this afternoon. Will you give the orders?"

Jones smiled. "I already have, sir."

But it was a disappointing visit. Mr. Delverton, emerging reluctantly from his study, where, Fessingham suspected, he had been fast asleep, admitted to having had a daughter, and at least to the possibility of a granddaughter. "I know there was a boy—likely lad enough by all accounts; they called him after me. Favor-grubbing, of course; but I was pleased, a little, I remember. Even meant to write and say so, but never got around to it, somehow. It seems so far ... for letters, I mean ... Anyway, the chit had made her bed. Used to write me, of course, from time to time. Yes, I believe she did say something about a girl—well, girls, you know." He shrugged them off. "Anyway, m'daughter died, years since, and the boy too—not so long ago—don't remember how I heard that, but bad news always travels. As for the gal—well, I suppose if she came here, I'd feed her. Could hardly do less, could I, as a Christian? But don't think I'm going knight-erranting across Europe looking for her. At my time of life! Let her father look out for her, I say. Can't think what she's doing jauntering about with the armies, anyway. Most unsuitable thing for my grandchild, if you ask me. No, on second thoughts I'm not sure I could receive her; not after that. As for cousins; first I ever heard of any; on our side at least. But her father may have them like rabbits, for all I know. Expect he has; you know how those Germans are. Sorry not to be more help to you. Drop of something before you go? Matilda!"

Fessingham had already encountered the housekeeper when he arrived, and had no wish to do so again. He made his excuses and returned to London no wiser than he had left it, but feeling rather sorry for the unknown Miss von Hügel.

The visit he paid to Trumpington was rather more rewarding. Mr. Barrymore was remembered with great affection by his parishioners. His daughter was another matter. "Seemed a nice enough girl, you understand." The landlord of the inn was quite ready to talk about her. "Then ran off, bold as brass, with some young lord or other, clear across England to Liverpool—and then home again, on her own—you couldn't help feeling sorry for her but sorrier for her poor old pa. Ruined herself, of course; talk all over the county; nearly lost him his parish, if you ask me. Lucky for him she took a notion to take her disgrace abroad. Married? No, I never heard tell that she married anyone—not much hope of that after what she'd done. Well, stands to reason the young man would only have abandoned her like that for reason good—and what that would be, you can guess as well as I can. My daughter was proper turned up about it—loved Miss Barrymore, she did; the trouble I had keeping her away from her after it happened; but you've got to think of your own, ain't you, sir? As for cousins—I never heard talk of any kin of hers, but that's not to say she had none. Nor yet that she mightn't have up and married one of them—it just don't seem very likely to me. And keep the same name, too? Something havey-cavey about it, I'd say. She always was a one that valued her own judgment above the rest of the world's. Asking for trouble—and found it, poor girl. Killed her father. Not at once, but gradually, what with disgrace, and missing her and all. No doubt about it, she was a good daughter—and ran the school a fair treat—before it happened, you understand; course we couldn't have a fallen woman teaching our children. Why, thank you kindly, sir, I don't mind if I do join you in a short one. No, I don't know as anyone here would know more about her than I do; I reckon to keep pretty well in touch with what goes on." And he proceeded to prove it by a series of probing questions directed at discovering the reason for Fessingham's interest in Elizabeth Barrymore.

Back in London, Fessingham was not surprised to learn that the further inquiries he had instructed Mr. Jones to make had drawn a complete blank: there was no record of a marriage between Elizabeth Barrymore and someone of the same name—or anyone else, for the matter of that. And nor had he been able to find out anything about a possible connection with a family called Vincent. It added up to a disquieting picture. Since Elizabeth Barrymore was entirely and Sonia von Hugel half English, it seemed elementary logic to assume that the relationship between them and Charles Vincent must be on the English side. And yet there was not a fragment of evidence to confirm it. The innkeeper, for all his claim to omniscience, had been unaware that Elizabeth had relatives in the Cotswolds, but Sonia's grandfather must have known. And the name Barrymore had meant nothing to him. As for Vincent, the name was common enough, but Mr. Jones, indefatigable in his researches, had been able to find no one who admitted knowledge of this Charles Vincent. At last, gloomily, Fessingham sighed, shrugged and sat down to write a long, admonitory letter to Denbigh.

Chapter 13

"Here comes 'my cousin says'." Sonia turned away from the window. "With news, by the important look of him."

"Sonia!" Elizabeth looked up from her work. "How often must I tell you—" Her voice came out sharper than she had intended and she stopped, coloring at her own display of temper.

"Oh, Barry, what's the matter with you?" Sonia crossed the room to stand over her anxiously. "You're not well, you know you're not. I wish you'd have the doctor."

"And have him prophesy woe! No, thank you. And don't worry about me, Sonia. I'm a little out of sorts, it's true, but nothing to signify. It's been a long winter. Ah, Mr. Haverton, how are you?"

"All the better for the news."

"Oh?"

"Yes. My cousin writes that the Allies have signed a new treaty at Chaumont: an alliance to the death against Napoleon. Now we shall see some action. Why, what's the matter, Miss von Hugel? Have I said something to entertain you?"

"No, no." But she was crimson with suppressed laughter at his variation on the phrase she had turned into his nickname, and Elizabeth had to save her face by intervening. "And what of the Congress here?"

"Being wound up. Caulaincourt's playing for time, that's all."

"And how long has he got? When do we march on Paris?"

"You may well ask. My cousin writes that the generals are still undecided. Well, you can understand it. No one knows how the Parisians are going to receive us, if we do get there ... Suppose, at the same time, they were to wage guerrilla warfare on us—and Napoleon were to cut our communications with Switzerland, which is all too likely ... Then where would we be?"

"In the soup." Vincent had entered the room while Haverton was talking. "Is your cousin back yet?"

"No. He says he and Castlereagh do not mean to return here, for the moment at least. I rather think, reading between the lines, that they are afraid of raising false hopes if they do so."

"Among the French, you mean?"

"Yes. You know how ready they are to take advantage of the slightest sign of wavering on our part."

"Well, can you blame them? You've wavered enough, in all conscience."

"You?" Sonia took him up on it. "Why don't you say 'Can you blame us,' and have done with it?"

"I only wish I could. But how can I be French, so long as Napoleon is in power?" And to Haverton: "Your cousin is at Chaumont still?"

"I believe so. If they have not moved, already, to Troyes."

"Box and cox with Bonaparte, eh? Well, I hope they have not, for it will most tediously prolong my journey."

"Your journey?" Sonia whirled, with a rustle of petticoats, to face him. "Charles, you cannot be proposing to leave us *again!*"

"I am afraid I must. A—friend of mine has just reached town, from Paris. I promised Lord Denbigh I would bring him to see him as soon as he arrived. This is important, Sonia."

"That's what you said last time." She was prowling about the room like an affronted kitten.

"It's still true. Sonia, believe me—"

"Believe you? Charles, why should I? Or rather, I'll believe, if you like, that you value these 'friends' of yours more highly than you do us, because you make it all too obvious. But as to the importance of these mysterious journeys of yours—why should I believe you?"

There was appeal in her voice now and his softened in response. "Because I beg you to. Rapunzel, you must see that I cannot explain—" A quick glance reminded her of Haverton's presence.

"I see perfectly well that you don't intend to. Women can keep secrets, can't they, Charles, so long as they don't know them. You told me that yourself, and vastly flattering I found it. Do you remember when we started on this

166

journey, Charles? We were to be comrades, you said. "Well"—she clicked her fingers angrily—"so much for your comradeship. We're just the excess baggage of your adventure, Liz and I—and that reminds me, what happens to us, pray, if the conference breaks up while you are gone?"

"Give me credit for a little foresight." He had been looking increasingly anxious lest, in her excited state, she should betray their true relationship—or lack of it—to Haverton. Now he hurried to intervene. "I have already made arrangements about that. If the Congress should break up suddenly, which I think far from likely, I have arranged with Lord Aberdeen that you will join the diplomatic cortege that will leave for Allied Headquarters. I shall be awaiting you there, my business, I hope, done." And then, on a note of unusual seriousness: "Sonia, I must beg you—Elizabeth, help me to convince her that this is important—and not only to me."

"I rather wish I could convince myself." Elizabeth looked at him thoughtfully. There had been a great change in him since they had first met. "You are serious about this, are you not?"

"Never more so. I think this journey so important that, frankly, I shall go, whatever you say."

Sonia jumped to her feet. "Precisely," she exclaimed. "You make yourself most delightfully clear, Cousin Charles." Her tone made a mockery of the familiar address. "So—there is no more to be said, is there? Mr. Haverton, our apologies for boring you with our family discussions, and indeed, yes I should be happy to take a turn through the town with you. I find the atmosphere indoors oppressive this morning." And then, over her shoulder. "Good-bye, cousin. Perhaps we shall meet again, some day. Liz, remind me, tonight, that there is a letter I must write."

"Sonia!" He moved towards her, then apparently changed his mind. "Enjoy your promenade." He opened the door for them, said a formal farewell to Haverton and then stood oddly still for a moment, silently watching as she made a little business of finding hat, pelisse and gloves for her outing.

At last, he re-entered the room, closed the door gently behind him, met Elizabeth's sympathetic eye and shrugged. "She'll write to her grandfather, I take it?"

"I imagine so. And, really, I cannot think it a bad idea. My plan, you know, has always been to get her to England. It will be much better if she is expected, has some hope of a welcome."

"A welcome! With the damaged reputation I seem to have contrived for her? You are too patient with me, Elizabeth. Your very silence makes me feel more guilty than any amount of reproaches would."

She smiled at him. "Believe me, that was not my intention. Truly, Charles, I do not blame you for anything. Indeed, I do not like to think what would have become of us if Sonia had not had the luck of meeting you. As it is, we are at least much nearer England."

"England, yes, but what about the fortune I promised you?"

"Oh, Charles, I never believed in that, nor yet in the brilliant marriages you and Sonia were to make. I have lived too long in the world to imagine that kind of miracle. If I can just get her safely to her mother's people, I shall feel I have done well enough."

He was pacing up and down the room now. "A country vicar! And a man who cut off her mother for her rash marriage! Have you thought, Elizabeth, what is going to happen when it comes out that we are none of us cousins?"

"Frequently. I try not to let it keep me awake at night. Sometimes I think that that engaging, devoted boy is the only answer."

"Haverton! For Sonia! You're out of your mind. She's worth six of him, and you know it." He had moved over to the window to stand gazing down into the street. Sonia and Haverton had just emerged from the house and crossed the road, Sonia hanging on his arm; her head thrown back, she was smiling at him as if she had not a care in the world.

"Elizabeth!" His tone made her cross the room to join him. "Take care of her."

"Of course." Her eyes followed his and she wondered if he was aware, as she was, that Sonia knew they were watching.

He turned impatiently from the window. "I ought to be on my way. Elizabeth, forgive me—and—try to make Sonia understand."

168

"I'll do my best." But she could not help wondering how much she herself understood.

Lord Denbigh's servants noticed that he was unusually restless. Leaving Châtillon for Chaumont, he had, for once, been repetitive in his insistence that any letters should be brought on, at once, by hand. And now, when Allied Headquarters was moving back to Troyes, the same scene took place. Once again, a servant was left behind with particular instructions about letters. "It is urgent!" reiterated his lordship, swinging himself up on to his horse.

"Yes, I somehow rather gathered it was," muttered the groom he had left behind. "Writes to England one day, and wants an answer the next—never saw his lordship so unreasonable. At least—not for years. Well, I wonder?" Since his audience was now entirely French, he got no further with his wondering.

The expected letter had still not arrived two days later, when Charles Vincent reached the house Denbigh and Castlereagh were sharing at Troyes. "Vincent—and a friend," Denbigh told Castlereagh. "And I've not heard a word from Fessingham as to his background."

"But the 'friend' is doubtless the emissary from Paris he promised to bring you?"

"I assume so."

"Then there's nothing for it but to see them—and sift them as best we may. Encouraging news from Paris might make all the difference just now."

"It might indeed—so long as we can believe it."

"I shall leave you to be the judge of that. See Vincent and his 'friend' first alone, will you?"

"And leave you as our second line of defense? Good."

Half an hour later, Denbigh reported himself convinced. "Of Charles Vincent, I admit, I still have my doubts, but as to the stranger—he is undoubtedly what he claims to be, an emissary from Paris, and with a message, at last, from Talleyrand."

"Ah. And that is—?"

"That we are crawling when we might walk. In fact, that Paris—or at least the better half of it—will receive us with open arms. There does seem, by the man's evidence—

he wishes, for obvious reasons, to remain anonymous—to be a considerable body of opposition to Bonaparte."

"And support for the Bourbons?"

"There, frankly, I am not so sure. That there is a royalist party is obvious enough—Vincent has had messages, before this, from the Duke of Dalberg, who seems to be its leader—but the most significant thing, to my mind, is that Talleyrand, in his own message, does not commit himself on this point."

"You mean we must go to Paris—and see?"

"That seems to be what it comes down to. Vincent does not think so, of course. Since he visited the Comte d'Artois he is a fanatical royalist."

"I wonder what he will say when he sees the King—if he ever does."

Denbigh laughed. "The descendant of St. Louis, in velvet boots. Yes, I wonder too, but that is neither here nor there. I have promised him that you will see them both, and if you find them as convincing as I have, take them to the Allied chiefs—and, most important, to the Czar."

"Yes, convince him and it's settled. There was no talk of Bernadotte?"

"None repeatable. I think that dream of the Czar's is just that—a dream."

"I hope your stranger can convince him of that. If he does, he will have done our cause a powerful service. As for Vincent—you still have your doubts of him?"

"None of his loyalty to the Bourbon cause. But of his general reliability—well, you must judge for yourself. I am inclined to think him dangerous just because of his enthusiasm; there is no fanatic so desperate as the adventurer who has found a cause at last."

"Yes. It's a pity we know so little about him. But you must hear from Fessingham any day now. Anyway, let us see your fanatic, and his convincing friend. How pleasant it would be to find ourselves in Paris for Easter."

That was a day of unusual activity at Allied Headquarters. Vincent and his companion saw Castlereagh, saw Nesselrode and Stadion, finally, late that evening, saw the Czar himself. He listened with his usual courtesy to what the stranger had to say about Paris; professed himself highly gratified at Talleyrand's message, but shook his head over the Bourbon claim. "Time enough for that when we are at Paris."

And still nothing was decided. The Emperor of Austria was at Dijon and must be consulted. Schwartzenberg was prostrated with an attack of the gout; the King of Prussia would follow any decision of the Czar's—when the Czar decided. And all the time, Vincent and his companion had to stay kicking their heels at Headquarters. It was hard to tell which of them took it worst. The stranger wanted to get to the Comte d'Artois, Vincent fretted over the position of his companions at Châtillon.

Denbigh, who had agreed with Castlereagh that Vincent must be kept under observation till Fessingham's report on him arrived, did his best to allay his fears. "Lord Aberdeen—and Haverton, of course—will look after your cousins if the Congress does break up: there is not the slightest cause for anxiety on their behalf."

"No? Not with Bonaparte on the rampage again? Anything might happen."

"It's his last fling, I promise you."

"I wonder. Something tells me that when Bonaparte makes his last fling, the earth will shake with it."

His anxiety reached fever point when the Czar gave his companion leave to go, with messages as vague as they were friendly, to the Comte d'Artois, who was believed to be still at Nancy. It was obvious now that, though ostensibly Denbigh's guest, he was being kept in a kind of protective custody. Then, one drizzling March evening, his chance came. An urgent messenger summoned Denbigh to Nesselrode's lodgings and for once he did not suggest that Vincent accompany him. Alone at last, Vincent did not waste a moment. A brief note, part defiance, part apology, for Denbigh and he strolled out to the stables. Here too luck was on his side. Denbigh's groom had accompanied him, and the stable boy saddled up Vincent's big chestnut readily enough. "You'd best not ride far, though," he warned. "The gates are closed at nightfall."

"I know." This was part of Vincent's plan. Once safely outside the gates, he settled down to ride steadily all night. There was no sign of pursuit, nor did he expect any. After all, he had never been told, in so many words, that he was a prisoner.

His spirits rose with the miles and he allowed himself to

imagine the meeting. It seemed, now he was on his way at last, an age since he had seen the girls, since he had watched Sonia walk away down the street, laughing and chattering with Haverton. She had been angry with him for going—had almost quarreled with him. And yet he was smiling to himself as he thought of that last morning and her angry little manner of a ruffled kitten. Had she, then, really minded his going? Did she—but there would be time for these thoughts later. Soon, he told himself, soon now—and set spurs to his horse.

The sun had risen now, with all the promise of a fine day. Would the girls be up already and at breakfast? Would Sonia jump up to greet him, to forgive him because she had been angry? Imagining the little scene, he turned his horse down the riverside promenade that led into Châtillon, then pulled up suddenly and listened, gray-faced. To what? To silence. Where were the sentries' challenges? The early morning bustle of the occupation troops? Faster now, pressing his tired horse on to confirm what, in his heart, he already knew. The town was quiet, empty, dead. The Congress must have broken up. Sonia had been right again.

Reaching their house at last, he knocked, but without hope. He could feel its emptiness already in his heart.

Marthe's first words, when, finally, she came grumbling to open the door, confirmed his fears: "You're too late, m'sieur. They left yesterday, with Milord Aberdeen and the other bigwigs—for Chaumont."

"Chaumont? But why? Headquarters are at Troyes." Anxiety piled on anxiety.

She shrugged. "How should I know? They're gone, is all I can tell you, and not best pleased about it either. Especially Mamselle Sonia. She was all for waiting here for you, but madame wouldn't hear of it—nor yet M'sieur Haverton. And of course they were right; I'd do my best for them, but—well, you know how things are, m'sieur. Lucky for you you'd pass as a Frenchman anywhere. But come in—you look worn out—and famished, too, I wager."

The house had the desolate look of a place hurriedly abandoned. Elizabeth's workbox, Sonia's embroidery, all the little things that had made it seem a home, had vanished. Marthe read his thoughts: "They packed up everything," she said. "Your things too. And what an argument they had about that. Don't look so anxious, m'sieur; they're well cared for. M. Haverton rides with them—Milord Aberdeen has them under his protection."

But Vincent's anxiety was as fierce as it was, apparently, unreasonable. He drank some of Marthe's good coffee, and ate a couple of rolls, standing, then went out to look at his weary horse.

Marthe followed him. "Mamselle had to leave her pony behind," she said. "She was in tears about that too, but I told her you were sure to come, and would take it to her."

His head lifted suddenly. In tears about that too, Marthe had said. Had Sonia cried, then, at the idea of leaving without him? Suddenly, everything seemed possible. Surely the luck was changing. With Marmion to spell his own chestnut, he should easily be able to catch up with the diplomatic cortege, which would move at the snail's pace of its slowest carriage.

"You want to go carefully." Marthe had been packing him a small bag of food. "Jacques was here last night—he'd taken English leave to bid me good-bye: the Little Corporal's on the march again, he says."

"Did he say which way?"

"No, for he did not know. But you want to keep your eyes open. I don't mind telling you I'm happy to know you're rejoining the young ladies."

"So shall I be—when I find them." Anxiety was driving him again. Marthe's quiet, competent preparations seemed intolerably slow, the time needed to saddle up Marmion too much to bear. But at last he was riding out through the streets that were crowded now with black-clad women going about the daily business of living, their wooden shoes clicking on the paved streets. He hardly saw them, nor noticed the glances, some curious, some amused that his odd figure drew as he rode down the street on the little pony, with his big chestnut following. Over and over again he told himself that his anxiety was absurd—out of all proportion to the facts. Marthe had told him that the diplomatic cortege had consisted of twelve carriages, with a well-armed escort of hussars and Cossacks. So guarded, the girls should be perfectly safe. It was no use. Something in his heart refused to accept these arguments of comfort.

Spurring on the willing pony, he came, a few miles out of town, on a sight that confirmed, all at once, the very worst of his fears. The last time he had ridden this way, he remembered thinking how untouched the country looked, with fields and woods shooting into the first delicate green of spring. Since then, very recently indeed, an army had passed, leaving the usual trail of desolation. Or—two armies? What had been happening here? And—more important—whatever it was, had the girls escaped it? Now anxiety, openly admitted, made the pony's steady pace seem a snail's. Concerned more with speed than with caution, he emerged too quickly from a little wood—straight into the arms of an Austrian picket. Luckily, he still had the pass Schwartzenberg had given him. The signature of their commander in chief made them his friends at once and in answer to his impatient questions they told him what they knew—which was not much, and what there was of it, confusing. Schwartzenberg, apparently, was still laid up with the gout: "That's why we retreated," explained one. "Or why we didn't advance," put in another. "Then Boney turns up—bold as you please, and it looked like we were going to retreat all over again." "But in pops the Czar, like the devil on horseback, and his Cossacks with him, and the next thing we know we're advancing again, and a bloody day we had of it, too, at Arcis-sur-Aube."

"Two days ago, that was," put in the other, "and what's happened to Boney since, his friend the devil may know, for I'm sure we don't."

"But who won at Arcis-sur-Aube?" asked Vincent.

The corporal in charge of the party shrugged. "Damned if I know. They *said* we did; well, we didn't retire, but neither did Boney—not that night, that is. We thought we'd be at it again in the morning, hammer and tongs, but, hey presto, come dawn, the Frenchies had vanished. What with that and no word from old Blücher for God knows how long, they're in a pretty state of confusion at Headquarters, I can tell you. There's talk of retreat to Switzerland; talk of advancing to Paris; your guess is as good as mine. Ladies? Twelve carriages full of diplomats?" He scratched his head over the question. "No, I've heard nothing about them, but I can tell you one thing, they're in trouble if they've gone to Chaumont; the tocsin was

174

ringing for the attack when we came past there last night. And you'd best go carefully if you're heading that way; it wouldn't surprise me if the French weren't between us and it. Boney moves fast when he moves, you have to give him that."

At this point, one of his companions interrupted him. "I heard tell of some ladies," he said, "when I was out first thing looking for forage—like getting blood from a stone in this country; I had to go miles—and then nothing but some rotten oats, half straw, for my pains."

"But the ladies—" Vincent interrupted what showed signs of being an interminable lament. "What of them?"

"I met a friend of mine; couple of miles from here, I suppose it was, he was talking about them. Came away from Chaumont in a hurry when they saw how the land lay there, and bivouacked with the army, a whole party of them, ladies and all, he said. Young ladies, they were, he couldn't get over it. Lucky for them it cleared up; fancy their sitting round a camp fire all night."

"And today? Do you know where they are now?"

"That's what my friend found so funny. When it came time to march this morning, the ladies' carriage was bogged in the mud; that's the worst of the thaw; the snow was bad enough but, believe me, this is worse."

"So what happened?"

"A mighty argument, my friend said. Leave their things and take a ride with some other lady, or stay with their things and part company with the convoy, and that's all I know. My friend left them still at it."

"Where was all this?"

The man scratched his head. "That I don't rightly know, sir, but I can tell you where I met my friend Michel." He did so at some length, with a wealth of countryman's detail. "But this was all two hours ago at least," he concluded, dampingly. "I shouldn't reckon they're there still."

"Where was the convoy heading?"

The man thought hard. "Towards Langres, I reckon; follow that road, and you might come on them—and then again you might not."

It summed up the situation with discouraging accuracy, Vincent thought, changing over to the now rested chestnut and turning its head down the little country lane the man had indicated. It would be little short of a miracle if he found either the convoy, or the two girls, supposing they had really decided to stay with the carriage. But—could they have been so mad? Admit—they might have. The carriage contained everything they possessed in the world. But the risk did not bear thinking of. If only he could stop thinking.

At least, the soldier's directions seemed to have been surprisingly accurate. There was the barn he had spoken of, and here the windmill. Near it, he met a considerable body of Austrian troops, ground his teeth over the inevitable delay while their officer examined his papers and once again put his question.

"The diplomats?" The man sounded amused. "Yes, they spent the night with us, and are off this morning to join the Emperor at Dijon. I suppose they would very likely spend tonight at Langres. The rate they were traveling they'll be lucky if they get there. As to ladies—there were some with them, that I do know, but that's all I know. Oh yes, I can tell you where we spent the night all right, and a damned uncomfortable one it was too."

Once again, Vincent listened carefully to the directions he was given and turned his horse's head down the rough farm track the officer indicated. "It shouldn't take you more than half an hour," were his last, encouraging words. "We've done nothing but go round in circles this morning."

Riding quickly along the track, Vincent allowed himself to hope a little. If the girls had insisted on staying with their carriage, he might well find them still on the site of the bivouac. If, on the other hand, they had accepted a lift, he assumed from Lady Burgersh, he should easily be able to catch them before they reached Langres. Then he checked his rising hopes. He might be on a complete wild goose chase; it might be some quite different ladies. He set his teeth and tried not to think of a story an Austrian friend of his had told him. This man, an officer, had seen a French lady, obviously well born, being carried off by Cossacks. He had rescued her and she had explained, gratefully, that she had been following her husband who was in Napoleon's army. He had left her in charge of his servant, only to learn, later, that the Cossacks had returned in force, and carried her off again. No amount of inquiry had discovered her, though he had appealed to the Czar himself. Her fate did not bear thinking of and he had kept the story from Sonia and Elizabeth for fear of alarming them unduly. Now, he wished he had told them ... At least it might have prevented their even thinking of staying with their baggage. Not much good either to try and console himself with the thought that, theoretically, the Cossacks were on their side. When it came to pillage, Cossacks were on no one's side but their own. Even their own officers could not always control them.

Hurry ... hurry ... He must be near the site of the bivouac now. It should, by his instructions, be on the far side of this little wood. And on the thought, from that very direction, the sound of shots. No time now for hope or fear. He set spurs to his horse and rode through the wood at a dangerous gallop, only slackening his pace as he reached its fringe to reconnoiter before emerging. The firing had stopped, but he could hear a confused noise of shouting.

In the field beyond the wood, a little group of Frenchmen were attacking a Cossack who seemed to be defending the body of a companion. And beyond them—Vincent's heart gave a leap—stood the familiar carriage with Sonia close beside it, her face white and set, her little gun in her hand. During their travels, he had done his best to improve her shooting, and now with a warm little thrill of pride, he saw her take aim, steadily, as he had taught her, and fire. Amazingly, one of the Frenchmen fell and two of his comrades turned to advance on Sonia. Vincent urged his horse forward, turning, as he left the wood, to shout an order to an imaginary body of men. The ruse worked; as he threw himself into the fray, the Frenchmen turned to flee pell-mell down the road. But the second Cossack had fallen now across the Frenchman Sonia had shot, who lay helplessly shouting oaths at his vanishing comrades. To Vincent's relief, they took no notice, but continued their headlong flight and had soon vanished over the brow of the hill.

Sonia was coming towards him, the little gun still in her hand. "That was timely." Her white face and trembling hand gave the lie to her casual tone.

"Thank God, yes." No time now for the thousand things he wanted to say. Instead, to the wounded Frenchman:

"Stay still, sir, if you wish to live." And then, to Sonia, with an effort at her lightness: "Good shooting, urchin. Now, keep him covered will you, while I disarm him? But where's Elizabeth?"

Something changed in her face. "Ill, in the carriage, But—the poor Cossacks?"

"Dead, I'm afraid, both of them. And as for you—"

The Frenchman was sitting on the ground, bleeding heavily from a wound in his leg. "God damn them," he said dispassionately after his vanished comrades. And then, to Vincent, "I assure you, sir, the fight was none of my seeking. This young lady will tell you that I did my best to dissuade those fools from attacking. I'm a civilian— you can see from my dress—I was merely acting in self-defense."

"It looked a pretty violent kind of self-defense to me," said Vincent. "Did he really try and dissuade them, Sonia?"

"Yes, indeed he did. He kept saying something about his papers."

"Papers, eh? By your leave, sir, I'd best have a look a them. No, I wouldn't resist, if I were you. You might get hurt." He found the papers concealed in a secret pocket of the man's greatcoat. "Keep him covered, Sonia, while I take a look." And then, "Good God, no wonder he didn't want to get involved in a wayside broil. Here's a letter from Napoleon to his wife." He looked through it hurriedly. "With a description of his plans. Sonia, can you help me get him into the carriage? We must not lose a minute. He's too weak, I think, to give trouble, and we can hardly leave him here. I warn you, sir, if you try anything, I'll kill you." He meant it and the Frenchman, now very pale, allowed them to help him along towards the carriage, which, Vincent had seen with relief, had already been extricated from the mud into which it had sunk. "But Elizabeth," he asked now, "what's the matter?"

"I don't know: a chill, perhaps, caught last night—we camped out, you know, with the army. Or—I don't know— maybe just nerves."

"Nerves? Elizabeth? Surely not."

"You expect us to be made of iron, don't you, Charles? Flattering, I suppose, that you think us so well able to take care of ourselves."

178

"I've been worried to death about you, Sonia. You must know that."

"Must I? More worried than about your beloved Bourbons?"

"Of course. What I feel for them is duty ... loyalty ..."

"And for us?" Her eyes were large and bright in her pale face.

"For you! Sonia—" He stopped suddenly. "But what happened to Haverton? Why was he not there to take care of you?"

"He left Châtillon with urgent dispatches for his cousin just before the order came to move. You thought we were safe with him, did you, Charles?"

"And Lord Aberdeen ... Lady Burgersh—" They had nearly reached the carriage. He looked at Sonia across the drooping body of the Frenchman. "No, I won't make excuses; I can't bear to have failed you like this, Sonia. If anything had happened to you, I'd never have forgiven myself."

"No?" She reached up to open the carriage door. "Look who's here, Elizabeth. Charles to the rescue—better late than never."

Elizabeth was huddled in a corner of the carriage, very white, and shivering convulsively. "Thank God," she said. "Are you all right, Sonia?"

"Oh, absolutely; there's nothing I like better than a midmorning shooting match. And here, please note, is my victim. You will not mind having him for companion, Elizabeth? He is quite quiet now."

The Frenchman began a feeble protest. "Surely you will bandage my wound before we go. Look how it bleeds."

"And give your companions time to come back for you," said Charles. "I think not, sir."

"That reminds me," said Sonia. "*Your* companions are a long time coming, Charles."

"Are they not?" No use admitting in front of their prisoner that he was alone, but Sonia's quick glance told him she had understood. "Where's your coachman?"

"Ran like a hare, when the French attacked," said Sonia. "If it had not been for those brave Cossacks—I'll never say another word against them. Were they quite dead, Charles?"

"Quite, I'm afraid." He propped the protesting Frenchman in the corner of the carriage. "I shall have to drive. Keep him covered, Sonia, and shoot to kill if he makes the slightest move. You know what a capable shot she is, sir." And then, to Elizabeth: "I am so sorry to find you thus. Will you be able to bear the motion of the carriage, do you think?"

"I shall have to." She managed a wavering smile. "But where are we going? To Dijon?"

"Dijon?"

"That's where the diplomats have gone," explained Sonia. "They sleep tonight at Langres."

"And that is the way those Frenchmen will think we have gone; if they should decide to come after us. But anyway, I am sorry, Sonia; Elizabeth, forgive me. I have no choice; I must take you to the Czar."

"To the Czar!" Sonia's voice rose. "And where, pray, is he?"

"At Arcis-sur-Aube; or was yesterday." He had been expertly tying the Frenchman's hands behind him as he spoke. "I am sorry, Sonia, but I must take him Napoleon's letter."

"You know, of course, that the French army is very probably between us and Arcis." She kept her voice light and low, in the hope that Elizabeth would not hear.

"Yes. We will get away from here, find some shelter where we can leave him, and lay our plans. Believe me, Sonia, it appalls me to have to expose you two to further danger . . . but I must."

"Duty calls, eh, Charles. As usual." She settled herself facing the Frenchman, gun in hand. "I warn you, sir, I'm in a very bad temper. I shall shoot you without the slightest hesitation. Very well, Charles, drive on, and God help us."

Chapter 14

Charles whipped up the horses and turned the heavy carriage away from the scene of the fight. They had lost dangerously much time already. But at least the horses were fresh from their night's rest, and the carriage uninjured. He was able to set forward at a good pace, congratulating himself, as he did so, that the diplomatic convoy had left the muddy road in such a state that it would be quite impossible for any pursuers to pick up the traces of their carriage. Still more important, he had come on a landmark that he remembered. He had come this way, once before, when going to Nancy and had spent the night with a family of passionate royalists in their small château deep in the forest. He remembered the way now, and also that there was a village a few miles this side of the château. Presently he stopped the carriage, jumped down and opened the door by the Frenchman.

"Out," he said. "This is as far as you go."

"What?" The man looked at the thick woods through which the road ran. "You cannot leave me here. It would be barbarous."

"There's a village a little further on. I shall send you help from there. Be grateful, sir. I might have left you where you fell." He propped him against a tree, gave him a flask of wine and a hunk of black bread from the provisions the girls had brought and left him there.

"You really will send him help?" Sonia asked.

"Of course. Do you think me a liar as well as everything else? I shall tell them we saw a man lying wounded back here and promised to send help to him. By the time they hear his story, we shall be safe away."

"Where?"

He told her about the royalist château. "They will do their best for us, I am sure. You must see that it is essential I take the news of Napoleon's plans to Allied Headquarters." For once, his voice was almost pleading.

181

"It's not much use my arguing, is it?"

"Frankly, no. But how is Elizabeth?"

"Not at all well; she does nothing but shiver."

"Wrap her in my coat." He handed it in to her. "I am hopeful that my friends the Loyets will take her in."

"And me, I suppose. I might have known it."

"We won't argue the point now." He clinched the matter by swinging himself back on to the coachman's box. A few miles further on, he stopped, as he had promised, in the village and ensured that the Frenchman would indeed be rescued by describing him as prepared to pay well for any help he received. Then, before he could be embarrassed by too many questions, he inquired the way to a town in the opposite direction to the Loyets' château, explained in passing that he was taking his sick wife to the doctor there, and drove out of the village on the road indicated. This meant a considerable detour, but it was still early afternoon when they reached the château. To his relief, it lay quiet in erratic March sunshine: no army had been this way.

He left the girls in the carriage and knocked on the door of the wing of the castle to which long years in opposition had reduced the Loyets. Then, as he had been told to do when he came here before, he stood back in the countyard so as to be visible from the upstairs windows. After a considerable interval, he thought he saw movements behind one of them, then, at last, the big door swung slowly open.

"You!" Charles Loyet stood, gaunt and haggard in the doorway. "Don't come any nearer, M. Vincent, we have the fever."

"The typhus?"

"I fear so. My wife. Wait, and I'll come out to you. They say it communicates itself less easily in the open air. But keep well away." He accepted Vincent's sympathy, but shrugged aside his offers of help. "My wife is beyond it; my son is with her. For myself, I am beyond caring. But you—what can I do for you? You would not be here without a good reason."

As briefly as possible, Vincent explained his position, ending with the vital question. "Is it true that the French army is between here and the Allies?"

"I am very much afraid so. But—spread out, disorga-

182

nized; I think it might be possible to get through. And I can help you. Before my wife took ill, I had completed the arrangements to move her and my son to Paris, away from the fighting. I have all the papers; could you not use them?"

"But you?"

"Our next journey, I think, will be to the graveyard. Don't trouble yourself about us; you are on the King's business. If, by giving you our papers I can shorten this war by even so much as a day—and hasten his return—it will be worth it to die here, where I have lived. Don't look so concerned, if you could see my wife, you would know there is no question of moving her. But—we must lose no time, nor should you be lingering here to catch the disease."

They planned, briefly and urgently. Elizabeth would pass as Mme. Loyet: "If you hint she may have the fever, they will not examine her too closely." He gave a brief, grisly list of symptoms to be quoted. Sonia presented a greater difficulty, since the third set of papers were for the Loyet's nineteen-year-old son. "That's easy," said Vincent. "She's dressed as a boy before; lend us some of your son's clothes, and she must do so again."

"Admirable. And as for you; you'll just have to pray they don't query your age. It will be dusk, which should help, and a hint of the fever should keep them at arm's length."

While Loyet hurried indoors for a suit of his son's clothes, Vincent returned to the carriage. Elizabeth had nodded off into an uneasy sleep as soon as it stopped and Sonia leaned out of the window to greet him in an anxious whisper. "She's asleep; don't wake her. What's the matter? Why were you so long?"

He explained, as quickly as possible. Her reaction was instantaneous: "The typhus? Frightful. But should we not do something to help them?"

"He says there is nothing to be done, and I believe him."

"So you cannot leave us here after all. Poor Charles. Instead, we are to be your cover once again. Is that it?"

"You could put it that way. At least, it means I can keep you with me."

"And you want to? Why, Charles—"

He was looking past her. "Here's M. Loyet. Be as quick as you can changing, Sonia. We must be through the French army before morning."

"You hope." But she was already turning away with the bundle of clothes under her arm to change, as Loyet had suggested, in the deserted main entrance hall of the house. He had chosen the clothes well, and a voluminous greatcoat and large tricorn hat went far to conceal any deficiencies. When she returned, with her own gown and pelisse hanging over her arm, Vincent looked at her with approval. "You'll do," he said, "in the twilight."

She made a face at him. "Thank you for those encouraging words. I'm glad to think I shall pass—in the dark. But what about the carriage? It has a very German look about it to me."

"I shall say I stole it from an Austrian officer."

"Enterprising Charles." She was about to open the carriage door, but Vincent stopped her.

"You'll have to ride on the box with me. No one would risk being shut up with a typhus case. I've propped Elizabeth up with all the blankets. She says she'll do."

"You mean, she'll have to."

"This is war, Sonia."

"I'm beginning to realize that . . ."

Loyet had hardly stayed to listen to their thanks, but hurried back to his wife. Charles helped Sonia up to the high coachman's seat and settled himself beside her. "You'll have to have a bad throat if we are questioned. Your voice would give you away at once."

"How encouraging you are." She croaked it at him in the deepest voice she could manage. And then, more naturally: "How pleasant it is up here. I'm so glad we lost that rascally coachman. I wonder where he's got to by now. I suppose you know where we are going?"

"I hope I do. There's a system of side roads that might, if we are lucky, take us around the edge of the French army."

"And if we are unlucky?"

"I've thought about that. If we are questioned too closely—if, in fact, they are going to search the carriage, I shall change my story and admit to being a French courier. I still have his papers, remember."

"You think you could get away with it?"

184

"God knows. One can but try."

"That might be your motto, I think, Charles. 'One can but try.'"

"I can think of worse ones."

"Well, really, so can I. We've come quite a way on it, come to think." She laughed. "And here I am, just the same, back where I started from, acting a boy. I can't tell you how pleasant I find it."

"Poor urchin. Is it so tedious being a young lady?"

"Unspeakably. Have you ever thought how you have let me down, Charles? You promised me a life of gambling and adventure, and what have I done but sit in drawing rooms and do embroidery."

"You don't call this adventure, for instance?"

"Ah, this is something else again." She drew in a great breath of evening air, fresh from the forest. "This is delicious. Just smell the pine trees, Charles, and listen to the quietness." And then, carelessly: "I wrote my grandfather, by the way. Philip took the letter to his cousin, to be sent in the bag."

"You're going to abandon me?"

"Taking a leaf out of your book, Charles. You've abandoned us often enough."

"But never willingly."

"All for the Bourbons, and the world well lost. For an adventurer, you have a wonderfully strong sense of duty. Is he really such a spellbinder, this Comte d'Artois?"

"I wish you could meet him; then you'd understand. He's a man—a leader . . ."

"You don't think that France might be a little tired of leaders? And besides, what about his brother?"

"The King? He's old and tired, and must be content to sit back, enjoy his position, and let his brother govern."

"You think he will? It hardly sounds like any Bourbon I ever heard of. Charles! I know I'm just a woman and not supposed to know a Czar from a sans-culotte, but I do beg you won't let yourself get in too deep."

"How could I? Think of the Loyets: they are ready to die for the Bourbon cause. Why should not I?"

"I'd much rather, at a pinch, that you lived for it. But, really, why should you? What have they ever done for you?"

"Don't you understand, Sonia, that's not the point. All

185

my life I've been an adventurer, a wanderer: homeless, rootless, with nothing but Charles Vincent to care about. Now, at last, I've found a cause worth fighting for, worth risking everything for."

"Don't forget, Charles, you've found us too. Are we not worth a little risk? Or—do you include us in your 'everything'?"

"Try to be fair to me, Sonia." She could hardly see his face in the gathering darkness, but there was no mistaking the appeal in his voice. "This is more important than any of us," he went on. "This is the peace of the world we are talking of."

"Peace?" Thoughtfully. "I hardly remember what it was like. But you really think these papers so important?"

"Absolutely. I saw the Czar, you know, just the other day, at Troyes. He was almost decided, even then, to risk all in a march on Paris. This information should settle it."

"And in the Bourbons' favor?"

"I hope so."

"And I hope they prove worth your devotion, Charles. From what I have heard, I can't help wondering . . ." She felt him stiffen on the seat beside her. "Don't be angry. I won't tease you any more. Your mind's made up, isn't it, so what's the use of arguing. Besides—I'm enjoying this." She leaned a little closer to him as the carriage swung round a corner. "I should like to drive on like this forever."

"So should I. If we only could . . ."

"Well—" He felt rather than saw the eager little movement with which she turned towards him in the darkness. "Why not, Charles?"

"Because—oh, God, Sonia, I'm not my own master."

"Not—what in the world do you mean?"

"Just that—No, it's no use, Sonia, don't ask me. We've been good comrades, you and I, adventurers together. Soon, I hope, the adventure will be over. It's been—I'll never be so happy again. You and Elizabeth, you're all the family I'll ever have. My mother hated me, you know. She used to scream at me, tell me it was all my fault—" He gave a savage jerk to the reins and the horses plunged forward. "I don't know why I'm telling you all this. It's not what I meant to say—"

"Dear Charles, what did you mean to say?"

"Nothing. It would be monstrous ... I have no right ... You deserve a golden future, Sonia, and I am almost beginning to hope that I see it taking shape for you."

"A golden future? Goodness gracious, Charles, what dream is this?"

The road here was deeply rutted and for a few moments he was fully occupied with the horses. Then, "One I had not intended to mention—and yet, I hardly know why not. You remember the terms of our partnership? God knows, I have failed you often enough, but I do begin to hope, now, that you are in sight of the good marriage we planned for you."

"Oh?" She drew a little away from him, while her eyes tried vainly to make out his expression in the dark. "What marriage, pray? You cannot still be harping on poor silly Philip?"

"No, no. But you cannot fail to have noticed Denbigh's concern for you."

"Denbigh? Good God, Charles, how can you be so stupid!" Anger fought tears in her voice, and won. "Are you quite blind? Denbigh indeed! He's concerned merely with my damaged reputation, and let me tell you, Charles, damaged it is. Just look at me now, and tell me, after such a midnight frolic as this, what hope there is for me, in respectable England?"

He turned sideways on the seat, intensely aware, as he had been all along, of how near she was: "Sonia! Let me—"

"Hush!" Her hand on his silenced him. "Look!"

For a fatal moment he had taken his eyes off the road. Now he could see the stir of movement ahead: they were rapidly approaching a French sentry post. Nothing for it but to go on and hope to brazen it out. His hand held hers for a moment of communication and reassurance. "Quietly," he said. "And in French."

"*Naturellement.*"

He was already drawing in his horses, and stopped at once at the sentry's command, his story and his papers ready.

"Typhus?" The man drew back a step. "You'll kill her driving through the night like this."

"No more certainly than she'll die if I don't get her to the doctor."

187

"Well, keep away from the army, for God's sake. We've troubles enough of our own. Give it to the Allies if you must, curse them."

"Are they so near?"

"You'll have your work cut out to avoid them. We lie back there." He gestured vaguely in the direction of Bar-sur-Aube. "They're ahead somewhere. Some say the Czar himself is at Arcis. You'd best watch out for Cossacks; they'd eat that boy of yours for their supper. He's very quiet, by the way. Is he sickening too?" At the thought he took another step backwards.

"Just tired. Say good evening, Jacques."

"My throat hurts," croaked Sonia in the deepest voice she could manage.

"Here." The soldier tossed the little packet of papers back to Charles. "Get going, for God's sake, and take the left fork at the bridge there. That should keep you clear of our outposts. As for the Allies—that's your funeral. I just hope you infect the lot of them. And"—his voice suddenly became human—"good luck to you."

"Thanks. We need it." Vincent whipped up his horses. And then, when they were safely out of earshot, but still in a cautious whisper, "No more talking. It's not safe."

It was almost night now, and with the darkening of the air, they could see, off to their right, the glimmer of many fires, where the French army was bivouacking, and hear the sound of voices, shouts, the neighing of horses, an occasional trumpet, all the manifold noises of an army settling down for the anxious night. Then, gradually, the sounds died away behind them; instead an owl called suddenly, very close, making Sonia, who was nodding, half asleep, start into wakefulness and huddle a little closer to Charles.

"Are you cold?" He was driving as fast as he dared in the near darkness.

"A little. Nothing to signify." Like him, she whispered the words in French. "Can we talk now?"

"Best not, I think. Just in case—"

She nodded, her head sleepily against his shoulder, but risked one more question. "How far now?"

"A long way, I'm afraid. All night, at this pace. But soon there will be a moon."

"You're always lucky, aren't you, Charles? But you

were going to say something, back there where we were stopped."

"Was I? I quite forget. Anyway, we'd really best not talk. And—take care not to go to sleep, or you may fall."

"So I may. That would be too bad, wouldn't it? Oh, very well, your obedient stone."

He drove on silently for a while, aware of her valiant efforts to keep awake. Once or twice, when she nodded off and her head dropped down on to his shoulder, he had to put out a hand at once to wake and to steady her. The moon came up at last, making strange shadows on the road ahead of him, dimming the glow of the campfires they had left behind. They had come several miles now since being stopped. He reined in his horses, an arm supportingly round Sonia, who had fallen against him, fast asleep. For an instant he let himself hold her like that, her hair, under the absurd tricorn hat sweet-scented against his cheek. Then, more firmly than gently, he shook her awake.

"What is it?" Half awake, she spoke in English.

"Bedtime." He jumped down from the high seat, turned and lifted her down. "Safe enough now, I think. Our next problem should be the Allied outposts. No need to talk of typhus to them." He had opened the carriage door as he spoke and bundled her in. In the far corner, faintly revealed by a shaft of moonlight, Eilzabeth stirred among her coverings, muttered something and fell asleep again. "Sleep well, urchin. You are already."

"It's not fair." But as she protested she settled obediently in her corner and let him cover her with one of the rugs that had fallen off Elizabeth.

"Things seldom are. Sweet dreams, Rapunzel." He closed the door, climbed back on to the box and set forward at the best speed the tired horses could manage.

He had been lucky in his choice of road. Nothing seemed to be stirring as the countryside held its breath between the two armies. Occasionally, a fox barked or an owl called; once or twice he passed through villages where not a light showed. For all the signs of life, they might have been entirely deserted. Perhaps they were. If not, their inhabitants were doubtless hiding themselves from the threat of war, as a child pulls the bedclothes over its head in the dark.

And no wonder. The moon had set and the first cocks were calling to each other from farm to farm when he entered a village whose desolation showed bleak in the first glimmerings of dawn. Here and there a building was still smoldering; the dark shadows along the side of the street were probably piles of corpses; dogs howled. At the crossroads, in the center of the hamlet, for it had been no more, when it had been anything, three dark unmistakable figures swung from an improvised gibbet. Of life there was no sign. Shivering, Vincent told himself that he must be getting near to the Allied army. Beyond question, the Cossacks had been here.

He whipped up his horses. No time now to be thinking of the horrors of war, nor yet of the rights and wrongs of it. If the papers in his pocket could shorten it by so much as a day, they must be delivered at whatever cost. He had taken the precaution, when he moved Sonia into the carriage, of stowing away his set of French papers in the deep, hidden pocket of his greatcoat. Now, he made sure that Schwartzenberg's invaluable pass was ready to hand. It was dog-eared now, and battered-looking with much carrying, its date, perhaps fortunately, entirely illegible. He had come to a fork in the road and took the branch that led to Arcis itself. Surely the Czar would be there, and there, too, would be the best prospect of rest and shelter for the girls.

But the Czar must come first. He made this clear at once when he was stopped by an Austrian picket. He had not dared think, through the endless night, of what might happen if he encountered a marauding Cossack band. And yet, only yesterday, two of them had died in the girls' defense. . . .

But with the Austrians all went smoothly. The information that he had come round the French army in the night roused their interest immediately. He must come, without delay, to their commanding officer.

He agreed at once, but when he had been taken to the officer—a mere junior—he made his position brutally clear. "I have news of the utmost importance. For the Czar, if possible. Or failing that, for Schwartzenberg."

"The old man? He's still laid up. But—the Czar? I can't disturb him at this ungodly hour."

"You'll be sorry if you don't." So far Vincent had said

190

nothing about Napoleon's letter. If possible, he wished to deliver it in person and make the best use of it he could for the Bourbon cause. "He knows me. Tell him my name, and that I've got urgent information. I don't think you'll regret it."

"I certainly hope not. It's true we're all at sixes and sevens here. If you've really got information . . ."

"I have. Let me write a line."

"Very well." He looked relieved at this shifting of responsibility. And then, as Vincent wrote rapidly, "And the ladies in the carriage?"

"Let them sleep there, for the time being. Here, if you send that to the Czar, I think you'll find he sees me."

And then there was nothing to do but wait and eat, while waiting, a strange but welcome meal of black bread and strong local wine that helped him to fight back, for a while, the fatigue that was graveling his eyes and slowing his judgment.

When Sonia woke, it was high morning. She ached all over, and was in doubt, for a moment, where she was. Then, the sound of a trumpet reminded her. When she had fallen helplessly asleep last night, they had been looking for the Allied army. The noises all round her suggested that they had found it: horses neighed, men shouted—listening carefully, she was relieved to hear that they shouted in German. Yes, they had found the right army. Indeed, from the sounds, they were in the thick of it. She peered cautiously out the window and was confronted by the large back of an Austrian trooper, obviously on guard over them. Well, that was something . . .

A movement in the other corner of the carriage made her forget her stiffness. In a bound she was at Elizabeth's side, and in time to prevent her from falling off the seat. She had waked in one convulsive movement. Her cheeks were flushed and her eyes very bright. She looked at Sonia without a trace of recognition and began to talk in a rapid monotone: "I must find her. Where is she? Sonia! Sonia! Don't go with him, they'll only stop you. Don't go with him, Sonia!" It was almost a shriek.

"It's all right, Liz. I'm here." Her hand on Elizabeth's forehead felt it fiery hot and sticky.

For a moment, Elizabeth's eyes seemed to focus on her.

"You're a man. What have you done with Sonia? I told her not to go with you. It's no use, I tell you ... no use ..." She rambled off into incoherent mutterings, her eyes vague again.

Sonia propped her up, the way Charles had done, as securely as possible in her corner, then moved across to the other door and opened it. No time now to be thinking of her odd appearance.

The soldier's back stiffened as he heard the door creak open behind him, but he remained rigidly at attention, facing the other way. "Hey, you, trooper! I need help." Beyond him, she could see the camp humming with activity. It looked as if the army was preparing to march.

"Yes, madame." Now he turned round, saluted and choked back a gasp at the figure she presented. "I beg your pardon, sir?" It ended on a question.

"Ma'am will do. It doesn't matter. My friend is very ill. Is there a doctor in the camp? Can you fetch him for me?"

"A sawbones? Well, naturally we've got 'em. But I don't know whether they'd be much good to your friend. Don't want a leg off or anything in that line, does she? Hey, Franz," he shouted past her over the carriage top, "d'you know whether the doctor's still about?"

She had not noticed that there was a trooper on guard at the other door of the carriage too. Now his round red face peered over the driver's seat, turned wooden and went a little redder still at sight of her. "He was about last night all right. I helped carry him to bed. Drunk as a lord, begging your pardon, ma'am. Well, not surprising when you think he'd been cutting 'em up steadily for two days, ever since the battle. Not much use this morning, I wouldn't think."

"Oh." Sonia assimilated this unpromising news. "In the town, then? She's very ill. I don't know what to do."

The two men exchanged dubious glances. "We were told to guard you here," said the first. "And anyway, they've most of them run—from Arcis, I mean."

"Surely one of you could go. There might be someone. At least, ask your officer."

After a brief debate, they agreed to this and the one called Franz went off at the double, while his comrade began an uneasy packing round the carriage rather like a mother cat round her boxful of kittens, Sonia thought, and then shivered at unwelcome memory. For a moment, she was back in the dusty stable loft helplessly watching the destruction of everything that had been her life. Well, not everything ... Elizabeth stirred and muttered beside her. It had not, after all, been quite so bad as she had thought. And for the first time, thinking this, she felt the justice of what Elizabeth had so often said to her. She could have achieved nothing by trying to intervene that day, except her own death. Could she perhaps begin to forgive herself for only watching and, worse still, listening to that scene?

Her thoughts flickered away to something that had lain warmly at the back of her mind ever since she woke. Charles ... dear, stupid, high-minded Charles. Maddening that they had encountered that French sentry just then. He had almost said—what? A soft little smile warmed her face. Darling Charles playing adventurer and too scrupulous to involve her. But was it only that? There was something else he had said, something less warm in the memory: "I'm not my own master." What could he have meant by that?

She would not let herself imagine the worst. If he had been married already, he would have told them. Her scrupulous Charles would never have lied, even by omission. What then? The Bourbons, of course, but how? "I'm not my own master," and then, soon afterwards, "Sonia, let me ..." Let him what? She had been teasing him, of course, about her own position, about England, and reputation. What had she nearly teased him into? She smiled again. Marry Denbigh, indeed! Or Philip Haverton for the matter of that. What would it have been like to drive through the night with one of them at her side? To be deposited, at last, so unceremoniously on the carriage seat? Imagine Philip doing that. She stretched out her trousered legs and looked at them meditatively. And what in the world would either of them say if they could see her now? At the thought, the secret little smile was back again, to disappear instantly at a renewed delirious muttering from Elizabeth. What a brute, after all, she was to be happy, actually happy, with Elizabeth so ill ...

But happiness blows where it pleases and with the best will in the world, she could not make herself miserable. Instead, she tried to make Elizabeth a little more comfortable in her corner of the carriage and bathed her hot forehead with spirits of vinegar.

The doctor, when he arrived, proved immensely unhelpful. Even the soldiers seemed less than optimistic about him, but insisted that he was the best Arcis had to offer. His hands were dirty, his breath stank of garlic and his only suggestion was that he should bleed Elizabeth at once. He produced a dirty black parcel from the pocket of his coat and unrolled it to reveal a sinister-looking collection of instruments.

"No." Sonia put herself firmly between him and Elizabeth. "No, thank you. Oh, thank God, Charles! Tell him to go away." No time now to be thinking of last night. Charles was busy at once dealing with the doctor. When at last the man had gone grumbling off, clutching the fee he had extorted, his first question was about Elizabeth.

"She's very ill." Sonia's white, anxious face and shadowed eyes made him furiously angry with himself, with everything. "What are we going to do?" Her voice shook and he could see she was near the end of her tether.

"Take her to Paris." Keeping his voice low and calm, he was intensely aware of their strange position and the watching, fascinated soldiers.

"To Paris? Are you quite mad?"

"Not at all." The two soldiers had withdrawn, now, to a respectful distance, but he kept his voice low. "I've seen the Czar and shown him Napoleon's letter. At last, it's decided him. Don't you see the preparations? The march on Paris begins this afternoon. We must get there first."

"For the pleasure of being besieged there? Charles, you're crazy."

"There'll be no siege. A couple of days' fighting at the most. Then—it will be over. Don't you remember saying that you wanted to see the end of the adventure? Well, here's your chance. And—where else can you hope to find the attention Elizabeth needs? Besides I have to go. I have messages from the Comte d'Artois—not to mention the Czar's."

"Oh, I see. What alternative have I?"

"None, I think."

She shrugged. "When do we start?"

"At once. Here come the horses now. They are bringing food for you to eat on the way."

194

"You mean to tell me that I am to arrive at Paris like this?" An expressive glance drew his attention to her costume.

"If we get there at all it will be on the papers Loyet gave me. Never mind, urchin, I told you once before, I seem to remember, that you make a gallant boy."

"Gallant fiddlestick! Paris—the capital of civilization—like this." And then, on an entirely different note: "Good gracious, Charles, look!"

It was indeed a surprising little procession that was approaching, since with one exception it was composed entirely of the immensely tall Cossacks of the Imperial Guard. The exception, a small man in drab civilian clothes, introduced himself with much respectful bowing, as the coachman who was to take them to Paris.

"You speak French?" Charles motioned the two Cossacks who were carrying an ornate luncheon hamper to put it into the carriage.

"*Oui, monsieur*. I am French. The escort will take us to the limits of the army. After that, I understand you have papers. As to horses—we must just pray to God—and pay."

"Quite so." Four enormous, miscellaneous horses were being harnessed up as they talked, and now the coachman climbed up to his box and the escort grouped itself round the carriage. Charles climbed in and sat down opposite Sonia. "This is better than driving." He opened the hamper. "Champagne, I'm glad to see, and cold chicken. A little unusual, perhaps, as a breakfast, but never mind."

"Good God!" Sonia watched him expertly loosening the champagne cork. "What did you do to the Czar?"

"Gave him the news he needed, that's all. I owe you something for catching that French courier for me."

"Being caught by him, you mean. I've never been so frightened."

"You hid it very well. You must be a lioness when you're feeling brave. Heaven defend me from being on the other side."

"That poor Frenchman: I do hope they are taking care of him. But were the papers he carried so important?"

"Important! I should rather think so. That letter of Napoleon's to his wife was worth an army to us. The Czar said so himself. You see, it was in answer to one from

Marie Louise warning him of the possibility of revolt in Paris if the war goes on much longer. It's what I told the Czar, of course, when I saw him before; now, at last, he believes me. And then, in his answer, Napoleon referred to his own plan of trying to take the Allied armies in the rear ... It leaves them no course so good as to take Paris and rely on opening up a line of communication through Flanders. So—the march begins."

"With us as outriders? And in all this luxury, too." She was eating a leg of cold chicken as she talked. "He must indeed have been pleased with you, Charles. Those horses are worth a fortune."

"It's worth plenty to him to have me reach Paris in good time. I carry his letters to Talleyrand."

"Oh, I see. Does that mean he has come down at last on the royalist side?"

"I wish it did. No, he's still hedging on that. I don't believe he's got over that crazy notion of putting Bernadotte on the throne of France. Though what he *says* is that he will await the decision of the French themselves. So you can see why it is so important that I get to Paris with the Comte d'Artois' messages."

"And the Czar sends you, horses, champagne and all. What a skilled diplomatist you are getting to be, Charles! I hardly recognize you these days. Life was much simpler when we were just playing cards for money. And quite as honest too, if you ask me. Thank you." He had contrived, with a good deal of spilling, to pour a little champagne into a glass. She raised it and smiled at him across it, the old teasing sparkle in her eyes. "I needed this. Dear Charles, don't look so serious. Drink some too and you will feel better."

If she had hoped to tease him into a more personal conversation, she failed. He was indeed looking serious. "Honest! What can you mean? Do you not realize that the fate of France may depend on what we are doing now?"

"Yes, that's just what worries me."

"If you'd met the Comte d'Artois, you'd understand."

"What a spell he's cast over you. But what about his brother? Do you remember what you used to call him? 'Louis the Undesirable.' And now look at you."

"Now I have a cause. It's what I've wanted all my life."

"I just wish I was sure it was the right cause. No, no,

196

don't start telling me all over again. And don't tell me that the end justifies the means either, because I won't believe you. Not but what it's delicious champagne. I just wish the carriage didn't jolt so." She smiled at him sleepily, out of an aching heart. Last night had been magic, today was—just today. Charles had remembered his cause, and his scruples. When would he have time to remember her? "What are you thinking of?" she asked.

"Talleyrand."

"Oh, Charles!" She settled down in her corner of the carriage. "In that case, wake me when we get to Paris. And Charles, look after Elizabeth."

"Of course. But I'm afraid you'll wake many times before we get to Paris. It's a long way, still, and a hazardous one."

"I know, but I'm so tired I could sleep through any number of hazards. Specially with you here to cope with them. Only, dear Charles, don't forget us among your causes."

Chapter 15

Paris! It was a pity, of course, to get there, after a surprisingly uneventful journey, in the dark, but even in the daylight, Sonia, who had almost lost count of the nights since she had last slept in her comfortable bed at Châtillon, would hardly have been able to rouse a spark of excitement. Somewhere between Arcis and here, the journey had turned into an endless nightmare, with Elizabeth's delirious mutterings for its leitmotif. When the carriage stopped at last, after so many temporary stoppages, at the great closed gates of a hotel in Paris, she hardly had the strength to ask the question.

"Whose house?"

Charles had to lean close to catch her words. "Mme. de Morne's. We shall be safe here."

"Safe? Oh dear, yes ..." She was almost too tired to care for that, or even for the odd appearance she must make. Charles had jumped down to talk to an ancient and reluctant concierge, now the great gates were slowly opening . . . With an effort, she pulled herself upright, and, when Charles opened the carriage door and made to lift her down, "No, bring Elizabeth," she said. "I can walk."

She could—just. The big house beyond the courtyard was quiet and dark. She did not even know whether it was very late or very early. She was aware of flickering lights, murmuring voices, an exclamation—of surprise—of pity? It did not matter. Someone had taken her arm to help her upstairs and along what seemed an interminable corridor, then she was in a room, being helped out of her clothes, surprised, for a moment, at the unfamiliar problems they presented. The bed was heavenly soft . . . someone pulled the covers up around her. She was asleep.

When she woke, light was filtering through the slats of closed shutters. From the courtyard below, she could hear a succession of comfortable domestic noises; the clink of a pail, voices, a girl's laugh and, further off, the melody of church bells. Could it really be only Sunday? The last few days, and even more their nights, had seemed to stretch out endlessly . . . If it was Sunday, it was the twenty-eighth-of March—she tried feebly to calculate, but fell asleep again while she was doing so.

When she next woke, someone was standing by the bed. The shutters had been thrown back, to let morning sunshine into the room. She looked up at the unknown face. "What day is it?" she asked.

"Monday morning. You've slept a long time, but M. Vincent said we had best leave you to it. I'm Mme. de Morne." She was a dark woman in her early thirties, with a handsome face that spoke at once of kindness and the habit of command. "I hope you feel better?"

"Much, thank you. You are wonderfully kind to a stranger."

"We are none of us strangers who work for the cause."

"Oh." Grasping this, Sonia realized that she was accepted as a royalist like Charles. But she was still too tired for explanations. Besides there was something much more important. "Elizabeth?" she asked.

"Your friend? Still asleep. The doctor says that the longer she sleeps, the better. Indeed, he is not unhopeful

198

that she may be better when she wakes; he thinks the crisis of the fever has passed."

"Thank God for that. So we did right to bring her."

"You did the only possible thing. Paris is crowded already with refugees. I do not like to think what might have happened to you."

Sonia found herself wondering exactly what story Charles had told this kind woman. It would be best not to discuss the past in too much detail before she had seen him. She moved impatiently in bed: stories . . . deceptions . . . call them lies . . . how tired she was of it all.

"You are tired still." Mme. de Morne reacted instantly to the movement. "Shall I leave you to rest some more?"

"No, please don't. May I not get up?"

"When you have had something to eat." She rang a hand bell that stood by the bed and gave the necessary orders. "M. Vincent is out. He was sent for, first thing, to M. Talleyrand's again."

"Oh. But—what's happening? What's the news?"

"Terrible. I had never believed it would be like this. Listen—can you not hear it?"

At first, Sonia could only hear the familiar, pleasant household noises, then, behind them, further off came the deeper, sinister sound she had heard so often that winter —the note of cannon. "They're here already?"

"Yes—I hardly believed M. Vincent when he warned me." She shuddered. "Our poor France . . . and now Paris. There was a regiment of cuirassiers yesterday; I saw them march through the town in their white cloaks, the music playing . . . They were back from Spain, on their way to the front. I saw some of them again this morning, clamoring at the barriers, their white cloaks stained with blood, their horses wounded too . . . The boulevards are crowded with peasants, with their cows and sheep and their poor little bundles of belongings. I was afraid for a minute they were going to mob the carriage . . . it's almost like the bad old days all over again . . . And yet, there were women walking in the Jardin des Plantes, dressed in their best, as if it was a day like any other day. And to think I have prayed, all winter, that the Allies would march on Paris and free us from Napoleon. Only—I had not understood it would be like this."

"Where is Napoleon?"

"Nobody knows. There is no news. We do not even know what the Empress is planning to do, nor the Court as a whole. But there is a rumor that the courtyards of the Tuileries are full of wagons."

"They will flee, you think?"

"I hope so. I could almost be sorry for the Empress, stiff and proud though she's always been, and the poor little King of Rome. There are all kinds of rumors going about; nobody believes the *Moniteur* any more. Do you know, just the other day, they held a solemn parade in the Empress's presence and handed over the Russian flags and swords won at Montmirail. But the couriers from the front show no signs of travel—a little dust would be more convincing."

"You think it's all over?"

"All over but the tears. But here's your breakfast. Eat well and try not to worry. M. Vincent has made admirable plans for our safety when Paris falls. We have been getting in provisions all day. He says at the last moment we must draw up a hay wagon to block the gate, close all the front shutters and make the house look empty. The looters are always in such a hurry, he says, that the slightest obstacle will stop them . . . But oh, my poor Paris. If I had known it would be like this . . ."

Sonia comforted her as best she could, her nerves all the time on the stretch for sounds of Vincent's return. The day dragged out endlessly, full of polite, desperate conversation. It was late in the afternoon when Charles appeared at last, and then he looked exhausted, almost desperate, Sonia thought. His eyes were dark-circled, the skin of his face drawn so tight over the bones that new lines were etched around the corners of his mouth. But his tired eyes lit up at sight of her. "Sonia, you're none the worse?"

"Not the least in the world. But you look worn out, Charles. What's happening? What's the matter?"

"What's happening?" His voice was bitter. "Talk—and more talk; and the Allies getting nearer every moment. You've laid in your provisions, madame?"

"Yes." Mme. de Morne also looked worn out. "Flour, rice, hams—we should be able to stand several days' siege. Should we put out the fires?

"No, not yet. Wait till you can hear the sounds of

musket fire as well as the guns. Then you will know it is time. But—how could I forget! Sonia, how is Elizabeth?"

"Sleeping much more peacefully. You were right to bring her, Charles. I hope—"

"So do I. But if there is safety anywhere, it will be here."

"Safety!" Mme de Morne's voice was almost a shriek. "If I had only known it would be like this."

"But think, madame, under Napoleon, no one was safe. Ever."

"You speak as if his reign was over."

"I think it is."

And indeed the first news they had next morning was that the Empress and the Imperial Government had fled in the night. "So much the better," said Vincent. "Now it will be possible to make peace and save Paris."

"Do you really think so?" asked Mme. de Morne eagerly.

"I'm sure of it. Talleyrand has not left with the Government. He arranged to be stopped at the barriers for lack of papers, and is back at his house again. Bear up, madame, it is only a matter of time now."

"Time." She shuddered. "And French blood flowing all the time."

"Not only French blood, madame." Sonia gave way to sudden irritation. "Germans and Russians are dying out there too, and the war is none of their starting." She caught Vincent's furious eye upon her, blushed and began an apology, but Mme. de Morne interrupted her.

"You're quite right," she said. "It is I who should apologize to you. But to see Paris like this ... The boulevards are thronged with the wounded this morning, with fine ladies in their feathers walking among them as if it were some kind of a peepshow. Good God! What's that?"

"A shell overhead. Nothing to signify—I hope. Tell me, what view do your upstairs windows command?"

"The servant's quarters? Come and see."

They hurried upstairs to a tiny attic bedroom whose two narrow gabled windows commanded a view of Montmartre. "Good God!" Mme. de Morne withdrew from the window. "I can't bear to look. Tell me what's happening."

"The Allies are attacking in strength. The defenses will

201

never hold. Half of them are mere boys, you know, this year's conscripts, hardly able to handle their arms."

"I know. Marmont told me the other day that he saw a conscript standing at his ease in the thick of the fray at Montmirail, doing nothing. Why? Because he did not know how to load his gun! Marmont had tears in his eyes when he told me. And it is boys like that, is it, who are out there, dying uselessly?"

"I'm afraid so. But, take heart, madame, it won't be long now."

That night, the moon shone with extraordinary brilliance. Paris was strangely quiet, its squares and streets full of the French army, bivouacking on the pavements, silent with exhaustion. From their top-floor window, Sonia and Charles could see the lights of the Allied campfires on the hills overlooking the city, and even hear the challenge and counterchallenge of the sentries ringing out sometimes in German, sometimes in Russian. The town was surrounded on three sides.

"Will it be tomorrow?" asked Sonia.

"Very soon. There have been meetings all day, and messengers going to and fro. Best of all, there's still no news of Napoleon. No one knows where he is. Yes, I think very likely it will be tomorrow."

"And then—what?"

"God knows. Nothing's settled; nothing's even planned. Talleyrand smiles that smile of his and says nothing. If only the Comte d'Artois were here!"

"Or Louis the Undesirable?"

"Sonia—don't!" He turned towards her, his face harsh in the moonlight. "Not now, not tonight. I can't bear it. There's too much already: don't you join against me."

"Against you? Oh, Charles, may I not even try to laugh?"

"Not now. Not about this. I tell you, Sonia, it's no laughing matter. It's the future of the world—how we are going to live for the rest of our lives—in peace, in freedom, or—slaves, as the French have been. And I . . . I may have some part to play. Try to understand that this is more important to me than anything. My life's not my own any more—I've staked it—I'm not free . . ."

"A slave, like the French?" And then, as he made an

202

impatient movement beside her, she put a gentle hand on his shoulder: "Charles, I do understand. Or—I try to."

"Thank you, Rapunzel." His hand went up to cover hers and they stood for a moment, saying nothing because nothing needed to be said.

Sonia moved at last. "Dear Charles, try not to take it so hard." And then, on an intentionally light note, "Well, it's late. Mme. de Morne will be wondering what's become of us, and besides, if we are to be sacked in the morning, let us by all means have a night's sleep first."

"There's nothing to fear, I promise you. The Czar has said all along that he intends no harm to Paris."

"I've heard old Blücher talk differently. They're not all saints like the Czar. Frankly, I wish it were tomorrow night, and all well. But you'll be here to look after us, Charles?" Frank appeal in her voice now.

"Sonia—if I can."

"You mean, if nothing more important comes up." Now, suddenly, she was angry. "I should have known. It's all very well to talk, but if the Bourbons whistle for you, it's good-bye to us: we must just take our chance with the Cossacks. Never marry, Charles; your wife might not quite like always taking second place to your ideals."

"Not if she cared? Not if she shared them?" Suddenly, his hands were hard on her shoulders as he swung her round to face him and gazed down at her in the half-light as if he were trying to read not so much her face as her heart. Despite herself, she leaned a little towards him, her lips ready to meet his. But the grip on her shoulders hardened as he pushed her a little away from him. "Sonia, whatever happens, forgive me . . . Think of me, sometimes, as one who loved you too well to—" He stopped, seeming to bite off the words.

"Charles, you're frightening me. What is it? What's the matter?" But she stood there quietly, intensely aware of the grip of his hands.

"It will all be over soon." He seemed to be talking more to himself than to her. "You will be safe in England, happy, I hope, and I—"

"Yes, you, Charles?"

"God knows. Hush." His hands clenched for a moment on her shoulders so that she caught her breath in sudden pain, then, gentle again, he pushed her away from him. "Yes, Mme. de Morne?"

"I said"—Mme. de Morne's silk skirts rustled on the narrow stair—"it's very late. There will be much to do in the morning. God help us."

"I hope He does," said Sonia.

She woke early, to a strange sensation of quietness. The cannon were not firing. Armistice? Or surrender? She dressed as quickly as she could and ran downstairs to find Charles, still in his greatcoat, drinking a cup of coffee in the dining room. "You've been out? What's happened?"

"It's all over. The French army withrdrew in the night; the Allies enter the city at eleven."

"Just like that?"

"Just like that."

"And where's Napoleon?"

"Ah, that's still a question. Coming up fast from the rear—but too late. The capitulation is signed and sealed. I hope to God he recognizes defeat when it's absolute."

"It will be most unlike him if he does."

Mme. de Morne was quite herself again this morning, and very busy making white cockades for her household. She sang as she worked, then broke off to say, "You see, I knew it would be all for the best. The Czar, after all, is one of the most civilized men in the world. He will not make us pay for Napoleon's faults. When the Bourbons are safely back on their throne, it can all be forgotten."

"You think so?" Sonia remembered her father's death and all the other scenes of violence she had encountered.

"I'm sure of it. You will see; they come as friends, not conquerors."

This opinion was confirmed by an early visit from an old friend of hers, the Russian Prince Wolkonski, who brought assurances of safety and protection from the Czar's Foreign Minister, Nesselrode. Wolkonski had come to Paris in advance of the Allied armies, to probe the state of public opinion. Mme. de Morne held out the cockade she was making: "There is your answer," she said.

"I wonder. You are very loyal, madame, but I must tell you I saw a group of young men in the street, as I came along, wearing white cockades, and shouting 'Vive le Roi!' People shrank away from them as if they had the plague."

204

"They're still afraid. You must remember the long tyranny we have endured. When the Allied armies are in control of the city, it will be another matter."

"You think so?"

"I'm sure of it."

"You may well be right. But some enthusiasm now, when it carried a risk, would be more convincing. What hope can there be for a king replaced on his throne by foreign arms? But, forgive me, madame, I know how little question there has ever been of your loyalty. I can only hope that what I see on my way back through the city proves more in line with your views."

After he left, the manufacture of white cockades went on harder than ever, but rather more quietly. It was punctuated now by an anxious sending about of messengers. Mme. de Morne and her royalist friends were busy arranging a demonstration that should convince the Czar.

Charles had been out when Wolkonski called, but returned in time to escort Mme. de Morne and Sonia to the Recamiers' house in the Rue Basse de Rempart through which the Allied procession was to pass. To Sonia's disappointment, the famous beauty was away, but her husband made them welcome and established them in a first-floor apartment, on a level with the boulevard. The first thing they saw was the group of young men of whom Wolkonski had spoken, still waving their white handkerchiefs and shouting *"Vive le Roi"*—but still pitifully few. Significant, too, was the atttiude of the silent crowds in the street, who neither molested them, nor joined in their cries, but looked at them almost with pity, as at predestined victims. It might well be true. "They're as good as dead men," whispered Mme. de Morne, "if Napoleon returns."

Charles Vincent had left them for a while to find out how the Allied armies were being received in the outskirts of the city. Now he rejoined them, but shook his head glomily in answer to Mme. de Morne's eager questions. It's bad," he said. "No white cockades, no shouting, nothing. Just silence, deserted streets, a few heads looking gloomily out of windows."

"It will be different when they reach this part of town."

"Yes, but it may also be too late."

There was indeed a considerable show of enthusiasm

when the Allied army reached the Place Vendôme and as it approached the window where Sonia sat she could see hands go surreptitiously into pockets, here and there in the road, and bring out white cockades, or white handkerchiefs. When the advance party of Cossacks of the Guard reached the head of the street, the shouting began: *"Vivent les Rois Liberateurs!"* called the Parisians, *"Vive l'Empereur Alexandre! Vive le Roi de Prusse,"* and, most often of all, *"Vive Louis XVIII"* and *"Vivent les Bourbons."* Even some of the National Guards had produced white cockades by now, while the group of young men who had seemed so forlorn earlier were skirmishing eagerly around the Allied sovereigns, trying to make themselves seem twice as many as they really were.

"What now?" asked Mme. de Morne when the procession had passed.

"The Emperor and the King of Prussia are to review the army in the Champs Elysées. After that—God knows. May I see you home now, madame? The crowds have thinned already—and I am anxious to get back to M. Talleyrand's."

"What does he say?"

"Nothing." Charles looked more exhausted than ever, and Sonia's heart bled for him.

"Did you get any sleep last night?" she could not help asking.

"Sleep? I don't remember. No, I don't believe so."

When they reached the Hôtel de Morne, Sonia urged him to come in with them and get some rest, but he refused. "There will be time for rest later. If you need me, I'll be at Talleyrand's. The Provisional Government's operating from there. Any moment the fate of France may be decided, and you talk of sleeping."

"Well, I can't help thinking you'd be a great deal more use to yourself and to others if you had had some rest. You look worn to the bone, Charles. At least, come in and eat something."

"Thank you, no. I'll get something there."

"If you remember to."

Elizabeth was sitting in the salon. Her recovery had been sudden and rapid, but she still looked pale and wasted to an alarming degree and accepted Mme. de Morne's greetings and congratulations listlessly.

It was so unlike her that Sonia could not restrain her anxiety. "Should you really be up, Liz? I'm sure it's too soon."

"I couldn't bear it any longer in bed. There's too much time for thinking. But, come"—with a visible effort—"tell me about the procession. How did it go?"

Mme. de Morne launched at once into an enthusiastic description of the royalist demonstration and Sonia listened and wondered at how optimism could exaggerate.

Philip Haverton came to call on them that afternoon. He and Denbigh, he explained, had ridden quietly into Paris after the procession was over. "My cousin preferred it so." Something petulant in his voice suggested that his own view had been different. "He's at Talleyrand's now. We met Vincent there, that's how I knew where to find you." There was something odd about his manner. Why was he so ill at ease? Any moment now, Sonia thought, he would be sucking the head of his cane the way he used to when they first met him.

"Charles is at Talleyrand's still?" She broke a silence that threatened to become awkward.

"Yes, along with all the rest of the world. You never saw such a scene! The Czar has moved in there, you know. He seems to think there's a bomb in the apartments that were prepared for him in the Elysée Palace, so he's playing safe by staying with Talleyrand. After all, no one would blow up the whole of the Provisional Government."

"Is that still there too?" Sonia was more and more puzzled by this curiously general line of conversation.

"Oh yes. It's an absolute madhouse. The Czar and his aides-de-camp are on the first floor, Nesselrode and his secretaries on the second and Talleyrand and the Provisional Government on the entresol. The stairs are lined with Imperial Guards, and there are Cossacks fast asleep in the courtyard. My cousin says it's as much as your life's worth to get a word with Talleyrand himself."

"How is Lord Denbigh?" Sonia suspected that he had regretted his reference to his cousin.

"Well, thank you." There was an odd note in his voice. "And you?"

"I'm always well, but Elizabeth has been ill since we saw you last." It was becoming necessary to explain away the strained silence in which Elizabeth had listened to their talk.

"I'm very sorry to hear it." Once again the oddly formal note.

What could be the matter? "You have not asked how we contrived to get here ahead of the army." Sonia found her own voice constrained now, having caught his evident embarrassment.

"Vincent told me a little of your adventures. I should have begun by congratulating you on your escape."

"Congratulate us on our heroism, rather." With an effort she recaptured the old teasing tone. "I never hope to be so frightened again in my life."

"I hope you may not be." He rose to his feet. "I must not keep you longer from your domestic duties."

"Don't be absurd, Philip. Domestic duties, indeed! You cannot mean to run away so soon. Why, you've not told us half your news." She was angry with herself as she spoke. If he really wanted to cut his visit so short, it was not for her to urge him to stay.

She could only be grateful when Elizabeth intervened. "Don't you be absurd, Sonia. Mr. Haverton has doubtless much business on his hands, today of all days. We must be grateful to him for sparing us as much as five minutes of his time." And then, in a tone oddly full of meaning: Good-bye, Mr. Haverton."

He exchanged a long look with her as he took the hand she held out to him. "Good-bye, Mrs. Barrymore." Why did he blush and stumble on her name? "It is true, I have a great deal to do. I called, in fact, to explain . . ."

"How busy you are. Yes, we quite understand, do we not, Sonia?"

"Of course we do." Sonia had her cue now, and took it gallantly. "And of course we are very busy too. We expect to leave for England as soon as the roads are open, do we not, Liz?"

"I hope so."

"To England! Will you really—" He stopped. "Forgive me, it's no affair of mine." And still confused, he took his leave.

"Well—" Sonia looked at Elizabeth. "What does that mean, do you think?"

"It means the masquerade's over." Elizabeth leaned

back on the sofa and closed her eyes for a moment. "I should never have let it begin."

"Nonsense," said Sonia robustly. "What else could we have done? And here we are, after all, safe in Paris, with the road open at last to England."

"Yes," said Elizabeth, "and you saw how Haverton looked when you said we were going there."

Sonia laughed. "I did indeed! You think our guilty secret's out? He knows we're not cousins? And has jumped—trust Philip—to the most sordid possible conclusion."

"I'm afraid so."

"Shall we make Charles call him out?" And then, more seriously, "Darling Liz, don't look so wretched. It will all come right in the end, I promise you it will. You only take it so hard because you have been ill. And after all, who cares about Philip?"

"If it were only Philip," said Elizabeth.

Chapter 16

The spring sun shone. Birds sang in the Champs Elysées, and under the trees the Cossacks, bivouacking, tethered their horses and went busily to work, as if they were in some country camp, mending their clothes, polishing the copper buckles and ornaments of their uniforms, and sharing out the booty which, despite every order to the contrary, they had contrived to acquire.

And yet, to the Frenchwomen who thronged, in their elegant, low-cut spring gowns to stare at this novel spectacle, they appeared the mildest of men, and many a black-pinafored French child had enjoyed a ride on their shoulders, or even in front of them as they sat, stiff-legged in their high saddles. It was only when men loitered too near that a sudden fierceness showed them for the savages they were. And there were stories, too, of what had happened in outlying villages where householders had been so foolish as to resist them, or where they had come upon an empty house, which they considered fair game. It was no wonder if they had plenty of plunder to share.

Aside from these stories, Paris was incredibly peaceful. "I can't believe it." Mme. de Morne had just returned from her morning drive. "How can those women go out and gaze at the Allied camp as if it was a raree show? How can we take it all so quietly?"

Elizabeth could not help feeling sorry for her. It was true that the French were hardly showing themselves in a heroic light, and though it could not be anything but a relief that there was, so far, no hint of guerrilla warfare against the conquering Allies—well, she could understand how Mme. de Morne felt. Even the news that Napoelon was now actually at Fontainebleau had failed to disturb the Parisians' curious calm. Or if they reacted at all, it was with fear that the fighting might start all over again.

"They're exhausted," she said to Mme. de Morne, "that's what it is. But I confess I wish people didn't keep telling me that they were always opposed to the Emperor, in their hearts."

"While cheering him to the echo. Yes, I know what you mean. Even now, when Talleyrand convoked the Senate, only sixty-four of them dared appear. What kind of a provisional government can they form? Oh—if only they would make an end of it and commit themselves once and for all to the Bourbon cause—"

"You think everyone would cheer that to the echo too? Well, you may be right, but you can hardly blame the Czar for going slowly on it."

"I know . . . but M. Vincent is in despair. He thinks there is still a chance of Bernadotte's being summoned. I'd rather die than see his wife queening it over Paris."

"Perhaps it will be a regency after all."

"For the little King of Rome? An Austrian to rule us?"

Elizabeth sighed and shrugged. She could not help feeling sorry for Mme. de Morne, but neither could she help a degree of impatience with her. It was a relief when a servant appeared to announce a visitor. But at the name, she felt her color drain away.

"Lord Denbigh?" Her first thought was of flight. "Tell him I'm not—no—" Her head went up. She had Sonia's battles to fight as well as her own. She had been convinced, from the first, that Denbigh must be behind the change in Haverton's behaviour. She owed it to herself, as well as to Sonia, to have it out with him. "With your permission, madame?" She turned to her hostess. "He is an old—acquaintance of ours."

"Of course. Show him in, Jacques. But"—Mme. de Morne was no fool—"I am afraid I shall have to leave you shortly; I have a million things to attend to. You will not mind?"

Denbigh was looking extraordinarily well, his fair hair bleached white and his skin tanned by the sun. Set in the brown face, his eyes looked bluer and more piercing than ever. They were fixed, at once, on Elizabeth, making her angrily aware of the very different change in her own appearance. "You have been ill. Philip told me. I am so sorry." He had already paid his repsects to Mme. de Morne.

"It was nothing to signify. I am better now."

"You do not look it. You should be out in the sunshine." He stopped. This was not what he had come to say at all. Now, he turned it off into a mere social exchange by speaking to Mme. de Morne. "Can you not persuade your guest that she would profit by exploring Paris a little. I can assure you that the streets are quite safe now."

"I know it," she said dryly. "I have just returned from watching my countrywomen exhibit themselves in the Champs Elysées."

"At the Cossack camp, you mean? Yes, I have been there too. I can understand your feelings, madame. But I believe Mrs. Barrymore has found that the Cossacks can be good friends, as well as savage foes. I was sorry that Philip was not there to protect you." As he turned to address Elizabeth once more, Mme. de Morne rose and made her apologies, quoting the million things she had to do. He made his adieux, held the door for her and then returned to stand over the sofa on which Elizabeth was sitting. "You look very far from well. What does the doctor say?"

"That I shall soon be better." Her voice was dry, lifeless.

"You are right; it is no affair of mine. I apologize. Besides"—he moved away from her across the room, gazed for a moment unseeingly out of the window, then came back to stand over her again—"I am come on a

211

painful errand. I am sorry not to find you looking better."

"So you have said. But if it is painful, shall we not do best to get it over with? Hard things are best said quickly." And then, when he still did not speak, "You have forbidden your cousin to visit us."

"Forbidden him? No. What made you think that? But—it is true. I have told him—" Once again he stopped in mid-sentence.

"What have you told him, sir? I think, at least, we have a right to know."

"That is why I am here. But you must let me explain a little . . . Your—" He stopped. "Charles Vincent, as you know, has been mixing himself most ardently in the Bourbon cause. I felt it incumbent on me to have some investigations made into his background. There have been too many double agents, too much betrayal. War is not a pretty business—"

"I am aware of that, Lord Denbigh. So you had investigations made; by your own—agents?"

"You could say so. Elizabeth—you must understand. This is more serious than any question of you and me. This is the fate of France—perhaps of Europe."

"Quite so. Let us forget the ancient history, and come down to cases. You had investigations made—in England, I presume?"

"Yes. And had a report—Philip brought it to me—that gave me much pain. Why? Elizabeth, why all the lies?"

"Surely you as a diplomat must know that there are times when a lie is a great deal more convenient than the truth."

"So you admit that they *were* lies? That you never married a cousin, a Mr. Barrymore? That neither that pretty little girl, nor Charles Vincent is in any way related to you? Elizabeth, you might have told me."

"Told you? What in the world makes you say that? It's bad enough that we should have met again, like this, but to be telling you the story of my life—I thank you, no."

"You're angry with me—and, God knows, I don't blame you. I've cut a sorry enough figure throughout, have I not? Of course, I see now, I was mad to believe my father and sister when they said you were dead. But I was young, Elizabeth, and they were my father and sister. I had no idea, then, that such treachery was possible."

She had turned away from him impatiently. "Must we go on talking about it? It's all over, years ago, forgotten, dead as last summer's roses. What we have to think of is the present—the very embarrassing present. So you've had a report on us from your agents, have you? And a very suspicious set of characters I'm sure it makes us seem. Posing as cousins .... running a gaming house ... no wonder if you warned that silly ward of yours against us."

"But Elizabeth, be fair. What was I to think?"

"Why, nothing to my credit, that's certain. Nor do I much care what you think—of me. My reputation's been gone these ten years and more. No"—an angry gesture silenced him—"we're not discussing that. We're talking of Sonia, who has her life still to lead. For her sake, I must try to make you understand. What would you have done, my lord, if you had found yourself, as I did last autumn, the sole protector of a girl so young, so charming, and so helpless as my Sonia?"

"Helpless? She never struck me, exactly, as that."

"No, I don't suppose she did, and I take a good deal of credit to myself for that very fact. She saw her father killed before her eyes, you know, and her home ransacked, first by the French, then by your Cossacks. All she had was me—and Charles Vincent, whom she encountered by chance."

"But—her family?"

"The Germans? An old, miserly aunt, and a cousin from whom I had been protecting her since she was twelve. And he the head of the family. He offered to marry her, in my hearing, to conceal her shame. That's what he called it. It would have been shameful to let her do it. And I'll say this for her, I doubt if she would have, even if I had been so mad as to advise it. So instead, I threw in our lot with Charles Vincent. The lies follow from that. Of course, now, here, in Paris, I can see that I was mad—and yet, I cannot see what else I could have done."

"But your idea—you must have had some plan?"

"Of course. To get Sonia to England, to her grandfather there. Have you had a report, also, on him?"

"I am afraid so."

"Oh." She took it squarely. "That is what I feared. He won't have her?"

"No, I'm afraid he won't. I am sorry to bring you so much bad news at once."

"Thank you." Mechanically. "But it is not exactly news, you know. Philip Haverton's behavior told me most of it. It was ingenious of you, sir, to contrive that there would be no need to forbid his seeing us again. Do you know, like an idiot, I had hoped to spare Sonia the knowledge of the full extent of our disgrace. Well, perhaps I should be grateful for small mercies: at least you have saved me the pain of telling her. Haverton's behavior has done the business for me. It remains merely to decide where we may best hide ourselves from our disgrace. A nunnery, perhaps, if they'll have us? But I beg your pardon, it is no affair of yours. Your inquiries were, of course, necessitated by reasons of state; their result an unlucky side issue—unlucky, that is, for us. From your point of view, it can only be good: to see your ward so easily cured of his infatuation must be the greatest comfort to you."

"The young brute. I wish I could give him the horse-whipping he deserves."

"But why? Be reasonable, Lord Denbigh. You told him of our masquerade with exactly that idea in mind. You cannot expect him, at his age, to be able to administer a *coup de grâce* as subtly, with such an air as you do. He was a little blunt, a little obvious, perhaps, but really it is to the good. At least, now we know where we stand."

"Nothing of the kind. Do you really believe that I have put the story of what you call this masquerate of yours about Paris? Or that I intend to do so? I told Philip because I thought it my duty—and to be frank with you, because I hoped that it might put an end to an affair that could not possibly come to good. You know as well as I do that Miss von Hugel doesn't care a button for him—oh, she enjoyed his adoration, what girl wouldn't? But that's all there was to it. Be fair, admit it."

"Why should I be fair? And if you are high-mindedly intending to conceal our shame from the world, what guarantee have we that young Haverton will do likewise?"

"The guarantee of his fear of me, which, I may say, is considerable. I have his promise. It is only for you to think of some reasonable explanation for the estrangement between them: I promise you, he will do everything in his power to substantiate it."

"Thank you." She inclined her head ironically. "What a powerful bully you have turned out to be. I would never have thought you had it in you."

"You've never forgiven me, have you, for failing you so. Well, I don't blame you. I don't believe I shall ever forgive myself. When I thought you dead—Elizabeth, I wanted to die too. And then—to discover it was all false: to be told that you had married. Can you imagine what I felt then? And that too was false. Elizabeth, I have been through hell."

"I can imagine that your pride must have suffered considerably, poor Giles." She colored, angry with herself for letting his first name slip out.

"My pride? You cannot really think that!" And then, ruefully, "Well, I suppose, to an extent you are right. To think that you'd forgotten me so easily—but, as you said, that's ancient history. It's the future we are concerned with: that is why I am here today. Now, at last, I have a chance to make you amends. Your situation is—difficult, to say the least. What I have learned, others may too. You were mad, you know, when you agreed to the scheme in the first place. What can the world think when it learns that so far from being cousins, you and Vincent met for the first time, under very shady circumstances, somewhere in Germany?"

"The worst, of course. I have known that for a long time. If they only thought it of me, I would not mind so much."

"Quite so. That is like you. And there is also your pose as a widow to be explained away. That is not going to hold water for a moment after the first group of English tourists reaches Paris. Which will be any day now. My sister is coming, you know."

"No, I did not. Then, I admit, we are lost indeed. I should think a Trappist nunnery, should not you?"

"It would hardly suit your Sonia. Elizabeth, I wish you would be serious. I begin to wonder whether you can, in fact, appreciate the gravity of your position."

"If I had not, Mr. Haverton's behavior would have undeceived me fast enough. Frankly, I think it too serious for discussion." She rose to her feet as if to end the interview.

"No, you shall not put me off so. I would not have

215

come if I had not a practical suggestion to make. You trusted me once, trust me again. Marry me, Elizabeth, and I shall be able to protect both you and your Sonia, for whom you seem to care so much more than for yourself."

"Marry *you?* Have you gone quite mad?"

"No, I have come to my senses. Here, at last, is the chance to make good the wrong I did you, years ago. I only wish the position in which you find yourself were twice as bad—"

"That I was really a fallen woman, you mean, instead of just appearing to be one? How kind of you, Lord Denbigh. Your name, of course, would be sufficient to cover many more indiscretions than I have involved myself in. And what do we do with Sonia? Since she is not fit to marry your ward, do we keep her on as some kind of a retainer—a governess, perhaps?" She colored fierily at the word, but then went steadily on. "And how delighted your sister will be to welcome me into the family—"

"That's exactly why we must be married at once and present her with a *fait accompli* when she arrives. Then, family pride will be on our side. You will be surprised how she will come round." He had taken her hand when he first made his declaration and had so far contrived to keep it, though struggling, in his. "It will be a nine days' wonder, of course, but soon lost in all the wonders of this extraordinary campaign. You will return to England as my wife, Lady Denbigh ... Under my protection, you will have nothing to fear."

"And nothing to hope for!" She pulled away the hand that had somehow, treacherously, remained in his. "I thank you, sir, but I'll not accept so great a sacrifice. To exchange my tarnished name for yours, to hide my shame behind your dignities—I tell you, I'd rather be publicly disgraced than so protected." And then, with an effort at calm: "Don't look so anxious. It's all over. You have made your gallant offer, and been rejected. Let the past be as it should be—past. The future is my affair, and at least I shall face it under my true colors."

"But—Elizabeth—I have done this all wrong; you misunderstand me on purpose—"

"On the contrary, I understand you very well. It does you the greatest credit, sir, that you have had me so much on your mind all these years, and most handsomely have

216

you attempted to pay what you consider your debt. Now, it is canceled. The obligation, if any, is on my side. You will add still further to it by helping me to get Sonia out of Paris before Lady Elinor arrives."

"I'll do nothing of the kind. Instead, I shall see to it that the first thing my sister does, when she gets here, is pay you a formal call. Why, what's the matter?"

She had burst into hysterical laughter. "A morning call from Lady Elinor! That will be the day. On the self-styled Mrs. Barrymore, and her disreputable protégée—oh, Sonia, listen—"

But Sonia, who had just entered the room, took one appalled look at her now helplessly sobbing friend and turned on Lord Denbigh: "What have you done to her? Don't you know she's been ill?" And then, in a very different tone, "Come, Liz, you're overtired. Lord Denbigh will excuse you, I know." She was already helping Elizabeth to the door. "Good day, Lord Denbigh."

At the door, Elizabeth paused and turned, still supported by Sonia's arm. "Yes, good day," she said, "and— good-bye, Lord Denbigh."

Left alone, he stood for a moment, gazing after them. Then, deliberately, he picked up his hat from the table where he had laid it and threw it with all his force to the ground. "Idiot," he said, "fool, bungler—"

What he said, later, to Philip Haverton left that young man white and shaken. "But ... but you told me ... you said ... what was I to think?"

"Nothing to any purpose, that is clear enough. I thought at the time that if you had been half a man, or really cared for the girl, you would have told me to go to the devil. Now, I tell you that if the slightest whisper of the business gets abroad through your means, I'll kill you, Philip."

"You mean that!"

"I am glad you have at least enough sense to see that I do. Now I am very busy. I should much prefer not to see you for some time."

"Should I go to them, sir, and apologize?"

"Good God, no. What use would that be? Just keep out of my sight, Philip."

Philip, very sorry for himself, was glad to do so, and plunged into the diversions that liberated Paris had to offer. He missed his passion for Sonia, but found gaming an adequate substitute for a few days, and lost a good deal of money in one of the gilded upstairs rooms of the Palais Royal. For the first time in his life, he was actually glad to see his formidable cousin, Lady Elinor, whose little party was the very first to arrive from England. Such meal as he had been compelled to eat tête-à-tête with Denbigh at the Hôtel de l'Europe had been so uncomfor able that any extension of their party must be a relief.

"You have lost no time," Denbigh greeted Henry Fess ingham who had alighted first from the capacious family carriage that had drawn up in the courtyard of the Hôtel de l'Europe.

"Yes," said Fessingham. "We were already at Dover when the news came. It is magnificent, is it not?"

"I hope so." He was interrupted by his sister's imperious voice. "Well"—she was standing at the carriage door— "am I to wait here all day? First we travel at what I still think a most unreasonable speed, and now, when at las we arrive, we must be left to stifle here while you gentlemen talk politics."

A look of friendly comprehension flashed between Denbigh and Fessingham, then, simultaneously, they moved forward with apologies and offers of assistance.

"Thank you." She let her brother help her down, then turned back to say, with every appearance of genuine concern, "Juliet, my love, are you quite done up?"

"Not at all, Aunt Elinor." Miss Cerne now appeared in the doorway, her looks confirming her words. They might have traveled fast, thought Denbigh, but they must have stopped, just the same, at the barriers of the city. His sister was always meticulously tidy, but Miss Cerne's appearance was a work of art. One directed, he wondered, at whom. Once more he and Fessingham ex changed quick glances. His own was questioning. Fessing ham's full of some unspoken apology.

Inevitably, it was Philip Haverton who sprang forward to help Miss Cerne alight. "Oh, Philip—" Lady Elinor apparently noticed him for the first time. "You will hardly remember my ward Miss Cerne."

"How could I have forgotten her?" Phillip raised th tiny gloved hand to his lips.

Juliet Cerne giggled. "Last time we met," she said, "you called me a plaguy nuisance."

"That was years ago! Where can Lady Elinor have been hiding you all this time?"

"At school." She made a little pouting face at him. "I can't tell you how tedious it was."

"Juliet!" Lady Elinor's voice was at its dryest. "My brother is waiting to pay his respects to you."

"Oh—I . . . I do beg your pardon." She blushed a child's comprehensive blush and held out the little hand to Denbigh, who contented himself with giving it a quick, firm squeeze and letting it go.

"Welcome to Paris, Miss Cerne. You are come, I suppose, to finish your education?"

She blushed harder than ever and muttered something almost incomprehensible about having left school. Lady Elinor intervened. "Surely, Giles, you need not make a stranger of my Juliet. She is come, of course, to keep me company when you men are busy with your politics."

"Juliet, then." He smiled down, very kindly at her from his great height. "And of course I am delighted that you will have company, Elinor. It is true, I shall be busy." Again a long exchange of glances with Fessingham. "But Philip, I know, will be happy to show you the sights of the city."

"Philip!" Elinor's tone dismissed him as negligible, but he hardly noticed. He had contrived, somehow, to possess himself of Juliet Cerne's hand again and was telling her, in an undertone, of the sights they must see together. "We are very tired." Lady Elinor took Juliet's other hand, ignoring Philip. "Tomorrow will be time enough to think of sightseeing."

Since Paris was crowded almost beyond bearing and Denbigh, for reasons of his own, had refused to be billeted on some unwilling French family, it took a little time and a good deal of negotiation before Lady Elinor and her protégée were installed in apartments that Lady Elinor considered adequate to her dignity. At last, it was all settled. Lady Elinor had grumbled herself to a stand-still about unaired French sheets, the churlishness of French chambermaids, dirt and high prices. "We are worn out." Her cold gray eye lit on Philip Haverton, who had been making himself useful in a thousand small, intelligent ways. "We will rest tonight and then, tomorrow, we will be fit to attend the performance of the opera you speak of." Now she was speaking to her brother, Philip once more relegated to non-existence.

"Good. I shall make a point of being here to escort you. And you, Fessingham?"

"I shall certainly hope to accompany you. It will be interesting to see how the Allied sovereigns are received."

"Oh, if it's politics again, good day to you. Come, Juliet, it is time to be thinking of our unpacking. We will see you, then, tomorrow." This she divided impartially between Denbigh and Fessingham, but Philip Haverton had Juliet's hand. "Tomorrow," he said.

"Well!" Philip had contrived to separate himself from the other two men at the entrance of the hotel, and Denbigh now turned to Fessingham. "You brought her."

"She brought me!"

"I collect I should thank you. Well, as a matter of fact, I do. But—the child?"

Fessingham laughed. "Poor child. I leave you to draw your own conclusions."

"I have. I was never so grateful for young Philip's existence in my life. Will you come to my rooms, or shall I go to yours? I have a great deal I must discuss with you."

"I expected so. That is why I have made myself so unpopular with Lady Elinor. Days are important now, are they not?"

"Important? They are priceless. Europe's fate for the next hundred years is settling itself under our noses—and the only man who seems in the least in control is Talleyrand."

"Castlereagh is not here yet?"

"No, he is expected daily, and so is Wellington. In the meanwhile—well, you will see for yourself."

"Go to the opera?" Sonia's voice rose in amazement. "Are you mad, Elizabeth? You know perfectly well you are not nearly strong enough. Why, you have not even been out yet."

"Then it's time I went. Shall we go and look at the Cossack camp this afternoon, or would you rather take a stroll in the Jardin des Plantes?"

"I'm sick of the sight of Cossacks—and the way the Parisiennes stare at them—but are you sure you are strong enough for the Jardin des Plantes?"

"Of course I am. The hothouses are dull, I know, but we can always go into the library if it rains. I am sure the air will do me good." She did not think fit to mention the real object of the excursion, which was to see how they were received by such acquaintances as they should chance to meet. It was not that she did not believe Lord Denbigh. If he said their secret was safe with him, she could be sure that it was; but Philip Haverton was another matter. She knew him too well to believe him capable of holding his tongue for long. It would be best to know what they would be likely to face at the opera that night. "Of course we must go!" She countered Sonia's reiterated objection as they strolled along the boulevard. "The Allied sovereigns' first ceremonial appearance, and we not there! Even Charles promises to be home in time to escort us."

"That will be a change." Sonia's voice was dry.

"Yes—he has been busy. I wish he did not look so fagged, so—I don't know, almost desperate at times. Has he talked to you at all about what he is doing?"

"Hardly, but it is only too clear that nothing is going as he hoped. It seems unbelievable that the Allies should still be prepared even to consider negotiations with Napoleon."

"I know. Poor Charles. I only hope he does not let himself be driven into any rash action. I have wondered, sometimes, about his friends. Have you noticed that there are some he takes care not to present to us?"

"Yes. I often wish we were still running a gambling hell."

"Sonia, don't say such things." Instinctively, she reverted to the old governess tone.

"Come now, Barry." Sonia's reaction was instantaneous. "We've gone a long way since those days. As for our reputations, from Philip's behavior we might as well kiss them good-bye."

It was the first time she had reverted to the subject, and Elizabeth was relieved to have her take it so lightly. It was equally a relief—and a surprise—to have Philip himself make a point, a few minutes later, of crossing the street to greet them with all his old courtesy. He walked a little way with them, exchanging polite nothings with Elizabeth, then took his leave. "Lady Elinor is come, you know. Shall we see you at the opera tonight?"

"Of course. I wouldn't miss it for the world." And then, as Sonia continued obstinately silent, "Lady Elinor here so soon? She must have had wings."

"Oh, they were at Dover already—had been for several days. Miss Cerne"—he colored—"her ward, you know, says the Ship Inn is more Gothic than ever. They were actually glad to get to France, dirty chambermaids, extortionate postilions and all. I am quoting Lady Elinor, of course. Miss Cerne sees everything through rose-colored glasses. Her enthusiasm is a pleasure to see." Once again, he colored, muttered something about commissions to execute for Lady Elinor and took his leave.

"Well," Sonia grinned at her companion, "now I understand everything. I have lost a lover, I fear!"

"It looks very much like it." Elizabeth gave a small secret sigh of relief. If Sonia believed Philip's sudden coldness to be the result of a new passion for the unknown Miss Cerne she would be spared much of the anxiety that was afflicting her. And in fact the various acquaintances they met had, so far, greeted them with their usual courtesy. It almost looked as if Denbigh had succeeded in silencing Philip. Well, she smiled to herself, if anyone could do it, he could. But Lady Elinor was another matter. She had never met her, but remembered all too well the change that had come into Giles's voice, years ago, when he spoke of her. It was from her influence, really, more than from his father's, that she had hoped to remove him when she committed herself to that wild American scheme. What a fool she had been. Only now, so long after the event, had she really understood that you do not escape from people by flight. Even if they had succeeded in getting to America, Lady Elinor's shadow, and his father's, would have always fallen between them. Whereas now . . .

She would not think of now. Least of all, would she let herself hope—for anything. If only they had not met again. Before that, it had been as easy as it was logical to hate him for what had seemed his betrayal. Hatred had warmed her, a pride like his own had kept her head high through the desolate years. And then he had reappeared, not faithless, as she had thought, but Giles, deceived as

222

she had been, the boy she had loved grown to a stature that surprised even her. She had clung to her hatred, almost desperately, but what could she do, watching him moving now, a man among men, dominating any company in which he found himself?

Yes, he had grown a long way. A long way away from her. That had been clear from their very first encounter and she had faced it, she hoped, courageously. How long had she managed to keep up the pretense of hatred? She shivered. Don't think about the long lonely years ahead. Think instead that if she could no longer deceive herself, at least she had kept up the pretense with him. It was a little comfort, though not much, that when his fine sense of honor had made him offer her marriage, she had been able to reject him without betraying herself. "I beg your pardon?" What had Sonia been saying?

"I said, you look positively hagged, Liz. Let's go home."

"Yes, do let us. We should both rest this afternoon if we are to enjoy the opera tonight, and I, for one, intend to do so." After all, Lady Elinor must be faced, and the sooner the better. As for Denbigh's promise that his sister would call upon her, well, as she had said, she would believe that when she saw it.

Her doubts on the subject would have been amply confirmed if she could have been present at an interview between Denbigh and his sister that same afternoon. It was the first time they had been alone together, and even now, Denbigh had only achieved the tête-à-tête by a deliberate request.

"She's a pretty child," he said, when Juliet Cerne had blushed and curtsied her way from the room. "If you like them silly."

"Silly!" Lady Elinor bridled. "She's as well educated as any girl in England."

"Oh—education. Yes, I expect she is. It was wisdom I was talking about."

"One hardly expects wisdom in a child of eighteen."

"Precisely. I am glad you take my point. One would no more expect it in Miss Cerne than one does in my poor Philip."

"Your poor Philip? I see nothing to pity in him. In fact, I was intending to congratulate you on his improvement."

"I am glad to think you see one. And I am really

223

delighted, Elinor, that you brought that pretty child to keep him out of mischief."

"To keep Philip—that is not what I meant at all."

"I rather thought not, but, just the same, that is what is going to happen. Dear Elinor"—he took her hand—"let us not quarrel. She's a charming child, but—not for me. I should make her miserable, and she would bore me to tears."

"But Giles, you should marry." For a moment she let her hand lie in his, and his voice was less strident than usual.

"I have been thinking the very same thing myself. But—not a child straight out of the nursery. Give me credit for a little judgment, Elinor."

"Judgment! You—Giles, I had not meant to speak of it so soon, but I had a most disquieting conversation with Mr. Fessingham, before we left London."

"Oh?"

"Yes. Is it really true that that young woman has bobbed up again?"

"Do you by any chance mean Miss Barrymore?" Ice in his voice.

"Yes—or should I say Mrs. Barrymore? I could hardly believe my ears when Mr. Fessingham told me she was parading about Europe, like the veriest camp follower, in the guise of a married woman. I always told you that was a miraculous escape of yours, and now, at last, I must have the pleasure of hearing you admit I was right."

"Do you really expect that, Elinor?" Deceptively gentle now. "Curiously enough, I had something rather different to say to you on the same subject. Do you remember telling me, years ago, that Miss Barrymore was dead?"

"Why—yes, I believe I did. It seemed the kindest thing, at the time."

"Did it so? That's your excuse, is it? You were protecting me, were you? Well, I am old enough, now, to protect myself—and Miss Barrymore too, who is in need of it. And—you are going to help me, Elinor."

"I?"

"Yes—you. If you wish me to forget what you did to me years ago. Or at least to try to. It was—wicked, Elinor. But no use talking of that. Only—now is your chance to make amends. Elizabeth's position here in Paris is precari-

224

ous in the extreme, and so is that of her friend Miss von Hugel. Henry Fessingham told you something of this, I know."

"He told me that your 'Elizabeth' was masquerading as a married woman and, as if that were not bad enough, pretending to be the cousin of some young adventurer— what's his name? Vincent. I saw him in the street this morning and if ever there was a hangdog, untrustworthy countenance, that's it. I can't think what possesses you, Giles, to imagine, for one moment, that the association between him and those two young women can be innocent. And running a gambling hell, too, from what I hear."

"I can see that you have not lacked for informants, Elinor."

She had the grace to look a trifle embarrassed. "Well, of course everyone knows that your happiness is my major concern."

"Precisely. I am grateful to you for putting it so straight. That is exactly why I ask you to pay a call on Miss Barrymore today."

"Call on Miss Barrymore! Are you run mad?"

"Far from it. I know your standing with the world quite as well as you do. After all, it has been your chief care all your life, has it not? Well, you have succeeded: no slightest breath of scandal has ever touched you: Lady Elinor Burnleigh is held up by mammas to their daughters as a pattern of correctness. Your approval carries almost as much weight as that of Lady Jersey or the Princess Lieven."

She did not like the almost. "What is that to the purpose?"

"Everything. If you call, publicly, on Miss Barrymore today, the rumors that are already current in Paris will be stopped as effectively as if she had been received by the Queen."

This was a happier note. She could not but look a little pleased at the comparison. "Well—you flatter me, but there may be something in what you say. I have heard it suggested, from time to time, that I would make a better patroness of Almack's than—" She stopped abruptly. "But this is all nonsense, and you know it. Just because I value my good name, nothing would induce me to call, publicly,

225

on two young women so lost to the commonest sense of propriety."

He was white with anger, but his voice was steady. "I ask you to accept my word, Elinor, that any scandal about Miss Barrymore and Miss von Hugel is entirely without foundation. You will be doing an act of merest justice—as well as of kindness—in extending to them your protection now, when they are so much in need of it."

"But why on earth should I?"

"Because I ask you. Because, if you like, you owe it to me for what you did before. No—wait a minute before you speak, and I will give you another reason, since I can see those do not appeal to you. I am serious about this, Elinor, and serious when I tell you that if you do not do as I ask, I will never, willingly, see you again. And if I am asked why I have made the break, I shall tell the story of the lies you told me, the letters you suppressed. It would be interesting, would it not, to see how your reputation as a paragon of propriety stood up to such a disclosure? You have made enemies, you know, with your fine moral distinctions, as well as friends. I can think of many people who would get acute pleasure in the propagation of such a tale. And of course there would be practical difficulties in it for you. I have always been happy to let you live in my houses—use my carriage—ride my horses. It would mean an end of all that, Elinor. I am sure yours is too lofty a spirit to let itself be swayed by anything so vulgar as financial considerations—but they do carry a certain weight, you know. Anyway, there you have it. A call this morning, some distinguishing notice at the opera tonight— and we continue brother and sister. Otherwise—"

She had risen to her feet. "You leave me no alternative."

"I rather hoped I did not."

To say that Elizabeth was astonished when Lady Elinor Burnleigh was announced would be putting it far too mildly. "Lady Elinor!" Her hand caught Sonia's. "Don't go!"

"She cannot wish to see me."

"I cannot imagine why she wants to see either of us. But we must be grateful to her for the call; it is a great service, you know."

"Lord Denbigh must have made her——"

"Hush!"

Elizabeth and Lady Elinor had never met before and each was perhaps equally surprised and disappointed at what she saw. For Elizabeth, the elegant aquiline society woman with the graying hair and faintly petulant expression was absurdly different from the imagined monster who had wrecked her happiness. Lady Elinor's surprise was perhaps more acute. She had intended Elizabeth and Sonia to be a pair of overdressed slatterns, at once gaudy and sordid. Elizabeth, of course, would be aging now, her figure spreading, her hair either faded or, better still, obviously tinted. The shock of seeing two frightened girls rise to their feet to greet her made her even more abrupt than usual.

"Miss Barrymore." Taking Elizabeth's hand in her lifeless one, she saw, with pleasure, that Elizabeth did in fact show some signs of her thirty years. There were lines around the fine eyes, laughter lines round the mouth. "Miss von Hugel." This was just a girl, dismissable as such. "Delighted to make your acquaintance." She did not sound it. And then, coming straight to the point: "You will forgive me if I say I would be glad of a few words with your—friend, alone."

Sonia, summing up their visitor with the unsparing eyes of youth, liked nothing of what she saw. She curtsied, gracefully. "Of course," she said. "You and Elizabeth must have much to talk of." A laughing, teasing glance in exchange for Elizabeth's pleading one, and she was gone.

"A charming child." Lady Elinor seated herself, unbidden, with a little sigh of muslin skirts. "No wonder my philanthropic brother feels concerned for her predicament. He asked me, of course, to call on you."

"We are honored—and grateful."

"Don't be grateful too soon, Miss Barrymore. I am come with a proposition for you."

"Oh?'

"Yes. You must have some idea of the kind of talk that is going around about you and that pretty protégée of yours. And Mr. Vincent, of course. I will not soil my lips by referring to it in more detail."

"I would not wish you to do that." A sharp exchange of glances registered Lady Elinor's recognition of a worthy adversary, but her voice was smooth as ever when she resumed:

"That, of course, is why Giles asked me to call upon you, as publicly as possible. My carriage is outside. It can hardly fail to be noticed. I promise, also, to summon you to my box at the opera this evening. I have some standing in the world. Thus franked, even after what has passed, you should have no difficulty in finding a respectable match for that pretty child, which I take it is your intention. I will even do my best to help you."

"You are too kind." Elizabeth contrived to keep all feeling out of her voice.

"On one condition."

"Yes?"

"That you refuse Giles in terms that make it impossible for him ever to approach you again."

"Refuse him?"

"No need to pretend astonishment. You know as well as I do that the mere memory of you has kept him from I don't know how many suitable matches. And now he has met you again—" An expressive shrug finished the sentence. "I will pay you the compliment of being frank with you, Miss Barrymore. Giles must marry. Our line is an ancient one; it must not be allowed to die out. I have found the very girl for him, and brought her to Paris with me. A charming child—she would make a good friend for your Miss von Hugel, and shall, if you will oblige me in this. And after all, you must see, yourself, that your marriage with Lord Denbigh is out of the question. It is but to give him the shock that will cure him—I do not care how you do it. That is your affair. And then, I promise you, I will bring Miss von Hugel out, ensure a good marriage for her, and for you"—here, at last, she lost countenance a little—"perhaps a pension—I do not know exactly how you are situated."

"You think Lord Denbigh will propose to me."

"Of course he will." Impatiently. "He's head-over-ears; it's worse now than it was before. And violent diseases, you know, react to violent remedies. When he does so, tell him—well, I leave it to you what you tell him. Cure him, and you have made me your friend for life."

"You give me credit for a great deal of altruism,

228

ma'am." Her heart was singing: He loves me, he loves me, all this time he has loved me.

Did it color her voice? Lady Elinor's certainly sharpened as she replied. "No, merely for some common sense. You must see that marriage between you and Giles is out of the question. You—Miss Barrymore—Mrs. Barrymore even—a name so tarnished, a family no one has ever heard of—"

Elizabeth rose to her feet. "May I show you to your carriage, Lady Elinor?"

"But you have not answered me."

"No. You should, I think, be grateful to me for that. But I have no wish to trade insults with you. So—good day."

Lady Elinor remained seated. "Insults! Believe me, Miss Barrymore, I had no intention of insulting you. I have told you a few plain facts—plainly. It is in your own best interests to listen to me, and I hope, when you think more of it, you will realize that it is. I will expect to see you at the opera tonight; you shall give me your answer then. I am sure, when you have considered, you will recognize how much it is that I have to offer—and how impossible is any other solution to the difficulties in which you find yourself. Marriage with you must mean ruin for Giles, the end of his career in the diplomatic service, the loss of the distinguished place he has held in society. Imagine him, lurking with you at one of his country seats, unable to hold up his head in the county—how long, in such circumstances, do you imagine that his infatuation for you would last? Divorces are rare, I know, but not impossible— and particularly not for someone like Giles. Do you really wish to play so high for the position of the discredited, the divorced Lady Denbigh?"

"I do not wish to discuss the matter any further. As for divorce—give me leave to get married before we consider that. And marriage, surely, and all its implications, is a question Lord Denbigh must decide for himself."

"On the contrary. You know as well as I do that he is bound to feel himself obligated to you. Of course he must propose for your hand. Even I recognize that. And equally, of course, you must refuse him."

"What would you say if I was to tell you that he had already done so?"

"What! And—"

"I refused him."

Now at last Lady Elinor was on her feet, grasping Elizabeth's unresisting hand in both of hers. "Miss Barrymore, I ask you a thousand pardons, I should have known that you were, in truth, a woman of principle. I promise you, I shall see to it that you never regret it. I have various positions at my disposal: there is the lady in charge of the home for distressed gentlewomen; she is getting on in years—or perhaps a wardenship at one of my almshouses—"

"You are too good." The hint of mockery in her voice was not lost on Lady Elinor, whose expression changed suddenly. "I have told you, because it is true, that I have already refused Lord Denbigh. I have made no promises as to what I shall do if he should ever ask me again."

"Don't trouble yourself about that." Lady Elinor was drawing on her gloves. "I shall see to it that he does not do so. But—a bargain is a bargain. I shall see you at the opera tonight."

"No bargain of mine, Lady Elinor, but of course we will be there."

Chapter 17

"Charles!" Sonia had hardly been alone with him since their strange moonlight encounter the night before Paris fell. Now, jumping to her feet as he entered the room, she dropped the dress she had been altering and went towards him, hands outstretched. "Something's terribly wrong. I can see by your face. What is it?"

"Nothing." Nothing I can tell you, said his voice.

"But there is. I know you too well—I'm . . . too fond of you, Charles. You must expect me to see when you are troubled. Something's been wrong ever since we reached Paris. Now, it's worse. You look—haunted, Charles. Tell me, please. You never know, just talking about it might help."

"It's nothing, I say. I'm a little tired, that's all."

"I can see that. If only that were all. But if you don't want to talk about it, I won't tease you, Charles. It's not your secret, is that it?" And then, when his silence confirmed her guess: "Oh, Charles, please be careful. We're worried about you, Liz and I. And please, for my sake, try to get some rest. We shall be late tonight at the opera, remember. Look"—she picked up the white dress and managed a lighter note—"shall I not be surpassingly elegant?"

"Yes, very pretty." He had hardly looked at it. "But then you are always elegant. Only—I came to say; to ask . . . I beg you and Elizabeth will not go to the opera tonight."

"Not go! For the Allied monarchs' first appearance? Charles, you are mad. Of course we are going. You know you said we must yourself. Oh, and Lady Elinor Burnleigh has been here this morning."

"Has she?" Amazingly, he sounded uninterested. "Sonia, do not ask me to explain but, please, believe me when I say it is best for you not to go."

"The scandal's as bad as that, is it? Never mind, Charles, I never believed in running away nor, I am sure, does Elizabeth. We had much best go and face it out."

"No, no, it's not that. It's nothing to do with you—or Elizabeth. I can't tell you more, Sonia. Only—it's not safe. Don't ask me."

"Not safe? Charles, sit down here." She pushed him gently but firmly down on to a sofa, then perched herself on the end of it. "We were to be fellow adventurers, do you remember? What concerns you concerns me too. And—don't make me say it, but you know there's another reason. Your secrets should be my secrets, Charles. Since I must share your unhappiness, surely I should share its reason. You know it's safe with me. I'll not tell Elizabeth even, if you don't wish it. But—not safe to go to the opera? Perhaps you don't need to tell me: perhaps I can guess a little. Who are these friends of yours who meet you so surreptitiously and have made you so unhappy? What are they planning? What have you involved yourself in? What's going to happen tonight, Charles?"

"Oh, God." Suddenly it was a cry from the heart. "What indeed. But—I can't tell you, Sonia; I've sworn."

231

"An oath you should not have, I'll be bound. I warn you, Charles, if you won't tell me what it's all about, I shall go to Lord Denbigh and warn him something's afoot for this evening."

"Lord Denbigh! Why did I not think of him?" He jumped up and took an anxious turn about the room. "I suppose despair makes one stupid. Sonia, I must see Lord Denbigh, quickly, in secret."

"You sound very desperate, Charles."

"I am. It's—Sonia, it couldn't be worse. They are going to assassinate the Czar, at the opera tonight."

"What?" And then, "Who? Not your friends!"

"They were my friends. But what can I do, one, against so many? They wouldn't listen to me. It's a miracle I got away." He was still pacing about the room, throwing disjointed sentences at her. "I didn't know where to turn, who would believe me. But—Denbigh's the answer. He will believe me. He will know what to do. Only, how can I see him, Sonia? Secretly."

"Leave that to me." She stood up. "Sit here, Charles. Rest. I must go and put my bonnet on."

"Your bonnet?"

"Yes. Did I not tell you that Lady Elinor Burnleigh paid us a most surprising morning call? Well—she left her glove behind. Or would have, if she had had any common consideration." She picked up one of her own. "I must return it, at once. What shall I tell Lord Denbigh?"

"That I must see him."

"Yes, but how?" She wrinkled her forehead in thought. "It won't do for Lord Denbigh to come here; that would be too obvious. We must meet by accident. But where?" She thought for a moment. "Of course. My dress." She picked up the white satin underdress that had pleased her so and gave it a crushing look. "A total failure—I shall rush to Leroy, the great dressmaker—and you shall pay the bill, dear Charles. Lady Elinor will doubtless need gloves, or a shawl or one of those vital last-moment nonsenses, and her henpecked brother will fetch them for her." As she talked, she had been deftly wrapping the dress up in tissue and packing it away in a vast, unmistakable dressmaker's box. "How embarrassed you will be, carrying this through the streets of Paris, Charles, and how surprised when you encounter Lord Denbigh on a

232

similar errand. Now, can I trust you to wait here and get involved in nothing more until I return?"

He kissed her hand. "Sonia!"

"Charles!" She smiled down at him. "There's a great deal to do before we are out of this scrape."

"We?"

"Of course. Your danger is mine, Charles, like your unhappiness. It's just—one of those things, I suppose. You little knew, did you, that day at the inn what you were getting yourself into."

"Sonia!"

"Charles!" She blew him a quick kiss from the open doorway. "There's no time to be lost. I must go. Stay here. Promise?"

"Of course. But—Sonia—"

"Later, Charles, later." She was gone.

Lady Elinor was surprised and far from pleased to be told that Miss von Hugel was asking to see her. "Encroaching—I might have known it. And I left no glove behind. A mere pretext. Tell her I'm busy."

The man hesitated. "She said to tell you there is a jewel in the glove, milady."

"A jewel? She's mad."

"And if, by any chance, you were unable to see her, she would be glad to deliver it to milord."

"To me?" Lord Denbigh was reading the *Moniteur* at the far end of the room.

"Yes, she seems to think it important that she see one of you."

"Then show her up, Jules."

Sonia told her story quickly and concisely and Denbigh took it in as fast. "I see," he said at last. And then, "Elinor!" He raised his voice to include his sister who had sat at the far end of the room, rather obviously dissociated from the conversation. "What do you need from Leroy?"

"Nothing." She folded her lips in her characteristic expression of disapproval.

"A pity. Miss von Hugel, what does she need?"

"A fan, perhaps? A white plumed fan."

"Of course. Very well, in half an hour then. Oh—and

233

do not be surprised if I bring my friend Mr. Fessingham. His taste in fans is excellent, I believe."

"Oh?"

"Yes, much better than mine."

At Louis Hippolyte Leroy's sumptuous establishment all was bustle and confusion. A characteristically French sense of the niceties of behavior had led every royalist lady to feel that she could not possibly welcome the Allied sovereigns in a dress that had graced the Emperor's court. Yards of white satin, muslin, lace and tissue were being sewed up in the big workrooms, the hall, even on the stairs. Sonia, arriving with Charles at her side carrying the huge bandbox had a moment of despair. There would be no chance of private conversation here.

But a black-garbed woman with a pincushion at her belt and a measuring tape wound round her neck was already moving forward to greet them. "Miss von Hugel? You are punctual. The dressmaker awaits you in the fitting room. If Monsieur will be so good as to bring the dress? You can see we are all at sixes and sevens here."

Two men awaited them in the tiny, cramped fitting room. Oddly, it was not Denbigh, elegant by the little window, but his older companion who dominated the scene. Sonia had heard of Fessingham from Philip Haverton and had thought of him as an old man. Now, curtsying to him and studying the craggy face and fierce gray-blue eyes she revised her opinion. This was a man. His age hardly mattered . . . But—those eyes . . . what was it about them? They had left her, now, to sum up her companion with the same quick, appraising glance. Or— was it the same? Fessingham's eyes and Charles's had met and held.

"Who the devil are you?" said Henry Fessingham.

"Charles Vincent." Puzzled.

"Vincent? And your parents?"

"What business is it of yours?" Once again the two gray glances met and locked.

Fessingham laughed a curious choked laugh. "You may well ask. I hope . . . I expect I'm mad. But humor an old man and tell me your mother's name."

"My mother's name? You're mocking me. It's quite other business I'm here on."

234

"That's as may be. Tell me your mother's name—or your father's for the matter of that. If you can."

"How do you mean that, sir?"

Sonia's hand went out to touch his in silent appeal. "Charles, answer his questions." She had been looking from one brown face to the other.

Fessingham deflected his compelling glance for a moment from Charles to her. "You're no fool. You see it too, don't you, girl? It was as if my youth walked in at that door." Again he laughed that odd, choking laugh. "Short temper and all. It can't be true, and yet—I can't believe it's otherwise."

"Your—" Charles looked from him to Sonia, whose hand still lay restrainingly on his. "You mean—"

"Your mother's name, ridiculous boy, and put me out of my misery. If this is a dream, I can't wake too soon. Not Vincent, though, surely?"

"No, no. She married again. He was my stepfather. She thought herself much above his touch: she was a Mlle. de Bondy. She went back to that name after my father"—he colored—"abandoned us."

"Lies," said Henry Fessingham. "I should have known it. The—" He stopped. "I beg your pardon, boy. I was forgetting, for a moment, that I referred to your mother as well as to my wife. She must have known about you when we parted. If *I* had, I'd have taken her back to England with me if it killed her. Where is she now, by the way?"

"Dead. These many years."

"Then we'll say no more about her. But as for us: What does one say to the son one did not know existed?"

"You're serious?"

"I'd hardly joke on such a subject. I've been lonely all my life. Now—it looks as if I shall be busy. How much trouble are you in, son Charles?"

"Enough."

"And involved with a woman, too, by the look of things." Somehow he had got hold of Sonia's other hand. "By what I see, you can't be entirely a fool, though you do not sound to have been conducting yourself altogether brilliantly. We shall have to put our heads together to see what we can do about you." For the first time he included Denbigh in the conversation.

235

"But are you sure?" Denbigh had watched the whole scene with his usual detachment and now came forward somewhat doubtfully.

"Sure enough. Look at him. And remember, I remember her. It was just the kind of trick she would have played. You were born, boy—what do you call yourself—Charles?—you were born at Coblentz—in, let me see, 1793. Your mother was Albertine de Bondy and proud as the devil. Thought she'd made a mistake the moment she'd married me. Oh well—I said I wouldn't speak of her. But I'm right, aren't I?"

Charles suddenly laughed the laugh that was so like his father's. "Near enough, sir. I was born just outside Coblentz, it's true, in 1793. And 'proud as the devil' describes her, though she was my mother."

"Well, there you are. A son ... I'd not have thought life could change so, all in a moment. And you're mixed up in a plot to assassinate the Czar tonight, eh?"

"I'm afraid so."

"I'm glad you have the grace to look ashamed. A fine lot of associates you seem to have found yourself, son Charles. Assassinate the Czar indeed! Who do you think's been protecting Paris all this time? Let Blücher have his way and there wouldn't be two stones standing on top of each other. What do they expect to gain by it, hey?"

"Chaos, I think, sir."

"They're right. With Cossacks running wild in the streets of Paris. They love their Little Father, you know. And—your friends?"

"Think it will be their chance to cut out Louis XVIII and put the Comte d'Artois on the throne."

"I see. Yes, there's a certain logic about that. The strong man, eh? Why not have Napoleon? Right, that's the picture. Now, what do we do? How much do you know? When? How? Who?"

"On his way into the theater. A bomb. I don't know who."

"Beginning to distrust you, are they?"

"I spoke out against it."

"Creditable, if not wise. So now they suspect you. A pity, that. But never mind. Tell me what you know and we'll plan accordingly."

"Best make it quick, said Denbigh. "This has been a

236

very long fitting already. You must be very hard to please, Miss von Hugel."

"I am," said Sonia, her eyes on Charles.

"Well," Fessingham summed it up a few minutes later. "Change the route, extra guard, watch your friends and—pray. I don't think we can do more."

"You won't arrest them?"

"No. It would create just the kind of scandal we are trying to avoid. No, prevention is the thing. Besides, I find myself a selfish old man. Now I've found you, son Charles, I don't mean to lose you again if I can help it."

"You mean?"

"Well—you said yourself you'd protested against their plans. Who do you think they'll blame if they are all suddenly arrested? Don't look so anxious, child"—to Sonia—"I'll arrest him too, if necessary."

"You cheer me unspeakably," said Sonia. But her eyes met Fessingham's in a long glance of mutual consideration and mutual approval.

"Don't want him locked up, eh?" said Fessingham. "I suppose you want him out for the wedding. Well, there's no accounting for tastes; he looks a doubtful enough prospect to me. Still, you'll get a devoted father-in-law, if that's any consolation. I'll tell you what; I'll save him for you if you promise me a grandchild a year."

Sonia blushed crimson and laughed. "But he hasn't proposed to me yet."

"Not proposed! Well, of all the young fools. Charles, I give you up. Compromised the girl all winter and never even got around to asking her to marry you. I'm not sure I won't marry her myself, just to teach you a lesson."

"How could I ask her, with my only prospect penury—and now, perhaps, the gallows? Sonia—you understand. I've loved you from the first moment we met."

"Oh?" She could not resist it. "When you called me urchin and made me pull off your boots?" And then, in explanation, to Fessingham: "I was dressed as a boy, you see, sir. He thought I was a Bavarian prince or something of the kind. And—he's been wonderfully good to me. You mustn't blame him for this trouble he's in. It was all on account of Elizabeth and me—we needed the money. He may have had no prospects—we had less. We could not be

237

anything but a burden to him. Whatever he's done, it was for us."

Fessingham smiled at her very kindly. "You're a good girl, I can see. So it was all your fault—hey? I like that. Son Charles, do you know how lucky you are? Well, take her hand, boy, and tell her you've got prospects now; enough for two, enough for twenty. I've had nothing to do, all my life, but make money, now, at last, I see some purpose in it. As if they cared—" This to Denbigh, for Charles had taken both Sonia's hands and pulled her ruthlessly into his arms.

"No—" Denbigh was thinking of Elizabeth. "But we must care for them. And time's running out."

"You're right, of course. At all costs, we must arouse no suspicion. Charles! Sonia! Children, it's time to go." And then, as Sonia turned in Charles's arms to raise her laughing, blushing face to his: "Allow me to congratulate you on your engagement, Charles. But if you intend to live to marry, you'd better lose no more time. As for your troubles, leave them to me. Behave exactly as if you knew nothing, and don't worry. If the worst comes to the worst, we'll visit you in prison, Sonia and I. What do you think, Sonia?"

"I think we're very lucky, Charles and I." Quickly, she reached up to kiss him, "Come, Charles, we must go." Once more, she handed him the package that had been their excuse to come.

The stairs were still crowded with seamstresses, but neither Charles nor Sonia saw them. Outside, spring sunshine was brightening the crowded boulevard. Sonia broke the strange little silence. "Do you think they may be watching you?"

"I'm sure of it." And then, "Sonia!"

"Charles." The electric current that ran between them as they crossed the street arm in arm made speech hardly necessary.

"You know how I've wanted to say it."

"I've hoped I knew. But did you really love me—right from the first? I think I rather hated you."

"I know you did. You hated us all, then, didn't you?"

"Men? Yes, I suppose I did. But not for long. How could I? Charles—what were you going to say, that night in the carriage?"

He shook her arm a little, lovingly. "What do you think? Only that French sentry saved me. It would have been inexcusable. I—involved as I was, to ask you to marry me. They made me swear a terrible oath, you know, when I joined them."

She shivered and clung more closely to his arm. "I knew you were in trouble. I've been so frightened for you." And then, with a little laugh. "And so cross with you. I began to think I'd never get you to say it! First that night in the carriage, and then at Mme. de Morne's ... Goodness, I could have screamed when she came chaperoning up the stairs. Charles! Say it now."

He slowed his pace to look down at her. "I love you, Sonia. I always have; I always will. D'you remember how you held me up with that little gun of yours? Like a furious kitten with all its claws out? How could I help loving you?"

"And you've kept quiet all this time?"

"Of course. What else could I do?"

"Dear Charles—you nearly drove me distracted, you know. You and your fine scruples, and your surreptitious friends—and all those journeys. Each time, I thought I'd never see you again."

"And you cared?"

"Wretched creature, of course I cared. And all you'd do was give me good advice and promise me a rich marriage. I could have boxed your ears. Did you think me a terrible hussy, Charles?"

"Desperate! I never knew what you'd be breaking next—and was always afraid it might be my heart."

"Oh, Charles"—she looked up at him with swimming eyes—"to think it's all over—"

"Not quite." He felt he must warn her. "There's still tonight."

"Yes—but your father will take care of that. I like him, Charles. He's got more sense in his little finger than you'll ever have in that handsome head of yours."

"Thank you! Maybe you'd best marry him after all."

"Perhaps I will at that. Anyone can see he's worth ten of you. Just think of all that money." She leaned a little closer, so that her curls brushed his shoulder. "Oh, Charles, may I tease you again?"

"My darling, always."

"Even about Talleyrand? But of course it will all be different now. How strange. Will you be a Whig or a Tory when you get to England, darling? What cause will you find to neglect me for when you're an English gentleman?"

"Oh, my poor love, have I been so impossible?"

"Of course. What else? And don't tell me it's all going to be different now, because I shan't believe you. I know you: there'll always be something—oh so desperately important. But you'll always come back to me, won't you, Charles?" And then, on a quite different note, "But, oh, poor Liz—"

"What do you mean?"

"We're so happy . . . so lucky. And for her . . . everything's wrong for her. I'm afraid. She had a visit from Lady Elinor this morning, looking like judgment itself. I don't see a chance of happiness for her. What shall we do? Shall we tell her?"

"About us? Of course. She's bound to see. Happiness does not disguise itself easily. Yes, poor Elizabeth . . . If Lord Denbigh had not been there, I would have spoken to my father about her; it's easy to see he's the most generous of men. She need never lack for anything."

"Except happiness? Ah, poor Liz."

But Elizabeth, when they joined her, showed no sign of misery. She was making herself a wreath of white flowers and singing as she worked. "Ah, there you are at last." She held it up for their inspection. "How do you like it?" And then, jumping up, "Charles? Sonia?"

"Precisely." Sonia moved forward to kiss her. "And Elizabeth, you won't believe it. We've got a father."

"A what? Is she mad with happiness, Charles?"

"No, it's quite true." The explanations that followed took so long that Charles suddenly exclaimed in dismay, "Look at the time! And we must be early at the opera. If you wish for my escort, you girls must dress like the wind."

"Charles." Sonia took his hand. "Must you go? I'm afraid."

"Nonsense, you don't know what the word means. And you know I must go. It's bad enough to be hiding behind my father's coattails like this. To stay away would be to confess cowardice. You wouldn't want me to do that."

240

"No, Charles, but go armed."

"Armed? In evening dress. Don't be absurd, my love."

"If you love me—" She broke off. "I know! My little gun. Take that, for my sake. Please, Charles, it's the first thing I've asked you."

He kissed her hand. "Since you put it like that, but I warn you, I shall tease you about it for the rest of our lives. I don't know what the children will say."

She laughed, and blushed, and had the last word. "They'll say their mother had a great deal of sense."

Denbigh and Fessingham were busy most of the afternoon making their arrangements and it was almost time to dress when Denbigh returned to his hotel. He found his sister waiting for him, alone, in the salon.

"You're late," was her uncompromising greeting.

"Yes. I've been busy. What have you done with the child?"

"I wish you would not call her that, Giles. Juliet is eighteen. She is getting ready, of course, and I should be doing so too, but I wanted a word with you first."

"Oh?"

"Yes. I paid the call I undertook to. I visited that"—she hesitated, then plunged—"that hussy."

"Are you referring to Miss Barrymore?" His voice was a warning.

"Or Mrs. Barrymore, if you prefer it. She's got assurance enough for any title. And means, she tells me, to have yours."

"What?"

"I never heard anything so shameless in my life. It was your fault, of course, for not telling me the whole story. Why did you not explain that you had already made your offer, and been rejected?"

"Because I thought it none of your business!"

"None of my business! Sometimes you drive me beyond all patience. You had already extricated yourself from the affair and never thought fit to tell me so. Have a little sense, Giles. I grant that you might, perhaps, be considered to owe the girl something for what happened long ago. Well, now that debt is canceled. She has had her chance, and rejected it. That's that, thank God. I told her

241

she should have all my support in marrying off that chit she's got under her wing—and for herself a post, or even a pension . . ."

"What kind of a post?"

"Oh"—she had the grace to look confused—"a wardenship of some kind. You know my charities . . ."

"Yes, I do. And what did she say to this handsome offer of yours?"

"That's where you had let me down. If you'd only told me you'd already offered, and been refused. As it is, she told me of it, bold as brass."

"Yes. And—"

"And had the unmitigated effrontery to add that she did not promise not to take you if you were to offer again. I've never been so angry in my life."

"She said that! Then, perhaps . . . What on earth had you said to her, Elinor?"

"Why, told her, of course, what a fool you had made of yourself for her sake all these years. When I think of the eligible matches . . . And now Juliet . . . a fortune . . . neighboring estates . . . most suitably reared, though I do say so."

"You told her about Juliet?"

"Of course. And that she had only to cure you, to free you—Giles, what is it?"

"Nothing . . . So you offered her your countenance, and—what was it? A pension and some delicious wardenship or other—"

"And she refused! That's what I'm telling you. She's entirely without shame, Giles. She'll have you, if it ruins you. You must see it now."

"I see that you've done me a great service, Elinor." To her amazement, he leaned forward to kiss her dry cheek. "We'll forget the past. Oh, I know you did not intend it, but never mind that. Told her I'd made a fool of myself all these years for her sake, did you? And Elinor, what did you say she said?"

"How many times must I tell you? She as good as told me she meant to have you if you asked again. Giles, have you gone quite mad?"

"I rather believe so. But come, this is going to be an eventful evening, we had best get ready for it."

242

Chapter 18

The Opera House was festive with white flowers and garlands. A group of young men were busy covering Napoleon's eagle emblem over the royal box with a white handkerchief. Everywhere, there were white flowers, white fans,
white dresses. Sonia turned to Charles. "Do you see anyone you know?" she asked.

"No. It's early yet."

"And look at the crowds already. When does he arrive?"

"Not for some time yet." Charles knew she meant the
Czar. "Ah, there are Denbigh and my father—" He still
used the word as if it were strange and surprising. "Will
you excuse me a moment? Sonia? Elizabeth?"

"Of course. But—don't be long." Sonia's hand, butter-
fly-light on his sleeve, underlined the request.

"How could I?" He was gone.

The box was too small to hold Sonia. "Let's go back to
the foyer, Liz. Please? Suppose something happened—"

"It won't. But—very well. Only, think a little, Sonia.
Don't you see that if you betray your anxiety, you betray
Charles? The conspirators will know, by the look of you,
that he's blown their plans. Pull yourself together, Sonia.
Think how often you've said you wanted an opportunity
for courage. Well, here it is. The decorations are exquisite,
are they not?" The big hall was filling rapidly, and a group
of Austrian officers had moved close enough to hear what
she said.

"Ravishing." Sonia took her cue. "Do you think the
Allied sovereigns will be much applauded?" And then,
convulsively catching Elizabeth's hand, "What was that?"

"Some disturbance outside, I suppose." Her hand, on
Sonia's, was at once a comfort and a warning. There was
a little bustle, now, at the main entrance. "It must be
almost time for the sovereigns to arrive."

"Elizabeth"—in a whisper—"I can't bear it."

"You must. Excuse me, sir." She leaned forward to catch the attention of an Austrian officer, with whom they were slightly acquainted. "Do you know what is happening outside?"

"Why—ladies!" He had not recognized them before, but now hurried closer to pay his compliments. "Some broil or other, I suppose. One must expect them in what is, after all, a conquered city. They'll tidy it up, all right and tight, before the monarchs get here. And heaven help whoever started it."

Elizabeth felt Sonia's hand writhe in hers. "Yes—quite so. Only—we are a little anxious because our friend Mme. de Morne is due to join us at any moment. It would be enormously kind if you would—"

"Go and see? Delighted. Anything to oblige a lady." He was gone on the word and Sonia's hand pressed Elizabeth's gratefully.

Time drew out interminably. Elizabeth kept up a gallant pretense at conversation, to which Sonia replied in erratic monosyllables. The room was very crowded now. "Why doesn't he come back?" asked Sonia under cover of the general babble of varied tongues.

"I don't know—oh." She saw Lady Elinor making her determined way towards them through the crowd, Philip Haverton and a young girl who must be Juliet Cerne in her wake.

"So there you are." Lady Elinor hardly troubled to acknowledge their curtsies. She had armed herself, for this occasion, with a lorgnette through which she looked at them, for a moment, with frank dislike. "I thought it my duty, as an acquaintance, to tell you that we have just seen your"—one of her significant pauses—"friend Mr. Vincent arrested by the French."

"Arrested?" Elizabeth had prepared herself to pretend surprise.

But, "By the French? Then all is lost." Sonia swayed where she stood and Philip Haverton moved instinctively forward to give her his arm.

"No, Philip." Lady Elinor was between them. "These two"—another pause—"young women have proved amply capable of taking care of themselves. You, Miss Barrymore—she raised her voice a little, so that no word should be lost to the crowds around them—"with your wide knowledge of the world, will, I am sure, understand why I do not feel able to present you to my ward here, nor indeed to continue the slight acquaintance that has grown up, much against my will, between us. Good day to you both." She inclined her head in a little, regal dismissive nod. "Come, Philip. Come, Juliet."

For a moment, Elizabeth, speechless with anger, thought that Philip was going to reveal, but Juliet had already moved away with mute obedience behind her patroness. One glance of abject apology from Sonia, and he turned to follow. But Sonia had hardly noticed the scene, nor did she see the curious glances of the people who had been able to hear and understand. "The French have got him," she whispered frantically. "What shall we *do*, Elizabeth?"

"Why, nothing. Talk, laugh if you can. Do you not see that now, more than ever, it must seem that we know nothing. Ah, thank God, there at last is Mme. de Morne." However aware of Sonia's anguish, and anxious herself on Charles's account, she had not been blind to the results of Lady Elinor's brutal snub. A rustle of whispers was working its way outwards through the crowd from where they stood, the target of all eyes. She was pale, she knew, but with anger. Sonia was white and shaking and she must be grateful that this would be misinterpreted as arising from Lady Elinor's insult. Her steadying hand on Sonia's, she moved forward to meet Mme. de Morne, the crowd falling away almost, she thought angrily, as if they were lepers. Well, socially, perhaps they were.

Mme. de Morne apologized, somewhat incoherently, for her lateness, visibly trying, all the time, to make out what was going on. But the signal had been given for the audience to take their seats; the Allied sovereigns were due to appear in a few moments; there was no chance to talk as they returned to their box. Half seeing, Elizabeth gazed out at the theater, now crowded to capacity, the glitter of jewels everywhere, the scent of the white lilies worn and carried by the ladies heavy in the air. The band had struck up, but the music of *"Vive Henri IV"* was drowned by wave upon wave of applause as the Czar and the King of Prussia entered the imperial box. Even through the turmoil of her feelings she had time to think, It's hardly decent. Covertly glancing sideways, she saw

245

that very much the same thing must have occurred to Mme. de Morne. Here, only a week or so ago, the applause was for the Empress Marie Louise.

Afterwards, she could never remember what the opera had been, but she rather thought that it was, of all things, *Oedipe*. Certainly she remembered the wave of cheering that stopped the performance every time the singers' words could possibly be stretched into a reference to current events. But she was too anxious even to be nauseated by this. Sonia, beside her, sat like an automaton, her eyes fixed, unseeing, on a point somewhere above the white garlands that decorated the opposite boxes. When the great velvet curtains swept to the stage at the end of the first act and the audience began to stir in its seats, Elizabeth touched her shoulder gently. "My love, remember."

"I am remembering. What else have I to do?" But she made a gallant effort to pull herself together and reply to Mme. de Morne's comments on the audience and, as a secondary concern, the performance.

As she talked, Mme. de Morne was patting her elaborate coiffure into place. "We shall be thronged with company in a moment," she said. And indeed Elizabeth could see that already the gentlemen in the various boxes were on the move, while the ladies stayed in place and held court where they sat. She wondered if Mme. de Morne would prove right. Should she explain to her what had happened before she arrived? But of course, she was being absurd. Lady Elinor's considered and public insult might have finished her and Sonia so far as English society was concerned, but this was France.

Though it hardly seemed so, she thought wryly a moment later, as a little crowd of Russian and Austrian officers entered the box, to be greeted with what struck her as excessive enthusiasm by their hostess. In the general exchange of greetings, she managed a moment's coherent thought. Charles might be dead now. And Denbigh? Why had she let herself enjoy that fantastic moment of hope after Lady Elinor's visit? Well, at least the delusion had not lasted long. It was over now. Only—hopelessness seemed so much worse after that brief spurt of hope. Well—what now? Almost as a distraction she made herself face the forbidding future. Italy, maybe? Mr. Fessingham would give Sonia a pension. They would live the life of

246

the discredited at—Naples, perhaps. And then, with remorse, Poor Sonia, it's worse for her than for me. She had more hope; her despair must be even greater. She pressed Sonia's hand, which had lain passively in hers all this time, only to feel it turn, suddenly, into a live thing.

"Look," said Sonia.

Charles Vincent and Denbigh were standing in the doorway of the box. "Come." Sonia's hand on Elizabeth's was insistent, they moved together to join the two men in the crowded corridor outside. "You're not dead." Sonia had eyes only for Charles.

"Far from it," Elizabeth heard him say, then forgot all about them. Denbigh had taken her hand, had contrived, somehow, to establish her in an alcove, was standing tall above her, looking down with eyes that said—what? "Well, Elizabeth?" Irrelevantly, absurdly, she found herself thinking, How well he looks tonight.

"Lord Denbigh." She had been trying, quite in vain, to withdraw her hand from his. "You should not be here."

"No? Why not, pray?"

"Because—you will not have heard." This was almost impossibly hard. "Lady Elinor—"

"Of course. I have heard. Philip told me; I'll say that for him. He tells one things. That is—partly—why I am here. It is lucky for Elinor that I have such cause to be grateful to her."

"Grateful?" In that case, why, indeed, was he here?

"Yes, grateful. She told me, this afternoon, that you promised her, if I proposed to you again, to accept me." His voice changed; around them, conversation buzzed in three languages. "Elizabeth, I've been all kinds of fool. When I asked you before, I really believe you thought I did it from a sense of duty. But you must know I've always loved you. Even when I thought you dead, I could not forget you. When I found you alive, I tried. I'll not pretend otherwise. The time for pretense between us is past; from now on all is to be clear and open. And of course, I was angry, furious to think you had forgotten me and married. I never forgot. But I would not let myself admit I remembered. When our paths crossed again at Châtillon I made myself keep away from you. Remember, I had a position to maintain."

247

"Yes"—dryly—"you told me once my situation was such that you felt unable to visit me."

"And you took it as a slur on your character? Oh, my darling, when I realized that afterwards I could gladly have shot myself. What I meant, of course, was Charles Vincent's harebrained entanglements. How could I, representing Government as I did, visit the house of a known spy? But even then that was not the real reason. I knew that if I saw you, I was lost. And so it proved; that blow on the head was the luckiest thing that ever happened to me. There's never been another woman in my life, you know. You're everything I want: wife, companion, friend. We'd have been happy in America, if we had only got there, years ago but, Elizabeth, I think we will be happier still in England. I have—I suppose I did not understand then—there are obligations connected with rank. You will help me face them."

"But"—she had given up the effort to free her hands, but raised great pleading eyes to his—"that's just it. Lady Elinor's right. You can't marry me; your career, your position . . ."

"Let me be the judge of that. Look, Elizabeth"—the blue eyes held her captive—"I'd marry you out of Bridewell if it was necessary. You've often talked of my pride: well, you're right: I am proud enough to know that my wife will be above comment because she is my wife. You're laughing—"

"I was thinking how little you've changed—and how much. I used to be able to talk you round."

"And so you still can—when my mind's not made up."

"But you forget, Giles"—how naturally she found herself using his first name—"I have a mind too, and it tells me I can't do this to you. Oh, perhaps you mean it now, but, think a little—suppose the time should come when you realized your sister had been right."

"It never will. It's no use, Elizabeth. I've turned your position: you might as well yield gracefully. The only argument I would accept from you would be that you do not love me—and, God bless her, I've got my sister's word for that. You promised her, you know, that you'd have me if I asked you again. Well?"

"Giles, it's not fair: she made me angry: I should not have said it."

248

"All's fair in love and war. So come, my love, yield gracefully, since yield you must. Your secret's out: you love me too." And then, his eyes still laughing down at her, he raised his voice so that it caused a little hush in the crowded corridor. "Miss Barrymore," formally, "will you do me the honor of becoming my wife?"

How long had it been since they had exchanged one of these looks of complete understanding? She was half aware of silence around them, of curious glances. How little they mattered. Nothing mattered, but the hand that held hers, the eyes that looked down so commandingly into her own. "Lord Denbigh"—she kept it as formal as he had—"you do me too much honor."

"It would be impossible." And then, as a little buzz of talk broke out again round them, "I warn you, Liz, look at me like that for one moment more and I kiss you, here and now."

Anything to break the tension that stretched almost unbearably between them. "Since when did you have leave to call me Liz?"

"Since I had leave to marry you. I learned it from Miss von Hugel, of course." He looked around. "Has she had a very bad half-hour? We had to arrest Vincent, for his own safety. You see it did not last long. But where is he?"

"The Czar has sent for him." Sonia's eyes were shining, her face flushed. Seeing the change five minutes had made in her, Elizabeth was not aware of the similar change in herself.

"The Czar? To thank him? Good. Fessingham thought it right he should be told. I suppose he has gone with him. Well, in that case perhaps I may have the honor of joining you two in your box for the next act. You are to congratulate me, Miss von Hugel."

"What? Not really?" She laughed and shook her curls at him. "And about time too, my lord. I was beginning to have visions of nursing my poor Liz through a decline."

"What a flattering thought. Elizabeth, have you really been pining for my sake?"

"Nothing of the kind," said Elizabeth. "I've merely been distracted by the responsibility of Sonia and Charles. You can't marry too soon for me, my love."

"Nor for me," said Sonia. "But come, the orchestra is striking up. Should we not return to our places?"

249

It was surprising how easily they made their way through the crowd with Denbigh's tall figure to clear the way. Back in the auditorium, all their eyes turned inevitably to the imperial box, where they could see Vincent's slight, elegant figure bent deferentially towards the Czar, who was talking earnestly to him.

"You'll be lucky if you don't end up at the Russian court," said Denbigh teasingly to Sonia.

"I'm so happy," she said. "Charles always wanted—oh, my God!"

It had happened so fast. Charles, standing behind the Czar, and looking out into the house had looked up, had paused in what he was saying and thrown himself in front of the Czar. At the same moment, a shot had rung out, from somewhere in the gallery above and he had fallen out of their sight.

Pandemonium in the theater. Denbigh had a hand on each of their shoulders. "Quietly," he said. "It may not be so bad as we think. Stay here. Promise not to move."

"Of course." Elizabeth's arms were round Sonia who was crying, with a child's abandon, on her shoulder. "But—look!"

The Czar had come to the front of his box and now held out his hand for silence. Gradually, amazingly, the hysterical crowd hushed. "Ladies and gentlemen," he spoke in his easy French, "quietly, I beg you. There is no harm done. A madman has been arrested." His eyes were on a corner of the gallery that the girls could not see. "And the gallant gentleman who acted so fast to save my life is unharmed." How could it be true? And yet, there was Charles Vincent, very white, but managing a bow for the Czar and a long, anguished look in their direction. "And now," the Czar went on, "if you will all kindly return to your seats, the performance can continue. The incident is over—to be forgotten."

The orchestra struck up all over again. "What a man," said Denbigh.

And, "He's alive," said Sonia. "I must go to him."

"Wait," said Denbigh. "You'll be sent for. Fessingham is there, remember."

"I can't."

"You must. He's all right. You saw. It's a miracle, but he's alive."

The curtain had risen; the performance was continuing. Five endless minutes passed, while Sonia sat obediently in her place, the tears following each other silently down her cheeks. Then there came a quiet knock at the door of their box. Denbigh was gone for a minute, returned and whispered something to Mme. de Morne. Then, "Your farewells," he whispered to Elizabeth. "Quietly."

Mme. de Morne kissed them both, whispered an oddly final farewell. Then they were outside in the corridor, where lights burned low. "How is he?" asked Sonia.

"None the worse." Denbigh had been talking rapidly to the Russian who had fetched them. "Shaken; nothing else. They're waiting for us in my carriage."

"Well, then," said Sonia. "What are we waiting for?" The empty foyer echoed oddly to her voice. Their footsteps sounded loud out of proportion as they hurried down the marble stair.

Fessingham was waiting for them at the main door of the theater, two Cossacks of the Czar's guard beside him. "It's all right," he told Sonia. "You saved his life."

"I? What can you mean?"

"You'll see." He had taken her arm and was guiding her towards the carriage that stood outside, also guarded by Cossacks.

Denbigh and Elizabeth followed. "I should break it to you," Denbigh began, but Sonia's anxious voice drowned his. "Charles." She was up the carriage step in a bound. "Are you really unhurt?"

His face showed very white in the uncertain light, but he held out a reassuring hand. "Entirely, thanks to you." His arm gathered her against him as the others followed her into the carriage. "Your little gun saved me, Sonia. The bullet hit it."

"My God." She was shaking now against the comfort of his arm. "Charles, promise me never to be a hero again. I can't stand it."

"Once is enough for any man." Fessingham's voice came bracingly as the carriage started to move. "But—I'm proud of you, son Charles. We're not doing so badly, you and I, Sonia."

"No." She was back in control now. "What a story to tell the children. I don't believe they will tease me after all, Charles."

"They'll never hear it." Fessingham spoke, suprisingly. "The Czar has ordained that tonight's incident never happened."

"What?" Sonia and Elizabeth spoke together.

"Yes. He's a powerful man, the Czar. And—he's right. It would do untold damage at this point. So—it never happened . . . Not that he's not grateful, Charles. Come to Russia, he says, and he'll prove it. And—he sent you this." The diamond ring caught fire from a passing flambeau. "He thought you might have a use for it."

"I have." Charles slid it on Sonia's finger and she closed her hand to hold it in place. "But—can he?" she asked.

"Obliterate the incident? I expect so. You'll see. You don't mind, do you, son Charles?"

"Mind? I should think not. I've been such a fool—"

"Not altogether," said his father, and Sonia laughed a little, contentedly, between them.

Denbigh and Elizabeth had sat silently, facing them, content just to be together. Now Elizabeth leaned forward to look out of the carriage window, and spoke for the first time. "I hesitate to interrupt so interesting a conversation," she said, "but surely the coachman has missed his way."

"Why, so he has." Sonia turned to look out of the window. "Where in the world are we?"

"I told you I had something to break to you." Denbigh's voice was full of laughter. "You are being abducted, ladies."

"Abducted?" asked Sonia. "What in the world do you mean? Should we scream and faint, Elizabeth?"

"I would much rather ask for an explanation."

"That's my girl." Happiness gave warm overtones to Denbigh's voice. "And an explanation you shall have. We thought it best, Fessingham and I, that young Vincent—or rather Fessingham, as we must get used to calling him—should leave for England without delay. The Czar's ukase is a powerful thing, but I doubt if it can prevent his erstwhile friends coming to certain conclusions in the morning. It will be best if he is well on his way to Calais before they can act on them."

"Not without me," said Sonia.

"Exactly. That's what we thought you'd say. And as a matter of fact, it makes sense. A party will be the best possible protection for him—and, we must face it, he is in

252

considerable need of protection. He has done a great service to the Allies tonight. I do not like to think what would have happened if that bullet had found its mark. But he has made himself a band of enemies who will stop at nothing."

"You mean—even afterwards?" Sonia's voice shook.

"That's what we are afraid of, his father and I. He involved himself, you know, with a very powerful secret society. Their reach is as long as their memory."

"But what are you going to do?" Panic in Sonia's voice now.

"Listen, child, and I'll tell you." This was Fessingham, speaking with calm authority. "He's going to disappear. There'll be a story, in the morning, that his body has been taken out of the Seine. And there's an end of Charles Vincent. Meanwhile, you two ladies are going to leave Paris, with Denbigh and me—and my son."

"Charles?"

"Exactly. There are some advantages to my profession. I have his papers all ready under his real name. Charles Vincent is dead, Sonia, forget him, and—long live Charles Fessingham."

"Well!" said Elizabeth.

"Well?" Denbigh's voice mocked her lovingly. "With which objection do you propose to begin?"

"Giles, it's all very well ... Our baggage is not of the slightest consequence, I suppose, but you yourself were the one who scolded me about the impropriety of traveling about Europe unchaperoned. Just think how you worried about Sonia here."

"It's nothing to the way I worried about you." He had produced something from his pocket that rustled in the darkness. "That's the other thing I had to break to you, my love. And incidentally, the reason why I was not able to come to you sooner. I have been busy this afternoon. Here is the result." He handed her a heavy piece of parchment. "Since you cannot possibly see to read it, you will have to take my word for the fact that it is a license for the marriage of one Giles Burleigh and Elizabeth Helen Barrymore, spinster."

"A special license!" And then, inconsequently, "You remembered the Helen."

"Believe me, I remembered everything. My love, will you

253

forgive me for doing it thus, in huggermugger? The only English minister in Paris is waiting for us at my hotel. Marry me tonight, and the tongue of gossip is stopped— not that either of us cares a rap for that. But it does also mean that we can be of some slight service to our young friend here. Why, what's the matter?"

She was laughing delightedly. "Oh, Giles, I do adore you. When I think how you scolded me for pretending to be Mrs. Barrymore."

"Of course I scolded you. I was so jealous I could hardly bear it. I don't believe I shall ever quite forgive that none-existent Mr. Barrymore. But of course you were quite right. Marriage is the only protection in a position of this kind. Only, this time, I intend you to marry me, and with every sanction and safeguard the church can devise."

"Lady Elinor said we would marry only to be divorced."

"Damn Elinor. If you mention her again on our wedding night I will shake you, Elizabeth. But—the carriage had slowed to a walking pace—"here we are. Miss Barrymore"—once again that odd note of formality— "will you marry me: here and now?"

She sighed, pleasurably, in the darkness. "Lord Denbigh, though, of course, with the greatest reluctance, I will." And then, on a ripple of laughter: "You'd never have dared bully me like this before."

"No. Is it not a lucky thing for me that we are being married now, not then. I am going to rule you with a rod of iron, Liz."

"Liz indeed. Sonia, what would you do if you were me?"

Sonia laughed. "Dear Elizabeth, for my sake, marry him. After all, think what you have gone through already for the sake of my reputation. Surely a little thing like marriage won't daunt you?"

"Very well," said Elizabeth. "But merely as a favor to you, of course, and with the greatest reluctance, Lord Denbigh, I consent."

"That's lucky," said Denbigh.

ON SALE WHEREVER PAPERBACKS ARE SOLD
— or use this coupon to order directly from the publisher.

BARBARA
CARTLAND

V2705	**Again This Rapture** $1.25 £ (#36)
V3389	**Against The Stream** $1.25 £ (#68)
V2823	**Audacious Adventuress** $1.25 £ (#41)
V3491	**Coin Of Love** $1.25 £ (#3)
V2921	**Debt Of Honor** $1.25 £ (#16)
V3473	**Desire Of The Heart** $1.25 £ (#1)
V3271	**The Dream Within** $1.25 £ (#62)
V3537	**A Duel of Hearts** $1.25 £ (#8)
V2560	**Elizabethan Lover** $1.25 £ (#28)
V2769	**Enchanted Evil** $1.25 £ (#5)
V2795	**Enchanted Moment** $1.25 £ (#40)
V3048	**The Enchanted Waltz** $1.25 £ (#26)
V3019	**A Ghost In Monte Carlo** $1.25 £ (#48)
V3627	**Golden Gondola** $1.25 £
V3239	**A Halo For The Devil** $1.25 £ (#55)
V2706	**A Hazard of Hearts** $1.25 £ (#2)
V3358	**A Heart Is Broken** $1.25 £ (#66)
V2539	**Hidden Evil** $1.25 £ (#27)
V3538	**The Hidden Heart** $1.25 £ (#10)
V2636	**The Innocent Heiress** $1.25 £ (#15)
V3564	**An Innocent In Paris** $1.25 £ (#24)
V3326	**Josephine, Empress Of France** $1.25 £ (Biographical Romance)

Send to: PYRAMID PUBLICATIONS,
Dept. M.O., 9 Garden Street, Moonachie, N.J. 07074

NAME

ADDRESS

CITY

STATE   ZIP

I enclose $_____, which includes the total price of all books ordered plus 50¢ per book postage and handling for the first book and 25¢ for each additional. If my total order is $10.00 or more, I understand that Pyramid will pay all postage and handling.
No COD's or stamps. Please allow three to four weeks for delivery.
Prices subject to change.   P-15

are you missing out on some great Pyramid books?

You can have any title in print at Pyramid delivered right to your door! To receive your Pyramid Paperback Catalog, fill in the label below (use a ball point pen please) and mail to Pyramid...